The Resident Agent

The Resident Agent

Mitch Stern

A Bad Susie Book

The Resident Agent is a work of fiction. Names, characters, places and incidents are the product of the author's imagination or are used fictitiously. Any resemblance to actual events, locals or persons, living or dead, is entirely coincidental.

Book cover design by Rebecca Stinson

ISBN Print: 978-1-7369392-0-8
       eBook: 978-1-7369392-1-5
       Audio: 978-1-7369392-2-2

For Bad Susie, my partner every step of the way.

Author's note: The FBI divides up the United States into territory administered by field offices, also known as field divisions. Field offices are named for the city where they are located. For example, the Newark Field Office has responsibility for most of New Jersey. Throughout a field office's territory, there are satellite offices. These are called resident agencies.

The leader of a field office is called a special agent in charge, abbreviated as SAC. When referred to in speech, one says "ess-ay-see," never "sack." The SAC has deputies, called assistant special agents in charge. When referred to in speech, one says "ay-sack," never "ay-ess-ay-see."

Table of Contents

Saturday

Rob Lawson stared at the divorce papers in his hand. They were held together with small binder clips at the upper left. Two copies. *State of Indiana, County of Marion, Robert J. Lawson vs. Kathryn E. Lawson.*

It had been an agreeable Saturday after a busy week. He had settled with his marine insurance company and found an apartment in the older, box-like white building on the curving road that ran over the hill, such as hills were in this part of western Florida, near Seminolacola Harbor in the City of Seminolacola, County of Shambia, just this side of the line from Mobile. The rented furniture had arrived yesterday.

Today, after a long run and a long swim and grouper for lunch, Rob did some marketing, fighting the urge to pick up another twelve pack of beer. The FedEx envelope rested against his front door.

The papers therein made him mad enough to find an open real estate office with a notary. He signed them, both copies. The realty secretary and a customer served as witnesses. He killed the rest of the day sitting at his rented desk in his new apartment with its beige walls and Walmart accessories. Good enough for him. Not at all suitable for Kathryn though. "Good enough" did not meet Kathryn's minimum standards.

In the end-of-day gloom, he jammed the signed papers into the FedEx envelope with a three-word note: "File these now."

He slapped his handwritten label on the envelope. The one addressed to his lawyers, not hers. He would drop it in the box for a Monday morning pickup.

Rob stood for the first time in hours. He went to the bathroom. He was hungry. He didn't want to go out. He didn't want to play games or stream anything. He had some Oscar Mayer bologna, Miracle Whip and white bread. He ate his sandwich and drank a Coke while watching commercials occasionally interrupted by Clint Eastwood doing Josey Wales, who dined mostly on tobacco.

Later, looking out at the night from the dark apartment, Rob saw the white steeple of the church at the bottom of the hill, bright in the moonlight above the oaks. He had seen the church and liked its name, Maritime Methodist. He could stop by in the morning and thank God for his survival. It was time to say something to the Big Guy.

Sunday

"Are you going to wear your vest, Reverend?" Keisha Nettles asked.

"You know I am, Love," Coleman Henderson Nettles tried to pull his suit jacket on while holding several five-by-seven inch note cards. He put the cards and his light blue suit jacket on their four-poster bed.

Reverend Nettles stared at her, a little embarrassed, as always, when his wife caught him out. She was taller than his five feet, five inches. And she was a heck of a lot prettier than he was handsome. Not to mention quite a bit younger than himself, too.

Today she wore a modest pink floral print dress. It didn't show much skin, but it hugged her narrow waist and stopped at the knee, baring those marvelous calves. Somehow, with his pug face, barrel chest and his call to preaching, he had won her.

"And don't forget, you have the meeting with the Bishop on Tuesday," Keisha said.

"Yes dear," Reverend Nettles said.

Keisha slipped his vest off the valet.

"Does that ring a bell, Reverend?" she said, holding the vest out so he could put it on.

"Yes, the vest." He forced a laugh to cover his embarrassment and slid his arms through the holes.

"The meeting on Tuesday? You said you would go with Melissa Simmons to the, the —"

"Ah, yes."

He put his jacket back on and picked up his notes. They left the bedroom together for church.

Reverend Nettles noticed the man during his sermon as he said, "Forgiveness is not easy, and it don't mean the forgiver is a coward." He made eye contact with the man. He was white, clean shaven, with parted, straight brown hair, and neat in his khakis and a button down. He was young, still in his thirties by the look of him. He perched motionless in the old stained pew, attentive and watchful.

Then it hit Reverend Nettles. It happened to him now and then, this feeling. He thought of it as the Holy Spirit communicating with him. He had learned not to talk about this feeling, recognizing early on it was hard for others to consider him normal if he talked about how the Holy Spirit occasionally said hello. He appreciated the feelings. Without them, he never would have had the confidence to flirt with Keisha. Reverend Nettles felt the Holy Spirit tell him the neatly dressed young man would solve his problem.

After worship, he and Keisha stood sweating by the scarred hardwood door in the May sunshine as they bid farewell to their congregants. Reverend Nettles spotted Melissa waiting for him. So did Keisha.

"You have to go see the Bishop this week," Keisha said.

"I know."

"Don't you go sacrificing again. She's reasonable, she'll understand."

"I know."

The Holy Spirit yanked his head to the right as the man left the sanctuary. He stood a little less than six feet tall and had an oval face with average features, marred only by evidence of violence to his nose. Muscles filled his shirt, more than a tennis player but less than a weightlifter. Their eyes met. For an instant, the man seemed annoyed. Perhaps he wanted to sneak by him and Keisha, Reverend Nettles thought.

Then the young white man smiled personably.

"Thank you for the sermon, Reverend. Very timely for me," Rob Lawson said, shaking hands. He had wanted to sneak by the Reverend and avoid the possibility of any personal questions.

The Reverend wouldn't let his hand go. "First time to our church, sir?" he asked.

"Yes sir." Rob tugged but the little man held firm.

"Have you ever been in a penitentiary?" The Reverend said, focusing 100 per cent on Rob.

"Reverend," Keisha lightly scolded.

"May I?" Rob tugged somewhat more strongly.

"Oh, yes," Nettles said, letting go. "I'm sorry. I'm the Reverend Nettles and this is my wife, Keisha."

"Hello," Rob said. "To answer your question, yes I have — to visit."

Rob watched something like relief cross the reverend's face.

"Well, sir, I am in need of some assistance. I was supposed to go with that young woman there to – please forgive me, this can be shocking – sit with her as we watched the execution of the murderer of her husband. I find now another matter has come up and I cannot make it. To be blunt sir, can I impose upon you to take my place and support Mrs. Simmons at the unfortunate event?" The Reverend asked, nodding his head in Melissa's direction.

Rob thought the little man had to be kidding. Rob planned to disappoint him and disappear into a glorious Florida Sunday, never to be seen at this place again. Out of mere curiosity, he followed the Reverend's nod.

Everything stopped.

Her thick, straight, dark brown hair flowed to her chest. She had large brown eyes spaced wide apart and prominent cheekbones. Her face narrowed to a somewhat pointy chin. She struck Rob as someone in her late twenties, maybe thirty. Her wide mouth grinned nervously under a button nose when she saw both men gazing at her.

She wore a cream blouse with a pointed collar and a tan skirt with flats. He wondered at that, as she couldn't have been taller than five-two or three. The clothes worked with her complexion, which was not quite dark enough to qualify as olive. She stood in a funny way, with one foot back and the other forward, feet at forty-five degrees. Slender and fit, Rob thought she might be a dancer. Maybe a dancer, but beautiful for sure.

The Reverend coughed. "What's your name?" he asked in a whisper.

"Rob Lawson."

"Melissa dear, come meet Mr. Robert Lawson."

Melissa's expression firmed up on her way to the gray concrete steps. She didn't walk up the steps as much as hovered, grace personified.

"Melissa, thank you so much for understanding how sorry I am I have to meet with the Bishop on Tuesday. I have been able to find a replacement, Mr. Lawson. Mr. Lawson, may I introduce Melissa Simmons?"

Rob shook her outstretched hand. Her grip was firm without being rough. Her eyes, though, they were deep and lively.

"Thank you Mr. Lawson, but I think I can get myself there and back," she said.

"Oh no, Melissa. Keisha and I feel very strongly you should have support in your time of need," the Reverend said.

"Um hum. And what makes you a person that can provide support, Mr. Lawson?"

"Well, for one thing, he's a lawyer," Reverend Nettles said.

"Accountant," Rob said.

"Uh, oh yes, accountant. I forgot."

"Forensic accountant, so I have some knowledge of convicts," Rob said.

Melissa eyebrows rose. Her head tilted slightly forward.

"How long have you two even known each other?" she asked.

"We go back a bit, Melissa dear. I'd feel much better if you had someone go with you," Reverend Nettles said.

Rob let the lie carry him along.

Reverend Nettles ended his part of the conversation by facing the growing knot of parishioners occupying the concrete landing. They kept coming, positioning themselves to talk to Nettles and Keisha, crowding Melissa and Rob down the steps. Melissa and Rob ended up facing each other on the lawn.

"I'm very sorry about your loss," he said.

"Thank you. I have to go to the playground now. Nice meeting you." She started walking.

Rob caught up. "Your turn to watch the kids?" he asked.

"Mr. Lawson —"

"Rob, please," he said.

"Rob, I can drive myself. I really don't want to put anyone out. I didn't ask Reverend Nettles to come, you know. He kind of assumed he'd be involved."

"Isn't that like a clergyman," Rob said, smiling.

Melissa looked up at him, frowning at first, until she caught the joke.

"You know executions are at midnight?" Rob asked. "Do you plan to drive back from Raiford right after?"

"I hadn't really thought about it. The victim-rights woman said I could get a hotel, but I didn't follow up. I think when the Reverend got involved it made it easier to think about just coming home the same night."

"Mommy!"

Oh great, Rob thought. A kid.

A cyclone fence coated in green rubber surrounded a playground of brightly colored equipment: swings, climbers, slides, a horizontal ladder and a wall. A five or six-year-old boy zipped around the fence. His natural form impressed Rob. The way the boy pumped his arms, leaned forward and controlled his legs made Rob wonder if he was already being coached. The boy ran to Melissa and jumped.

Rob thought he was going to knock her down, but she caught him easily. All she had done was move her left foot back a bit.

"Who are you?" the boy asked.

"I'm Robert."

"Oh."

"And who are you?" Rob asked.

"Jules! Mommy, I'm hungry!"

"Ok, we'll go home."

"I want tacos!"

"One minute Jules. I'm sorry Mr. —"

"Rob."

"Ok, Rob. I'm sorry, but —"

"Why don't we talk about it? I'll give you a call later."

Melissa's smile switched on and off. She considered him for a long moment. He really liked those eyes. He wanted to see her again.

"Hey," he said gently, "it's a long way back from Raiford and it will be late at night. I'm sure you'd rather be with Jules the next morning. If I do the driving, you can rest."

Her smile stuck this time, slight, but Rob would take what he could get.

"Let me think about it," she said.

"All right. Need a lift?"

"Nope, we're right there." Melissa pointed to some garden apartments, built in the newish block-like style, down the street.

She and Rob exchanged numbers and they said their good-byes. She put Jules down. They walked hand-in-hand for a few steps before Jules squirmed out of her grip and ran ahead.

Monday

Melissa usually wore pink scrubs and her hair in a ponytail at work. Today she would finish up her shift at HCA Western Regional Medical Center, affiliated with the Medical University of Western Florida, with Old Mr. Maygarten.

"Good afternoon, Mr. Maygarten!" she said, entering his room.

"God dammit, what the hell are you doing here again?"

His lower lip quivered. Mr. Maygarten was a veteran and they were all the same, at least the VA referrals were.

"Let's see those legs, Mr. Maygarten."

"Don't you touch them, God dammit."

"Come on, we have to stretch."

"If you weren't so lovely, I'd fire you."

"You can't fire your PT Assistant, Mr. Maygarten. I come with HCA."

Melissa started stretching him out from the top, working his rectus femoris in the front and his biceps femoris in the back before finishing on his gastrocnemius (medial and lateral) and tibialis anterior down below. She gently pulled and pushed throughout his range of motion.

She noted three treatment units on his chart, having done two and adding the required extra unit as instructed. She didn't like it, but the job paid her enough keep Jules in daycare, pay her bills and carry her Civic, so she did as she was told. After all, it came with rights to the fitness center!

Melissa swung by the Allied Health break room and picked up her gym bag. She badged out and ran down the stairs.

She jogged across Indian Trail Road to get to the three-story Fitness Center. Everything was brand new and she used it all. She loved being able to get in some serious training while still picking up Jules by five.

Melissa changed into a baby blue Asics tank top and navy running shorts. She made her way upstairs to the strength training area. She thought of Matthew, her murdered husband. She guessed she had him to thank for this lifestyle. He had bought life insurance without even discussing it with her.

She owed Chucky Duaphin some thanks too. He watched after her money now. Matthew had worked for him in his insurance and financial planning business. Chucky had arranged everything. Without him, she didn't know what would have happened after Matthew's murder. Thinking this led to thoughts of the execution, which made her nervous. It made her want to work out.

As Melissa did various dumbbell and machine-based exercises she thought of the man Reverend Nettles introduced her to on Sunday. He seemed pleasant. She thought Reverend Nettles knew what he was doing, but she didn't remember ever seeing the man before at Maritime Methodist. Lawson had called yesterday to confirm he would drive her. She had still been somewhat uncertain, but he had insisted nicely.

The truth was, in the end, she wanted someone there with her. Only there wasn't anyone. She had friends, but they were mostly other mothers with young children and she didn't want to impose on them. Her sports friends, girls she knew from competition, were mostly still single but also mostly out of the area, and family, well, that wasn't really an option. They were up north anyway. She mounted a treadmill. Melissa set it for eight minutes a mile at a two percent incline with a twenty-four minute countdown. In the end, she thought, it was all right this Lawson person was coming.

"Mommy, can I have tuna fish on my PB and J?" Jules yelled through the closed bedroom door.

Melissa studied her reflection in her Target vanity. She wore a Chanel knock-off dress, so blue it was almost black, with white trim around the ends of her short sleeves and hem. Melissa liked the knee-length dress because it clung to her in all the right ways. She had combed her hair with the part on the side. She gave herself a once-over in the mirror. Maybe she shouldn't do her best for an execution, she thought.

"Mommy!"

"Yes you can." She knew he meant 'sandwich' when he said 'PB and J.'

"With chips?"

"Yes."

"And Coke?"

"No."

"I want to cut it!"

"Let Lila do it."

Lila was her savior. She was a neighbor woman who would sit for Jules for free if Melissa would let her. Truthfully, she wasn't successful in getting Lila to take money all the time anyway.

Melissa studied her reflection. *How had this happened?* she asked herself. How had she ended up alone with a child? How had she become a widow? She put her lipstick on and went out to face her fans.

The master bedroom led to a kitchen with a large island. Jules stood on a chair watching Lila trim the crust off his sandwich. Melissa couldn't believe how lucky she was to have him.

Lila, a matronly sixty-year-old, her short hair colored blonde, stood about five-two and beamed like a grandmother.

"Wow Mommy, you look beautiful!" Jules said.

"You do," Lila said.

"Too much?" Melissa asked.

"It's his last day," Lila said, shrugging.

Melissa nodded. She smoothed her dress down and exhaled sharply. Suddenly, she felt restless.

"Can I make something for you to eat?" Lila asked.

"No, I'm too nervous."

From the L-shaped kitchen to the island, the room continued to a dining/living area where they had a round table, their couch and their main TV. The glass doors to the balcony were past the couch. Melissa started toward the balcony doors and then changed her mind.

Lila carried Jules's plate to the table with a glass of milk. Jules hopped on a chair and began to eat.

"I don't know about this Robert person," Melissa said, taking a seat on the couch.

"Well, if Reverend Nettles knows him, he ought to be all right, don't you think?" Lila said, pulling out a chair and sitting next to Jules.

"I just wish I had met him before. I don't remember ever seeing him at church. Have you?"

"I don't know. I think I would have remembered him, him being smokeshow and all."

"Lila!"

"Mommy, are you going on a date?" Jules asked.

"No honey. I have to go to a meeting." Then to Lila: "I don't think he's so hot."

Melissa actually couldn't remember exactly what he looked like.

"If you say so," Lila said.

"Doesn't this seem creepy?"

"What?"

"Going to a, this thing, with a stranger?"

"But Reverend Nettles —"

"Yeah," Melissa said, waving Lila's comment away.

Melissa gazed out the glass doors. Thick, dark green leaves set off a powder blue sky. This will end it, she thought. Everything will be new after tonight. No more unfinished business. Matthew will really be gone.

Her eyes were completely dry.

Rob had driven around the condo complex to get the lay of the land. He parked in a visitor's spot near Melissa's place. Her building had been built on a slight rise and concrete steps led to a porch area serving the front door. A large green bush grew on the left. It obscured quite a bit of real estate behind it, plenty of room for someone to hide. Rob disapproved.

Everything seemed okay.

He enjoyed the anticipation he felt walking up to the door. More than her hotness, something about this woman fascinated him. He had no illusions of a post-execution hookup, but there might be an opportunity to keep seeing her. He might even consider going to church regularly for that.

There were two sharp raps at the door.

"I'll get it!" Jules shouted.

Melissa stood. Lila followed Jules, who fumbled with the lock. Lila opened the door.

"Hi!" Jules shouted.

Melissa was glad he had worn a suit. It was gray. He wore a stripped blue tie and a white shirt with a button down collar. It made her feel a little better about going with him.

"Hi," Rob said to Jules as he came in, scanning around the room.

"Are you going on a sleepover with Mommy?" Jules asked.

Lila giggled.

Rob's grin turned mischievous. Melissa thought she saw a glimpse of what he looked like as a little boy.

"We're going on a long drive."

"We better get started," she said. She picked up her purse and a sweater, and turned to Jules. "Mind Lila and don't stay up too late."

"Can we go to Lila's?"

"No honey, please stay here. Not too much television," Melissa said.

She bent down, kissed him, tousled his hair and thought he didn't favor Matthew at all.

"You don't mind if we use 98, do you?" Rob asked.

"No, that's fine."

They were in his ten-year-old aspen-green Ford F-150 driving alongside the white sand of the dunes and the brilliant oranges of the sunset. Out here there were still piles of hurricane refuse; litter, palm trees, branches, wood from broken houses. His suit jacket hung behind him in the extended cab area of the 4x4.

"Do you think we're dressed ok?" Melissa asked.

"Yup, I think so," Rob said.

"I don't want to honor him, but at the same time, I want to be respectful."

"I know what you mean. He's a criminal and all, but he's going to die tonight."

He caught her shiver out of the corner of his eye.

"That's what I thought, too," Melissa said.

Her hands were in her lap. She didn't fidget. They passed Fort Walton, Destin and Santa Rosa. Rob turned onto 331 North. After a quick stop for a Subway and coffee for him and just the coffee for her, they made up some time on I-10.

"You know where we are going? You don't have a GPS or even your phone," Melissa said.

"I know where we're going," Rob said.

He floored the accelerator to get around a semi.

"How is that, anyway? I mean, how do you know? What is it you do? Really, who the hell are you? Reverend Nettles said he knew you, but now I'm not sure. Where are you taking me? I want to know!"

"Hey, now. Hey, we're driving down I-10 to Florida State Prison. I'm an accountant by training. I'm between jobs at the moment and I went to church to give thanks because I rode out the hurricane on a thirty-six-footer. I know where the prison is because I've been a visitor from time to time. Not an inmate. I mean, I've been to see an inmate or two."

That sounded stupid, he thought.

"I see. Who did you visit?" Melissa asked.

Rob laughed briefly and without humor.

"Not like that," he said, "it was more like professional."

"An accountant visits clients in jail?"

"It's complicated."

"And what do you mean 'between' jobs? Do you work?"

"I'm living off the money from my old job. I'm thinking about what comes next."

"What does that mean?"

He hoped someday for her forgiveness as he readied himself to lie.

"I sold a business," he said. "I'm living off the money from the sale for now, but I'm getting back in the mood to work."

"You have to be in the mood to work?" she asked.

"Not to work so much as decide. Should I go back to accounting or try something different? Maybe something like building bulkheads. With global warming, I bet that's a growth field."

He chuckled. She didn't.

She settled back into her seat.

They drove on.

A ragged line of maybe fifteen protesters milled about the gate to the penitentiary. Rob and Melissa followed the photocopied directions to the death house. After they finished with the magnetometer, they met with Sharon, the victim-rights lady. She led them into the gallery.

Metal office chairs with gray cushions squared off in front of a large window in rows. A wall air conditioning unit fought the heat. The white room smelled of fresh paint. New linoleum flooring contributed to an overall sense of good repair.

They would have to stand to see the gurney, Rob thought.

There were other witnesses. Rob supposed one particular group sitting together on the far left were family members of the teens Jimmy Tank Gubbs, the prisoner, had killed as they hooked up in a car. Rob guessed they were tax-paying civilians. It had been a thrill kill, Rob remembered. The victims had no known connection to criminal activity.

Most of the other victims Gubbs had admitted to killing had been criminals. He had made those admissions after he had been convicted for the murder of Matthew Simmons, Melissa's husband.

The other witnesses consisted of a rundown, worked-over bottle-blonde who was so high on something she could stay upright only by leaning on Sharon, and a pair of young Hispanic men with hard, hard eyes. Rob wondered what scam they had perpetrated to get in. Between the two of them, they had three solid teardrops tattooed on their faces. Fifteen years hard time. Gang members for sure.

They listened to a monotone lecture about what was and wasn't appropriate behavior from a cadaverous bureaucrat from the Florida Department of Corrections. Then they waited.

Melissa held her back ramrod straight. Under the harsh florescent lights, the skin of her face gave the impression of having been pulled taut across the underlying bones.

No one spoke. At eleven forty five, the communications director for the prison arrived and asked if there were any objections from the witnesses to Gubbs addressing the group.

Melissa digested the announcement. She peered at the others.

"What do you think?" Rob asked in a whisper.

"I don't know. It seems like an obligation, to listen to him, I mean. Like it is part of it," she said quietly.

"Anyone object?" the bureaucrat asked.

Melissa shook her head.

"We'll listen," the younger gangbanger said.

"Now, you don't have to let him speak," Sharon said to the woman next to her.

"Huh?" the woman replied.

"We don't object," a gray-haired man in his 50s wearing Dockers and an expensive golf shirt, the oldest of the far group, said.

The communications director nodded and disappeared.

"It won't be long now," Rob said.

Melissa started biting around her left thumbnail.

A short time later, the death party entered the chamber. Gubbs, the prisoner, held the center. Two uniformed guards, both stout middle-aged men in stab-resistant vests, flanked him. Another two men were in washed-out suits, one gray, the other black. A collared priest walked directly behind Gubbs.

The white priest, who Rob guessed was in his mid-sixties but looked eighty, could have been a burned out activist who had stayed at his menial sustenance job a few decades too long. His salt and pepper hair, parted in the middle, hung down to his shoulders in greasy strands. He stood a head taller than Gubbs. His mustache covered his upper lip and grew down around the edges of his mouth. His black jacket didn't do much to hide a pronounced belly.

Gubbs himself, a white male about thirty, blue-eyed, thin and hollow-cheeked, wore prison orange. His hands were chained to a thick leather belt, tan, wrapped tightly around his waist. He carried book bound in leather. Rob recognized Gubbs's shuffle. Although he couldn't see, Rob knew his ankles were shackled.

Gubbs was radiant, blissfully happy even. His blond hair had been neatly cut, combed and parted. His face, ravaged by years of drug use and what Rob supposed had been poor hygiene, showed historical evidence of having stopped many fast moving blunt objects. Gubbs should have been a feral predator without evidence of intelligence, cornered and sullen; maybe even scared. Instead, he was positively . . . jubilant, Rob thought.

Gubbs cleared his throat. They heard the tinny sound out of hidden speakers.

"Y'all, I'm Jimmy Tank Gubbs. Thank y'all for lettin' me speak. Thank you."

With that introduction, Gubbs became Jimmy Tank forever more in Rob's mind.

Jimmy Tank faltered. The priest whispered something in his ear. Jimmy Tank nodded.

"Um, y'all, um, I know I did wrong. That's why I stopped them appeals. I done it. I want to thank Father Clyde before I start talking. Father Clyde showed me to the Lord and I want to thank him for that. I'm sorry. I done wrong. But now I know Jesus loves me. He loved me before, but I didn't know it. I had to come here and meet Father Clyde. I stopped them appeals before but it was out of anger. But now I know."

Jimmy Tank dipped his head and inhaled deeply. He shook his book. He looked out at the spectators again.

"I done confessed truly and I know the Lord Jesus Christ has forgiven me and accepted me into the Kingdom of Heaven, but I know I got to apologize. I'm sorry, you Harrises and you Taylors, I'm sorry for what I done to them kids. I was evil. Father Clyde says I got to stop off in purgatory some and I know I deserves it. I'm sorry.

"Yo, Hector, and you – yeah, I know you Pablo, I'm sorry too for Richard. I mean Ricardo. I'm sorry 'cause I was an evil sinner, but you should know Ricardo was self-defense. He was coming at me. No matter, I'm sorry.

"I got me the true contrition. I know I'm going to heaven after some purgatory time, but I can do that. I can do time. I made confession. I confessed it all to my Lord and Savior.

"Now you, Ms. Simmons . . . ."

Jimmy Tank Gubbs turned his head from side to side. Then he locked it straight ahead. He focused on a something behind them, farther back than even the back wall of the little gallery.

"I, I'm sorry. I'm sorry, Ms. Simmons, but I didn't kill your man."

Here Jimmy Tank's mien changed. For the first time, the joy fled his face, replaced by trouble.

Melissa gasped. She grabbed Rob's upper arm. She had quite a grip, Rob thought.

"Okay Jimmy," the older of the two men in suits said. "Come on now. It's time."

"Yessir." Jimmy Tank shuffled to the gurney. "Y'all, please forgive me even though I done wrong. I've confessed and the good Lord Jesus Christ put his hand on my heart to let me know he forgives me. Please, you do it too. You, too. I'm sorry."

Father Clyde slipped the book out of Jimmy Tank's had. They helped him up on the gurney. Jimmy Tank disappeared below the ledge.

At first Rob was content with attending the execution of a common criminal and not actually witnessing it. He thought he could sit through it and not actually watch. After all, he told himself, he was here to support Melissa and she had made no sign of wanting to get up.

Suddenly the act of witnessing became important to Rob. His government was about to take the life of one of its own, a man who had committed unspeakable acts. Journalists reported Jimmy Tank had confessed to twelve murders total. Even so, his was still a life.

Rob stood up.

"What are you doing?" Melissa asked.

"Maybe we owe it to him. As a citizen, I mean, I owe it to him to witness his death," Rob said.

Melissa thought about it for a minute and then stood up herself. She took his hand.

He liked that.

The gangbangers stood next. Two men in the other party got up.

Thick brown leather restraints held Jimmy Tank to the gurney. He was smiling. Two men in scrubs approached his left arm. One blocked their line of sight, but at what Rob thought was the insertion of the needle, Jimmy Tank closed his eyes. He started moving his lips rapidly. Rob thought they must be pushing the cannula through.

The men stood back. Rob could see tubing hooked up to the connecting hub. Jimmy Tank was left alone. He did not open his eyes. His lips slowed, then stopped. After about twenty minutes, one of the suits announced Jimmy Tank had passed.

Rob hustled Melissa toward the truck. They blew by a reporter who wanted an interview. They drove back the way they had come, through darkness so complete they could have been in a can of black paint.

"Care for something to eat, maybe a drink?" Rob asked.

Melissa shook her head.

She chewed on her thumb until they were on I-75 almost at I-10.

"Do you think he was telling the truth?" she asked.

Rob risked a glance. Shadows half hid her pensive countenance.

She was giving Jimmy Tank's statement some weight, Rob thought.

19

Rob chose to believe Jimmy Tank had been a crazy killer and the world was better off without him. But under the circumstances of his wanting to keep seeing Melissa, he thought of a more tactical answer.

"Maybe enough to look into it," Rob said.

"Like investigate it?"

"I was thinking more like researching. Did you keep up with the case at all?"

"No," she said, turning her face to the window. "It wasn't a very good time."

"Why don't I do some research and when I'm done, I'll give you a call?"

"Okay."

Rob drove on, damned pleased with himself.

Tuesday

Rob woke refreshed for the first time in a long time. Skipping his new tradition of two slob hours in front of the computer or the TV, he shaved and dressed. He chose a pair of olive expedition pants and a tan button-down shirt with a collar, which he wore untucked. He was famished, which was strange as he hadn't had much of an appetite recently. He carried his laptop down the block to the Coffee Service Café.

The whitewashed brick building with the red and white striped awning had never come across more inviting than right now. At a table from which he could see both doors, he ate a cheddar cheese omelet, bacon and toast. Over coffee, he read articles on Jimmy Tank from the Seminolacola News and Journal website.

Matthew Simmons as a victim created the initial momentum. The first headline read: "Rising Executive, Former NFSU Three Season Varsity Athlete Murdered – No Suspects."

Simmons had been shot to death in the parking garage of a shopping mall. His car, a new red Chevy Camaro, had been stolen and his wallet was missing. The police carried it as a robbery gone bad. Articles on Simmons's murder had eventually tapered off until Jimmy Tank's arrest. Rob kept reading. The reporters referred to Jimmy Tank by his last name, Gubbs.

Some weeks after the Simmons murder, the arresting officers had observed Gubbs driving a late model Chevy Camaro around Diego Circle. Officers told the court they were familiar with Gubbs, and had run the license plate number as he was unlikely to own such a vehicle. Results had come back with a violent felony hit and stolen want in the Simmons murder/robbery.

The officers had turned on the car, causing Gubbs to flee. During the chase, a pistol was thrown out the driver's window. Gubbs wrecked out and was arrested at the scene. The officers recovered the pistol and tests later determined it had fired the bullets that had killed Simmons.

Reporting slowed once again until it trickled off to nothing. The nothing went on until jury selection. The News Journal covered the trial, short as it was. After his sentencing, there wasn't much more press until Gubbs dropped a bombshell: he fired his attorneys and forbade appeals. He spoke to one national reporter long enough to tell her to go do something to herself she could not broadcast on TV and then clammed up all the way to injection time.

Good patrol work, Rob thought, but why the rush to the death chamber? Rob paid up and left the cafe.

It was hot outside, but not nearly as hot as it would get, so he decided to go for a run on the shoulder of Bayside Drive. He never got tired of the scenery: green foliage and turquoise water.

Soon sweat stung and it became hard to breathe. He pushed through it for two miles out and two miles back. He skipped lunch, showered, changed, and cranked up his truck.

Rob's first stop was the main police station at the southern terminus of I-295, the rump interstate running down from I-10 to the center of town. The public entrance to the worn stucco building opened to a waiting area of faded linoleum tile and molded plastic chairs. He asked the desk sergeant for Detective Lowery King.

"Detective King is busy," she said, clicking away at a keyboard.

"Hey," Rob said in the most solicitous manner he could manage, "could you tell him it's Rob Lawson?"

The Sergeant glared at him from behind her reading glasses.

Rob tried to look endearing.

She picked up the phone.

Lowery "Hoss" King pushed through the substantial wooden door separating the offices from the public. Hoss was big and solid, with a long face and thinning light hair. He hadn't removed the napkin from his collar.

"Rob, how you been?" Hoss stuck out a hand and saw the thick brown sauce on it. "Well forget that. Come on in."

Moments later, they faced each other over Hoss's desk with its mounds of paper and Styrofoam-encased remains of sauced-up, smoked pig parts.

"Been a while," Hoss said.

"Yup," Rob said.

"Go out of town?"

"No, hunkered down mostly."

"Uh-huh. Oh, well, condolences; condolences on your loss."

"Thanks Hoss."

"How's the wife?"

"She left me."

"Oh?"

"Yeah."

"Sorry."

Rob watched Hoss worry a rib and sip his sweet tea.

"Well," Hoss said, "you come by for more than spreading joy and cheer?"

"Yeah. Jimmy Tank Gubbs."

"He dead, Rob."

"Yup. I saw it."

"You were there last night?"

"Yeah. Met the widow at church and ended up going with her to give moral support in her time of need."

"Ugly as sin, she was?"

"You know it. Big old mole on her nose."

"Shit, boy," Hoss said, smiling, as he wiped his hands.

"The thing is, Gubbs went out of his way to say he didn't do the Simmons job. He copped to the others in his last words, but not to Simmons."

"So?"

"So, I'm there with old lady Simmons and I said I'd look into it and report back. The emphasis is on 'report back,' if you get my drift."

"Sure, I get it."

They smirked at each other.

"So the thing is," Rob said, "I need to get more than what's in the articles to take back to her."

"I got you, brother. Set while I dig for a minute."

Hoss drank some tea and typed away on an ancient desktop workstation. He read a little, typed a little, frowned, and read some more.

Then he read a three-paragraph narrative of the investigation aloud.

"Paper's said the same thing," Rob replied.

"So? That's it," Hoss said.

"What's with the frown?"

"What frown? Nothing."

"Can I read his statement?"

Hoss pounded on a few keys with rigid forefingers. "No statement."

"Declination?"

"Come on, Rob."

"Crime scene report? Property list of the decedent? Vic's wallet found on Gubbs, et cetera?"

"Damn it, Rob."

"Photos?"

"Ro-ob," Hoss said in a slight sing-song.

"What was the frown?"

Hoss shot him some stink-eye but said nothing.

"What about the arresting officers?" Rob asked.

"D. Randall Hargrove and William "Wee Willie" Washington Jefferson? Good *po*-lice is what," Hoss said.

"A troubling file is good *po*-lice? Say, is that with a hyphen?" Rob asked.

"Shit, boy."

"That frown, was it because of good *po*-lice?"

"Now Robert, are you asking because you want to get in with that widow lady, or are you all looking at D. Randall and Wee Willie? No hyphen, by the way."

"I'm not with them anymore."

Hoss jabbed a key with authority. Rob thought if Hoss had been reading from a file folder, he'd have slammed it shut.

"Well then, go on an' make up something to get into widow lady's pants. She was a gymnast and a diver you know."

"Oh?"

"Yup. She and Matthew Simmons were big athletes at West Florida State University up there. She was national ranked but never could get to the Olympics. I knew of her after she got to NFSU. She switched to diving there. Should be a quite enjoyable lay."

"Oh?"

"'Oh' my ass, Rob. What you want?"

"What about those cops?"

"You ain't with them no more, you go on and worry about flexible widow ladies with big life insurance payouts."

"And if I am with them?"

"Come back when you know if you is or if you isn't. Either way, I'll tell you to make sure you have your own life insurance in place."

"Oh? Is life insurance necessary?"

"Maybe it is," Hoss said, picking up a rib bone and leaned back in his chair.

"You always say something like that about good *po*-lice?" Rob asked.

"Rob, now, none of that. None of your fancy questions, turning me around and shit. I'm giving you good information. You take it or you leave it. I need to go back to work."

"Okay. Hoss, what do you make of Jimmy Tank shutting down all his appeals?"

"Don't make nuthin' out of it. Or care. No, wait, how about a sudden development of civic duty? Maybe he decided to save the taxpayers the cost of the appeals."

"Civic duty, yeah, right. You're a poet, Hoss. One last thing. If I want to talk to Hargrove or Washington Jefferson, where would I find them today?"

Rob met Hoss's glare with as innocent an expression as he could manage.

"Damn you, boy." Hoss logged back in and typed once more. "D. Randall is off today and Wee Willie is coming on now. You might be able to catch him on the ramp. Now git."

Wee Willie could barely sit still in the scuffed up briefing room.

"One last thing," the patrol sergeant said, "snatch and grab hijackings are up in Plainsview. Be sure to swing through several times. That's it, hit the street and stay safe."

Wee Willie exhaled. He had no time for foot chases. What he did have time for was dinner, like right damn now. As soon as he cleared, he'd go get himself some shrimp. Wee Willie was a large black man in his late thirties. He kept his tightly curled hair fairly short. He had round cheeks, a double chin and extra baggage around the middle that made him feel bad.

He picked up his gear and headed outside. As he checked his black-and-white (really it was black and cream like the Highway Patrol) for damage (he'd been burned by the officers going off watch before) a white boy approached him.

"Officer Washington Jefferson?" the white boy asked with the demeanor of a missionary.

Wee Willie guessed him at thirty-five or so. The white was almost six foot and in shape. His 'happy to sell you' attitude chapped Wee Willie's ass. Dickhead wanted something for sure, Wee Willie thought.

"Do I know you?" he asked.

"No sir. I'm Robert Lawson and I'd like to ask you a few questions about Jimmy Tank Gubbs."

Reporter, Wee Willie thought. Not so hippie, but a reporter for sure. Willie never talked to reporters.

"Public Affairs inside," Wee Willie said.

"I'm not a journalist. That was some arrest. You knew to turn on the Camaro just because Gubbs was driving it?"

Willie rubbed his rumbling stomach through his ballistic vest.

"You do-gooders give me gas." Willie belched. "You ain't going to save him, you know."

"I know. He was executed last night. I was there."

Wee Willie tried to come up with an angle for this boy but couldn't.

"Why you asking?" he asked.

"I'm verifying some facts for the family of one of the victims."

Wee Willie squinted at Lawson.

"No you ain't. Don't know what you are doing, but you ain't doing that. You do-gooders get on my nerves. Public affairs officer is inside. I'm going to work."

Wee Willie opened the trunk as if the white boy wasn't there. He lobbed his gear bag in and made his way around to the driver's door. It seemed like this Lawson, who was in the way, would stand his ground. Wee Willie kept going.

Lawson stepped back.

Good for him, Wee Willie thought.

The seat groaned as Wee Willie fell onto it. He slammed the door shut. Hot as hell, he thought. The odors of tobacco-infused spit and sweat were both familiar and reassuring. He started the car and the air conditioning.

Lawson got the message and walked away.

Wee Willie checked the gas and sure enough, those days bastards hadn't filled the tank. He'd have to swing by the municipal pumps before he could get his shrimp. But first, he grabbed his phone.

Rob, parked and idling, pointed his own air conditioning vents at his torso. He could see Wee Willie, who had not moved. The officer's head bent forward. Rob wondered who he was texting. Rob grabbed his own phone. He decided to dial instead of text and connected with Melissa's voicemail.

"Hi, it's Rob. I've got some information. Maybe we could get together tomorrow and I'll tell you about it. Maybe after work? I bet you pick up Jules. Maybe after? Maybe for coffee? Won't work, I guess. How about dinner? Like a date – no! Not a date! Just dinner. Uh —" and here, mercifully, the system cut him off.

"That went well," Rob said out loud.

Wee Willie had driven away. The ramp was empty, save one cruiser in a spot near the end. Rob put his truck in D for go.

Much later, Ali Barkr, a student at Bayview High School, felt trouble coming. He had uncharacteristically been added to a private group online as Saladin, his username. Excited at first, he started to suspect something was up because the others only ignored him. He felt he should exit, but like looking away at a car crash, he could not bring himself to do it. His apprehension grew. Finally, the pack turned its attention to their prey.

"Who's going to the dance?" came up on screen.

"u know."

"WHO bitch."

"Sand nig," 57Chev posted, as if Ali wasn't even there.

Ali Bakr couldn't stand it and couldn't stop himself. He posted "FUCK U ALL BIN LADEN LIVES DEATH TO YOU ALL."

Ali, a junior at Bayview, immediately left the group and slammed down the lid of his laptop. He knew he shouldn't do things like that, but they made him so mad.

He slumped down in his seat and stared at the weak light pooling on his desk in his single-family home in north Seminolacola. He was sure his parents, immigrants from Egypt, were asleep. They both worked hard. His brother was away, doing super at the University of Michigan. Only Ali couldn't fit in.

He kicked his trashcan.

Ali had delicate, almost feminine features and deep brown eyes. His dark curly hair defied all control techniques known to man and he had the slim build of a footballer, a soccer player, which he had been until they had run him off the team.

There would be snickering again at school tomorrow.

How the hell could he get them to stop, never mind even like him? His parents were no help. His father flat out didn't understand and his mother kept telling him he was her baby, although she was mad at him about his schoolwork. Even his brother, Hamda, did not get it. Everybody loved him. He'd had no difficulties at all and had sailed into a top university. Ali hated everybody. He hated them and felt like killing them.

The tears came. He turned out the light.

Wednesday

Rob thought Josiah Waller, a tall, angular, patrician white man in his middle fifties with a full head of wavy gray hair was one of those modern lawyers who got off on appearing empathetic. He met Rob at the metal, imitation wood-covered blast resistant door of the reception area for the US Attorney's Office of the Western District of Florida himself.

Waller's rolled shirtsleeves exposed squash player's forearms. A loose tie complemented the subtle checked trousers from his suit. He had steered Rob to a couple of armchairs in front of his desk, separated by a small pine table.

"Thank you for seeing me on such short notice. Congratulations," Rob said. "How long have you been up here?"

"Thank you. I did take an extended vacation after resigning from the States Attorney's Office, did some sailing, but it's been about three months now," Waller said, lacing his long fingers around the top knee of his crossed legs. "Forgive me, but what is your interest in the Gubbs matter?"

"Friend of the family. Mrs. Simmons asked me to go along with her to the execution."

"That sounds like fun."

"Hell of a good time. We were both struck by how Gubbs admitted culpability in the other murders, but not the murder of Matthew Simmons. What do you think about that?" Rob tried to look innocuous.

"Are you a lawyer, Mister . . . ?" Waller asked.

"Lawson. No. Accountant."

"You sound like a lawyer."

Waller had a high, brittle voice.

"I'm not," Rob said.

"You were at the execution?" Waller asked.

"Yes."

"They are fairly shocking affairs. I thought they stopped allowing the convicts to make statements. I think you were rattled, quite frankly."

"Melissa agrees with me."

"Ah, it's *Melissa* now, is it?"

Rob smiled, as if in on the joke. "What do you think about Gubbs's statement?" he asked.

"I think I convicted him beyond reasonable doubt. The trial lasted four days, excluding voir dire and motions, and the jury was out 90 minutes, which included a lunch ordered from a restaurant. They waited forty-five minutes for their food to arrive. Do you see what I am getting at? Forty-five to get lunch, forty five minutes to eat lunch. I think nothing of it, Mr. Lawson."

"Nothing?"

"Nothing. I think it was the ranting of a deranged mind. What are you really up to?"

"Just finding out what happened, Mr. Waller."

"Tread carefully, Mr. Lawson," Waller said, standing up.

"I'm sorry, is that a threat?" Rob asked, remaining seated.

"Not on my part. Consider it some advice. If Officers Hargrove and Washington Jefferson hear about you asking questions merely to impress a lady, you'd better have your will executed."

"Executed? That's pretty funny," Rob said.

Waller blushed.

"Why is that? Are they in the habit of killing people?" Rob asked.

"You ask interesting questions, Mr. Lawson. Please forgive me. I'm due in court." Waller gestured at the door.

Sure you are, Rob thought, as he left.

"Oh, I have fixed him. You know I have fixed him," Kathryn Lawson, Rob's ex-wife, said. She popped the cherry out of her Manhattan into her mouth and grinned wickedly.

She was back home in Indianapolis.

Grace wondered what she was doing in Pipers Restaurant with Kathryn. They had been in the same group at university, but Grace had been one of the corps and Kathryn one of the principals. Grace, a little big-boned normally, but now, once again pregnant, felt rather large. She thought herself pretty enough, with creamy skin and blonde hair, but she had no illusions.

"I have a plan," Kathryn winked. "Are you sure you don't want even one drink?"

Grace shook her head and rested her hand on her belly. Kathryn kept talking.

On one hand, Kathryn's text had excited Grace. The invitation was an unexpected opportunity to catch up and hear the gossip. With two kids and one on the way, she didn't really have the time to Facebook much anymore. Also, the invitation was for Pipers, and she craved their French onion soup and Chesapeake crab cakes like nothing else this time around. Even so, Grace was having a serious case of the second thoughts.

"You carry the weight so well," Kathryn said. "I wouldn't have guessed you have others!"

Kathryn didn't carry weight. Not now, not back in school. In fact, she had not changed a bit: tall, shapely and beautiful. A perfect fall of rich light brown hair framed her square-ish face and reached her shoulders. She had cheekbones to die for. Her eyes, though, Grace thought, were something else. They were big, brown and deep, but they could show a merciless streak, as they were doing now.

The soup arrived and Grace dove in. The quality of Kathryn's gossip did not hold her attention. She ate, drank her water and barely listened until she caught Rob's name.

Grace had a soft spot for Rob. He was kind of handsome in a nice way, like not intimidating. And he had been easy to be around. They had never hooked up, but Grace would have been all-in.

"Divorce papers," Kathryn said.

"What? You did what?" Grace asked.

"Sent him divorce papers." Kathryn sneered.

Kathryn's fundamental misjudgment of Rob left Grace speechless.

"You don't think that will make him come running? You bet your ass it will," Kathryn said.

Grace didn't think Rob would respond to a cracked whip at all.

"Well, aren't you going to say something?" Kathryn asked.

"Uh, Kathryn, I don't think that is the way it's supposed to work," Grace said.

"What do you mean?"

"I mean, threatening divorce is extreme, don't you think?"

"Extreme? What about me? After what happened? He owes me."

"It happened to both of you."

"No," Kathryn said with a short shake of her head. "No. No it didn't. Besides, what you say is nonsense. He'll come. He'll have had enough and come on back up here."

"But what if he signs them?"

Kathryn rolled her eyes dramatically. "Grace, that is about the stupidest thing I've ever heard you say. He wouldn't sign them."

And right then it occurred to Grace she really didn't like Kathryn at all.

"Kathryn, why did you call me?"

"I'm back in town and I want to see my friends. I thought you'd like to be the first one out with me."

"I do, I do. But what about Summer or Hailey?"

Kathryn ran her fingers around the rim of her water glass.

"They couldn't make it."

Grace didn't say much more and didn't protest at all when Kathryn offered to get the check. Grace got into her Town and Country and drove to Costco and then the obstetrician. When she finally got home to her four-bedroom colonial in Perry Township, she was tired and hungry. And she had to pee.

Rob parked in front of a rundown strip mall in the Plainsview neighborhood of Seminolacola. Plainsview was too far inland, Almost to I-10, for a sea breeze to offset the crushing heat. The mall was brown stucco, baked to oblivion. Chunks down to the wire mesh were missing. Several store fronts were empty. Rob pulled into a spot by the anchor establishment, a boxing gym.

The gym smelled of sweat and mildew and ammonia. There were the same two full-size boxing rings. The familiar six heavy bags and three speed-bags, all patched with gray duct tape, ran along the wall by the locker room. Room, as in only one.

"Hah! Hey, where you been?" Gravelly-voiced Fat Floyd Furness hadn't changed either.

The big black man ruled his domain from a throne, a torn-up old kitchen chair. His legs were spread wide and his large belly rested on the stained yellow seat. He had sweat through a short-sleeved button-down shirt and held a quart cup of tea with a red straw through the lid in one massive hand. The other rested on his ham hock of a thigh. His broken nose and the generous scarring around his eyes told anyone he had walked the walk.

"Here and there," Rob said. "You know how it is, Fat Floyd."

"Heh hey, you knows I do."

Rob and Fat Floyd shook hands. Rob tried some pre-emptive pressure but Fat Floyd crushed his hand like he was cracking walnuts, without any sign of criminal intent.

"What you think about dat kid?" Fat Floyd asked, nodding at the closest ring.

A black teenager with sculpted arms, impressive pecs and an attitude smirked at him from the far corner. He wore black trunks with a green flash and sixteen-ounce gloves. Two friends assisted him, although exactly how was not apparent. They were in dirty sweatpants and t-shirts.

Five Hispanics congregated around the near corner. One had clearly taken a beating.

"You Mexaricans got anything else? You got anything else?" The black boxer taunted.

They conferred in a tight knot. One of them stripped off his shirt. They relieved the beaten boy of his gloves and transferred them to the new fighter, who walked to the center in a wife-beater and khakis, hands up and ready.

The Hispanic boy gave up two years of age, height and reach to the much larger African American teenager, who was damn near six-foot tall. They circled each other. The Hispanic boy darted in and hit his opponent with a flurry of technically perfect punches. As he scooted back out, the black fighter landed a powerful blow on his forehead.

The punch had blazed out from his waist, Rob noted. The black fighter was so contemptuous, or lazy, he failed to even bring both fists up. The punch knocked the Hispanic boy back so hard his lower half couldn't keep up with his upper half. He backpedaled a bit before hitting the mat.

He sprung up though, and a brawl ensued. The Hispanic boy abandoned what could have saved him, his form, in favor of wild strikes that had little effect on his opponent. The black fighter pummeled him back, a Marcos Maidana wannabe, pounding away and eventually landing enough powerful blows to end it.

"Okay you all, okay," yelled Fat Floyd.

The Hispanic boys, fifteen-years-old to an individual, helped their wounded champion out of the ring.

"Yeah," the black boys yelled. "Yeah, get on."

"Dat boy can do it," Fat Floyd muttered to Rob, "but he too proud. He too proud."

"You gonna take me on, fat man?" the victor called out.

"Tyrell, them boys is one thing, you bein' eighteen and them not, but full-time fightin' is another. Go on back to school," Fat Floyd said.

"How about if I take that white motherfucker right there. You take me on then?"

"You can't take him, Tyrell. Go on, git outta here," Fat Floyd said.

"Floyd, what are —" Rob started to ask.

"Chah!" Fat Floyd cut him off. "Boy ain't got no respect," Floyd muttered to Rob.

"Go on home, boy," Floyd said to Tyrell.

"What you say, old man? You ready for night-night?" Tyrell said.

Rob read Fat Floyd's silent request on his features.

Tyrell smacked his gloves together. "Whitey! You get me?"

"Nighty night mother fucker!" one of Tyrell's friends shouted. Hilarity ensued. "He old, called him Honkey, bitch," the other said.

"I'm too fat these days to do it myself," Floyd muttered to Rob. "They got to go back to school."

"A little sumthin'-sumthin', bitch?" one of the boys taunted.

More laughter.

"I'll change," Rob said.

"There's eight-ouncers in the locker room," Fat Floyd muttered. "Kid will never notice."

Rob stripped off his clothes and put on a ripped tourist t-shirt, dingy US Olympic trunks from long ago and a pair of worn boxing shoes. The eight-ounce gloves hung from a hook behind the door.

Back on the gym floor, Fat Floyd taped him up amid a growing chorus of insults.

"I gots to get this kid oriented right. He can fight, but he's going down the wrong way. Boy on the right clocks. I don't want Tyrell following him onto a corner sellin' dat shit. Short ride to dead like that," Fat Floyd said.

"So you want him to beat me up?" Rob said, putting on his head gear.

"Sheet boy, he ain't gonna beat you up. You drop him in the first round even after a year of nothing but HBO. He'll punch you twice and then drop both his left an' his right. You takes them hits on you arms. Make sure you ready to give him you right cross." Fat Floyd finished taping up the laces.

"Whatever you say," Rob said, stepping into the ring.

"He can hit, now."

"Great," Rob muttered.

Tyrell danced around his corner. "Don't worry white man. You old. I'll take it quick on you."

More laughter. Rob's adrenaline kicked in.

"Tyrell, where's your headgear?" Rob asked.

Tyrell and his friends shot each other theatrical 'get real' smirks.

"Get the fuck in here, bitch," Tyrell sneered.

Rob bit down on his mouth guard.

"Ding!" Floyd said.

Rob put his hands up. Tyrell had already covered some distance and wound up for a knockout blow.

Rob charged. He landed a stiff jab before Tyrell, startled and knocked off balance, bounced his punch off Rob's head.

Tyrell needed to take two clown steps backwards to regain his stance. Rob shook his head to regain his concentration. Even retreating, Rob felt the punch through the padding.

Tyrell ran at him.

Everything decelerated, giving Rob time to think. He saw Tyrell drop his right a little, no doubt his set up for the planned punch. Rob stepped right, brought his hands up and leaned in to take the blow on the most padded part of his headgear. As Tyrell launched, Rob shuffled back a little bit.

Or started to. Tyrell was so fast, he landed the blow with most of its force square on Rob's forehead. It rocked Rob, but he kept moving back. Tyrell's second punch rocketed out of the gate, and it landed, but Rob was far enough away so it merely hurt. As Fat Floyd said, Tyrell lowered both gloved fists almost down to his stomach.

Rob leapt. He landed firm and pivoted sharply, throwing a cross to Tyrell's exposed chin. Rob got his pelvis and shoulders into it. His fist, covered with half the padding of Tyrell's, landed on the boy's jaw.

Tyrell collapsed on himself. He fell with a look of surprise half-formed on his face.

Rob retreated to a corner.

Tyrell didn't spend much time on the canvas. He managed to get to his knees quick enough. He hadn't gone all the way out, but he was groggy.

"That's it," Fat Floyd yelled.

Only one of Tyrell's friends entered the ring to help. The one Fat Floyd said was a low-level dealer bopped his way to the door, followed by his entourage.

"Yo, man?" Tyrell shouted.

His friend merely threw up an extended middle finger as he passed into the harsh hot sunlight.

Tyrell huddled with his remaining corner man. Rob stepped between the ropes and jumped to the floor. Fat Floyd untied his gloves.

"I knowed it would happen. I knowed Tyrell be selling himself as a hitter. Street hustler probably wanted to turn him into muscle," Fat Floyd said.

"How'd you know I could take him?" Rob asked.

"Boy could make a fighter, but he needs to get serious. He can hit, but he need to learn the rest of it. You now, you a thinking fighter, even if you can't punch as hard."

"Well, I'll take that as a compliment."

"Take it how you want. By the way, you know I'm sorry about what happened."

They got his gloves and head gear off.

"Yeah, I know. Thanks. Hey Floyd, what do you know about a pair of *po*-lice, D. Randall Hargrove and Wee Willie Washington Jefferson?"

Fat Floyd slyly eyed him sideways. Floyd glanced down at the floor. Then he pointed his gaze upward to the Devine, followed by a big show of peering at Rob sideways again.

"You sure you want to ask?" Fat Floyd said.

"They're dirty?" Rob asked.

"Shh!" Floyd scanned the nearly empty gym.

"Come on, Fat Floyd. It won't come back on you."

"You making crazy talk. Them *po*-lice be crazy, too. They be shifty. Shifty and mean. D. Randall owns rent houses and uses Wee Willie to collect. They got no heart and put folks on the street in a hot minute."

"That don't make them dirty."

"I know it. D. Randall gots a hand problem. There's always a witness done go missing and whatever and he done do some damage, you know?"

"I know."

"Those boys — D. Randall mostly I guess 'cause Wee Willie don't do shit he don't have to — never make an arrest what don't stick."

"So? Maybe they know what they are doing."

"Maybe, except I heard one time too often many them arresteds didn't do it."

"Nobody has ever done it."

"Chah. You asking me, or what? Maybe one time too many alibies be good up front and then not so good after D. Randall gets through with them."

Rob put away his head gear and handed the light gloves to Floyd as he thought about this new information.

"You going after them?" Fat Floyd asked.

"I'm not sure I have a reason to," Rob said.

"If you do, name your beneficiary."

Rob couldn't stop himself from chuckling.

"They're going to kill me?"

Floyd didn't laugh.

"D. Randall gots a hand thing, sure, but I also hear people he got trouble with stop turning up," Fat Floyd said.

"Like who?" This time Rob asked.

"You mind me. Take care."

"Give me a name Floyd. Who?"

"You better start on the speed bag. You got slow while you been gone."

Melissa and Rob settled in at their booth in Emerald Oyster and Steak, an upscale restaurant on the southern edge of the Seminolacola Historic District. Dark wood paneling, a polished hardwood bar with brass trimmings and vinyl tile flooring passably imitating pink pavers set the mood. Rob wished he had picked one of the tables with chairs. He felt as if he was sitting a football field away from Melissa and he wanted to be closer.

Melissa had pinned back her hair. Her outfit, a long-sleeved, pink paisley blouse worn over her blue jeans, was chaste but pretty. Her rolled-up sleeves revealed tan forearms. He had worn pressed beige cargo pants and a brown-checked short-sleeved button-down shirt with a collar.

The server, a tall hairy guy in black named Nick, brought their drinks — a Coke Zero for her and a Maker's Mark with one cube for him — and took their orders.

"Just a cube to open it up," Rob said, promising himself he'd stop after this one.

"So you said you found out something?" she asked.

"Oh, yeah," he said with a grin. "Yeah, a few things. The facts in the papers," and here he repeated the narrative in clipped, authoritative tones, "matches what's in the police report."

"You read the police report?"

"Yeah."

"How did you get a copy of the police report?"

"I asked. I know a guy."

That impressed her, Rob thought.

"But more interesting was the feedback I got on the officers," he continued. "They fell into this arrest, which is not a problem, but I when asked one about it, he –"

"Wait, you spoke to them?"

"One of them, yeah."

"You spoke to him? How did you find him?"

"I asked around at the station. He was coming on duty. I approached him there."

"You walked into the station and asked them? What did you say?"

"I introduced myself and asked if he had a minute to talk about Jimmy Tank."

"Oh my God. I could never do that. Weren't you afraid? What did he say?"

"Not much. He got real short with me. Of course, he assumed I was a reporter."

"Oh. Was he mad?"

"More like annoyed. Anyway, I've learned a few things about the arresting officers. Nothing dramatic, but curious stuff. I'd like to keep looking into it."

"Like what?"

"I'd rather not say just yet."

Rob hoped she'd express some continued curiosity. He wanted to keep seeing her.

"Okay," she said. She sipped her Coke.

Great, Rob thought.

"But there is this," Rob said. "Did you know Jimmy Tank dismissed his lawyers and cancelled his appeals?"

"I remember someone calling about it, but to tell you the truth, once they explained it to me, I thought it was good."

Nick brought their food, broiled sea bass for Melissa and a steak for Rob.

"How do you know so much about this stuff?" Melissa asked.

"Oh. Uh, I was a forensic accountant. Some of the policing must have rubbed off on me."

"But you said you sold a business?"

"Yes, an accounting practice. Like I told you, I've been living off the proceeds." The lie almost choked him. "I can't do it forever, so it's time to make some decisions."

"You said something about bulkheads?"

"I'm thinking about building and repairing bulkheads. It's hard work, but lucrative. I could start something in the construction line."

"You don't sound so sure."

"Nope – my innate laziness. Sitting in an office has its attractions, especially when it's a hundred twenty-five in the sun. What do you do?"

Rob listened to Melissa tell him all about her work as a PT Assistant. The upshot was she and Matthew had gotten married and pregnant, and she hadn't finished her education, though she thought about going back for it.

Nick passed by. They both declined dessert.

"I'm really lucky about how Matthew arranged things. There were two insurance policies and some savings, so I can work part time and handle the payments for the condo and my little Civic on an assistant's salary," Melissa said.

"That's great," Rob said.

"I know I need to get my DPT, but I'm, like, I'm making it. I mean, I can pay my bills, get a workout and still spend time with Jules. I'm so thankful. I want things, like, stable, you know?"

"Sure."

Nick put a black five-by-eleven inch folio on the table, closer to Rob than Melissa. Rob scooped it up.

"Shouldn't we split the check?" Melissa asked.

"Nah," Rob said, "Use your half for extra boxes of mac and cheese back at the house."

They continued their conversation outside as they strolled down the brick sidewalk. The streets of the few blocks of the historic district were gray cobblestone. They passed hundred-year-old storefronts that housed bars, restaurants and other businesses, some tourist orientated and others not. The street lamps of worked iron, reminiscent of gas lights from long ago, came on as the sun set.

"You can hardly tell the hurricane passed through," Rob said.

"Yeah, it's normal here," Melissa said.

"Let's get some ice cream."

"Oh no, I can't. I'm stuffed."

Two men stepped into their path. The shorter one, about five-foot seven, had a narrow face with a combination of Hispanic and Indio features, a salt-and-pepper goatee and short brown hair. He wore a seersucker suit in traditional blue and white with a white shirt. His tie, patterned in squares of different shades of blue, hung loose. The other was white, taller, and wore a dark bowling shirt and tan pants with cargo pockets. Both were in their late thirties or early forties. The taller man was stocky. Both stood with their feet shoulder-width apart and their hands down.

Melissa moved closer to Rob. She grabbed his upper arm. It felt good.

"Boss wants to see you," said the taller man in a Chicago accent.

"I'll come by in the morning," Rob said.

"Afraid not."

A late-model blue Chrysler 300 pulled up to the curb. The shorter, Hispanic man opened the rear passenger door. Rob ducked a bit and spoke to the driver.

"Hello Chris," Rob said.

"Sorry to bother you Rob, but we need to see you at the office. Does the lady need a lift?" Chris, a white man in his late forties, said.

Melissa's eyes were wide and her lips pursed.

"Are you comfortable driving my truck?" Rob asked Melissa.

"What's going on?" she asked.

"I know these guys, it's fine. I'll come by in about an hour and pick up my truck. Here's the keys. It's okay."

From the back seat, Rob saw Melissa clutching his fob with both hands. She appeared worried. Rob casually waved.

Soon all four men were in the car and heading north.

"Sorry about upsetting your plans for tonight," Chris said.

"No problem," Rob said.

"You on a date?" the taller man from the sidewalk asked.

"Sort of," Rob said.

"Oh? Where's Kathryn?"

"For the love of God, Leo," Chris said.

"We are very sorry about what happened," the Hispanic man said.

"Thanks Steve."

They drove to a SunTrust Bank building. Chris carded the door open. They called an elevator.

"She's gone," Rob said.

"Gone?" Chris asked, surprised.

"She went home about nine months ago. She sent me divorce papers, like last week. I signed them and mailed them back."

"Shit," Leo said. "That's shitty."

After a ride up, they stopped in front of a considerable wooden door. A black metal, case hardened combination lock with an LED readout had been installed above the silver doorknob. A keypad with black buttons and white numbers was attached to the wall nearby. A dark plaque read, in three lines of white General Services

Administration lettering: "FBI, Seminolacola Resident Agency, Tallahassee Field Office." Chris bent to work the lock and then patted his chest.

"Crap. Steve, I forgot my glasses. Can you open up?"

They switched positions.

"Hey Chris," Rob said, "it sucks you couldn't be in here waiting. The guys could have brought me in to see you glaring as the light of one lamp cast menacing shadows. No Maddie tonight? Or Kay?"

Chris shrugged. "Maddie retired and Kay couldn't stay."

The combination lock clicked loudly. Steve opened the door. Chris produced his access badge. The alarm squawked. They all ran in as the door closed. Chris punched in the code.

"My office," he said.

They passed through a second inner door. Chris led the way through the dark cube farm to his private corner office. Rob lowered himself into one of two armchairs in front of a large desk. Steve remained standing behind and a bit next to Rob. Leo leaned against the door jamb. Chris plopped down in his leather chair behind the desk.

Rob knew Chris's office by heart with its two telephones, two computers with multiple monitors, the mementos in the hutch behind him: challenge coins, law enforcement plaques, a Director's Award statuette.

Chris lifted his hands up and brought them down, flat palms striking the desk.

"Look, Rob," he said, "I needed to see you anyway. I used up all your sick leave and all your annual leave to keep you on the books. I kept you out on leave without pay for as long as I could. Now the LWOP period is exhausted. The Assistant Special Agent in Charge and the Administrative Officer are all over me to get rid of you. Not to mention with you taking up a position but not doing anything, we're understaffed and the others are carrying the weight.

"On top of that, Esteban here," Chris pointed at Steve, "gets a call from Hoss. On top of everything, we find out you're freelancing a public corruption case. Rob, you gotta be on the team. You can't do this stuff as a private citizen and expect us to protect you. If nothing else, those cops will eat you up if you keep going. So, here's my question: are you coming back to work or not?"

There it was, Rob thought. Did he want to come back to the FBI or not? Was it time to build bulkheads, or should he go back to full days of administrative FBI bullshit so he could work really bad, bad guys on "overtime?"

The other men had their interview faces on.

"I mean it. Tell me now. Tonight. Tomorrow at zero eight hundred I pull your plug, Rob. I'm sorry about before and I'm sorry about Kathryn, but this is it. I have to know now," Chris said.

Rob missed this office. He missed the guys, both here and on the division SWAT team. He thought of his first big case.

Three of his six years in the Bureau had been spent structuring a fraud case against some Canadian wiseguys running small cons on old folks throughout the US. He had one hundred thirty-two victims in twenty-seven states. He was there when the Royal Canadian Mounted Police rounded them all up in Windsor. He remembered how it had felt when he told a few of the old timers in person.

He remembered how it felt when Director Muller presented his credentials to him. He still had the photograph with the Director and his family, taken right there on the stage at Quantico. Even Kathryn had beamed.

Chris must have been reading his mind because he unlocked his desk drawer. He put Rob's black credentials wallet on the desk, then his badge in a belt clip, his Springfield Armory .45 ACP pistol in its holster, extra magazines and his BlackBerry. His building and office badges came last.

Rob exhaled sharply.

"I'm in," he said.

Smiles broke out around the room. They all shook Rob's hand.

"Great, now tell me. What have you got on the Seminolacola Police?" Chris asked.

Rob told him everything, and it didn't take long.

"That's about a whole lot of nothing," Chris said.

"One other thing," Rob said. "He does a McVeigh after sentencing. Dismisses all his lawyers and cancels all his appeals."

"So? First bit of sense he had in his life," Leo said.

"I see what you mean," Steve said, "that thing with the lawyers. It's not normal. But in the end, what you got is some good police work, Rob."

Steve Guerra assignments were Criminal Enterprises and the Violent Crime Major Offender programs, making him the closest with the police and sheriffs in the territory. The fact he shared Army experience with many of the officers only made them tighter.

"Rob believes him," Leo said.

Leopold Kladsko, half Polish, half Italian, former Army himself and former Chicago Police too, called it as he saw it. Leo worked Terrorism and headed up the West Florida Joint Terrorism Task Force.

"No, he doesn't," Chris said. "We don't do crusades around here. Tell me you don't, Rob."

Chris was the Supervisory Senior Resident Agent — the boss. He was much closer to fifty than the others and putting on some desk weight around his beltline. He was in his retirement post and everyone knew it. With less than 24 months to go to qualify for his pension, Rob knew Chris wanted avoid trouble, if possible.

"Yeah, I guess I do," Rob said.

The three men fidgeted and avoided each other's eyes.

"I mean, not enough to go on a crusade, but enough to do some due diligence," Rob said.

"So you think the State of Florida executed an innocent man?" Chris asked.

"No, not innocent. He admitted to twelve murders. Innocent of the charge that got him to the death chamber, maybe."

"Yeah, something minor like that. Couldn't you have picked something less loaded for your comeback case? Like maybe the Governor taking bribes or the chief justice being a Klan member?"

"Sorry Boss."

"He's back five minutes and he wants to light the RA on fire," Leo said.

"Robert, really, why?" Steve asked.

"What are you thinking?" Chris asked. "We'll draw down every death penalty activist on this, not to mention wall-to-wall journalists. There is enough here to keep them fed for weeks. After this case Seminolacola PD will hate us for the next fifteen years."

"There are no journalists anymore," Leo said, "only lazy infotainers."

"If you're pushing me," Rob said, "I'll tell you this — no detective was assigned to the case."

"Bullshit!" Leo said. "Hoss had it."

"No bullshit, Leo. Hoss had it after the fact. There is no evidence to indicate a detective ever interviewed Gubbs. Nothing in the file, nothing in the press."

"Maybe he declined," Leo said.

"No record of it, according to Hoss."

"So what's your theory?" Chris asked.

"The officers set up Gubbs and he had a compelling reason to go along."

"So you think the cops killed the decedent?" Chris asked.

"I don't know. Maybe."

The office was silent as each man thought about the implications.

"Here's what I want," Chris said. "You show up on time tomorrow and do your Blood Borne Pathogens course. After, you open this up as a civil rights preliminary. While you are waiting for permission, you either prove or disprove the existence of any statements, interviews, or declinations he made with detectives. If you find one, we close this bitch immediately. Got it?"

"Yes, Boss."

"To be sure, what I mean is I want this closed before it gets opened, and even formally titled, clear?"

"Yes Boss."

"Great. Welcome back. Get out. I'll lock up." Chris pushed the gear to Rob.

In the restroom outside the FBI suite, Leo and Steve waited as Rob threaded his holster back on his belt. He tried to lay his shirt on top of the .45.

"You know what you got here?" Leo asked.

"Yup," Rob said.

The shirt bunched up on top of both the large pistol and the magazines and BlackBerry. It looked ridiculous. Rob went about tucking his shirt in. He clipped the badge in front of the holster.

"This can cause a lot of bad blood if it gets out," Steve said.

"Yup," Rob said.

"Well, you follow the money. There will be money in this case, if it's real. Find it and follow it and you'll find the players," Steve said.

"There won't be any money, Steve," Leo said. "Rob, you know what you got here? You got a big stinking pile of dog shit. Come on, I'll take you home."

"I should call the police," Melissa said again, as she paced from her kitchen to the living area. "It's been longer than an hour."

"I don't know," Lila said, "he said he was fine." Lila sat on the dark brown leather couch in the fully carpeted living area. She wore a white t-shirt and green pastel stretch pants. Her hands were clasped in her lap.

Melissa had counted on Lila since about two minutes after she and Jules had moved in, not long after the murder. Lila, a neighbor, had walked over, introduced herself and never really left. Lila liked Melissa, but she loved Jules.

Melissa and Jules had ended up in a condo that was more than she had ever hoped for. There were two bedrooms off the common living and dining area, one on each side, and a loft over the living area. Jules played up there all the time. A large sliding glass door opposite the kitchen led out to a broad deck with a killer bay view. Two bathrooms, off street parking and a small complex pool for Jules made it perfect. She had no idea how she had been able to afford it. Thank God for Chucky Durant, she thought.

"What if he doesn't come back?" Melissa asked.

"For you, he'll come back," Lila said.

"What a thing to say."

"You'll see. He likes you."

"He does not."

"Sure he does. Why do you think he keeps talking to you?"

"He's checking things out."

"Sure. He has nothing better to do but read about what the monster did. He likes you. Besides, he has to get his truck."

Melissa started to respond but a light knocking interrupted her. She ran to the front entrance and yanked open the door.

"You really should check through the peep hole before opening it, especially at this time of night," Rob said.

"I did," Melissa said.

Rob paused on his way in for a quick scan around the room.

"Hi," Rob said to Lila.

Lila caught Melissa's eye and pointed at Rob.

He wore a huge intimidating black pistol in a black holster on his hip. The small gold badge clipped to his belt had a slight mitigating effect, but still.

"I've got some explaining to do," Rob said.

Melissa stood by Lila. "Yes, you do," she said, with her foot tapping.

Rob grinned sheepishly. Melissa melted a bit and thought she could get in real trouble here.

"Did you babysit for Jules tonight?" Rob asked Lila.

"Uh-huh."

Rob pulled some cash in a money clip out of his pocket. He counted off three twenties and handed them to Lila.

"You don't have —" Lila said.

"Take it," Melissa said. She snatched the bills out of Rob's hand and passed them to Lila.

"Well?" Melissa asked.

"I don't want to hold you up Lila," Rob said. "Do you need a ride?"

"Oh no, but I'm staying anyways," Lila said, crossing her legs and folding the bills.

He smiled again. She was beginning to really like his smile. Explanations first, though.

"I'm all ears," Melissa said, with snark.

"Well, first off," he reached for one of the white chairs with wicker seats ringing the glass table they used for meals, "may I sit?"

Melissa waved him down but remained standing.

"Thanks. First off, I have to apologize because I told you a lie."

"Just one?"

There was that grin again.

"Just the one," he confirmed. "I haven't been living off the sale of a business. I'm on a leave of absence from the FBI, where I'm a special agent."

"You're an FBI agent?"

"Yup."

"You expect us to believe you're an FBI agent?"

"Yes."

"What about the accountant stuff?"

"I am an accountant and worked as one before coming into the Bureau."

"Oh. Why did you leave?"

"Not leave – take leave. I had some family issues to work through."

"I see you don't wear a wedding ring," Lila said.

"No wedding ring," Rob said.

"Are you married?"

"I was."

"Was your divorce part of the family issues you worked through?"

"Yes."

"You are single now, right?" Lila asked.

"Lila!" Melissa said.

"Yes. Well, divorced," Rob said.

"I can go now," Lila said. She waved animatedly at them both on her way out.

"Should I walk her home?" Rob asked.

"No, she only lives across the street and over a little. What about picking a business to start?" Melissa asked.

"That was true, too. I've been on leave without pay. I was thinking about leaving, really on the fence about going back to the Bu, up to about a half an hour ago. It was time to make a decision. I needed to go back or to resign. If I didn't do anything, I'd get terminated."

They wouldn't have like, shot him or something, Melissa thought. She wondered if she'd heard him correctly.

"I mean fire me," Rob said, as if he could read her mind.

"Oh. So you knew about prisons through your job?"

"Yup. I've been to Raiford several times to interview inmates."

"Oh. Did Reverend Nettles know?"

"No. Look, I'm sorry. I've been through a lot lately. It's more than I'd want to bring up on a first date, especially one where we were going to watch the execution of your husband's killer."

"A date? Now we've been on a date? Was it a date? You FBI guys have some interesting ideas about what makes a date."

"Not exactly, no. Not a date."

This time he fought against his grin. It only worked a little.

"Uh-huh. Do they – you – traditionally grab people off the street when you want to talk to them? Maybe they do in the FBI," Melissa said.

"No, not traditionally, because traditionally, when we do try it, they run away."

"Huh?" Melissa asked.

Rob laughed.

"No, we don't" he said, "that was something else. I got into a little trouble for asking those questions at the police station."

"Why? Why would a police officer be upset at some questions?"

"Sometimes people behind the badge are a little sensitive."

"But still, why pick you up off the street?"

"It's my fault in a way. I was living on a boat until the hurricane. I had to move into my apartment after and I hadn't gotten around to telling anyone where I lived, so they came to find me."

"They couldn't call?" Melissa asked, joining him at the table.

"I wasn't answering," Rob said.

"I see. I'm not happy with you right now."

"I can tell."

"So what do they think about the execution?"

"You have to keep anything we discuss to yourself."

"All right."

"They don't think there is much. Chris, my supervisor, is only letting me go to check out some irregularities and then close it up pronto."

"It will be hard, but I'll try to keep that to myself. What do you think?"

"Something may be up. I have this urge to close a gap or two. If I don't come up with something fast, I'll have to drop it."

Melissa tried to organize all this new information: Rob was in the FBI, there was some issue with the investigation into what happened to Matthew, and Rob thought of the trip to Raiford as a date. On the one hand, Melissa thought it was creepy, to think of an execution as a date. On the other, she was getting to like his grin.

"I had a good time tonight," Rob said.

She was having a hard time staying mad.

"Me, too," she said.

"Do you forgive my subterfuge?"

"Is that what you call it?"

"Yeah, that's what I'm going to go with."

She nodded slowly.

"So what now?" he asked.

"Now you can go home."

She got up and retrieved his keys from the counter. He stood and she dropped them into his outstretched hand.

"Can I call you again?"

She laughed.

"Something funny?" he asked.

"I think it's cute you call," she said.

"I'm sorry I lied to you." He put his hands on her upper arms and kissed her forehead. "I'm going now, but I'll *hit* you tomorrow."

She let him out and went about straightening up the kitchen. Eleven thirty and work tomorrow, she thought. She mechanically ran through the tooth brushing and face cleaning. After changing into silk shorts and a matching tank top, she padded on her bare feet to check on Jules. He lay on his back, his beautiful hair covering his face. A feeling of love welled up in her chest so powerful she felt as if she could barely breathe.

In her own bed, she lay under a sheet with her hand resting on her stomach.

She started to feel thick in her middle.

It was supposed to be over, she thought. Matthew was dead, and so was the guy who killed him. Now this FBI person shows up from nowhere. How strange.

The bloated feeling grew.

That grin, she thought. And his bod was *lit*.

She started to feel uncomfortably full, even though she hadn't eaten in hours.

He thought taking her to a prison was a date.

She couldn't stand it anymore.

She shot upright. The sheet was off and she was on her feet, walking to the bathroom with purpose, like taking the floor. In front of the commode, she felt compelled to stick her fingers all the way into her mouth, to the back of her throat. She felt it start.

Melissa used both hands to hold her hair back. When she was done, she knelt on the cold tile, backside on her heels, spine straight, shoulders back.

She was going to have to watch herself, she thought. That hadn't happened in years.

Melissa wiped her mouth with the back of her hand.

Senior Patrol Officer D. Randall Hargrove drove his marked Seminolacola Police Department cruiser north on Bayside, way out of his sector. The new Chevy Impala police package had a three point six liter vee six, six-speed automatic transmission, heavy-duty power disc antilock brake system, heavy-duty police suspension, and a hundred seventy amp alternator. He loved the black and cream color scheme influenced by the Florida Highway Patrol, even though he hated FHP.

D. Randall was on duty, sharp in his City uniform, a forest-green, short-sleeved shirt and matching trousers with a three-inch wide Sam

Brown belt. His six-pointed star rode on the right and a few hero bars were pinned above his left pocket. He liked the whole package.

When D. Randall stood, his full height reached six-foot one. He had the fading physique of a former jock and had to wrap his ballistic vest around a slight paunch. He wore a flattop and sidewalls and shaved every day. D. Randall believed in officer presence.

D. Randall was proud of himself and his department. He didn't agree with a lot of the new-fangled community policing, but it did not affect him much. The Seminolacola city fathers and one mother wanted the city safe for tourists with crime contained to the appropriate neighborhoods and they didn't care too much about how it got done.

D. Randall was down with that.

He saw the reflection of the moonlight on the dark glassy water of the bay. He drove one man tonight and didn't have to consider what a partner wanted to do. If he wanted to drive off his beat and out of his sector to gaze at the bay, he did it. Everyone else could shut the –

"Two Twenty-Four, it's the domestic violence at 967 Grunion, cross street Bellaire. Adult son left location, advising he would get his eye-oozy and kill stepfather. All units, 224 is one man," the even female voice of the dispatcher said.

"Two Twenty-Four en route," D. Randall replied.

"I see 205 and 313 marking en route," the dispatcher said. "There's a request for an ambulance on this one. I'm holding it."

D. Randall keyed his handset to indicate *thanks*. He timed the lights and arrived, barely late, to see four cars parked on Bellaire waiting for him. He drove past and they fell in behind him as he turned onto Grunion.

967 stood at the end of the cul-de-sac. A middle-aged black woman in a housedress waited on the lawn with her hands on her hips. A black man of about the same age rested on the one-step stoop, elbows on knees, head in hands. The street dead-ended into a tall lush hedgerow. The small one story houses were run down enough for it to be noticeable in the moonlight.

"Two Twenty-Four arrived," D. Randall said into the radio.

"Ten-four. I have 205, 313, 214 and 113 on scene," the dispatcher said.

D. Randall stopped the car at an angle and stood behind the door, his hand on his pistol. The hedgerow hadn't been trimmed in years. He had his Streamlight in his left hand, resting on his shoulder, the powerful beam pointed at the thick wall of green.

"Two of you boys watch them – they're making me nervous. I can't see through them," D. Randall said.

Two of the other officers deployed to cover the hedges.

"Say baby, what we all got goin' on here?" D. Randall asked the woman.

"See here, my boy done smacked my mans upside the head with my phone," she said.

"Your phone? No iPhone did that."

"You know that, uh-huh. It was my old phone, the one with the turney dial. I still gots it in my parlor."

"How's he doing? Does he need an amb-lance?"

The man shook his head.

"Say baby, come on up here," D. Randall said.

He abandoned the cover of the cruiser and visually inspected the area. The woman in the house dress sauntered to the car and D. Randall met her at the front of his unit. He switched his Streamlight to under his arm, pinning it to his body, and without a word he stuck his hand into the right pocket of the woman's house dress. He came out with a nickel plated .25 automatic pistol and placed it on the hood of his vehicle out of her reach.

"Your mans be hitting on you tonight?" D. Randall asked. "You look okay."

"Naw, he a good man. He works. He works hard. He and my son fuss because my son don't work. They fussed and my boy done pick up the turney dial phone -"

They heard him first, bashing through the hedges. A tall, thin, twenty-year-old black man crashed through and passed by the sentinel officers. The skin of his face shone with sweat. He wore a hoodie, not a good sign this time of year, D. Randall thought as he started running. The kid had both hands on an Intratec Tec Nine submachine pistol, another bad sign.

The young man half stumbled toward his stepfather, raising the ugly weapon with its protruding single stack magazine.

As D. Randall got up to speed, the two officers drew their pistols. The prospective shooter picked up D. Randall and started moving the pistol in his direction. D. Randall reached out with both hands. He grabbed the shooter's wrist and the pistol's hand guard. He twisted the weapon up, held the wrist down, pivoted, and shoved his left hip into the shooter's stomach. D. Randall planted his feet and twisted his torso to the left, flipping the wanna-be shooter.

The young man landed hard. D. Randall ripped the pistol all the way out of his hands and backed away. Two more officers jumped the young man, cuffed him up, and started searching him.

The woman hadn't changed her position.

"This him?" D. Randall asked.

"That's him," she said. She spit on the street. "He a good boy. It's just . . . ."

"Yeah," D. Randall said. "I know."

Thursday

Rob woke before the alarm and dressed in a blue t-shirt and jeans. He strapped on his .45, a pair of handcuffs, an extra magazine, and his BlackBerry, putting it all under a short-sleeved blue-on-white checked shirt. After a light breakfast, he packed a gym bag.

Rob drove his pickup to the RA through a beautiful Gulf Coast morning, nothing but blue sky and sunrise. He got the denial buzz when he tried to badge in.

"Damn," he muttered.

He had hoped to sneak into his cube. He thought about his options and, after admitting to himself he didn't have any, rang the bell and looked up into the surveillance camera mounted on the ceiling.

A moment passed. A buzzer sounded. He opened the door and stepped into the small waiting area, no more than six-foot square. In front of him was a thick glass panel with a silver speaking hole. The second door would not open until the first door closed behind him.

Kay Yanuk stood behind the glass. She let him in and met him with a broad grin and a hug. She had let her straight blonde hair grow out a bit, down to her shoulders. He knew she was forty-two years old. She stood about five-feet, five-inches tall, wore a pair of khakis and a black Counterintelligence Division polo shirt.

"I am so sorry Robert. About everything," she said, holding him out at arm's length.

"You heard about Kathryn?" Rob asked.

"Yeah." She let him go as she squinted up her face in a sign of sympathy. "I'm sorry I couldn't be here for the intervention, but I called Chris right away after."

"Thanks," he said with a shrug. "You're not aging, Kay, you're getting younger."

"You lie, sir. I do my cardio and watch what I eat and I still keep getting broader. Steve and Leo are out and about already and Chris hasn't come in yet. Hey, I gotta go to the Navy base, but there's coffee on."

"Thanks, Kay."

"We'll catch up later."

Nothing had changed and Rob wondered why he was surprised. The office sported the same beige walls and gray carpeting. It had work stations in walled-off cubicles for fifteen employees.

In Rob's time in Seminolacola, they lost two special agent positions, an investigative analyst position, and the long unfilled receptionist position. All this meant more work for the survivors.

Rob made his way to his cube. Outside of a stack of official and semi-official paperwork, it was the same as he had left it. His binders and books were there, as were his personal files. He went through his cabinets and drawers. All his protein bars and batteries were gone.

Rob powered up his computers, one for the secret enclave and the other unclassified. It would take long slow minutes before he could do anything as the dated hardware couldn't handle all the programs HQ regularly forced on the machines.

His desk phone indicated he had messages. He didn't relish wading through a million "where the hell are you?" rants.

Coffee, he thought.

The break room shared the middle of the office with a conference room and a storeroom containing their gun safe. He'd have to check and see if his M-4 carbine and Remington 870 shotgun had been picked up by someone from the SWAT team. He needed a range day. He was out of scope on all his weapons. Something else for the task list.

His mug formed up with the others on a tray in the break room, which housed a refrigerator, snack cabinet and a short bookcase they had converted to a coffee service. The black mug had been a gift from Kathryn and bore the white inscription: "If I Learn Any More, I'll be a Threat to National Security." She had bought it when she had still liked the FBI.

He wiped away the dust and poured himself a cup.

He toured the space as he sipped. The cubes ran along the walls meeting at Chris's corner office. The other two walls of the square space were lined with floor-to-ceiling filing cabinets. Various items occupied the space on top: a three-hole punch here, a roll of the clear thick plastic bags used to seal drug evidence there and rolls of evidence tape everywhere. A painting of snow-covered pines in the mountains hung undisturbed, coated in thick dust.

We like our consistency, he thought, as he passed the room with the National Crime Information Center terminal in it, and the cube where they had set up the equipment to download audio from the solid state body recorders. His welcome home lap completed, he got to work.

He started with the phone messages. Thankfully, his mailbox had filled up. The most recent, from months ago, were automated vendor calls or routine headquarters queries.

Then came the phase where colleagues called to check up on him. They were split between concerned and sympathetic or complaints about lost investigative opportunities caused by his absence. The latter weren't friendly. Friends went on an apology call back list.

He deleted them all.

The phone rang as soon as he put down the receiver.

"FBI," Rob said.

"Welcome back, Robbie. Do I keep you on the roster or let you go?"

Rob recognized Howell "HM" Trotter's voice. HM for Howling Mad. He was the SWAT Team's senior team leader.

"I thought I'd be off by now."

"What can I say? You've got the best STL in the Bu. The obvious being covered, I've got to know, in or out?"

In a way, that's how it started in the first place, Rob thought. Perhaps he should quit SWAT. Then again, without Kathryn, the call outs would be easier to handle.

"I'm in," Rob said.

"Listen, I'm out on a limb here. Check the safe and make sure your M-4 and the scattergun are still there and confirm with an email. The next monthly will be . . . June 4th and 5th. Be ready for the SWAT fitness test and to qualify with everything. Get qualified on your pistols, will you? I got chits out to the SWAT Operations Unit on you like you would not believe."

"Will do, HM."

"How you doing, brother?"

"Kathryn left me."

"Shit. When it rains, it pours."

"Yeah, but no more running out of the monthlies for wife maintenance."

HM laughed. "We're real sorry about all this, Rob."

"Thanks."

"It'll be good to have you back."

"Thanks, man. It'll be good to be back."

HM hung up and the computers were finally ready to use. Emails were similar to the phone messages, with the most recent being all Bureau and All Field Office miscellanea.

Rob opened his case management software.

"Crap!" he said aloud.

His docket showed fourteen cases, six of which had deadline requirements: four backgrounds and two civil rights, and eleven leads. Chris had reassigned all the items to him last night. It would take the rest of the morning for Rob to sort this out. Fair enough, he had been squatting in a slot for a year. Time to pay up. Rob knew the background investigation deadlines were tight. He started with those.

D. Randall drove his city cruiser into the wooded lot on the north shore of the bay, out of the city in Santa Rosa County. The lot wasn't wide but it was long enough and green enough to hide a mobile home, his city car and his personal pickup. Nowadays he had to skirt the downed tree limbs he hadn't finished clearing after the hurricane. He parked between a screen of twisted buttonwood trees and the trailer.

D. Randall was tired. He kept his hands on the wheel and stared out the windshield. He thought of all he had to do today: evict Auntie Kenna from one of his rent properties in town, go out to the ranch and check the power, and fool with his yard tools here.

He felt a twinge in his back as he stood and wondered if he'd pulled something dropping the boy with the Tec Nine. D. Randall stripped his shirt off on the steps to his front door without loosening his Sam Browne belt. He yawned as he let himself in.

The neat little trailer was his home of record for the police department, but otherwise he really didn't have a home. He had the ranch on the river, the luxury condo across the bay at Gulf Point specifically for seducing vacationing ladies, single or otherwise, and rent properties he stayed in from time to time, if they were vacant. He liked the trailer during his work-week. It was close to town.

D. Randall lowered the air conditioning and grabbed a beer from the fridge. Once in the modest bedroom, he showered up. After, he removed his badge, hero bars, name plate and rank insignia from his shirt. He balled up his uniform and jammed it in the laundry bag and had a panicked thought. What if he hadn't gone to the dry cleaners?

He checked the closet and exhaled with relief. A fresh one hung there, still in the bag. He laid it out for tonight. He transferred all his insignia to the new uniform, complete with cardboard backing.

D. Randall crawled into the queen-sized bed and drank himself to sleep during *Live Emerald Coast* on the TV, ignoring the buzzing of his phone.

He woke to a pounding on his front door. He reached down behind his night table for a pistol – not his department issued weapon. He had used duct tape to fix a nylon holster back there. He came out with his trusty old Colt Python. He checked the time and cursed. Then he waited.

The pounding continued.

When it became apparent his visitor wasn't going to either go away or come in all the way to the bedroom to get shot, D. Randall decided to get up and shoot him through the front door. On the way to the door, he recognized Wee Willie through the curtained windows. D. Randall threw the bolts.

"Sheet, Wee Willie, you almost got smoked. What the hell is with you?" D. Randall asked.

Wee Willie had sweat through his t-shirt. His washed-out, off-duty cotton sweatpants drooped under his ample belly.

"Look man, some reporter is diggin' around Jimmy Tank's thing," Wee Willie said. He was short of breath and wide-eyed.

"Jimmy Tank. Shit. Man, what you waking me up at 1:00 pm for this shit for?"

D. Randall grabbed yet another beer from the fridge for himself. He didn't offer one to Wee Willie.

Wee Willie eyed the cold bottle.

"Well?" D. Randall asked.

"Well, he's asking around. That's why," Wee Willie said.

"What did he know?"

"Nothing."

"Has he talked to anyone else?"

"Don't know."

"He up from Miami? *Miami Herald?*"

"What?"

"Does he work for the *Miami Herald?*"

"Don't know."

"TV?"

"Don't —"

"Yeah, I got it. Get out of here Willie. I'll see you later."

"Yeah, but —"

D. Randall pushed him out the door and locked it behind him. He dropped into one of his kitchen seats. He sipped his beer. He thought it through.

"Who gives a shit?" he said out loud, when he was done thinking it through.

He was still tired. He felt around for the small glass jar in his freezer, finding it behind a can of coffee. He screwed off the top and scooped out two pills. He liked these tranks, they helped him sleep. He popped two and chased them with the rest of the beer before going back to bed.

Rob hammered out administrivia until he could not stand it anymore and then headed to the gym for a workout. At lunchtime, Leo followed him home to park the pickup and drive him back to the office. Chris had assigned Rob the oldest car in the Resident Agency, a Buick LaCrosse V-6 in Mocha Steel Metallic, a perfect color for surveillance. For a car with 84,000 miles on it, it passed muster.

He banged out two quick background interviews and reviewed his Jimmy Tank notes while running the Buick through a car wash. Rob had learned Father Clyde was, in fact, Father Clyde Laughlin. If first names were good enough for Jimmy Tank, they were good enough for Rob.

"Father Clyde it is," Rob said to the girl wiping down the car.

He thought about her in National Crime Information Center entry format: White/Female/27, 5'7"/98 lbs./Build Thin/Hair Blonde/Eyes Blue/quarter-inch scar left forehead/ruddy complexion and low body weight consistent with chronic meth use.

She winked at him.

Once in the car, Rob texted Steve, the most Catholic Catholic he knew. Steve advised he could find Father Clyde at St. Pious's, in the Angelsea neighborhood. Rob burnt rubber executing an illegal U-turn across four lanes and a double yellow. The game was afoot.

Croyden Pogue, LLP still favored the old ways. The lawyers wore suits or conservative dresses, cisgender appropriate, and honorifics were often heard in their paneled offices on East Ohio by Monument Circle. The firm had been servicing Indianapolis since, well, since there had been an Indianapolis.

"Mrs. Lawson on the line," his paralegal informed him via intercom.

Fanning "Frank" Nodel put down his kale and camembert on whole wheat to pick up the telephone. He looked the part of a partner, six feet tall and a little round at about 240 pounds, with a gray fringe around a bald pate, and wire-rimmed glasses, but he was still a senior associate.

Frank was late to partner at Croyden, but he had felt it coming since he had switched to family law. Although he was only in his early 40's, he exhibited a weary sympathy clients in family court liked – thus, his referrals had gone up, as had his billable hours.

In this case, however, he could not get the client, Kathryn Lawson, to trust him at all. Frank hated to think ill of his clients (uncommon among his colleagues, he knew), but Kathryn was quite the pistol. No matter, he thought, because with this call, their association would cease.

"Kathy?" Frank asked

"Kathryn, yes?" she said.

"Yes, sorry. I'm happy to let you know your divorce was final as of this morning. Congratulations." Frank used a fairly jaunty tone. He knew how badly she wanted this.

"What the hell are you talking about Noodle?"

That was what she called him, *Noodle*.

"Your divorce, Mrs. Lawson. Mr. Lawson's lawyer filed the papers this morning." He switched to a more business-like tone as he felt the situation go down-the-old-toilet.

"How the hell did that happen?"

"At your direction," and against my advice, Frank thought, "we sent him the papers to sign. He signed them and sent them to his lawyers, who filed them. I told you there was a chance this would happen."

"You told me? Who do you think you are?"

"Yes, Mrs. Lawson, I told you this would happen, and I advised you in person and in writing you shouldn't do it. You also should not have waived the appearance."

"He was *supposed* to call me."

Well he didn't, Frank thought.

"I'm sorry," he said.

"You should be. For what my family is paying you, you should have been able to handle this the way I wanted. I'm coming down. I want to talk to you."

"Don't make the trip, Mrs. Lawson. I'm grabbing a sandwich at my desk before running to court. I won't be here," Frank said.

Unfortunately, he spoke into a dead line.

And Fanning "Frank" Nodel chuckled because now he had an excuse to go home straight from court.

Rob parked next to the St. Pious rectory, a small, neat, brick cape. The lawn sported a sharp edge along the concrete walk to the front door, not typical for the neighborhood. He knocked and presented his credentials.

"Father Laughlin? Clyde Laughlin? I'm Rob Lawson and I'm a special agent with the FBI. Can I have a minute of your time?"

"I recognize you from the execution," Father Clyde said. "Come on in."

"Thank you."

"Tea?" Father Clyde asked.

They stood in the white kitchen of the rectory. Seeing clean paint, sound black and white game-board linoleum, and newer cabinets surprised Rob.

"Sure," Rob said. "Looks like you've caught up on your sleep."

The bags under Father Clyde's eyes were a little smaller and his skin color a little healthier. His hair, clean now and still parted in the middle, had been cut back to his collar. His mustache had been repulsed to the natural borders of his lips. It knocked years off his apparent age. Rob put him at fifty now.

"Jimmy Tank took a lot out of me," Father Clyde said. He waved Rob to the black build-it-yourself table and joined him with the mugs.

"New kitchen?" Rob asked.

"Um hum. Wondering where we got the money?" Father Clyde said.

"Big donors in Angelsea?"

"No, but there are some elsewhere in the diocese. Cookie?"

Father Clyde made a roundtrip to the counter for a cookie jar made in the shape of a friendly waving Pope John Paul II.

"Do you want to find out about the legitimacy of his repentance, or if he really didn't kill Mr. Simmons?" Father Clyde asked.

"Both, I guess," Rob said, nibbling on his biscuit, sipping his tea and trying to look innocent himself.

"So you come in here, flash your creds and show me a salesman's smile, and I'm supposed to violate the priest-penitent relationship?" Father Clyde asked. His manner was mild, but Rob saw the steel behind the facade.

"No, I —"

"I'm talking to you because I have known Steve for years and he asked me to, okay?"

"Okay."

"I'm not going to divulge any confidential information."

"Okay."

"When was the last time you went to confession?"

"I'm not Catholic, Father."

"Ah," Father Clyde said. "Sorry. Are you a Christian?"

"Yes," Rob said.

"Do you go to church?"

Rob's first thought was to deflect the question, but he could tell the priest had something to say. Rob didn't want to give him an excuse not to say it.

"I've been going to Maritime Methodist," Rob said.

Rob felt a little guilty. One time didn't really constitute *going*.

"Yeah," Father Clyde said. "Coleman. He's solid as a rock and that Keisha is something else." Father Clyde sighed. "So be it. I've been a chaplain at the prison for some time. I go out on a rotational basis with the others and was there when Jimmy Tank arrived. Of course, I knew about the Simmons murder. WWJD, right? I went to see him. Truthfully, I expected a quick rebuff. Check the box, you know?

"There was no brush off. He was very interested in the idea of forgiveness. He asked about the mechanism for redemption in the Church. At first, I described generally how it works. In subsequent meetings he showed continued interest, so we explored the topic deeply. We also studied the Gospels. I'd have started with Genesis, but by then he had cancelled his appeals, so time was an issue.

"As we continued to meet, he wanted to learn about confession and last rights. He told me his people were Cajun, so I went ahead and assumed he was baptized in the Church. We went at it from a mainstream Catholic perspective. It seemed to be what he wanted."

"Did you talk about the murder?" Rob asked.

Father Clyde wagged a finger.

"Just like Steve," Father Clyde said. "Straight to the point. I can't tell you about things he said under the protections of confession, but we did discuss his crimes. I am convinced his confession to the police regarding his prior murders was heartfelt and honest."

"I see. Now you may think I'm simple, but —"

"I do not think you are simple, Special Agent Lawson. I know you have a master's in accounting and big firm experience. I know you are very well regarded by your peers. I also know what you have been wrestling with recently."

So Steve had briefed Father Clyde. Fair enough, Rob thought.

Father Clyde paused. Rob thought he wanted to give Rob a chance to speak, but Rob chose not to. After a moment, Father Clyde continued.

"Everything about the Simmons murder was said during confession."

"I see. Do you think his turn to religion was honest?"

"I do. He knew where his situation was taking him. I truly believe he was making his peace with Our Lord."

"Did he kill Matthew Simmons?"

Rob expected a sharp rebuke, or at least a rebuke. Instead, Father Clyde tipped his mug and studied the dregs.

"I should clean these before they stain," Father Clyde said.

He rinsed both mugs in the sink.

"I'm sure you had a fruitful discussion with his mother," Father Clyde said.

It wasn't a question.

Rob thought about pushing it and getting a name and location for the woman. He was about to ask when Father Clyde turned off the water and left the room.

Rob got the message. He showed himself out.

Another school day closed for Ali Bakr. He ended this day as he usually did, hanging back at his locker as the school emptied. He liked to walk home after the rush. It lessened the chance of having to hear the insults or see the distain as he passed by.

He had dressed carefully today in his favorite three-quarter-length sweatpants. The dayglo green stripe matched the euro print on his athletic shirt. He had the perfect amount of gel in his hair and his backpack was thin enough to qualify as cool.

It did not matter, though. He was still an outsider, although today he had been mostly ignored, making it an excellent day.

Ali slammed his locker shut. Most of the other kids had left. Foot traffic was limited to the after school activities kids moving about purposefully, and losers dragging themselves in the direction of out. He hoisted his backpack and headed for the main entrance.

In the home stretch, down the long hall heading straight out, as he was coming up on the last staircase, Kelly Ann MacDonald appeared. As usual, she blew him away.

She was in his grade and had straight black hair. There was a little flip to it at the end of her shoulder-length tresses and she mostly wore it with bangs in front and barrettes holding some behind her ears. It set off her white skin and blue eyes perfectly. She was kind of tall, almost as tall as Ali. He loved her clothes. Today she wore a form-fitting white blouse and denim Capri pants.

He had never exchanged more than a few words with her at a time but she was cool in the rare instances when they did talk. He could remember the details of each conversation, down to what had been said. Also as usual, her earbuds were in and her full-to-bursting backpack weighed her down. She had the reputation of chasing A's.

Ali shadowed her out of the building. He'd done it before. Even though he lived north of school and she lived with her Mom in a sketchy complex east of Bayview High, he occasionally trailed her home. The first time he had done it, years ago, he was curious as to where she lived. The handful of times since, he did it because he liked to watch her.

Ali stayed on her. He let her get a little further away (he wasn't creepy after all). The two of them walked through the floral, sweetly fragrant afternoon humidity with Ali enjoying himself considerably.

All went well, with Ali fixated on Kelly Ann's swinging backside, until he stopped following her when she crossed the last big street before her complex. Ali liked to end it a little early because he thought it less likely he'd get noticed. It had always worked before.

"Hey raghead, MacDonald only likes whites!" Ali heard someone shout from behind.

He heart sank to the soles of his running shoes. Danny Martin, a varsity athlete, had lowered the window on the passenger side of a new red Camaro with black tinted windows so he could sit on the door, legs in the car, arms on the roof.

"Forget it raghead, you won't get anywhere with her!" Danny yelled.

"Fuck you infidel," Ali shouted instinctively.

"Check you tomorrow asshole! Slap it out at school, bitch!"

The driver of the Camaro, Ali couldn't see who it was, stomped the gas and they pulled away. Ali heard another boy yell, "sand nigger!" He didn't recognize the voice.

Ali felt the pressure build in his gut again and the tears leaked out. He started running and ran all the way home. At his house, he barged through the front door. Nobody was home. He slammed the door shut and went to the kitchen. He grabbed a handful of Chips Ahoy cookies. He paced about for a minute, jamming cookies into his mouth.

He ran down the hall to his parents' bedroom.

His parents had a fancy hardwood bedroom set that was out of place in their crappy room, which needed painting. The queen-sized bed, two nightstands, low dresser, high dresser, and wardrobe filled the space. Ali, still with his backpack on, with crumbs around his mouth and sweat dripping from his run, opened the top drawer of the tall dresser. He pushed aside his father's white boxers and stared at a blue steel Ruger .38 revolver with large wood grips and a four-inch barrel, and a box of shells. His chest heaved as he worshipped the pistol and dripped sweat on the floor.

Gray clouds formed fast as the afternoon waned. The atmosphere thickened in the surprise dark. D. Randall had sweat through his polo shirt as he watched his hired Mexicans drag Auntie Kenna's stuff out to where the grass met the broken, faded asphalt of the Plainsview street. The Sherriff's Deputy was gone, the gift of a crisp $50.00 in his pocket.

D. Randall's head pounded. He really didn't want to be here. He hated these lowlifes. He knew what he had to do next; it was the only way to get this place cleaned up and back on the market. He went inside.

Auntie Kenna was a sloppy black woman with two ankle biters hanging around. D. Randall didn't know or care who the kids were. It was time to get the old bitch out. The kids were lying on her, the weird one with her thousand-yard stare and the boy talking to himself. He toyed with the strands of Auntie's soiled denim cut-off shorts.

Auntie Kenna herself lay on a blue bean bag chair. Elderly in appearance, Randall knew her to be forty-eight. Her head flopped about as she tried to focus. She shot heroin and must have shot some when Gillis served the papers. Her high was kicking in full now.

"Come on Auntie, got to go," D. Randall said.

"What you mean?" she said.

"Come on."

D. Randall kicked her in the stomach. The girl, possibly nine, did nothing. The boy stood up. He grabbed her arm and pulled.

"Come on, Auntie," the little boy squeaked.

Auntie Kenna vomited on her black tank top.

"Fuck," D. Randall said, sick of this shit.

Walk back out to the truck. Pick up the cheap red tool box from the bed. Walk all the way back to the house. Sigh. Throw the latch on the box and pull a pair of disposable rubber gloves out. Sigh again.

D. Randall grabbed Auntie Kenna from behind, holding her under both arms. He shuffled backwards, dragging her on her heels, to the small pile of worn household goods outside and left her there. The boy moped after them, gazing at the broken cement of the walkway. The second trip consisted of the girl, half dragged, half carried, and the bean bag chair. He put the bean bag chair next to Auntie Kenna and lifted the girl onto it.

Wee Willie startled D. Randall as he drilled holes for the hasp he would use to lock up.

"That reporter gone talked to Father Clyde," Wee Willie said.

Lately, Wee Willie never had solutions, only problems. Wee Willie and D. Randall's headache worked together to pissed him off.

"So? What do you want me to do about it?" D. Randall said.

"Well, he could find out something."

"From Clyde? Clyde don't know shit."

"But he know people who do."

D. Randall rested the battery-powered drill on one hip as he thought it through.

"The mother?" D. Randall asked.

"Yeah man, I think so," Wee Willie said.

"Fuck. Go ahead and handle it."

D. Randall went back to work. He heard Wee Willie scuff his feet a little. That pissed off D. Randall even more. Can't the retard handle anything?

"What you mean, handle it?" Wee Willie asked.

D. Randall sighed.

"Make her go away, Willie. Now get on out of here," D. Randall said.

"Go away like how?"

"Like . . . away."

"That'll take money."

"Spend some, Willie."

"You going to reimburse me?"

"Yeah, I'll reimburse you."

"Like last time?"

"Not like last time."

"How much?"

"Willie, if you don't fucking skedaddle, I'll use this here drill on your left eye."

Leo let Rob into the otherwise empty RA. Rob ran through his emails. He had a phone message from Hoss King, the Seminolacola detective. He thought about the work he had to do on his leads and on his cases with firm deadlines. He thought about it and decided to work on finding Jimmy Tank's Mom anyway. He remembered something about her in the newspaper articles. He checked his notes. There it was, from a newspaper interview: EvaJo Gubbs.

Rob trudged back to the small room housing their National Crime Information Center terminal. It held the antiquated terminal and dot matrix printer on a beat up wooden desk. He had to squeeze by some gray metal file cabinets to sit in front of it. He typed in his login information and waited. In a moment green letters on the black monitor informed him his login had expired. Back at his desk he called the Criminal Justice Information Service to reactivate his credentials. They told him how to do it on the intranet. He hung up with a curse on his lips.

"What's up?" Leo, the Resident Agency's Counterterrorism Agent, asked, from the entrance to Rob's cube.

"My NCIC logon expired and I need to do a lookup," Rob said.

"Great! I'll do you a favor and run your check, and then I won't feel bad about hitting you up for a favor with a case."

"Uh oh."

"No, not bad. The regular shit. What you got?"

They ran EvaJo Gubbs for a Florida Driver's License. Nothing. Variations of the name were no help. They ran Jimmy Tank. He had a license, but when they tried Jimmy Tank's address, no EvaJo came up as an affiliated driver.

"Let's go to my desk," Leo said.

There, they went out on the internet and ran names and addresses through a paid commercial data provider, which returned a multitude of choices to their query. By comparing what they knew about Jimmy Tank, they were able to narrow it down.

"Here," Leo said. "EvaJo Trysta Moorer."

The service produced all her identifiers and an address history dated to the present, as well as a long list of civil judgments.

"Let's go to NCIC," Leo said.

They went back to the crowded little room. There they logged in on Leo's credentials again. They ran EvaJo, but not for a DL. Leo ran her in the criminal history section. The data slowly loaded. Leo paged down through entry after entry: check fraud, personal use narcotics, assault, public intoxication.

"Mother of the Year," Leo said.

"Wants and warrants?" Rob asked.

Leo ran it.

"Nothing but two Failure to Appears on a pair of misdemeanors," Leo said, "but this address matches the last one on the service list."

"That's a start," Rob said. "Now, what have you got?"

"You know those safe houses in town – the terrorist ones?" Leo asked.

"I remember the one. There's another now?" Rob asked.

"I think so," Leo said. "Traffic has picked up and we've got them contacting some known cells out West. No pertinent contact with the local Muslim population and no threat streams here, but we're watching the houses close. The overtime for the JTTF officers is crushing the budget and Chris is getting cranky.

"I also got a kid making threats on social media. Behavioral Science says he's faking, but Headquarters is all spun up. They want twenty-four/seven, they want a complete background, they want blah, blah, blah. You gotta help me. We have to figure out a way to get this guy off the radar. The JTTF is stressed out to the max."

"Is there that much traffic?" Rob asked.

"That much coming and going. Remember the car bomb that fizzled in Atlanta?"

"Yeah."

"The car was bought here, in Crestview."

"Okay. What are you thinking?"

"Some surveillance, I need pictures, before I do a knock and talk. I figure scaring the shit out of him will shut him down."

"You sure?"

"Like in guaranteed?" Leo shrugged.

"Well, if Headquarters wants us to do the full court press, shouldn't we do it?" Rob asked.

"What's gotten in to you? We don't have the resources to chase supervisory wet dreams and this is making Headquarters rock hard. The only reason the Hostage Rescue Team hasn't come down and killed the little bastard is I've been telling Washington he's grounded because he isn't doing his homework."

"Homework?"

"Do me a favor, read the stuff and let me know what you think. The behavioral assessment is already in the file."

"Yeah, no worries," Rob said.

Rob was very worried. Leo's way forward made him uneasy in an all-purpose sense of uneasy. Also, he had his documentation, cases and leads to do. Surveillance was time consuming.

"Give me the file number and I'll get up to speed," Rob said.

"Thanks man. I want to avoid charging this kid if he's faking."

Rob wrote up his stuff on the Gubbs case, thinking about Melissa the whole time. The rumbling in his stomach made him think about dinner. He put those two things together and reached for his cellphone. Nerves stopped him cold.

And what about Jules? He wasn't sure about a kid. The more he thought about it, the more nervous he became. Before he could totally fall disintegrate, he decided to go for it. After all, he was an FBI agent. What could possibly go wrong?

He started with a general text about the state of the investigation. When Melissa responded, he asked her if she wanted an update. She bit. He texted a suggestion: he could brief her up over dinner.

"You pick the place," he sent, "someplace Jules likes."

The phone remained silent. The seconds ticked by. He thought he had pushed it too far. He felt like an idiot.

"Already cooked. Can you come here?" she sent back.

Rob felt like a million bucks.

Wee Willie felt like shit. He didn't like it when D. Randall talked to him all rough like he done. Now he had to waste shit. First he wasted the cash to set up a pre-paid cell phone from a box store. He had to waste his day off on a trip to Mobile as he flew west on I-10 in his mint black 1986 Grand National. The one with the turbocharged V-6. He kept it show quality.

Wee Willie rubbed his rumbling stomach through his light blue stained t-shirt. He reached into the pocket of his gray sweatpants to check the cash he had on hand. He had enough, so he took the next exit.

As he ate a convenience store burrito and drank a thirty-two-ounce Coke, he fumed about D. Randall. EvaJo didn't have to go. What was D. Randall thinking? Homicides only brought scrutiny.

"Shit," Wee Willie said to no one in particular on his way to his car.

Again up on the freeway, he used the new phone to text the Master Blaster. There was no answer, so as he crossed the state line, he called.

"Yo, it's me. Call me," Wee Willie said to the voicemail.

Nothing.

He called again near the tunnel and when he got voicemail again he hung up. Wee Willie drove on to where he knew the Master Blaster lay his head at.

Jules stood on a chair in front of the cook top. He stirred the Kraft Mac and Cheese. Melissa grinned, enjoyed the scene.

Then she grimaced. What had she been thinking, inviting Rob? She lowered her head until it rested on her hand. Is he expecting anything?

"Mommy, do you have a headache migraine?" Jules asked.

"No honey. I'm just tired," she said.

"Do you want a nap?"

The doorbell rang.

"I'll get it! I'll get it!" Jules hopped down and sprinted to the door.

Too late to do anything about it now, she thought.

And there he was, smiling like a boy, all adorable and clean cut. She liked his blue-and-white checked shirt.

"I hope it was all right, but I brought some root beer for Jules," he said.

He also held a bottle of white wine and two glasses. Nice move Rob, but what are you expecting, she wondered.

"Mommy, can I? Can I?" Jules shouted.

"Sure. Come on in."

They ate some of Jules's mac and cheese, and a fillet of tilapia with parmesan cheese and some broccoli. Publix had French bread fresh, so she had bought some and they had a little with butter. They both had wine. She eyed the half-full bottle and, in spite of herself, she invited him to stay as she bathed Jules. They shared the rest of the bottle in the living room.

"I don't normally do this," she said.

"What, have dinner?" Rob asked with a smile.

"No, drink during the week."

"We're not drinking, we're having some wine."

"Oh, we're having some wine."

"Well, maybe drinking a little. Do you have another bottle?"

Melissa directed him to a room temperature Riesling. Rob found a corkscrew as he shared what he had found out and where he wanted to go next in the investigation. He brought back two glasses of the wine over ice, and the bottle.

"It's so sad, what happened," Melissa said. "It seems so pointless, so random, almost like winning the bad lottery."

"Uh huh. Was there anything strange going on with Matthew?"

The question embarrassed Melissa. The butterflies started. She breathed deeply.

"Melissa?" he asked.

She had a hard time catching her breath.

"Robert, Matthew and I were not in a good place," she said. "He was real rigid and I was having a hard time with it. He did not want me to finish school, and I wanted to go back and get my DPT."

"I see." Rob topped them both off.

She drank off half.

"Why did you marry him in the first place? You were both kind of young for it."

"Yeah," Melissa said. Whenever she thought of Matt, familiar conflicting emotions flooded in. She sipped her wine. "You have to understand, I had been competing seriously in gymnastics. I never had time for a boyfriend, or even a life. I lived away from home all my teenage years and only socialized with the other girls.

"When we finally knew for sure I wasn't going to break into the top level," she said, "it was such a letdown. I couldn't even decide what to do. Coach got me a scholarship down here at West Florida State but my heart wasn't in it anymore. They put up with it and switched me to diving. That's where I met Matt. He was a swimmer."

"Uh-huh."

"He was really cute," she said, and giggled.

That was a sign she'd had too much. She warned herself to slow down.

"You two hit it off?" Rob asked.

Melissa really liked the timbre of his voice.

"Yeah. He, like, paid a lot of attention to me. And he could get so jealous so quickly. I had never experienced anything like that."

And the sex was really great, she thought. Should she say they did it all the time before Jules? Probably not.

"Anyway," she said, "his family was conservative, like old-fashioned in a really nice way. They were very close. They were church goers and I liked that too. That's when I started going regularly. Do you go all the time?"

"My parents do. I hadn't been for a while. I rode out the hurricane on my boat so I thought I'd check in and say thanks. But we were talking about you and Matt."

"You have a boat?"

"Had. I used to live aboard a Monk 36. It didn't make it. It caught a fatal case of hurricane."

"Oh. Anyway, Matt and I became exclusive quick, and I liked it. We started talking about marriage. To me, it felt like a fairy tale. I had some convincing to do with my parents, but we got married. I got pregnant with Jules my senior year. Matt had already graduated and had a great job with Chucky."

"Chucky?"

"Charles Dauphin of Charles Dauphin and Associates. Matt was one of the associates. They did financial planning and consulting with old folks with money and stuff. Matthew was a finance major. Chucky has been great through all this. He set up this condo, invested Matt's and my money, and processed the life insurance, too. Because of him I can live here working part time as a PT assistant. This way I'm home with Jules a lot."

"That's great. We were talking about you and —"

"Oh yeah. So after Jules, Matt started acting differently. I had said *love, honor and obey* at our wedding, but I guess I didn't really think about the words. After Jules, I learned super quick what Matt thought about them."

"Which was?"

"Bottom line? Me, home with Jules, period. At first it was what I wanted too, but . . . ."

She thought he was kidding. Then they had argued. Should she say something about how he had been gaining weight? She hadn't liked it. She had lost her baby weight fast. He hadn't pushed a bowling ball out *his* hoo-ha. What right did he have to get fat? All he had to do was work and work out. And treat her right. She did everything else, everything with Jules, cleaned the house, shopped and cooked. Melissa liked men shredded, like ole Robby here. She bet if she got him to take off —

"Melissa?" Rob asked.

She had bent forward. Her forehead rested on one hand. The other held her empty wineglass. Shit, she thought. She straightened up and tried for a grin. Her eyes were wet.

"You okay?" Rob asked.

He handed her a handkerchief. Who still carried handkerchiefs? She wiped her eyes.

"Thanks. Yeah, I'm okay. Robert, we were in trouble. His temper was getting worse, he was working long hours at the office and also here at night. Right here at the kitchen table. I definitely supported it mostly, at first. Then he would get upset if I even came close when he was doing it. I had to sit over there when he worked like, over *there*." She gestured vaguely across the room.

"He became so secretive. We couldn't ever talk about his work, either. Then all he wanted to do on the weekends was drive around to construction places, like where stuff was being built."

"Do you remember which ones?" Rob asked.

"What? Oh. You know, the ones around. And he was going to strip bars. I wanted to go back and finish my PT degree and he was very against that. It was getting rough."

She didn't remember when she and Rob had switched to the floor, but they were sitting close to each other with their backs against the couch. She studied him, really examined him, and saw some concern, but also saw he was relaxed. He started leaning toward her.

Uh-ho, she thought.

Then they were kissing. Gently and slowly at first, and then things quickly progressed. She had not kissed someone deeply for some time. He knew what he was doing, she thought. She felt his hand on her waist. She broke the kiss and tried to stand up.

"Ouch!" She banged her knee on the coffee table and fell back onto the couch.

"Gracefully done. Are you okay?"

"Ow. Yeah."

Rob stood. He reached out and she clutched his hand. He helped her up and she ended up in his arms. She leaned her forehead on him, her right arm around his waist and her left hand flat on his chest next to her head. Got some pecs in there, she thought.

"You better go. Jules gets up early."

"All right."

"Not too fast," she whispered.

"All right."

After she closed the door behind him, she leaned against it and put her face in her hands.

What are you doing Melissa Simmons? she asked herself.

Wee Willie looked around until he found Master Blaster's wheels at Master's latest girl's crib, a small brown Florida Cracker with a generous setback in a neighborhood not too far east from where St. Stephen's met up with Dr. Martin Luther King, Jr. Avenue. Wee Willie parked on the dirt where the lawn should have been. In addition to Master's newer black Tiburon, a clean four-wheel drive Toyota Tacoma jacked up on thousand dollar tires shared the driveway. Wee Willie knocked on the door and obeyed the shouted order to enter.

The girlfriend wasn't home. Master Blaster and some freak Wee Willie didn't know were passing a bong and chilling to some Tory Lanez. Both men were shorter than Wee Willie expected for enforcers. The muscular Master, clean shaven with neat short cornrows, in an Under Armour t-shirt and biking shorts, leaned back on a torn brown leather couch sucking hard on the bong. The freak was next to him, head back, impenetrable Ray Bans in place. His curly goatee and stringy hair did not inspire confidence. Freak wore a Falcons t-shirt and tan cargo shorts.

"Yo, I got to talk to you," Wee Willie said.

Master finished his hit. "So talk," he said.

"It's business."

"So?"

"In front of him?"

"Yeah, in front of him. He my new partner. Sniper, say 'what-the-fuck' to a customer."

"What the fuck," Sniper muttered.

"Sniper? You hired a sniper?" Wee Willie asked.

"Yo, dude been to the sandbox. Like a hundred confirmed. He the man," Master said.

"You was in the Army?" Wee Willie asked him directly.

"Special Operations, mother fucker. Shot the Big Five Oh," Sniper said.

Sniper didn't stir as he spoke. His head stayed back. He spoke so softly Wee Willie could barely hear him.

Wee Willie had no idea who or what the 'Big Five Oh' was. This sniper annoyed him.

"Nigger, who are you?" Wee Willie asked.

"I am the Sniper Stefon."

"Sniper Stefon? What the hell kind of white-boy shit is that?"

Sniper Stefon adjusted his position slightly on the couch.

"Now look here," Wee Willie said, facing Master Blaster, "I need —"

The sound of a hammer being cocked stopped Wee Willie in his tracks.

Sniper Stefon had stood, drawn the largest revolver Wee Willie had seen in some time, a nickel plated gargantuan, and thumbed the hammer back. It was now pointed at Wee Willie's face.

Shit, thought Wee Willie. His Smith and Wesson was in the car.

"Whoa, hold on girls, y'all chill now," Master Blaster said, very focused and very calm.

Master stood up and padded in his socks between the men. He very gently rested his hand on Sniper Stefon's forearm. Sniper started lowering the pistol while keeping his arm rigid.

"The Sniper don't like to be questioned, my man," Master said to Wee Willie. "Yo man," Master said to Sniper, "why don't you fix you rod so's we can talk, yo?"

Sniper didn't respond.

"Yo, he a customer," Master said.

"Well, for a motherfucking customer," Sniper muttered.

He lowered the hammer by resting his thumb on it, pulling the trigger and easing it forward.

It was not lost on Wee Willie that the little shit had his piece pointed at Willie's own foot. Mother fucker, Willie thought.

"Let's sit down, bitches. Wee Willie, what you got for me, man?" Master asked.

Sniper Stefon sat back down. Wee Willie expelled his breath in relief. He chose to sit in a ratty armchair far from Sniper.

"So you know that thing?" Wee Willie asked.

"Yeah, that product thing up river?" Master replied.

"No, this other thing from back a bit. The thing with Jimmy Tank."

"That thing, yo."

"Yeah. We got a problem."

"Don't you all."

"Yeah, uh, EvaJo got to go."

Sniper Stefon snickered.

"She do?" Master asked.

"Yeah. She got to go, you know what I'm saying?"

"How far she got to go?"

"I think all the way."

"You ain't sure?"

"I'm sure. She got to go, man."

"Ok. Same price."

"No way bitch. EvaJo is a meth-ed out crack whore. She ain't like a man who kill yo ass. Two and a half."

Master thought about it. Sniper passed the bong. He pulled down a long drag.

"Three," Master finally said.

"Aight, three, mother fucker."

Friday

Supervisory Special Agent Jack Au of the Counterterrorism Division Terrorism Finance Section at FBI Headquarters in Washington, DC drove to the Hoover building on Pennsylvania Avenue before dawn. Although parking privileges at Hoover were normally above his pay grade, he had earned a temporary parking pass today because Terrorism Finance was expected at the Counterterrorism Division's Assistant Director's morning meeting, every morning, finance business pending or not.

Jack's section chief, who should have been the one to attend the meeting, was on travel. The assistant section chief, who should have covered the meeting in the chief's absence, was busy at home in his bathroom crapping out fifty years of collected digestive material in preparation for his birthday colonoscopy. Jack's unit chief, next in the pecking order, could not have cared less about face time. She told Jack the job was all his. At least it qualified him for the parking pass.

The good news was Jack did not have to put himself at risk by actually speaking today. The bad news was Margret Tauvr Au, his two-and-a-half year old daughter, had kept them up all night with various demands for everything from soda to another episode of *Peppa Pig*. Not the end of the world, he reminded himself. All he had to do was remain upright as he backbenched in one of the smaller Strategic Information Operations Center conference rooms.

He managed to stay awake as they quickly covered the most pressing international and domestic terrorism cases, collected intelligence, operational support issues and where the

Counterterrorism Division Fly Team special agents were heading to next before his mind began to wander.

"It looks like his mother isn't going to let him go. He's having homework issues," the International Terrorism Branch section chief said, his foghorn voice sounding thin through the television speakers. They were piping him in via a secure video conferencing system.

The comment jerked Jack back into the here-and-now. He must have missed something. An FBI counterterrorism case revolved around a kid and his homework?

A gray-haired supervisory intelligence analyst sitting directly across the room from Jack smiled at him and nodded in the affirmative, as if reading his mind. *Welcome to the asylum*, the analyst's grin said.

Rob poured himself a cup of coffee in the RA break room. Today he wore a tan short sleeved button down shirt, open, a black t-shirt, and black jeans. He whistled as he thought of Melissa's kiss, her taste, her touch – light as a child's. Her smell, floral, with a hint of something stronger underneath.

"Gimmie some of that," Leo said as he entered, dressed in a pressed white shirt, blue club tie and slacks. He extended a mug with "Hate the Police? Next Time Call a Crack Head" written on it. "You gotta help me with this high school kid. I got three phone calls from Headquarters before 6:30 this morning. I gotta tie this guy off. You read that shit?"

"Yeah, I read it. I'm with you. He's blowing off steam. What's your plan?" Rob asked.

The dulcet tones of the RA doorbell rang.

"This morning I'm going to the courthouse to get a subpoena for email content on all accounts associated with the house going back three months. I want to open a source at the school and get more background on the kid: like is he at risk? Grades, social development, permanent record, whatever. I need help. You free after lunch?"

"Permanent record?" Rob asked, struggling to keep a straight face.

"It's too late to review Leo's permanent record. We already hired him," Chris the supervisor said, walking into the break room. "Hoss is here."

Hoss King strolled in behind Chris. He wore a dark-blue golf shirt with the Mizuno logo and tan Dockers. His shirt was out, no doubt covering his Smith and Wesson semi-auto and maybe some handcuffs. He loosely carried a brown kraft eight-by-eleven envelope.

"Coffee?" asked Chris, who didn't wait for an answer before handing Hoss a blue mug with the letters *BOA* and the winged emblem of the elite Polish counterterrorism team on it.

Rob poured.

"Thanks," Hoss said. He did not add sugar or milk, stir or even sip the coffee.

Rob held the pot out, offering, and Chris waved it away.

The four men stood around, observing one another.

"So, what brings you up here, Hoss?" Chris finally asked.

"Uh, I need to speak to Rob."

"Great! Let's go to my office. You can speak to him there," Chris said.

"Uh," Hoss said.

"My office."

Chris led the way. Leo waved at them, staying put. Hoss and Rob brought their coffees.

"What's up, Hoss?" Chris asked, after they were in their respective seats.

"Well now, Boss, I —"

"Rob?" Chris asked, interrupting Hoss.

Rob shrugged, eyebrows up.

"You two don't have an appointment?" Chris asked.

"Nope," Rob said.

Hoss glared at him.

"So, what's up?" Chris asked again.

Hoss rubbed the top of his thighs. "I heard you been to see Father Clyde Laughlin," Hoss said.

"Yup, yesterday," Rob said.

"Why does that bring a Seminolacola detective to the RA before shift change?" Chris asked.

"It's after shift change," Hoss said.

"Bull shit, Hoss. I saw you parked by the Starbucks watching us when I drove up at 6:50, before shift change. Now one more time, and only one more time, what's this about?"

Hoss raised his free hand, palm forward.

"I give, I give," he said, "I came to ask Rob here to lay off D. Randall."

"You personally or officially asking?" Chris asked.

"Now Chris, I'm officially on time off and not even here. We're just asking, can y'all lay off D. Randall?"

"Who's the *we*?"

"This conversation was supposed to be 'tween me and Rob here," Hoss said.

"Overtaken by events. What's in the envelope?"

"Medical records. Results from my fitness for duty exam."

Chris and Hoss locked eyes.

"Is this coming from the Chief?" Chris asked.

"Chris," Hoss pleaded.

"No, what's up?"

"Now Chris, see here —"

Chris picked up the telephone and started dialing.

"Shit, Chris," Hoss said. He leaned in and pressed the switch hook on Chris's phone. "Important parties at the Department want you to think about laying off D. Randall. Jimmy Tank was a royal piece of shit. He deserved to die. D. Randall is very well connected. Now isn't the time for this."

"When would be?"

"We'll let you know."

"No way. Absolutely not. Good-bye Detective King."

"Wait a minute, wait one minute," Hoss said, his nerves gone and demeanor far more certain. "Okay. Listen. Maybe now is the time. Let's get him."

"What have you got?" Rob asked.

"Not too much. No one is talking yet. No one is betting y'all are looking into it for real. Everyone is afraid y'all will stir the gumbo and then quit. Nobody feels froggy, they don't want to jump. Like y'all, I think the Gubbs case stinks like three-day-old hammered horse shit. The thing is, no one is talking. No one ever talks about D. Randall."

"Why not?" Chris asked.

"I noticed some time ago people have a habit of disappearing when they say things D. Randall don't like."

"So what are you saying, Hoss? Officer Randall kills people?" Chris asked.

Rob could hear the edge in Chris's voice. He was back in his no-more-bullshit mode.

"No-ooo, not exactly. Now listen here Chris, you just aren't getting it about D. Randall. That old boy knows people. He's connected around here. He stayed a patrol officer all these years to keep his flexibility, you see. He got real estate around town, he goes to the right parties even as a *po*-lice, he does favors for people, for the *right* people. He knows people."

"So you're saying he mis-uses his badge for personal gain?"

"Something along those lines, sure."

"Why aren't the internal affairs guys on it?"

Hoss didn't reply and Chris didn't press him. They all knew the two Seminolacola IA detectives were no more than personal disciplinarians for the Chief.

"I see how you're going to be *our guy*. I'm tired of this Hoss," Chris said. "Have you got any information on wrongdoing committed by this officer?"

"I'll help y'all. That's all I'm going to say," Hoss said.

"What about you?" Chris asked Rob.

"I got a lead Jimmy Tank's mother knows something. I'll track her down today," Rob said. "I'm also going to swing by the Crystal Suites where the victim was found. Something the wife said makes me think there may have been some trouble with the marriage. I want to ask around. Then I'll drop some subpoenas for his financials."

"Do the first two but don't go down to the US Attorneys with this great big pile of nothing you have asking for bank records. Come back after you do the first two things and we'll talk."

"Yes, Boss."

"Don't 'yes, boss' me. Just do it. Get something or close this mess. This will only blow up in our faces and if it does, you're coming down with me," Chris said, pointing at Rob. "And I'm taking you down with us, too, Hoss."

Hoss stayed silent.

"Okay, enough, gentlemen. We've spent too much time on this as it is. You," Chris pointed at Rob again, "go hunting. You," Chris pointed at Hoss, "we'll call you when we need you."

Dismissed, Rob walked Hoss to the door. Hoss stopped in front of a credenza and put the envelope on it.

"Don't go underestimating D. Randall, Rob. Not just in manipulating the power structure, but even one-on-one," Hoss said, his panhandle accent much diminished.

"Power structure?" Rob asked. "Are you turning into an activist, Hoss?"

"I'm not kidding, Rob. D. Randall will fuck you up."

"He's not even going to get that close."

As the doors closed on Hoss, Rob grabbed the envelope and fairly ran back to his cube. It felt thin for the printout of an investigative file. On the edge of his chair, he worked the clasp and opened it. All the sheets were eight-by-eleven inch pages of printed automated case file data. Even the crime scene photos were inkjet printouts. Rob started reading.

The receptionist at the US District Courthouse on St. Raymond's Street buzzed Leo through the security door on sight. They exchanged pleasantries as he breezed past her desk on his way to Pamela Eswago's office. She handled national security issues for this branch of the Northern District of Florida.

The offices of the Assistant US Attorneys ringed the floor, with paralegals and administrative staff occupying cubicles in the middle.

The different hues of brown making up the office's palette reminded Leo more of a private law firm than a government office.

"Special Agent Kladsko, what brings you down to these hallowed halls?" a tall, sharp-featured man with a full head of gray hair asked.

"Where do I know you from?" Leo asked.

"Josiah Waller, formally with the State's Attorney's Office," Josiah said.

"Oh, you got picked up as an AUSA? Congratulations," Leo said, shaking hands with the man.

It never hurt to make friends with the new AUSAs, Leo thought.

"Yes, thank you. What brings you up here?"

"I need to see Pam. I need a subpoena for emails in a terrorism case."

Leo started walking again. Josiah joined him.

"Is there a threat in town?" Josiah asked.

"Not if you ask me, just kid stuff. Headquarters, however, has their panties in a wad."

"I see. Is there anything else interesting going on down at the office?"

"New guy rounding out his docket?" Leo asked.

The impertinence seemed to shock Josiah.

"I've got to make my mark. You know how it is," he said, recovering quickly.

The men had arrived at her office.

"Yes, *my* agent does know how it is, Josiah. Go find your own cases," plump, pretty Pam said from behind her desk.

She wore lots of hair, a dress with purple flowers printed thereon, a black blazer and a diamond encrusted wedding band.

Like a politician facing a tough question during campaign season, Josiah retreated with a companionable wave.

Rob did a little more research on EvaJo Trysta Moorer, Jimmy Tank's mother, and narrowed down the addresses to three he liked. After cross-referencing and double-checking, the one he liked the most was an apartment up in Tarkiln's Ford, north of town. The

Google Earth satellite image was far from complimentary. He decided to bring a partner.

Rob walked through the RA. Everyone had gone. He stood in the common area in front of Chris's office reviewing his options.

"What's on your mind?" Chris shouted from behind his desk.

Rob cursed to himself. He had forgotten Chris's lines of sight from behind his desk and broke the first rule of RA life: "don't let the supervisor see you doing nothing."

"I've got a home address for EvaJo. I was looking for someone to come with me," Rob said.

"Why?"

"Sketchy neighborhood."

Chris checked his watch.

"It's early enough. The mopes are still asleep."

"What if I get jammed up, up there?"

"One Ranger, one riot. Get going."

Rob left the parking lot about ten seconds later. He drove north along the bay. When the wetlands thinned into the Shambia River, he made a left toward town. The old industrial economy had long ago gone bust and the new service economy had not yet boomed in Tarkiln's Ford.

Rob stopped in front of the apartment building. It would not have surprised Rob if it had been converted from a motel: a flat roof over three stories of rooms opening onto walkways. Black paint flaked off the railings and lines of rust ran down to the asphalt parking lot, its cracks so old the grass growing up through them needed mowing. Tired cars and listing trucks rotted away in spots demarcated by disappearing white lines. Overgrown landscaping beds and fading signage did nothing to help.

A cable TV truck, newish and clean, stood out.

Rob parked. As he walked up the stairs, the cable guy stepped out of one of the apartments, buttoning his uniform shirt. After putting forth a studied successful effort at ignoring Rob, he jumped in his truck and went on his way.

Another satisfied customer, Rob thought.

He walked up to the third floor and found EvaJo's place. Standing to the side of the door, he knocked. No answer. He knocked again. He heard what sounded like movement inside.

"It's Rob," he shouted.

Nothing.

Rob knocked again.

"What?" A woman's voice shouted from inside.

"I got your money," he said, not loud enough to bring out the neighbors, he hoped.

He heard footsteps. She worked the deadbolt from inside. A chain, no more substantial than a breath, stopped the door.

"Slide it through," a female voice said.

"You're going to have to open up, EvaJo," Rob said.

"Hey, you ain't Rob!"

"I am Rob. Please open the door."

"You ain't no Rob I know."

Rob shoved his foot between the door and the jamb as EvaJo tried to slam it shut.

"Move, you asshole!" she shouted.

"It's about Jimmy Tank. C'mon EvaJo, I'm with the FBI."

"The FBI? You're full of shit."

"Most of the time, but not now," Rob said. He waved his credentials.

"Whatever! I'll open it."

Rob moved his foot. The door closed and for a moment he thought he had lost her. Then the chain rattled and the door opened.

"What's this about Jimmy Tank?"

EvaJo Trysta Moorer had been run through the ringer. She had a stained light blue robe wrapped around her boney frame. Her eyes bulged out of their sockets and her ears stuck out of her stringy, dirty hair. A yellowing bruise marked the left side of her tired white face, which was stained with old makeup.

"I'm here to warn you. The IRS is coming for you about the money Jimmy Tank gave you," he said.

"Bullshit! Ain't nobody know about that. Hey, you gonna take it away?" EvaJo asked.

Rob's adrenaline began to run. He told himself not to get too excited at the idea Jimmy Tank had come into some money before his arrest.

"Not me. Not my jurisdiction. But you never paid no taxes on it."

"Didn't have to. It was a gift."

"Don't you know about the gift tax?"

"You're bullshitting me."

"Not me. I don't want it and it's okay by me if you didn't pay on it. I hate the IRS too. I just need to ask you a few questions."

EvaJo muttered as she pawed through the litter on the warped top of an old buffet.

"You know what," she said, as she found and lit a cigarette. "Fuck you. That's what."

"Sure EvaJo. I have an idea. Why don't we both wait here for the IRS agents. They'll be coming by soon."

"Don't matter anyway, smart man. The money's all gone."

She sucked deeply on the cigarette.

"Don't matter? The crime is when you first got the money and didn't pay the taxes. They don't care there's no money now." Rob wondered how much longer he could keep this up before he fell apart laughing.

"All right!" EvaJo shouted, thrusting her bony hands, long fingers splayed out, including the two holding the cigarette, up and down in front of her in frustration. "What do you want anyways?"

"How did the money thing work?"

"Can't a boy give his moms a gift?"

"C'mon, EvaJo, it wasn't like that."

She took another long drag on the cigarette. "You the Eye?"

"Yup."

"Y'all got money, don't you? I mean, more than them cheap Seminolacola bastards?"

"Sometimes. How did it work with Jimmy Tank?"

"I was in Biloxi working the casinos." EvaJo knocked an old pizza box off a ripped baby-puke yellow ottoman and sat down. "He showed up and said he been working the oil rigs and got himself a lot of money. First he said it was overtime. Then he said it was a disability. I ain't stupid you know. He brought me back here and got me my car and set me up just top shelf in a condo. He was a good boy."

She slipped into a thousand-yard stare. Her rheumy eyes were wide and unblinking. The cigarette burned slowly.

Rob went down on one knee. He made sure he was low enough to look up at her.

"EvaJo," he said quietly.

"I wasn't no good mother. *At* mothering. I do meth and I'm a whore and I wasn't a no good mother, Mr. F—B—I, and that's the truth. That was me. He had nothing to thank me for, but he was a good boy."

"I know EvaJo," Rob said. "How did he bring you the money?"

"First he brought a check, but I don't have no bank. He went away, but he came back. He came back to me and got me. He brought me back to town and set me up with the car and the condo. He gave me cash. He said like as not he wouldn't be around. That's when he got busted for that thing."

She slipped back into her stare.

An adrenaline rush shook Rob up. This was beginning to sound like something. He knew he needed to stay unruffled to keep the information flowing. The EvaJos of the world had a finely tuned instinct for survival, and if she picked up on his excitement, she might clam up and disappear.

"EvaJo, do you remember where the condo was?" Rob asked.

"What? Oh. Down by the water on Gulf Way. Not the really best one, the tall one, but the one next to it."

"You still got the car?" he asked.

"Naw, wrecked it. It was a sharp, four-door Pontiac jobby. Got some settlement and had the little rice-burner next but that got repo'ed."

"Did Jimmy Tank ever take you to his bank?"

"Oh yeah, makes me laugh. White Sands Bank and Trust. Jimmy Tank called it . . . ."

"Yes?"

She squinted slyly at him.

"He called it cocaine bank. Get it? White Sands?"

EvaJo cackled and hugged herself.

Rob forced a smile.

"Hey, uh, do you think . . . ." EvaJo's sentence dangled in the air.

Rob stuck his hand in his pocket and fingered two bills. Using the practiced motion of all agents everywhere, he slipped his finger around the second bill and produced only the one twenty.

"Thanks," EvaJo said, focusing on him fully now. "Hey, uh, you seem really nice. Would you —"

"How about the time, EvaJo," Rob said. "I have to run. Got a meeting with the boss."

"Yeah, sure," she said. "Sure you do."

Rob knew the buildings EvaJo had mentioned. They faced the Gulf of Mexico on the west of the bay. The barrier island started to their east. The view was all gulf out to the horizon. There were only these two high-rises in the area. Everything else was three stories or less. EvaJo had identified the older, shorter of the two. Rob pulled into one of the few spaces in the small parking area by the main entrance.

The building next door was fifteen stories of modernist luxury with lots of glass, black steel trim and yards of boat slips in the back. Neatly trimmed grass covered small beds in the front.

EvaJo's former abode did not measure up. Its five stories of stained cement and small windows had no more spirit than a 1970's office building. Weeds choked the small beds and there were no boat slips out back. Rob entered through a narrow, smudged glass door.

The small tiled foyer had a rust-red couch and two gold armchairs, all covered in fraying ticking. Rob saw a glass door labeled *Office* on the left. A large white woman with an ugly scowl waited therein. She had parted her bright blonde hair in the middle and drawn eyebrows on her fifty-seven-year-old face with a pencil.

Rob waved through the glass. Her scowl deepened. Rob entered the office.

"How are you today?" he asked cheerfully.

"What did one of thems do now?" she said.

"Huh?"

She smacked her gum.

"What did one of my classy tenants or occupants or whatever the hell the little pricks are do?" she asked.

"What do you mean?"

"You a cop, ain'tcha?"

"Well, yeah, but —"

Her arm pivoted on the elbow she had been resting on the table. Three fat fingers went vertical, one of which sported a ring with a huge gold globe on it, and they motioned him closer.

"Lemme see it," she said.

Rob approached the desk and presented his credentials.

"Damn," she said, "the fucking FBI. One of them done it for sure. I bet you're here for Ling Po up on four, ain'tcha? Gonna take him in?"

"Where are you from?"

"Where the hell else — Jersey! I mean, who else can smell cops? I smelled you from up on the freeway. 'Course, youse ain't real cops. You gonna ask me about Ling Po?"

"Not today. How about EvaJo Moorer?"

She made a sympathetic sound with her tongue against the roof of her mouth.

"She's dead, ain't she?"

"Not yet. What makes you say that?"

Rob got an eye-roll in response.

"What'd she do?" The office lady asked.

"Nothing really. Did she buy or rent?"

"Rent. Second floor front. You know, she's a quality person. Deep down. Really deep. She makes me so sad."

"Why is that?"

"Well, I mean, why was she here, you know? Someone like that. We ain't high class but we ain't white trash. She was kind of dumb. Old Gordon taught her gin. She racked up a couple a hundred in losses. 'Course, I heard she paid in trade, if you know what I mean."

"You really got your finger on the pulse of this place. I'm Rob." Rob held out his hand.

"Dolly Patel." They shook.

"Patel?" Rob asked.

"Don't ask. Divorced. Anyways, she rented until she couldn't pay anymore. We carried her two months. She left before we had to evict her."

"Dolly, could you tell me the owner she rented from?"

"Yeah, the condo board. The board owns a few units and rents them out."

"You wouldn't happen to have the file on hand, would you?"

"Sure do."

"Can I see it?"

"Not without a subpoena."

"C'mon, Dolly. She doesn't rent here anymore. What duty have you got?"

"You ain't getting in that file without a subpoena, G-man. Now, if you happened to ask me . . . ."

Dolly drew out the *me* and impregnated the pause.

"Where she banked?" Rob asked.

"I sure as shit couldn't tell you White Sands Bank and Trust."

Dolly made a rolling forward motion with both her hands.

"Account number?" Rob asked, pulling out a notebook.

Dolly rattled it off.

"You remember it? You sure?"

"As sure as shit, cutie pie. Now get outta here. I got work to do."

"Got anything going?" Leo asked Rob.

Rob had gone for a run and eaten at his desk.

"Finishing up a subpoena application for Jimmy Tank's mother's bank account information," Rob said.

"Oh? Got something?" Leo asked.

"According to Mom, Jimmy Tank came into a large amount of cash. He told her several stories as to how he got it. They both banked at White Sands. Wish me luck."

"Good luck. Want a ride to the US Attorney's Office?"

"Humm?" Rob said, instantly suspicious.

"C'mon, come with me to the high school. I gotta look into my guy. I can't do the weekend without trying something."

"Oh, yeah. What the hell, let's go."

They filed the application and drove to Bayview High School. The long, low flat-roofed school occupied a large corner lot formed by the intersection of Bayview Avenue and Alexander Street. Two wings, forming an L shape, made up the classrooms and offices. Nestled behind were parking lots, playing fields and a separate building housing the gymnasium. Leo and Rob drove slowly, surveying staff and teacher cars.

"Leo?" Rob asked.

"Cruising the bumper stickers. Ah hah!" Leo said, pointing at an older Taurus with a FOP sticker near the licenses plate.

They crawled forward.

"There," Leo said.

Rob saw a Tahoe with an Army Strong window sticker.

"Our kind of people," Leo said, grinning.

"Leo, you're not writing down the numbers."

"Nope."

Leo parked in front of one of the dilapidated bungalows on Alexander Street.

"Leo, what are we doing?" Rob asked, on the sidewalk, in the heat.

"I want to see him come out," Leo said.

"See who come out?" someone asked from behind them.

"Tyrell Brown, ain't you all academic and shit," Rob said.

Tyrell from Fat Floyd's had snapped back into school mode. He wore a black tank top under a black and white print shirt and baggy black pants. He carried a thick backpack.

"Yes, sir. I gots me some catching up to do," Tyrell said, a bit of shyness under some urban posturing.

"Sir?" Rob asked.

"I spoke with Fat Floyd. He told me you be FBI."

"So that makes me a *sir*?"

96

"No. Your right cross make you *sir*."

Rob had to laugh.

"Could we spar, you know, sometime?" Tyrell asked. "Maybe you could show me a little something, something."

Rob cocked an eyebrow.

"Fat Floyd said you was chill," Tyrell said.

"Sure. Sure, we can."

"Thanks," Tyrell muttered.

"Hey Tyrell, do you know Ali Bakr?"

"Yeah, I knows him. You don't think he did nothing, do you?"

"Should we?"

"Hell no. That sand nig-, uh, kid can't deal with the frat boys. They all over him like."

"You got fraternities here?" Leo asked.

"You an agent too?"

"Fraternities?" Leo asked.

"No, none here, but those shits that go to them. The white ones. Anyways, Ali ain't nothing. He'd rather do art on the computer than anything else."

Tyrell chuckled.

"What's so funny?" Rob asked.

"He really likes Kelly Ann MacDonald."

"Who's she?" Leo asked.

"Oh, she a bad kitty. She fly with real white skin and black hair. She got them blue eyes. Not going to lie, a little bit on top but the greatest —" and here Tyrell brought his hands up to about waist height, vertical, fingers spread and slightly bent, cupping air. He grinned at the two men, who were not amused. Tyrell wiped his palms on his trousers. "Um, she a good girl. She even do her family's laundry at the laundromat."

"Which one?" Leo asked casually.

"The one with them Vietnamese. It be two blocks down on 7th."

"How do you know all this shit?" Leo asked, his exasperation showing.

"She a *lady*, man. I know about all the ladies. It be my business to know. Gotta know to make butt," Tyrell said. He started walking away. "See you at Fat Floyd's, Mr. I!"

"So much for low profile," Rob said.

Peak heat had sweat running down Rob's back and blurring his vision. He really wanted a cold drink. Rob leaned against the car and crossed his arms.

"You know that kid?" Leo asked.

"Not really," Rob said.

"I already spoke to the DARE officer. Bakr doesn't cause any trouble. Outside of his social issues, he's a model student and a normal kid."

"So was Mohamed Atta."

Leo glared at him.

"What?" Rob asked.

"Don't go getting stupid on me. I know the difference between a troubled kid and a terrorist. This guy is blowing smoke. How about this, we get him a girlfriend and that distracts him from putting crap out on insta-chat-twitsville and the next thing we know, the Assistant Director of Counterterrorism has time for shitbirds trying to buy Stingers in Detroit."

"But what if —" Rob said.

"It's on me. I accept full responsibility," Leo said.

"No, I meant what if he really is a nutjob? What if we put him on this Kelly girl and he's really a nut?"

"He's not a nut. He's just a kid and he's already on Kelly. I got an idea all he needs is a push to ask her out. Once she says yes, he'll be too busy for the web."

"Leo, how do you know?"

"How do I know what?"

"How do you know he'll stop? Hell, how do you know they'll hook up?"

"I don't. I don't know any of that shit. You want a guarantee? Buy a certificate of deposit. The DARE officer said he suffers from having an older brother who was a stud. Soccer star and academics. I think this kid needs a break and, if he gets one, he won't be my problem anymore."

"If you say so," Rob shrugged.

"Hey," Leo said, "you free tonight? I'll birddog the Rua Gait Laundry. If she's there, I'll reach out."

Rob thought about all the work he had pending.

"Yeah. I need to run up to the Crystal Suites and ask a few questions, but I'll listen for you."

Rob snaked through the neighborhood and jumped on I-295 north. There was an exit directly into the vast parking area of the Seminolacola Agorally mall and the companion Crystal Suites hotel, up near the intersection with I-10. The Agorally chain of luxury shopping centers had pioneered integrated retail, professional, lodging and dining spaces throughout the South. Rob headed for the three-deck parking garage nestled between the mall and hotel to examine Matthew Simmons's murder scene.

He drove up to the second level, where Matthew's body had been found about as far from any mall or hotel entrance as one could get. He knew the area both from the crime scene photographs, and from prior experience. He had spent hours here following Kathryn around, holding her bags, bored to tears.

Rob parked and let the car idle. He never thought he would get divorced. His parents were still married, bobbing along contentedly on Maryland's Eastern Shore. He had always assumed if he did his duty as a husband, he and his wife would stay together forever. Perhaps there would be some ups and downs, but certainly no divorce. Divorce happened to other couples. And yet, now he felt almost nothing; a little sadness maybe, but nothing else.

He got out of the car.

Rob scanned for cameras. The nearest one covered the doorways to the mall and hotel, and a small chunk of the deck, but not the twelve or so spots at this end.

Rob had been taught the trick to examining a crime scene was to scrutinize a small section of floor before moving on to the next, and so on, and to do the same for walls and the ceiling. Rushing or a lack of concentration could lead to missing evidence. As his class supervisor at the FBI Academy liked to say, missing evidence would "displease the Director," along with a host of other infractions.

What Rob saw was a lot of concrete. There weren't even traces of blood in the cracks. They must steam clean the deck regularly. Overpriced inventory paid for a lot of atmosphere, he thought. He didn't know what he expected to find but finding nothing disappointed him.

"What brought you here?" he asked out loud.

Rob considered the hotel entrance.

"What brought you here?" he asked again.

Rob trekked across the acre of concrete to the hotel entrance. The automatic glass doors glided apart and let forth a refreshing blast of arctic air. He entered a sea of wintery colors: ivory, pale blues and a mellow orange.

The hotel labeled this the Sky Lobby. Rob stood to the side at the front desk. Eventually, a hospitality industry professional inquired after his needs. Rob asked for the security manager and was told to wait. He stretched out in a comfortable armchair facing windows with stunning views of the mall roof.

"Mr. Lawson?"

The question jerked Rob awake. A clean cut if rather large-around-the-middle Hispanic man in his mid-thirties did the asking. He wore his dark hair in a flattop and had on a French Blue guayabera with khakis. He carried a radio in his left hand.

Rob jumped to his feet and stuck out his hand.

"Sorry, comfortable chair. Rob Lawson of the FBI."

"I know who you are." The man briefly shook Rob's hand. "What can I do for you?"

"And you are?" Rob asked.

"Officer Cintron."

"Officer Cintron?" Rob asked.

"Yes, Seminolacola PD. Working an extra job. What can I do for you?"

Cintron's sentences were clipped, his affect flat and his gaze hard.

"I'm with the FBI," Rob said, pulling out the black leather wallet holding his credentials.

"I know who you are."

Rob closed the credentials case and slipped it back into his pocket. He kept Cintron's stare.

"Do we know each other? Have I offended you somehow?" Rob asked.

"No."

"Then what's up?"

"What's up with what?"

"The hard-assed attitude, my friend."

"I'm not the one with the attitude and we're not friends. I keep asking you what you want and you keep not answering. What do you want?"

"About two years —"

"Yeah, the Simmons murder. I know. I didn't work here at that time."

"Well in the institutional memory, what —"

"There ain't none."

"Ain't none what?"

"Institutional memory. That it? I got work to do."

"What the hell is up with you?" Rob asked.

Officer Cintron stepped closer. Rob slid a half a step back on his weak side and brought his arms up by folding them across his chest.

"Tough guy, huh?" Cintron muttered, not missing the significance.

"Tough enough," Rob said.

"I'll tell you what's up with me. I don't need you fed guys questioning good police work. Jimmy Tank belongs dead and D. Randall and Wee Willie put him there. Good job, I say. You need activity? Go fuck with a raghead. Now if you'll excuse me, sir, I have to go back to work."

Citron strode away, with purpose.

Rob sighed.

He walked down a curving staircase to what he thought was should be called the ground lobby but probably wasn't out into the mall.

The boys in blue were talking, he thought. Bad news. He'd have to start watching his back now. More than usual, even.

He realized someone walking next to him matched his pace. He looked over and an attractive brunette smiled up at him.

Rob finally recognized her. Melissa thought the way his face opened completely in surprise was super cute.

"Are you stalking me?" she asked.

"Oh, yeah. Your purchase isn't helping me behave any, either," Rob said.

She shifted her Victoria's Secret bag from a one-handed grip to behind her legs with both hands through the cutouts. She had justified the purchase by telling herself she didn't have to sleep in a large t-shirt all the time. Though, really, she had been thinking about Rob. She felt the predictable heat rising in her cheeks.

"You weren't supposed to see that," she said.

Rob grinned as he caught the implication. He licked his lips.

"Ah, so where are you off to now?" he asked.

She could not decide if she was grateful he changed the subject or disappointed because the flirting ended.

"I have an appointment with my financial planner. You know Matthew worked for him, for Chucky Dauphin?"

Melissa pointed to the office tower at the end of the wing of the mall.

"So you said. Mind if I tail along?" Rob asked.

The request made her feel a little queasy. Wasn't it too private? she asked herself.

"Why?" she asked.

"I'd like to ask him a few questions. Then it'd be a lot easier for us to get a drink, logistically speaking," he said.

"Oh, logistically speaking. I see," Melissa said, steering them toward the elevators.

Rob thought Chucky must have hired a decorator. Frosted glass doors led to a waiting area with leather couches and cherry wood trim. An easel supported a poster for a real estate development project, an artist's rendering of a modern high rise with a view of the neighborhood. Something about it pulled at Rob, but he could not nail it down.

"We don't need to sit. He'll come right out," Melissa said.

The receptionist showed them to a conference room. The cherry wood theme continued, with added black accents. The conference table stood on the largest Turkish rug of Milas reds and yellows Rob had ever seen.

"Here he is. Hi Chucky. This is Rob. He's with the FBI. He's investigating the execution," Melissa said, presenting a cheek.

Chucky froze as still as a surprised rabbit, ignoring the cheek. He was a pudgy white man of about thirty-five. A fringe of blond hair circled his head. The sleeves of his dress shirt were rolled down and buttoned. His stripped tie hung loose around his neck and over his stomach. Forms were neatly arranged on the conference table.

Rob showed Chucky his credentials.

"Go ahead, kiss her," Rob said.

"Oh, yeah," Chucky said.

He leaned in and executed a quick peck, all the while watching Rob.

"We're not really investigating the execution. There were some civil rights allegations that came out of Jimmy Tank's arrest. A preliminary investigation, we call it. We ask a few questions, write a quick report and close it up," Rob said, doing his best to signal harmlessness.

"There's no problem, is there?" Chucky asked, regaining his composure.

"Should there be?" Rob asked.

"You're with the FBI, you tell me," Chucky said, moving the nearest form a bit. "But you know how these things are. Like when some technicality gets a murderer off, you know."

"He's already dead."

"Well, there's that taken care of. Mel, my clients don't habitually bring friends to meetings."

"Oh, we bumped into each other downstairs," she said.

Her brow furrowed and Rob thought she would question him about his characterization of the investigation in front of Chucky for a moment. It passed and her face cleared.

"We're going for a drink after," she said.

"Oh," Chucky said.

Ah-hah! Rob thought. Master Chuck has zeroed in on the hot young widow and Rob's being there is a wrench in the works. Seeing as the forms on the table were standard privacy agreements, one from Fidelity, another from Vanguard, and a third from a house he'd never heard of, Foreman Investments, there was no reason for Chucky to bring Melissa up to see him. Perhaps the real reason for the visit was for Chucky to see her.

"If you guys want to discuss business, I can step out," Rob said.

"Wonderful," Chucky said.

"No it's —" Melissa started to say.

They laughed, Melissa honestly, Rob thought. Chucky forced it, his little eyes hard as rocks.

"You can stay," Melissa said. "What are we doing?"

"Signing privacy statements," Rob said.

Chucky's features scrunched up around his nose in annoyance, but he recovered fast.

"Yes, signing necessary forms and a few other things," he said.

"What do you have her in?" Rob asked. He didn't want to let Chucky off the hook just yet.

"I don't discuss —" Chucky started to say.

"Index funds," Melissa said. "I don't mind throwing myself over a vault, but I can't stand being risky with money. Index funds outperform two thirds of fund managers every year. Right, Chucky?"

"Yes."

"See, I've been listening. Hey, Rob would like to ask some questions about Matt? Let me sign those and I'll hop out and call Lila. Then you guys can talk."

"Questions about Matt?" Chucky asked after watching Melissa walk out.

"Yes. He worked here?" Rob asked.

"Yes, we hired him off his internships. He was a quick study and a hard worker."

"About how long had he worked here?"

"Five years, more if you count the internships."

"Had those problems smoothed themselves out?"

Chucky did the rabbit thing again.

"I can't imagine what you are talking about," Chucky said after a moment.

"Everything was going okay?" Rob asked.

"What problems?"

"I thought Melissa said something about some problems."

"Oh, those. No, everything was superb. Really. His contacts in the sports community, here and throughout the South, were bringing in business. Matt was popular with the clients. He was bonusing well for someone so young. What problems did Melissa mention?"

"Oh, I don't remember. What problems were there?"

Chucky slid into one of the chairs. He started turning it back and forth.

"I've never attracted someone like Melissa. I think she's wonderful. More than hot, but I also *like* her, if you know what I mean. I knew I loved her when I first met her. When Matthew was alive, I always felt a sense of loss when she was around, like I had dated her and lost her to him when of course I never had. I'd never even met her until Matt started working here. But I felt a weird sense of loss after I met her. You know what I mean?"

Rob joined Chucky at the table with the best sympathetic mien he could muster.

"You probably don't," Chucky continued. "Anyway, after Matt died, I thought about trying with her. I thought about it and hesitated and thought some more and then I decided to go for it. I made up with these privacy forms for her to sign and got her up here. And here you are. With her. Another stud."

Rob had never thought of himself as particularly studly.

"Can you leave, please?" Chucky said, spinning in his chair, turning his back to Rob.

Rob walked into the reception area and caught sight of the real estate project poster again out of the corner of his eye.

"I've got it," he said, snapping his fingers. "That's the stalled construction on Brownsville at Cody! I knew I had seen it before."

"Is it?" Melissa asked without any real curiosity.

The last time Rob had seen the site, flimsy cyclone fencing surrounded one and a half floors of raw concrete sprouting weed-like strands of rusting rebar.

Moments later, Rob and Melissa were drinking gin and tonics at the bar in the Macaroni Grill.

"Did you get to ask him all your questions?" Melissa asked.

"I'd say I learned more than I wanted to, actually. What do you think of him?" Rob asked.

"I like him. I'm thankful to him. He was there after the murder. He collected up all of Matthew's pay and bonuses and the life insurance and invested everything for me. He got the townhouse for me and Jules and even now he pays our standing bills out of an account here and everything. If it wasn't for him, I'd have to be working fulltime and wouldn't have the money for Lila or time to stay fit."

"I see."

"I'm supposed to be going for my DPT and my full-on PT license, but I like life and everything as it is now. We set it up so I could go to school part-time and I really haven't even thought of going back. I feel like I can deal with a part-time job and Jules, and I can stay calm. I don't know about handling anything else now. I have Chucky to thank for that."

"Ever thought of going with him?" Rob asked.

"Like a relationship? Not really. He's always been rather fatherly. I know he's not real older than me, so maybe like a big brother. Frankly no, it's never come up."

Rob decided not to risk another one of those questions.

"Why do you ask?"

Busted, Rob thought. Might as well spill it.

"Chuck mentioned something in that vein," he said.

Rob now expected half an hour of Melissa examining the ins and outs of Charles Dauphin's feelings and desires. But he got something else instead.

"Odd," Melissa said, with a pinched mouth and creased brow. "A woman can usually tell when someone's interested," she said, giving Rob a shy, sly glance, with her cheeks a bit red, "and I never picked up on any interest from Chucky."

Ending this line of questioning right here worked well for Rob.

"Does Jules like Buccaneer Bob's?" Rob asked.

"He super likes it."

"Let's go get him and have dinner there. What do you say?"

Rob switched out his Bureau car in favor of his truck and collected Melissa, who had driven home to get Jules ready. In no time at all, they were together driving east on Highway 98. Jules rode on his booster between Rob and Melissa. The three of them wore sunglasses against daylight undiminished by thunderheads. Jules sang along to a Disney medley playing on Melissa's iPhone, his long black hair bouncing as he bopped to the music. When they crossed the line into Navarre, Rob pointed at a paint store parking lot.

"That's where my boat ended up after the hurricane, there in the lot," Rob said.

"That was yours?" Melissa asked.

"The one with the pole in it?" Jules fairly shouted the question.

"Yup, that was the one."

"I wondered about that boat. How did it end up there?" Melissa asked.

"I thought I could ride out the storm on two hooks in the Intracoastal. I was wrong," Rob said.

"You were on it?" Melissa shouted.

"Yup."

"But the telephone pole! Were you on it when the pole went into the boat?" she asked.

"Oh yeah."

"Shut up!"

"That is awesome!" Jules shouted.

"I hadn't been really scared until then. She'd been dragging and I had no idea where I'd end up. Then one hook grabbed and the boat swung so it pointed straight east, down the highway. I hoped that would be it and I'd make it when there was this really loud 'bang.' The pole shot through the hull with enough force to rock the boat hard. Water poured in, which was lucky because it ended up settling the boat down.

"It listed about forty-five degrees, but everything worked out. It didn't drag anymore and as the water receded, she touched bottom, leaning over with the telephone pole sticking up. That's why I was in Maritime Methodist that Sunday. I thought I ought to say thanks to the Big Guy."

Rob's mind drifted to the dark terrifying night of the hurricane. His memories were of noise, movement, vibration, and growing fear - real fear - as he realized he had made a bad, bad choice. There was nothing he could do in the boat, with its small engine, besides ride it out.

"Anyway," he continued, "it says a lot about a Monk 36. Tough old scow. I'm sorry I lost her."

"They could fix it," Jules said.

"Not that time, little man. The insurance company took it away."

"You could get another boat," Jules said.

"Maybe I will. Would you come on it?"

"We could be buccaneers!"

They drove into the parking lot of Buccaneer Bob's, where they ate a little and played pirate a lot.

Saturday

Rob drove up to Fat Floyd's for his workout first thing in the morning. The gym smelled the same as always. Fat Floyd sat in his same chair, at the same angle. Rob waved at him. Floyd waved back. It was inhuman to have a conversation this early on a Saturday.

Rob suited up and, after a quick stretch, began his workout. He circuit trained boxing style: calisthenics, rope jumping and bag work for about forty-five minutes. He showered and changed into a green Hawaiian shirt, layered over a black t-shirt and blue jeans; his big .45 on his hip, magazines, phone, and handcuffs on his belt.

He went to see Floyd.

"Hey, now I know you're back. Ain't no average type person in here this early on the weekend," Fat Floyd said.

"Floyd," Rob said, making sure no one listened in, "you got any contacts at the Crystal Suites?"

"Up at Agorally Mall?"

"Yeah, that's the one."

"Yeah, I know this little ole gal working housekeeping. You keep her out of it?"

"No worries. I need to know who's turning tricks up there and the house dick is frosty."

"Seminolacola PD got that place all tied up. I told you, them freaks ain't going to want to talk about D. Randall."

"They don't know it comes back to him."

"You born yesterday? Sure they do, G-man. You can bet they do. I'll text your ass. I need you to give my gal a taste, you know? A good-sized taste."

"We'll see what she can give up. I'll do the right thing. Thanks, Fats."

"Thank me if you don't turn up dead!" Fats shouted at Rob's back as Rob left.

Rob stopped on the way to the office and picked up a bran muffin and some yoghurt. He banged on the front door of the office to see if anyone else had come in before he started messing with the combination lock. After a moment, to Rob's surprise, Chris let him in.

"Rob, two words: blood borne pathogens, as in the Blood Borne Pathogens course you haven't finished yet?" Chris said, making room for Rob to pass.

"Yes, boss."

Rob meant to do the online training that morning, along with investigative paper, and to perhaps move some of the background investigations along, but when he got into his email the administrivia bogged him down. The source coordinator had learned he was back and sent a list requesting reports for sources that were already closed. The Primary Marksmanship Instructor sent him a nastygram about his missed quarters and the victim witness coordinator wanted to talk to him about a case that pre-dated Rob's entering on duty with the FBI. The emails sucked him in with their apparent potential for low-key, fast resolutions. By the time his BlackBerry buzzed, the morning had slipped away.

Fat's text had a phone number and name: "Manny."

Rob scooped up his keys and snuck out the back door before even thinking about logging on to Virtual Academy. After a flurry of texts, Manny finally agreed to meet at an Alligator Stu and Bar-B-Que restaurant across from the mall off I-10.

Rob drove around the block and then the parking lot. Inside, he accepted a booth and facing the door. Late brunch/early lunch time shotgunned patrons around the dining floor. The odor of simmering garlic, basil, oregano, pepper and onion hung in the air. After a moment, a wide, middle-aged African American waitress rambled over. She leaned against the booth.

"What choo havin' baby?" she asked.

"Diet Coke for now, please," Rob said.

"You stay scrawny drinking that stuff, baby."

"That's the idea."

"Sure enough."

She strolled away, rolling her big hips and gazing around the restaurant, with its fake stuffed alligator hanging from the ceiling and newly manufactured antique junk on the walls, as if it were her swamp and everyone else was merely living in it.

A gorgeous young black woman arrived. Sweat shone on her midnight-dark skin. Strands of black, tight curls framed her face and hung down around her neck. She wore a man's white -stunningly white against her skin - t-shirt and skinny black jeans. The v-neck showed some championship cleavage and Rob though only someone with legs like hers should be allowed to purchase jeans like that. Tension compressed her lips under her broad nose. Careful almond eyes searched the dining area before landing on Rob. She marched straight up to him.

"Fats send you?" she asked, contempt dripping off every word.

Whatever image he had conjured concerning *Manny* in his mind disappeared with a whiff of her jasmine fragrance.

"Manny?" Rob asked

"Well, who was you expecting?"

"A short, wrinkled-up, old Jewish man with a Yiddish accent and a hairy mole on his chin."

Manny tried hard not smile, but a small one escaped before she repaired her mask of urban attitude.

"Mandelana," she said. "Momma appreciated the Struggle."

"I'm Rob. Thanks for coming out."

"Yeah. Fats said you'd take care of me?"

"I can give you a little now, or a lot more if what you tell me pans out."

"What you doing here, girl?" The waitress asked, having silently materialized. "What you doing here with this man?"

111

"Escort, Donita," Manny said. "I'm working escort with him. White do you right."

"Don't you sass me. Who are you?" Donita asked Rob.

"I'm Rob. I'm a university advisor," naming the first job he thought of.

"What you want with Manny?"

"Donita, he knows I got my BBA," Manny said.

"We want her to consider attending Vanderbilt for her MBA," Rob said, the school coming to him out of thin air.

"I bet. You want something Manny?"

"Coffee. And give me the Cajun Baked Fish Sandwich. To go. Mr. Lee be paying."

Donita strolled away.

"Thanks for the softball," Rob said.

"Fats said you'd take care of me. It'll pan out. How much?" Manny asked.

"Depends," Rob said.

Manny shifted on the bench and leaned forward. "See here, you ain't far wrong with that Vanderbilt shit. I'm going to Morgan State up in Maryland for my MBA in August and I need me some green, you know?"

"I'll take care of you. But let's go for what's behind curtain number one, smart girl. Shoot straight with me and it will work out in your favor. How long have you been at the hotel?"

"A while. I'm a supervisor in housekeeping."

"Were you there when the man was murdered?"

"The white man got shot in parking?"

"Yup, him."

"I started a little after. Not too much."

"You know they executed his killer."

"Jimmy Tank Gubbs. I saw it."

"You did? What's he to you?"

"Nothing. I can read a news feed, Robert E."

"Fine. I need to know who works the house," Rob said.

"What do you mean?"

"Who turns tricks at the hotel."

"You po-lice?"

"Not exactly. Feds."

"What you need to know for?"

"Jimmy Tank may not have done it."

Manny snickered and turned away.

"What's up?" Rob asked.

"If he was in the Community, would you be asking?"

"I would."

"Sure you would."

"Look at me, Manny."

She did. He saw scorn there. He saw hate in those almond eyes. He saw contempt displayed all over her exquisite face.

"I would," he said.

They played guts poker for a long moment.

"They don't hang out in the lobby any more, old man," Manny finally said.

"So, how's it done?"

"Phone and apps now."

"Any regulars?"

Manny thought about it. Finally, she pulled a wrinkled yellow sticky out of her pocket and slid it across the table.

"Chloe Baxter. Talk to her. Don't mention me," she said.

"What does she know?"

"Just talk to her."

"Talk to who?" Donita asked, delivering Manny's sandwich.

"No one," Manny said, grabbing her bag and walking out.

Donita and Rob watched her go.

"You want anything?" Donita asked him.

"Huh? Oh. How about a small sausage and shrimp gumbo?" Rob said.

The black and cream Seminolacola PD cruisers were equipped with laptop computers. A bracket held them in place near the radio. The police software thereon had a messaging feature and D. Randall, in uniform and on duty, pounded the send button.

He had parked in the shade formed by a section of I-295 overpass. Asphalt had been poured between two of the streets and around the wide concrete columns holding up the interstate. D. Randall liked the squat.

"Message me back you fucking prick," D. Randall muttered.

Wee Willie drove up and parked next to D. Randall, facing the opposite direction. He lowered his window. Wee Willie was in a state. Sweat poured off his face even in the air conditioned car and he nervously gawked at everything. Beyond him, a young white officer typed away two-finger style on the laptop.

"Wee Willie! You done brought a friend," D. Randall said.

"Ah, yeah," Wee Willie said. He turned to his partner. "Hey, me and D. Randall want to talk."

"Go ahead," the young officer said, concentrating on his keyboard. "You won't bother me."

"Yeah man, that's great. Give us a minute?" Wee Willie asked.

"Hello? I'm kind of busy serving and protecting. You all talk away." The officer stopped typing and referred to his notebook.

For fuck's sake, D. Randall thought.

"Excuse me," D. Randall said softly.

"What?" the officer asked testily, turning his gaze back to the laptop screen.

"Eyeballs on me, you rookie fucking prick," D. Randall said, smiling.

The rookie looked at him. D. Randall thought he might have annoyed the Rookie a bit, seeing his frown and all. D. Randall kept smiling. The rookie started to crack. He silently appealed to Wee Willie for help and when none came, turned back to D. Randall. His face fell as his confidence drained away.

"Get out of the car and walk to the corner there, right fucking there. Serve it and protect it. Wee Willie will call you back when we're done, understand?" D. Randall said, still smiling.

"Yessir," the officer said.

He saved his work, grabbed his hat and ran to the corner.

"He talked to Eva – fucking – Jo," D. Randall said, abandoning any pretense at displaying mirth on his face.

"Now D. Randall, I, now —" Wee Willie stammered.

"The prick is F-fucking-B-I," D. Randall said, cutting him off.

"Shit."

"No shit. Shit."

"We're fucked."

"Don't go getting all fucked up about it. I got to confirm it. Even if he is FBI, he's got shit. Thing is, EvaJo got to go."

"Yeah. Yeah man. I see it."

"Yeah, you see it. If you had taken care of this already, she'd have been gone. Thing is, Wee Willie, our boy —" D. Randall checked to make sure the rookie was still serving and protecting. "Our boy got nothing. Them that can give him something need to go, you know?"

"Yeah."

"Fuck yeah. Handle it this time. Before I meant go, but now it's *go*, you know what I mean?"

"Yeah, thing of it is, Master Blaster —"

"Fuck Willie! Shut the fuck up. Go! Got it?"

"Yeah, I got it."

D. Randall really needed a trank. A trank and a beer.

"Two Twenty-Four," the female dispatcher said in her monotone, "it's the wreck, on 295 southbound, just south of Exit 7, multiple with injuries. Fire on the way."

"Two Twenty-Four," D. Randall said into his microphone, confirming he heard the call. "Willie, come on up there with me. Let's swing around to Bren and get up on it. I'll check out the wreck, you don't get too close. I'll tell you to set a flare line or close it up."

D. Randall didn't wait for a reply. He threw his idling cruiser into gear and floored it. He lit the car up and used the air horn as he blasted around turns.

He knew the highway undulated at the location of the wreck and therefore wanted Wee Willie to hang back a bit, on the top of one of the high sections crossing a side street, to lay a flare line if necessary.

D. Randall got up onto 295 north and didn't have to worry about overshooting the wreck. The daytime traffic had already backed up three hills. He put the cruiser onto the shoulder and activated the siren.

"Ten-four, 105, I show you joining 224," the dispatcher said.

D. Randall topped the last rise before Exit 7 and saw destruction.

"One-oh-five, close it at Exit 6, everybody off. Dispatch, I'll take a supervisor and another unit up here," D. Randall said. "Let's start with two amb-lances and line up but hold two more."

D. Randall counted four cars and a tractor trailer, the trailer being a tanker with flammable and explosive placards on it. The action had crushed a dark compact car. Another car, a large blue Volvo, had been T-boned by the tractor and the two remained locked together, having entered into an intimate relationship. A teal Japanese minivan and a black GMC Yukon were smashed up in the right lane. The interstate was completely blocked.

D. Randall parked on the shoulder, about twenty-five yards up hill. Hot gasoline vapor assaulted his face as he exited his car.

"Dispatch, we got a gas spill. Call for Hazmat," D. Randall said into the microphone clipped to his epaulet.

He hiked down to the wreckage. Adults milled about. Some children, tweens and a littler kid, surrounded a sobbing woman by the minivan.

"D. Randall, what you got?" shouted Officer Henry Gilcker, walking up the shoulder on the northbound side.

"We got a crap load of crispy critters unless we get this parking lot moving. I'll check with Wee Willie to make sure he's got it closed off and then we'll empty this bunch via the shoulder," D. Randall said.

"Check, check." Gilcker stepped over the barrier and headed up the traffic stream.

D. Randall reached up to key his microphone. By force of training and habit, he scanned the area. The nine-or-so year old from the minivan held a phone up as if to video or take a picture, pointed at the tractor trailer, and walked backwards between the cars.

"One-oh-five, have you got the high — Oh SHIT," D. Randall said into the mic.

A tricked-out Subaru Impreza raced down the left shoulder. He swung his head forward and saw the boy standing in the way, concentrating on his picture.

D. Randall pushed off and sprinted along the cars as he heard the scream of the turbocharger coming up from behind. When he came abreast of the boy, he reached out with his left arm and grabbed the boy around the middle. He pivoted and jumped, landing on the hood of a Gold Mist Cadillac STS. He waited for what felt like a millennia for the Subaru to slam his legs, which were taking their own sweet time bending in.

He felt a sharp smack on his heel as the Subaru sped by. It spun him and the boy on the hood. He heard his belt gear scratch through clear coat and paint. He didn't let go of the boy until they stopped, their feet, having taken the long way around, pointed at the tinted windshield. The boy jumped up on the hood.

"Did you see that! Mom, did you see that! I think I got it on video!" he jumped down. "Did you —"

Mom, still crying, ran to the boy and slapped his cheek so hard D. Randall felt it himself. Then she gathered him up into her ample bosom and continued wailing for all she was worth.

D. Randall, who not only saw it, but lived it, lay his head down on the hot hood of the Cadillac, the bright sun blasting right through his closed eyelids. His shoulder and his heel ached.

"I have *got* to get a new job," he said, to no one in particular.

A cup of coffee steamed on Rob's desk as he typed furiously, trying to catch up on his reports. He had sent the number Manny had given him a text asking for a date before leaving the Alligator Stu and Bar-B-Que.

His BlackBerry buzzed.

This was the return message.

"Do I know you?" Chloe texted.

"We never met," Rob wrote. He decided to gamble. "I got ur name from WW."

"Ain't heard from him. How is he?"

Interesting, Rob thought. "He good. Can we meet? It's business," he said.

"With WW, I know what business. Now?"

"Yes, to make plans."

"Ok. 3? Where?"

"U pick."

She named her choice.

"Of course," he said aloud.

He grabbed his keys and got moving. He headed north from the office, working his way northwesterly through the city. The strip malls and homes thinned out. Before he reached the city limit, he drove onto the concrete plain surrounding a windowless, neatly-painted white box of a building sitting all by itself. Purple lettering on a black sign proclaimed: "ECGC, The Premier Gentlemen's Club of the Emerald Coast."

A handful of cars and trucks parked close to the front door, taking up less than ten percent of the available spots. Despite the emptiness now, Rob knew the lot did fill up. The club brought in trade from college, military and highway traffic, even getting some customers from Mobile. Rob surveyed the area and saw nothing out of the ordinary, so in he went.

"No cover before up 'til the end of happy hour, dear," said the old lady behind the hostess desk.

Inside, there were bars along the walls and multiple dance stations throughout the room. Two main stages with their ubiquitous poles were at the front and back. Tables, chairs and booths were situated on different levels one step up or down, making for tricky maneuvering for drunks, Rob thought.

Today's crowd clustered around the one main stage where the only dancer performing could have worked on the side as a fitness model. She sported fake tits, cut musculature and a sheen of sweat as she held herself perpendicular off the pole while dancing to some Techno. Only one bar had a bartender, a girl-next-door brunette. Rob chose a table where he could face the door and see the stage at the same time.

The brunette came around and he ordered a beer. Rob's vision had adjusted and he picked up more details. There were two large muscular men standing at the far end of the open bar. They wore black ECGC t-shirts and lounged like bored lions. Bouncers. Rob sipped his beer.

He fought off offers of more beer and lap dances. After about three dancers, none of whom were as compelling as the first, Rob started to entertain thoughts of leaving. The bouncers were checking him out and did not appear to like what they saw.

A petite, effervescent blonde bounced in, bouncing shoulder length hair and waving. Smallish breasts bounced under a tank top and the hem of a super mini bounced along in time. She bounced herself down at Rob's table.

"Hi!" she said.

"Hi. Samantha?" Rob asked.

Her eyebrows went up and her mouth formed a large "O." She spun her head around to see if everyone else was as surprised as she was at his idiocy.

"No, silly. Didn't you call me? Call for Chloe?" she asked.

"Oh yeah, sorry. How *are* you?" Rob asked.

"I'm *fine*, but could really use a drink, yeah," she said.

I bet you're fine, Rob thought. Her glassy eyes and nervous energy spoke volumes. He gestured at the bartender and Chloe ordered a vodka cranberry.

"So, what's the business? I don't do group, but if it's a party, I can get more dates. If you have the money, of course." Chloe leaned in and caressed his thigh under the table.

Rob grinned and winked and reached for his credentials.

"It's not quite like that, Chloe. I'm a special agent with the FBI and I'd like to ask you some questions," Rob said.

He held the cred case below the table. Chloe had to duck her head to see it, half smiling as if it were a joke she needed to work out.

"Fuck!" She tried to stand up.

Rob grabbed her forearm and pulled her back down.

"Ow!" she squeaked. "You're hurting me!"

The boys from the bar started walking.

"Chloe, tell them you're fine or I'll show them my badge and say you're a snitch," Rob said in low serious growl.

"No," she said, afraid.

119

"Tell them."

"What up, Chloe?" the nearest one asked.

Rob let her go. He sipped his beer and ignored the bouncers.

"Yeah, Beau, I'm chill," she said with forced gaiety.

The bouncers returned to their positions at the bar.

"Thanks," Rob said, all good humor and deference again. "Can I ask you a few questions?"

"What about?" Chloe rubbed her forearm dramatically.

"Chloe, do you remember a man that was murdered two years ago at the Allegory Mall? Shot in the parking area?"

"No, I don't know nothing about that," she said, peering around like a trapped rodent.

"Sure you do, Chloe. We have the records from your phone," Rob lied smoothly. "We know it all."

Chloe squinted at him.

"Why are you coming only now? Why are you asking me after Jimmy Tank is dead?"

Jackpot! Rob thought.

"It's like a cold case, Chloe. Like on TV."

"Like the regular detectives couldn't solve it so you're doing it?"

"Something like that, yes. But solve what, Chloe?"

"Oh, Wee Willie said the man was cheating us sex workers and he wanted to set the man up, get him to pay."

Rob's blood ran cold. It was all he could do to keep his shock from showing.

"What was the plan?" he asked.

"I was supposed to hit on him and give him a blow job in the parking lot near the hotel. Then we would both get busted."

"You agreed to that?"

"Well, it wasn't like I would get busted for real, silly. Only he would. It was all official. Like you know, I was undercover or something."

"What happened?" Rob asked.

"Nothing." Chloe said.

"Nothing?"

"Yeah, nothing. Can I have another drink?"

"Wait, Chloe, nothing happened?"

"Nope. I did hit on him and sent him my digits. He texted and we planned to meet, but Wee Willie called and said not to come, saying it was off."

"Meet at the parking lot?"

"No, but at the hotel, in the hotel bar. It was before I got banned from there."

"Where did you hit on him?"

"In here, stupid! He came in here regular like."

"Oh? Did he have a girl here?"

"No, he would sit in the back and drink a couple of beers. Always after work. For happy hour, like. Hand out some dollars but nothing else."

So that's why she's talking so much, Rob thought. Nothing happened from her perspective.

"Weren't you concerned when you saw he had been killed?" he asked.

"I *was*. Wee Willie said it was a terrible coincidence, how he got robbed by Jimmy Tank just before the 'operation.' That's what he called it: the 'operation.'"

"Got it. Give me the phone number you use for Wee Willie."

"Don't have it no more. It don't matter. He changes his phones all the time."

"What number does he use now?"

"I don't know. I haven't heard from him in a long time. Since then even."

"Did he pay you?"

"I don't remember," she said.

Chloe developed a sudden curiosity in the current pole dancer.

"If you could remember, not saying you did, but if you could, how much did you get, assuming you could remember?" Rob asked.

"Five bills, for nothing!" she squealed gleefully, hunching up her shoulders.

She had held it together as they talked but whatever she was on kicked in. She slumped deeper into her chair.

"Hey," she said.

"Hey," Rob replied.

"You know, you're a fine piece of man flesh and I'm getting a little horny. Why don't you take me somewhere? It'd be for free."

Rob kept smiling at her. He thought about how the hell he had wound up in an Emerald Coast strip club with a sexy but stoned prostitute propositioning him while he wore a .45 on his hip and carried FBI credentials. He thought about how ridiculous it was to feel bad about rejecting Chloe's advances, but he did.

"I got to report in, the boss is waiting on me," Rob said.

"Sure. You just don't want to fuck no whore."

"No, really. He's tough that way. I tell you what, why don't you tell me where you stay at and maybe we could hook up another time?"

Chloe laughed in his face, but provided her identification details and contact information anyway. Rob felt a little better when she zeroed in on a dancer whose shift had just started on one of the side stations. So much for what he had thought was feigned attention.

He fractured a few traffic laws on the way back to the office. He needed to write this one up posthaste.

Leo hadn't intended to interrupt Rob mid-way through his report on the Baxter interview. He thought he would be catching Rob at supper.

"Hey Rob, you won't believe this, but the Ali kid is hiding behind the bushes in front of the laundromat and the girl is in there! You gotta get up here. We can close this out in a second," Leo said.

"Have you been following Ali?" Rob asked.

"No, I swung by the laundromat to check it out and everyone was here. Time to help me facilitate young love. Get up here."

"On my way."

"Your buddy was right. This is one heartsick kid. This thing is gonna work." Leo disconnected before Rob could comment.

Leo enjoyed watching Ali peer in at Kelly Ann. Ali was all teenager: messy black hair and dark fuzz growing on his olive cheeks. He wore a purple polo and green knee-length shorts. Ali scrunched himself up to hide behind the dark green foliage. His blue book bag dropped off his shoulder, ignored on its way to the ground.

Leo couldn't wait for Rob to get there.

Ali had been crouching for some time. Worried someone might object to his being there, he did his best not to look conspicuous, which meant to him he had to hold some weird positions. His back ached and he was thinking of going home. He decided after one more peek at Kelly Ann, he'd take off.

"Ali Bakr?" a male voice asked.

Ali literally jumped in surprise. He saw two men, one super old and the other merely old. They were both taller than Ali, with dark hair and shaved faces. The older one wore a light blue sport coat, white shirt, no tie, blue Dockers and had big muscles. The other one wore an open shirt and a t-shirt.

"Shit, you scared me," Ali said.

"Listen, Ali," the older one said. "It's about to get scarier, but hang with me. I'm Leo Kladsko. This is Rob Lawson. We're Special Agents with the FBI."

Both men pulled out large leather wallets and flipped them open like on TV. Ali saw their photos, and the blue "FBI" in the middle of the white credentials. First he thought about how cool this was and suddenly he remembered the posts he'd been writing.

"Oh shit," Ali said. "Shit, shit, shit." Ali danced around nervously.

"Ali, it's not like that. We just want to talk to you," Leo said.

"Are you going to tell my parents?" he asked, tears welling.

"Let's just talk for a minute," Leo said. "Take a deep breath."

"Okay. Okay," Ali said, gulping air.

"Listen, Ali, it's about the things you've been writing online."

"But how would you know what I was writing? You're reading my posts because I'm Muslim," Ali said, suddenly mad.

"Settle down, kid. We're reading your posts because every teenager's mom living in territory formerly making up the Confederate States of America has been reading your posts. They read them and call FBI headquarters because your hurting Jody's and Susie's feelings."

"What?" Ali asked.

"Never mind. A lot of people have complained about it. That's how we found you."

"You're not in my computer?"

"No, not at all."

"We get copied after the fact," the younger old dude said.

"Ali, we have to ask. What's going through your mind when you write that stuff?" Leo asked.

"Oh. Um . . . nothing," Ali said. That feeling he got when the kids give him shit came back.

"Nothing? Ali, you have to give us some more. What's this all about?"

"Well, see, the other kids at school are all on me on account of I'm Egyptian and we were advanced when the white male patriarchy was still drawing on cave walls and they always make fun of me," Ali said, pushing the embarrassment down inside himself.

"So you write that stuff?"

"It's what they expect." Ali felt his anger rise. "That's all I am to them, so I write it. I'd never hurt —"

And here fear shut Ali up. Sweat started pouring out of him. He held on to his backpack strap so hard his knuckles turned white.

Ali had put his father's pistol and the box of ammunition in his backpack before he went out, after his parents had left the house.

He had taken them without thinking, on a whim. He wasn't going to do anything or anything like that. He had even forgotten he had them.

"You were saying?" Leo asked.

Ali thought about running, but then figured running would make it worse.

"I'd never hurt anyone." Ali licked his lips and shifted his weight.

"We know, Ali. We think this is all nonsense. But I have to ask you. Are you a terrorist or planning a terrorist act?"

"No! I would never do that. Why are you even asking me that? You're only asking me that because I'm Muslim! That's racist," Ali said.

"Anti-Semitic, maybe," Leo said. "If you thought I was asking you if you were a terrorist because you're an Arab, that would be racist."

"What?" Ali asked, thinking the old guy was nuts.

"Anti-Semitic, Leo?" the younger old man asked.

"Yeah. Arab Muslims are a Semitic people."

"What? What are you two talking about?" Ali asked.

"Never mind. Listen, Ali, you gotta stop writing that crap. People are worried and that means we get all up in your business," Leo said.

"Yeah? Or what? I got free speech."

"You sure do. You can write whatever you want. Do it on a blog. Do it in print under your own name. Spray paint it on a wall at school, but whatever you do, stop posting inflammatory anonymous shit, got it?"

"What if I don't?"

Leo let his anger show. He jabbed a rigid forefinger into Ali's chest.

"If you don't promise me you'll stop it now, today, and mean it, I'll throw you in my car and drive you straight to your parents and tell them everything."

Oh shit, Ali thought. His Dad would yell at him and his Mom would kill him. Ali remembered the gun. Between the fear of his parents and his still having the gun, he lost control, but only for a moment.

"You're not going to search my bag are you?" he asked.

Ali saw the two men exchange a quick glance.

"No, Ali," Leo said, "we're not going to search your bag. But I'm adding to the deal. You have to promise me you'll stop posting that shit, got it? And, one other thing. You have to walk in there and say hello to Kelly Ann."

"What? No way."

"Way, yo. You walk in there and say 'hi.'"

Ali checked it out. Kelly Ann was loading a dryer. She wore her hair up, a pink cropped tank top and gunmetal knickers with an orange stripe down her fine thighs. She was so hot Ali forgot about his parents and the gun.

"What if she laughs at me?"

"So? You'll know it's time to move on. But you gotta do it to stay out of trouble."

"No, I can't do it. She'll make fun of me."

"Sure you can. She won't make fun of you. Even if she does, you have to man up and give it a try. If she tells you to pound sand, you'll know you tried. But I'll tell you a secret."

"What?"

"Now I don't know much about girls, but I'll tell you this: even when girls tell you to pound sand, they sometimes come around later all by themselves. So if she tells you to get lost, be a gentleman on your way out. We'll even give you a ride."

Ali's felt his heart pounding. He thought about it and tried to work it out in his mind.

"What do I say?" Ali finally asked.

"You carry in two cold Cokes, walk up to her, and say: 'I thought you could use some company.' Then you give her one of the Cokes."

Sensible, Ali thought. Now was the time. Maybe now *was* the time

"Wait," Ali said, "I don't have any money to buy Cokes."

"Come 'ere."

They clustered around the trunk of Leo's Chevy. In among the black nylon gear bags, a milk crate full of stuffed manila folders and jumper cables, a cooler held center stage. Leo produced a six pack of Cokes in glass bottles.

"Take two."

Ali smiled up at the gruff man and swung a strap of his backpack on his shoulder. He heard the distinctive rattle of the bullets in their box. Ali's muscles tensed up. He breathed deeply, risking a glance at the agents at the same time. The older man smiled and the younger one looked confused. Ali needed to do something fast.

"Thanks, sir. What should I say again?" Ali asked Leo.

"Walk up to her. Say: 'Hi. I saw you in here. I thought you could use some company.' Then hand her one of the Cokes."

Ali couldn't wait to get away from these guys. He should never have taken the gun out of the house.

"Yes sir. I'll do it."

Maybe, Ali thought, once he went in these guys would leave. He grabbed the Cokes and entered the laundromat.

"Leo, did you hear something funny in Ali's backpack?" Rob asked.

"This is it, that girl is going to take the Coke and then, no more posts. Our boy will be too busy," Leo said, taking a bottle for himself. "You want a Coke?"

"No thanks. Leo?"

"What?"

"Did you hear something funny in the backpack?"

"No. Did you?"

Not wanting to get caught by Kelly Ann, they avoided standing in front of the window. Leo could not see Ali's progress, but they did have coverage on the door. Every second Ali doesn't come out, Leo thought, is another step closer to "mission accomplished."

Leo wished Rob wouldn't ask questions.

"I thought I heard bullets rattling, like a box of ammunition," Rob said.

"Uh-huh."

"Did you hear it?"

"No, Rob, I didn't hear bullets rattling around his backpack."

Leo kept his eyes on the door and said a little prayer the kid stayed inside.

Seconds grew to minutes.

"Leo, why do you think Ali was so protective of his pack?"

"Well, it could have been he was scared shitless. Or it could have been he had his stash in there. Pot or whatever. Or," and here he stared hard at Rob, "it could have been he was nervous because he thought two grown male perverts were hitting on him. Assuming he was protective of his book bag, what do you think was up?"

Rob paused. Then he said "I guess I don't know."

"Come on, let's go check on Casanova," Leo said.

They inched around the corner of the building to get an angle.

"Yes," Leo hissed.

It the white of the interior and the glare of the neon signage, Kelly Ann leaned against a washer and sipped from her Coke as Ali talked a mile a minute.

"Think we should go?" Leo asked.

Kelly Ann's Coke came away from her lips. She grinned. They both started laughing.

"Our work here is done. Let's make like trees and leaf," Leo said.

Monday

The early morning sunlight blasted through the low-bid General Services Administration shades. Rob squinted as he typed at his desk. He could hear rapid clicks from Kay's keyboard. They were the only two in.

Anxiety had brought Rob out of a deep sleep before his alarm had gone off. He had dressed in a conservative blue suit, white shirt and red and blue striped tie and driven in. Fortified with his bran muffin, yoghurt and break room coffee, he'd been typing since before 7:00.

Rob was significantly behind on his paper for what he was now thinking of as the Hargrove case. His backgrounds were late and he hadn't even opened his leads or the two case referrals Chris had recently dumped on him.

Rob felt bad about it. His slob Sunday yesterday did not help his outlook at all. He had slept through church, dragged around his apartment doing laundry and bills, and killed the afternoon watching baseball. He did not even text Melissa, who had not texted him either, come to think of it.

Rob heard the beeps of someone coding in. The front doors worked in quick succession.

"Lawson, get in my office, please!" Chris shouted as he stomped his way to his desk.

"Coming, Boss. You want some coffee?" Rob called out, cringing at the sound of such obvious ass-kissing.

A high pitched snort-laugh emanated from Kay's cube.

"How about you get on up here?" Chris replied.

Expecting heavy weather, Rob grabbed a steno pad, pen and his mug, hoping to signal casual subservience.

"Dammit Rob, you can't take off a year, then come back and tell me to go screw myself," Chris started as soon as Rob entered the doorway.

"Boss, the —"

"I don't give a shit. You can take forty-five minutes to do a required training. It gets a lot of visibility from the front office."

"Yes Boss. I can —"

"Don't give me that 'I can' crap. You should have. Get it done."

"Yes, Chris," Rob said, turning to go.

"Not so fast. I looked at your background investigations. You're nowhere with them. Do I have to remind you they have Budeds?"

"No Chris, I —"

"Why haven't you even finished one?"

"I —"

"You haven't opened your SARs. What's going on in your head?"

"They —"

"No movement on your other investigations."

"Sir —"

"No other case has paper in the file, only your capital punishment dog."

"It's been moving kind of fast."

Rob's mind seized involuntarily on some case details and didn't quite catch what Chris said next. Rob stood there, mug, pen and notebook in hand, waiting for the next salvo.

"Well?" Chris asked.

"Sir?"

"Tell me about it."

"About what?"

Chris's eyebrows were up in the middle and down at the edges, and his mouth opened slightly. Chris held that expression for a beat of time, and then his face hardened.

"Double Entry Bookkeeping," Chris said.

"Uh . . .," Rob said.

"Do you have anxiety, Rob? Depression? Are gender identity or sexual orientation issues getting in the way of your casework?"

"No."

"Why don't we do this. How about you take a moment and tell me about your execution case! Who's the dead guy? Simmons?"

"Oh. Yes, Simmons. So, to start, the subject in the case made a heartfelt declaration of innocence in the offense that brought him to the death chamber. He admitted to other murders against his own interest, after conviction and not in pursuit of a plea agreement. By then he was under the influence of his renewed religious beliefs and a prison clergyman, but he continued to deny murdering Simmons.

"Upon investigation, I determined the arrest was without significant detective input and strangely simple. Sometimes it goes that way, but in this case the record does not support the conclusion the department conducted a full, complete investigation into the matter."

"Yeah, I remember you said there was no detective work on the case. Can you prove it?" Chris asked.

"Yes. Hoss brought the file. It's bare bones. Crime scene work, report from the responding officer and the duty homicide dick's note opening the file. The next entry was the actual arrest, followed by Jimmy Tank's brief confession." Rob said.

"So you're telling me they did nothing on the case?"

"Nothing. No interviews after the first day, no property recovered except the car, nothing went to the lab except the gun and there is no indication anything was entered into NCIC."

"Not even the car?"

"Not even the car."

"How'd the arresting officers know it was Jimmy Tank?"

"On view. In their report, they reference their knowledge Jimmy Tank wouldn't drive a car like that, so they turned on him to pull him over and investigate."

"How did defense counsel challenge them?"

"I don't know, sir. I haven't ordered the transcripts."

"Do it. Let's find out who the witnesses at trial were and what they said. I want them interviewed."

Chris swung his chair to look out the window and thought for a moment.

"Jimmy Tank's confession. Was his lawyer there?" he asked.

"Nope. Jimmy Tank waved and sang," Rob said.

"Odd, isn't it? A career criminal not waiting for counsel?"

"Yes, sir."

Chris thought some more.

"That's still not enough for anything meaningful. What else do you have?" Chris asked.

"I interviewed Jimmy Tank's mother. She stated Jimmy Tank obtained a large amount of cash, some of which he shared with her. He bought her a car and set her up in a condo."

"You can prove this?"

"I interviewed the rental agent at the condo, pulled the motor vehicle records and subpoenaed the bank records."

"What do they say?"

"They support her statements about the cars."

"No, dammit, the money. Tell me about the money."

"Oh. The records aren't in yet."

"Call on them today. I want them. I want the money substantiated."

"Yes Boss. I also found a prostitute who stated Wee Willie instructed her to take a run at the decedent. She did so and arranged to meet him at what would become the crime scene. At the —"

Chris spun around in his chair to face Rob and slammed both hands down on his desk.

"Why the hell didn't you start off with that! Write it up. Send the preliminary to both Civil Rights and Public Corruption. I want a draft beforehand so I can call the ASAC. What do you have backing her story up?"

"Nothing yet."

"Is she internet or pager?"

"Pager and Smartphone."

"I want her historicals ASAP. Nail this down hard, Rob. You need help?"

"Yeah, I'll need some for Chloe, the prostitute. Maybe Kay can help me with another interview?"

"Go ask her and let me know what she says. Get on the writing this morning, but I want you and Kay interviewing her this afternoon, as soon as she gets up, before she starts popping, snorting or smoking."

"Yes Boss."

"Another thing. You better start asking yourself why they killed him," Chris said.

"The State of —"

"Not the dipshit. Simmons. No one goes through all this merely to prove they can."

"Yes Boss."

"This is growing into an FBI case after all."

"Yes Boss."

"Well, you won't solve it standing around here," Chris said. "Get to work."

D. Randall sipped a fresh mimosa on the deck of the Sundowner Marina clubhouse. He liked the building's exterior of gray weathered Cyprus. He waited for Wee Willie over a breakfast of thick cut bacon, eggs and hash browns with onion, and had already drunk two of the cocktails. Now, even after he promised himself he'd stay sober, he was on his third.

He wore a roughly woven cotton pullover in faded white, exposing chest to solar plexus, a pair of tennis shorts and sandals. D. Randall hid behind the sleekest of TAG Heuer sunglasses. The bay was flat except for the ripples kicked up by a warm breeze. The morning sun made the water sparkle like so many diamonds.

"Hey," Wee Willie said, gasping, as he barely made it into the chair beside D. Randall. He put his wallet, keys, smartphones and the burner phone he had been using on the glass tabletop.

"Where the fuck you been?" D. Randall muttered.

The deck was mostly empty, with the nearest people being a group of four, two couples, old enough to be retirees, sitting three tables away.

"You bitch, you just called me, man. You called, I'm here, and I want some breakfast," Wee Willie said, waving at the young man behind the counter to indicate he wanted to order.

"Fuck your breakfast," D. Randall said, waving the man away. "Listen here, *bitch*, that motherfucker you and EvaJo talked to, I'm sure he's a motherfucking FBI prick."

"Shit."

"It gets better. He done interviewed Chloe."

"No shit!"

"Keep it down, shit-for-brains. Now listen to me. Chloe can put you and Simmons together, you know what I'm sayin'?"

"I know."

"You got to do the thing. Chloe got to be in a situation where she can't put you and Simmons together. You were supposed to give her money so she could go to California."

"I did! She moved and everything. She was gonna star in fuck flicks. It must have worked for a while, but she done circled back again."

D. Randall was about ninety-five percent sure Wee Willie was full of shit. He probably pocketed the money and sent her away on her own, maybe as far as Tallahassee.

"This is your number one priority. Use those shitbirds you picked up in Mobile," D. Randall said. He had every intention of turning those pricks in to Alabama State Bureau of Investigation as soon as convenient. "You got about a New York minute."

"Sure thing, D. Randall," Wee Willie said, waving the young man out from around the counter again.

"Fuck eating, Wee Willie. Get the fuck going," D. Randall hissed as he stood.

Wee Willie glared at D. Randall as he put a twenty and a ten on the table. He strode off the deck and thought about sitting in his truck until Wee Willie got moving too, before it occurred to him he didn't really care. Once behind the wheel, with the engine running and air blowing, D. Randall thought Wee Willie could end up expendable, too.

The first few notes from "Requiem for a Dream" played out of Melissa's phone, music she had used on what had probably been her greatest floor routine ever. She had set the tone to play for incoming texts. She stopped walking to check it out.

"What are you doing?" Rob's text asked.

She thought it was cute he wrote out all his words.

"Going home. I have to get Jules early," she wrote.

She started walking again. She wore her scrubs and her gym bag hung from her shoulder. Her phone went off again.

"You and Jules have time for lunch?" Rob wrote.

"Just me. I get Jules at 1:30."

"Nice. Where?"

Melissa felt deliciously mischievous.

"Meet me at my place."

Kay had been away from her desk and Rob had not been able to line her up for the afternoon. He went back to his writing as he waited for Kay. Not that it mattered. Melissa's text had driven all thoughts about work out of his mind.

Rob saved his current document and calculated his ability to successfully leave the office and get to his car while avoiding supervisory scrutiny. Best case scenario, he'd be back by two, even if he had to pick up some actual lunch on the way. He listened hard.

The RA was quiet. He logged off and headed for the back door. Rob stumbled on a cardboard box of documents by Steve's cube. He stomped around and crashed into a cube wall, and then froze. After a slow ten count, he slipped out.

Rob ran down the stairs and out the lobby doors. Once in his Bureau issued Buick, it was all shaved traffic lights and rolling stops on his way to Melissa's condo. The possibilities, he thought, were endless, although he mostly had only one on his mind.

As Melissa considered the texts she and Rob had exchanged, she thought he could easily come to the wrong conclusion. She didn't think there was anything wrong with a nooner, but she wasn't sure now was the time in their relationship. She started to get nervous.

Melissa arranged her plastic cutting sheet, chef's knife and an assortment of vegetables on her darkish Corian counter. She washed her hands and started chopping. She figured she had time to dump a can of tuna into the salad, and maybe some shredded cheese. She finished cutting up the Romaine, carrots, red peppers, a little onion and some celery.

She thought of Rob's smile and his broad shoulders. She thought about the way he handled himself, balanced and confident. Melissa didn't care for messy men, and she liked Rob's trimmed, combed hair and his clean shaven face every time she saw him. She put both hands on the counter and wondered what his workouts were.

She glanced down at her scrubs. Oh, no, Melissa thought. This would not do. She needed to put on something nice.

She heard a knock on the door. Three short confident raps.

Melissa grimaced as she brought her hands up to shoulder height and shook them, fingers straight and wide open. Her knees were bent and she leaned forward.

Well, she thought, she was trapped. She went ahead and answered the door.

Melissa skipped around the counter and ran like the gymnast she used to be, with those little hops and locked elbows. She stopped short, smoothed her hair back and patted down her scrubs. She exhaled and opened the door. The rubber sweep slid across the carpeting.

"Hi," Rob said, grinning his grin.

"Hi!" she said, a little too loud.

Melissa skipped off to the kitchen. With her back to Rob, she closed her eyes hard in embarrassment, but collected herself before turning around.

"I'm making some lunch," she said brightly. She thought she sounded like a lunatic.

"Umm, lunch," Rob said, walking toward her.

"It's salad," she said, picking up the knife and gesturing with it.

"Uh-huh," he said.

Rob stopped right in front of her and gently drummed the counter with his strong fingers.

"You look great in those scrubs," he said.

"Thanks. Thanks for lying. I should have changed for you," she replied.

She kept her competition face on but fell apart inside. Was she ever capable of not sounding like a candidate for involuntary commitment?

"That knife for me?" Rob asked.

"Oh, no." She put it down. "Hey, um, I don't want you to get the wrong idea about this," she said.

"Uh, huh."

"I didn't mean for this to be a —"

"No, of course not."

He came closer.

Melissa felt herself start to blush. To cover, she turned away. She pointed at the kitchen clock.

"We should eat. I have to get Jules in an hour," she said.

"Uh, huh."

Rob stopped right up against her back. She really wanted him to kiss her. She didn't move. He hesitated. The clock ticked.

"The hell with it," she said.

She spun around and reached under his arms, up to his shoulders. She angled her face up. She felt him embrace her.

They kissed.

She expected something more forceful than the gentle warmth of his lips.

"What the hell is this?" someone shouted.

In an instant Melissa found herself behind Rob. She couldn't move around him to get a better line on who was in her house. She was stuck.

Rob had balled up a handful of her scrub blouse in his left fist and held her firmly behind him. She grabbed his upper arms and stood on tippy toes, trying to see over his shoulder.

"For Christ's sake, Kathryn! After all these years! You could've gotten killed!" Rob said.

Rob pointed his massive pistol at a woman who had great hair, long loose curls of golden brown falling below her shoulders, and whose beautiful features were temporarily arranged in a very ugly manner.

"Oh, now you're going to shoot me. Go ahead. Go ahead and shoot, moron," this Kathryn said, fists on hips. "Go ahead, but won't the Director be *displeased*?"

That last word dripped with contempt.

Kathryn wore a skin-tight sandstone mini-dress that showed some great cleavage, better than her own, Melissa thought. Were those Jimmy Choos in red suede? They must be killing her Digitorums and Hallucises, but the shoes were gorgeous. And what the hell was this Kathryn doing in her house?

Melissa heard Rob sigh. He let go of her and holstered his pistol, smoothing his jacket over it.

"Melissa, meet Kathryn. We used to be married. Kathryn, this is Melissa. It's her house you're trespassing in," he said.

"It's your fault, stupid. Five years of you driving around in circles with me, making me late, keeping me from the damn bathroom or wherever I needed to be, surveillance detection routes my *ass,* and with *her* you run straight here. Are you paying for it today?"

Rob screwed his eyes closed, giving Melissa the impression he was in great pain.

"And as soon as I'm out of town, you run *straight* to your little whore —"

"Kathryn!" Rob shouted sharply, bringing Kathryn up short.

"Hey!" Melissa shouted. "This is my house!"

"So, you entertain married men in your palace, princess? Homewrecker," Kathryn said.

"Dammit, Kathryn, we're divorced," Rob said.

"We are not divorced! You were supposed to call me when you got those papers, imbecile," Kathryn said.

"Why? You ran out, you sent the papers, and you had your lawyer tell my lawyer you waved the appearance. Screw you, Kathryn. You got what you wanted."

"I wanted you to call me!"

"Why the hell didn't you call me?" Rob asked, the volume of his voice rising. "Never mind. I'm tired of your shit. You wanted a divorce, you got one. We're done."

"You didn't even try to call me for 9 months."

"I called and called for the three months prior. Why didn't you call me back?"

"I was grieving. You should have come up to see me."

"So was I. Didn't you think we should have been grieving together? Here? Where we live? Why the hell should I have chased you halfway across the country? You belonged with me."

"Indianapolis is not 'halfway across the country,'" Kathryn said.

"Hey, I see some potential for significant sharing and all, but maybe you two should do this somewhere else?" Melissa asked.

Melissa liked Rob, but she didn't need a ringside seat as they worked through their issues.

"Did he tell you what he did to our son?" Kathryn asked, malice on her face and in her words.

"It was an accident," Rob said.

"Ask him what he did to our son," Kathryn said, smugly this time.

"It was an accident." Rob glared at Kathryn.

"No, Rob, not an accident. You fucked up!"

"No, you god dammed bitch, you fucked up!" Rob shouted. He changed his stance to face Kathryn squarely. He leaned in and pointed at her for emphasis.

Melissa thought he was about to lose it, and him with his big, big pistol.

"You fucked it up, you god dammed selfish bitch," Rob continued. "It always has to be about you, doesn't it? You never got it, did you? It's about service. It's about you and me in service to our country! And it was about our son. Not your need to go shopping."

"I never signed up for that! You're the one who is selfish! Always the cases, running out to the sources and the fucking SWAT Team! You never asked me about any of it! I don't even want to live here!" Her attention shifted to Melissa. "You know what lover boy here did? He killed our son! Sleeping Beauty killed our son!"

Shocked, Melissa immediately thought of Jules.

Rob turned his back to both of them. His shoulders were strangely hunched. He had locked his knees and elbows. Melissa noted both of his hands were clenched fists.

Nobody was talking. Thick silence permeated the condo.

"I think you better go, Kathryn. Please leave now," Melissa said.

"Oh, I'm not done with the two of you," Kathryn said in a weirdly gleeful way. She crossed her arms and shifted her weight decisively from one foot to the other.

"Yes you are," Melissa said.

Melissa still kept a landline. She picked up the cordless handset from a silver V Tech base station. "Get out or explain it to the police."

"Fuck you," Kathryn said.

"No, Kathryn. Fuck you," Melissa said.

She held up the phone so Kathryn could see the keypad. Melissa's hands were shaking. She dialed 9-1-1. She brought he phone to her ear.

"Shambia County Joint Communications, what is your emergency?" a Spanish-accented female voice asked.

Kathryn's eyes widened. Her mouth made a little "o" but she said nothing. She spread her hands out at waist level and jerked her head around.

"I've got someone in my house. She won't leave. She burst in here and I can't get her to leave," Melissa said.

"What is your address?"

Melissa gave it to her.

"Shit," Kathryn said. She used quick small steps in those tall Jimmy Choos to turn her body to the door. When she had her desired trajectory, she launched into a clacking run without a backward glance.

"It's okay, ma'am, the person left," Melissa said.

"She's gone?"

"Yes, it's all right now." Melissa closed the door and locked it. "She's gone."

"Is anybody injured? Do you need an ambulance or a police response?"

"No, it's all right now."

"Okay. Is there anything else I can help you with?"

"No. We're fine."

"Okay, have a safe day."

The line went dead.

Whenever Rob thought about Benjamin, sorrow and regret enveloped him like some kind of unpleasant blanket. He also felt his grief physically. It manifested itself as a unique pain in his stomach. A current of embarrassment flowed through and around it, because in the end, it was his fault.

Earlier, nearer to Ben's death, there had been a whirlpool of despair spinning and pulling at him. For a long time, his pistols had figured prominently in his mind as he swam as hard as he could to stay afloat. This time, embarrassment crashed into him like a tsunami.

How the hell was he going to explain this to Melissa? She'd never let him near Jules again. He was sure she was about to throw him out.

He stood in the quiet kitchen for what seemed like long time. He could not bring himself to face Melissa. He stared out the kitchen window. He had a great view of a cypress branch in front of a brick wall.

He felt her arms wrap around his torso. He felt her cheek against his back, about even with his shoulder blades.

"Tell me about it," she whispered.

A following wave of relief lifted him and passed under him. He tears leaked out of his closed eyes. He rested his hands on hers.

"We had a boy, a wonderful boy. Benjamin. I pestered Kathryn to get pregnant. She said she wasn't ready. She wasn't even working. We were getting by on my Bureau salary only. Well, eventually it happened, probably a surprise for Kathryn. He popped out pretty and perfect and was a total dream. Almost from the beginning he smiled whenever he saw me. I think that bothered Kathryn."

It more than bothered her, Rob remembered. It drove her crazy with jealousy. Melissa didn't need to know it. You never get a second chance at a first impression, his Dad liked to say, and Kathryn had made one hell of an impression for sure. No need to pile it on.

"I eventually made the SWAT team. It's a corollary duty, meaning in addition to regular investigations, so it increased my time away. Training and jobs could last several nights. Kathryn complained a lot. Most days, she liked to hand me Ben as soon as I walked in the door. If I was late or had to travel, I'd hear about it for days.

"When Ben was almost three, we had a gang round up over two nights and three days. We planned to get them all at once, there were forty-one subjects, but it didn't quite go down the way we wanted. For some reason, almost half of them were not where they were supposed to be.

"Once the arrests started, we had to press the gang. They were hyper-violent and flight risks. If we messed it up, we'd spend years chasing these guys down. As it was, starting at about sunset the first day, the killings began. They were killing each other, competing gang members and associates by the handful while they were running from us."

"Here, in Seminolacola?" Melissa asked, doubt in her voice.

"No, in Jax. You may have read about it, a year or so ago?"

"Oh yeah, I remember. Wasn't it a terrible gang war?"

"Yes, job after job, round the clock. Get a follow-on warrant, hit a place, miss, get another warrant if necessary and so on, all night long for three days and two nights. Finally, we wrapped it up. By the end, Jax PD SWAT, the Highway Patrol TRT's and the whole Violent Crime Task Force had jobs.

"I should have stayed with a friend in Jax and driven home later, but I really missed Ben, and I knew Kathryn would be furious whenever I got home, so I thought I'd suck it up and be done with it.

"When I got home, as soon as I got in, she started yelling, waking Ben. He started crying. She jumped all over me about needing some 'me time.' There I was, in my living room, in my tactical gear, stinking because I had been in it for three days, holding an M-4 and my gear bag, listening to my kid screaming and watching my loving wife hightail it out to the mall.

"I fed Ben and put him down in front of *Toy Story* in our den. He wanted me to watch it with him, so I sat down next to him on the floor. My plan was to get him settled — just a few minutes — before I showered.

"I fell asleep sitting upright. Ben toddled out the back door, fell in the pool and drowned. He had pushed his way through the screen. I slept until Kathryn came home. The rest of the day was a nightmare. I thought it would never end."

"Oh my God, Rob. I'm so sorry," she said.

She hugged him tighter.

He could not hold it together any longer. He spun around and crushed her in a hung as the tears flowed.

"He was such a good boy," was all he could say whenever he could suck in a lungful of air.

"Shhh," Melissa said. "Shhh now."

He could not tell her about fear tore through him when he saw Ben's body floating in the pool. He could not tell her of how he jumped in, gear, guns, phone and all, and pulled him out. How he knew as soon as he touched him Ben had been long dead. How he started CPR anyway and ignored Kathryn's yelling until he couldn't any more, and how he shouted her down to get her to call 911. He could not tell her how hard he worked on Ben, or how he fought with the paramedics when they tried to get to his son, or how the local cops had to tackle him as the paramedics carried Ben's body away. He did not mention the months he drank away. He couldn't bring himself to tell her everything.

She caressed his back. He managed to get himself under control. Eventually she stepped back, running her hand down his arm, taking his hand. She didn't look at him, but led him out of the kitchen, to her bedroom.

A brown quilt and beige sheets, in comfortable disarray, partially covered the king-sized bed, a brown walnut four poster. It came with two matching night tables and an armoire. He stumbled over a white laundry basket full of balled up clothes. He ended up in a sitting position facing Melissa. She stood between his legs and rested her hands on his shoulders.

"I'm so sorry," she said, pushing him back.

The iron strap constricting his lungs let go and he enjoyed a full breath. He let her push him down. She eased herself on top of him and kissed him gently. He slid his hands around her waist.

They were going to be late picking up Jules.

Melissa thought Rob needed some tenderness, and she knew exactly how to get him to accept some. She did not think of herself an expert on men, so often they were nothing more than big boys, but she knew in her heart what this situation called for. She kissed him again. He kissed her back.

She liked the feel of his shoulders under her hands and of his hands on her waist, underneath her scrubs top. She liked how strong his hands were. He held her like he meant it. Melissa had wanted to do this for Rob, but she was getting into it.

Rob started to say something but stopped as she slid her top off. She regretted wearing her comfortable cotton bra, as plain as could be. Rob reached up, but she parried his hands.

"Let's take this jacket off," she said, pulling at it.

Rob had her move down on him a little and then shucked it off himself. They dealt with more challenges: the .45, extra magazines and handcuffs on his belt; the tie around his neck. He and Melissa had to disengage completely. In no time, there was a pile of clothes and FBI equipment on the bed, her scrubs on the floor. Melissa felt the desire curl in her belly and her need to be touched.

He reached out to her, obviously ready, and she could tell she surprised him when she pushed him back down on the bed. She wanted to be on top, to be in control, to be responsible for his release. When it was done, she wanted to soothe him and ease his pain.

They kissed again. She pressed against him, her breasts against his chest, her hands caressing his shoulders. He ran his hands along her back. She hoped she was as ready as he was, and risked positioning them to go on, briefly wondering if it was too soon.

She had her answer as they smoothly came together. She grinned. She kissed him as she started moving against him. She rose up a little, briefly breaking their kiss for more air, and he cupped her breasts, palming her nipples. He tried to roll her over, but she stopped him. They continued moving together, and it wasn't long before a climax surprised her, taking her breath away as her muscles contracted tightly around him. He wasn't far behind. Moments later they were cuddling quietly, which was where Melissa wanted them. She did not want him to speak at all.

"I did some drinking after," Rob admitted, quietly.

"Shhhh."

"Too much drinking."

"Shhhh."

Melissa put a finger to his lips, then caressed his face.

They lay there comfortably until growing shadows reminded them to get Jules.

Chloe Baxter slowly woke, glad to be in her own comfortable bedroom. As she stretched, she realized she didn't need any Crystal right now. She wouldn't have turned some down if she had any, but it wasn't pulling at her at the moment.

Chloe lived in a gated apartment complex on the edge of Plainsview's southern boundary, near the beach. Probably more like facing the beach, to be honest, which was some ways away. She liked to tell people she lived *on* the beach, even though it really wasn't true. Chloe also liked to tell people her complex was high-end, which was. Higher than some, anyways. There really was, like, a gate in the fence, but really, no guard or anything where you drove in.

She lay on the white sheets in her white bedroom in a white tank top and panties. She liked white and this place *was* white. There was some color around, trim and shit, but all her furniture was white, so she felt it worked out super well.

Chloe had moved in only since she had started concentrating on dating and dancing, having quit telemarketing, which sucked. Chloe stretched and yawned. She had danced last night and the exertion had knocked her out. To top it off, she hadn't had a date, so she hadn't used before falling asleep.

The truth was Chloe liked showing herself off, it was a turn on. Hell, the real truth was she liked sex. Not every date was a chore. She writhed a bit, thinking about those Army guys from the night before and how appreciative they'd been of her, and drew her fingertips across her stomach with her left hand. She thought of the tall one, the blond guy, and brought the fingers of her right hand to her mouth. As her hand caressed her stomach and a finger slid in her mouth, the image of the tall guy solidified in her mind.

Her phone blared the first few notes of "Five Little Monkeys," interrupting her ministrations. She decided to check the message. It could be a date.

"Got u from ww," the incoming message said.

Chloe did not recognize the number. She marveled to herself about how she *never* heard from Wee Willie anymore and now she had heard about him twice in as many days. This had to be a date, she thought.

"My friend," she sent.

"Cuming to town. Need to add party to bizness."

"U got the rite person," Chloe sent.

"Can you meet now? Need to discuss."

"Sure where?"

"Can we cum to u now?"

Chloe hesitated. She never brought clients to her home place.

"We was hoping for a little party now just swooped in."

Hmm, a date, Chloe thought. She could use it. Not to mention the money. After all, Wee Willie had sent him. It was like Wee Willie introduced them.

Then another message: "it cool ww is connect."

It was like they got her! Like they were reading her mind, she thought.

"We'll pay extra a room fee," the person sent.

Wow, she thought.

"'K will send address,"

"Cool, ww told us where."

Damn him, Chloe thought. She hated him for giving out the address of her new place on the beach.

"Motherfucker, why did you send it like that?" Sniper Stefon said with a sneer. "Bitch'll be out of there quicker than shit."

Master Blaster was getting tired of Sniper Stefon.

"Let's go," Master said.

He opened the door of the car, a plain Chevy Malibu in Red Jewel Tintcoat Master had bought a day ago from a White Prep crackhead halfway into his swirl down the drain. Fucker will probably report it stolen as soon as his binge ended, so Master had switched the plates and felt confident they would escape detection for the moment, as far as routine police observation went.

"Brah," Sniper said as he got out.

Sniper had started to worry Master. He had been high strung before they left, a little nervous, and had blown a little coke on the way. An Army guy with a hundred-plus confirmed kills ought to be rock fuckin' solid before a job.

Master slipped on some black leather gloves as they walked to the gate. He liked black. Today he wore a black bowling shirt with white trim and knee-length baggy black shorts. He had on mirrored go—fast sunglasses. The thick weight of his Glock nine between his back and his waistband calmed him.

Sniper wrapped his dark mood in a white tracksuit and a white ball cap with a stiff flat brim, worn somewhat sideways. Master made sure he had the towel.

Master had driven out to the complex the night before. He had shot out the security camera with a BB gun and broke the spring in the lock to the pedestrian gate.

"You got the key?" Sniper asked, his hand out, palm up.

"Amateur," Master said. He pushed through the gate.

"Bitch," Sniper muttered.

This was not the way Master thought a former Army sniper should act. Where was the professionalism?

Apartment doors fed out onto exposed walkways. Master liked the style. It made him think of a luxury motel.

The plan was they would talk their way in and Master would find a seat. He'd talk Chloe into sucking his cock and when she knelt in front of him, Sniper would choke her with the rolled up towel. Master liked the plan, but Sniper still worried him. The Army time should have made the Sniper reliable. Reliable and steady.

They stopped in front of Chloe's apartment. Master nodded at Sniper, who nodded back. Master knocked on the door.

"Just a sec!" they heard a woman yell.

A slight blonde woman opened up after a minute.

"Now you be fly, yo," Master said. The compliment flowed; he meant it.

Her blonde hair had a tossed, windswept quality to it. Her blue eyes appraised Master and he thought she liked what she saw. He was into her small upturned nose and round little mouth. She wore a pink robe made out of a shiny material, open, showing some fine little titties under a white tank top. Master appreciated stiff nipples. Maybe they'd party a bit before he let Sniper kill her.

"Two of you. More the merrier," she said jovially.

Master checked out the apartment from the doorway. Mostly everything was white. Other than the need for a few touch-ups, he liked it. He saw a loveseat on the far wall, maroon with stylishly arranged tears and split seems. Perfect, he thought. He stepped over the threshold, trailing his fingers over her hip as he passed by on his way to the loveseat.

"So what we was thinking —" Master started to say.

"No!" Chloe cut him off with a panicked scream.

BANG! The sound, muffled and loud at the same time, cut her off.

Master drew his Glock. Chloe fell backwards as if she had been shoved. Her hands fluttered by her mouth, like she was waving away the after effect of too much hot sauce. A red flower of blood stained her fine pale chest, a little high but still low enough to indicate the bullet had gone through her sternum.

"What the hell did you do?" he hissed at Sniper.

Sniper stepped fully into the apartment and tried to use a heel to close the door. He missed.

"Got it done, man. Ain't no fucking around with no crack whore, brah."

Sniper had rolled up his towel into a tight cylinder around the barrel of his huge revolver. Master knew it to be a .357 magnum. Sniper still held the towel against the pistol, though the weapon was at rest down by his waist. A spray of red stained the end of the towel.

"Shit man! That was NOT the motherfucking plan." Master checked outside to see if the shot had gotten anyone's attention. He did not see anyone out in the bright Florida heat. He closed the apartment door.

Chloe tried to breathe, gasping audibly.

They both watched her.

She focused on Master. He saw fear and a plea for help in her eyes. Then she gazed straight up at the ceiling. She tried to breathe again but coughed instead. The cough lifted her torso off the floor and shot blood out of her mouth. Tears ran down the sides of her face to the floor.

"Fuck this bitch," Sniper said.

He leaned down, put end of the towel against her forehead and yanked the trigger. Even expecting the blast, Master jumped when it went off.

The shot sprayed blood and bone on the linoleum. A puddle grew, absorbing the splatter. Chloe's hands were still. Her knuckles rested on the floor, palms facing up. Her fingers curled a bit. She had stopped blinking.

"Yeah, that's the shit," Sniper said, laughing.

Anger coursed through Master. He had definitely wanted a piece before it went down.

"Let's go, bitch," Sniper said.

They locked the door on their way out.

The clearing of the air with Kathryn and making love to Melissa blew like a stiff spring breeze through the winter waste of Rob's head. He still felt a mixture of guilt, embarrassment and terrible sadness about Ben, but actually having told Melissa about it had eased the pressure a great deal. He tapped along with a Green Day song off the good-time radio and headed back to the RA.

He had wanted to stay with Melissa for the rest of the afternoon but the thought of all he had to write up had sent him on his way, leaving with Melissa as she raced to pick up Jules. They had kissed deeply, but made no plans for later.

Back in his cube, Rob reviewed the emails and put out a few fires. HR at headquarters city wanted to see him. In person, which meant he would have to make time to drive there.

Rob started writing. Every interview he'd conducted in last few days needed its own report and he was behind. As a supervisor, Chris tolerated only so much of that. Rob didn't come up for air until he noticed the bright orange and reds of a splendid sunset. He saved his current file and checked the RA for anyone else in vain. Everyone had gone.

Rob organized his cube and packed his gear. He checked the classified safes, the supervisor's safe, the firearms cabinets and any drawer which for whatever reason dreamed up by Headquarters in Washington required daily documentation as to its secure integrity. All was in order and, with briefcase in hand, he kicked the phones over to Headquarters in Tallahassee, set the alarm and locked both doors.

He drove south and managed to talk himself into stopping by Melissa's to check in. Rob thought it would be a lovely gesture considering their afternoon. He rolled slowly through the small parking lot of her building just as it grew dark and, finding no available visitor spots, parked on the street.

"Oh, hi!" Lila said brightly as she opened the door.

Her wide-eyed grin bordered on manic, causing Rob to question her connection to reality. Lila, in her pink Quacker Factory tunic with three-quarter-length sleeves, rhinestones and matching Capri pants, struck him as one of those simple sorts who suffered from a surfeit of optimism.

"I'll tell Melissa you're here," Lila said.

She brushed a strand of her blonde hair behind an ear with her pudgy fingers. After taking three steps into the hall, which led to the bedroom, she shouted news of Rob's arrival in a false whisper.

"Oh. I'll only be a minute," Melissa shouted back.

"She'll only be a minute," Lila said to Rob, walking back to him. "She's putting Jules to bed. Can I get you something?"

He was ferociously hungry, but decided to wait for Melissa. Maybe he could turn this into dinner out, especially if he could keep Lila at the apartment.

"Is there any Coke?" he asked.

"Mel keeps Coke Zero. How about some Coke Zero?"

"Terrific."

Lila waved in the direction of the living room. "Why don't you sit and I'll bring it out."

A moment later Lila was next to him on the brown leather couch, watching him sip his drink. Rob thought he better get a conversation going before she decided to leave.

Before he could think of anything to say, Lila spoke up. "Melissa told me what happened today," she said.

"Ah. Sorry you had to hear about it," Rob said.

"Your ex-wife doesn't sound very nice."

"She wasn't at her best."

"And I'm so, so sorry about your little boy."

"Thank you." Rob did not want to talk about it.

"It's so sad when you lose a little one. They really don't deserve it, do they?"

"No, I guess not."

"I mean, they're so sweet. They all need to grow up and live perfect lives, don't you think?"

Lila said this in an affected manner sounding to Rob a lot like baby talk ramped up for adults.

"I wonder how God could take them," she said.

"I don't know."

"I don't know either," Lila said, concentrating on him intently and nodding sympathetically. "We have to get past it and keep going. We need to know it's in God's hands and look to Jesus for help."

Rob liked going to church and did so when he could. Admittedly it was not as much as he should, but he did not care much for all the jargon.

"We just have to accept it and move on," Lila said, rubbing her thighs.

"Yes," Rob said.

"It must be hard."

"Yes, it is."

"The Lord doesn't give us burdens we can't carry."

And how the hell would you know, Rob thought. He had enough discipline to think it, rather than say it, but this line of conversation always stressed him out.

"We have to trust in the Lord," she said.

He wanted to bark at her, but instead he held it together.

"Well, someone who hasn't been through it really doesn't know what it's like," Rob said.

He hoped she would not be too offended, but he needed her to shut up.

"I *know!*" she replied. "When Bernardo killed my April and their two little ones, my life was just torn apart," Lila said.

Rob did not think he heard her correctly. His confusion kept him silent.

"Yes." Lila's head nodded, up and down, up and down. "It was *terrible*. He seemed like such a good man. He worked hard. We thought he would be good for April."

Lila peeked at Rob slyly, narrowing her eyes and smiling.

"She met him after she got clean," Lila said nodding again. "He was in air conditioning. A *good* job, it was."

"Yes, a good job," Rob agreed, trying to catch up.

"Yes. He yelled at her a little, but really, April could do that to a person. Even though he was, you know . . ."

Rob had a hunch he should add 'Mexican' or 'Hispanic' here.

"One of them," she said. "We thought he was good for her. And those two little babies."

"Of course," Rob said.

"Bernardo was in a bit of a bad patch. He was laid off when his company was bought out. He didn't expect a layoff. He was out of work and then the unemployment ran out. They started arguing. I helped them when I could. I wanted to do more, but with Fred gone, well, you know.

"Now my April could be difficult, and I tried to tell her not to get on Bernardo's nerves the way she did, but she had the stress, you know. She had a condition and she didn't always take her medication.

"Then he and April started arguing more and more and those little babies, Maria and my Juan Pablo, he was twenty months, well, they were typical. At three-and-a-half and almost two, who wouldn't have a handful? And with that yelling; I tried to take them, but April was very protective.

"One day the police called me at work. They sent a car for me. I knew it was real bad. They don't never send a car unless it's real bad. Uh-huh. I went right with them. They told me Bernardo had gotten a pistol from somewhere. They thought he shot April and Juan Pablo first. After, he ate breakfast and waited.

"When little Maria came home from the county child development on that little bus and ran up to the house, he was right there. He opened the front door and shot my little angel at her own steps. There were witnesses.

"He walked out of their house and right by his little girl. He stood out in the street, shouted something, nobody could tell what — even though some of them could speak Spanish — and shot his own head off. Uh-huh. Yes he did."

"Lila, what can I say? I'm sorry for your loss," Rob said.

Her story froze him there on the couch, with his Coke midway between his mouth and the coffee table, embarrassed for himself and sorry for her.

"Well don't you apologize at all. It wasn't your fault. There wasn't anything you could do then," Lila said.

"Excuse me?"

"We couldn't do anything then. But now we can. We can pray. Let's pray for Juan Pablo and Maria and your little boy. What was his name?"

"Benjamin."

"Okay, Benjamin."

Lila pushed the coffee table away from the couch and grasped his hand in both of hers. She knelt and tugged at him. Part of him wanted to pull away, but he also wanted to kneel with her. Uncertainty made him motionless. She tugged at him again and he acquiesced. He put his Coke down and knelt beside her. She held his hand tightly.

"Dear Lord, dear God the Father, you have our angels, our Maria, Juan Pablo and Benjamin; you took them when they were still children and we don't know why. Maybe they were too pure to stay. Please protect them and take care of them. Please tell them we think of them always and we are coming to be with them. Dear Jesus Christ, please forgive them and us our sins, all of us. Amen."

"Amen," Rob said quietly.

He had expected her to rattle off some canned prayer. This was much better. He knelt there, strangely content, thinking about Benjamin, holding Lila's hand.

"Well," Lila said after a minute, "enough of enough." She let go of Rob and stood up.

"Melissa, why don't you get out here?" Lila yelled. "You have a hungry man in your house. You and Rob go out and get something to eat. I'll stay with Jules."

"Bless you, you're a saint," Rob whispered, meaning it.

Lila winked at him.

D. Randall rested his forearms on the balcony railing of his high-rise beachfront condo, the one held in the name of a business he did not officially own. Wearing nothing more than boxers, he picked at the sweaty label of a cold beer. Easygoing Gulf waves sent up the sound of gentle breaking on fine sand. The stars and a section of moon put out just enough light to enjoy the scene. Yet even after a trank and several beers, even with the dark condo behind him and the clear sky above, the soothing sounds of the Gulf had no effect on him.

It was supposed to be over by now, he thought. Once Jimmy Tank got the needle, it was supposed to be over.

The more he thought about it, the more certain he was EvaJo had to go. Hey, he thought, it rhymes. Maybe he could start a new career jumping around a stage with his hand on his cock, rhyming shit. What he could not do was wait for Wee Willie's Master Shithead and the Fucktone to get around to it.

He had some clean plates for the borrowed Corvette parked downstairs. He had a burner phone. He had EvaJo's number. He wanted to be able to put this away, put the situation behind him and far away, but shit kept coming up. It was all about tying up the loose ends. He was ready.

"Shit," he said to no one, as he pushed off the railing to stand up straight and get dressed to go out.

EvaJo had to go.

EvaJo bummed another drink off the seedy guy. They were part of a high-and-drunk crowd in Betty Mack's, a club in a windowless building made of concrete construction units on the edge of Tarklin's Ford. It stood all by itself in a prairie of broken up asphalt that had once been a real parking lot with stripes and everything.

Whoever ran Betty Mack's had stripped the walls down to the concrete and exposed mechanicals, and then painted everything black. They used black laminated pressboard for the bar. The black and silver chairs sucked, by general consensus. The drinks, however, were cheap, and nobody minded the pharmacopeia in the restrooms. A country-dance-techno track pounded out of industrial strength speakers.

EvaJo liked it here. She could always turn a trick or score as she got fucked up on well-whiskey and Cokes. There was no particular dress code, but the resident bikers set the tone. EvaJo herself wore a leather vest and black skinny jeans. She thought her look was on point and maybe even sharp enough to cruise the hotels and truck stops off I-10. She hadn't decided what she wanted to do tonight, past scoring enough Crystal. Her new friend next to her at the bar, a tall, thin, hairy crewman off a shrimp boat, had bought her two drinks and could likely be a customer.

EvaJo drew off half her cocktail and batted her eyes at her next-stool neighbor, who burped, heaved and threw up his last few shots, beers and nachos on the bar in front of him.

"Goddamit asshole, get the fuck outta here!" yelled the bartender, an unsympathetic, unnatural redhead of particularly obese proportions, as she threw a dirty rag into the middle of it all.

EvaJo couldn't remember her name. She could not remember much lately. She did notice, however, her young sailor's most recently ordered shot stood forgotten and untouched. EvaJo did not remember what he was drinking, but scooped it up and downed it anyway. She picked up her own drink and transferred the EvaJo Show to an empty table near the door. She felt her phone vibrate.

"You out," the text read.

"Im out," EvaJo responded.

"Me 2 u available"

"4 what"

"Party whatev u want"

EvaJo wished she recognized the number.

"What do u want," she countered.

"Round the world im holding"

That sounded like a plan, EvaJo thought. Still, she wished she had the number from before, like from an introduction. Her desire to get high competed in her damaged brain with her desire not to get ripped off or murdered. She tried to think it through.

"No u from Shaina," her correspondent sent.

Shaina the bitch, EvaJo thought. But it *was* a reference. EvaJo bit her lip.

"In town and lonely u available" he sent. At least, EvaJo assumed it was a "he."

She was about to answer when she saw this: "where u at ill pick u up im at tgi near tarklinsford"

TGI Fridays! EvaJo thought. It was nice a classy guy wanted her for a change. His being down the road was like it was meant to be or something. It made her feel a lot better about everything.

"At Betty Macks," she sent.

"Meet me in lot in 10."

At ten? EvaJo asked herself. Oh, EvaJo thought. It's past ten. She repeated "oh" to herself twice more. She emptied her glass, made it to her feet and wobbled off toward the front door.

In the parking lot, swaying gently and squinting into the glare of the streetlights, EvaJo waited. It occurred to her he maybe meant ten *minutes,* not 10:00 pm. She hadn't needed to shoot her drink after all.

EvaJo was so intent on making sure she recognized Mr. Right Now, she paid no attention to the loud arrival of the custom Corvette. In spite its roaring into the parking lot and drifting to a squealing stop right in front of her, she jumped when the passenger door opened, revealing a handsome white man, maybe 40 or 45 or so, with bright teeth and a military haircut. He had muscles under a green and white golf shirt.

"Hey EvaJo, you're hot tonight," he said.

Things were getting better and better.

"Aren't you going to say 'hi,' EvaJo?" he said.

"Hi," she said, feeling girlish.

"Hi. I'm Randy. Why don't you hop on in?" he asked, as he held out a closed fist.

His big fist creeped her out. Randy opened it. There were two small foil packets in his palm.

"Why don't I?" EvaJo asked, smiling.

Randy kept up a steady patter of small talk as they drove. When they stopped, EvaJo noticed they were in the dunes at the Gulf.

"We should talk about our date," she said, her mind firmly on the foil packets, which she could really use right now.

"Here, why don't you take this," Randy said, giving her one of the packets. "I've also got . . . ." He produced a glass pipe, a lighter and the other necessary paraphernalia.

She held the packet in the fingertips of one hand and the pipe and the other stuff in the palm of the other.

"I was thinking $400 for around the world, you know, like the rest of the night?" Randy asked shyly. "Oh, and I've got two more hits."

EvaJo had a question on the tip of her tongue but before it formed in her head, Randy spoke again.

"Why don't you light up?" he asked.

She went to work on the foil packet, forgetting her question. When she was done smoking both packets, which held less than she'd hoped, she leaned back in the seat and relaxed.

"Say baby," Randy said, "how about we get down to business?"

EvaJo thought about saying okay, but instead merely faced her host. She knew what he wanted. She closed her eyes as that handsome face closed in for a kiss.

D. Randall knew it was best to go ahead and kiss EvaJo, despite the sanitary issues and the mess meth had made of her face: sagging skin, pockmarks, scabs. As disgusting as it was, he knew this would go down easier if he kissed her. He slid closer to her, close enough to cover the gap between the bucket seats. He leaned on her and pinned her left arm with his torso. He reached behind her head with his right arm and supported it as their lips met.

Her lips were rough and her mouth was dry. Her tongue barely responded.

D. Randall kept it up as he reached across her body with his left arm and grabbed her right wrist. He casually lifted it to his own right hand and gently, but firmly, grabbed it. He brought his left hand to her throat. Only after he pinched off both her carotid arteries did he break the kiss. He leaned back far enough to see her face.

He watched her eyes open slowly halfway and close, and then flutter open. She pushed against him, not enough to budge him at all, and tried to pull away. He increased the power of his grip on her wrist.

"There now, girl, this won't take but a bitty bit," he said.

Her eyes went wide, displaying a lot of white. He felt her arch her back. She tried to swing herself free but, because of the drugs and the lack of blood to her brain, she hardly shifted her position. In a moment she had stopped moving altogether.

D. Randall started counting. He counted until after he felt her death rattle against his cheek. When he was sure she was dead, he rolled back into his own seat. He put his head all the way to the headrest and rested for a moment. He was tired, real tired.

"Sorry, girl, but it had to be. Probably more merciful than what you were likely gonna get, going on the way you was," he said.

D. Randall sucked in a deep breath. He had a towel to put under her and cleaning supplies in the small trunk. She was sure to vacate some postmortem number ones or twos during the drive to her interim resting place. It was a perfect spot, involving water and solitude, where no one would wander by for a time.

As always, his plan was perfect.

Tuesday

Rob woke in his own bed, squinting against the sunlight.

"Shit," he said. He had slept through his alarm.

He reached for the clock, dreading the worst. 6:23 am. Not so bad, he told himself.

Rob planned a long day of typing, telephone calling and online training. To maximize keyboard time, he decided against a midday workout at Fat Floyd's, so he got up and searched for his running shoes. An hour later he was showered and sneaking into the RA via the back door with coffee and a muffin.

Rob fired up his computer. He started the file management software, the intranet browser and his email program, up to Secret on this enclave. He opened, but did not pause to read, the three financial Suspicious Activity Reports in his queue. He did the same for his leads and distributions. He started his blood course, but did not pass the introduction.

He gulped down the coffee and tore into the muffin.

Now he felt ready to start his Jimmy Tank paperwork. He had already opened the file with a summary memo and put in the newspaper clippings. Father Clyde was already done. He needed to add Hoss's file, but as that was a pain in the ass with the slow scanners they had, he decided to write up Chloe Baxter's interview first. When finished, he saved the document and scanned in his notes. After a brief break for more coffee, he proofread the report, fixed some typos and electronically signed it.

"Rob? Chris wants to see you," Kay said.

Rob picked up a pad and pen and made for Chris's office with Kay following. Hoss and another person, a black female, were waiting with Chris. They wore department polo shirts with embroidered cloth badges, and cargo pocket trousers. Hoss's were tan. His partner's were dark blue.

"Rob, Hoss has some questions for you," Chris said.

This sounds like trouble, Rob thought.

"Rob, meet Shalonda Hodges. She's new with homicide," Hoss said.

Shalonda was stout, about five-foot-five and in her late thirties with round cheeks and straightened hair.

He and Shalonda shook hands. No one said anything. Hoss and Shalonda stared at Chris. Chris investigated the ceiling.

"So, someone's dead," Rob said.

"Well boy, you don't let no moss get on you," Hoss said.

"How did you know Chloe Baxter?" Shalonda asked.

"Shit!" Rob stamped his foot.

"Jesus Shalonda," Hoss said.

"Someone had to start it," Shalonda said, shrugging her shoulders.

"Your cell number is in her phone," Chris said.

Leo ambled up, sipping coffee, and leaned against the doorframe.

"Yeah. I interviewed her two days ago," Rob said.

"At her place? At night?" Chris asked.

"Chris!" Hoss said.

"Let's cuff him now," Leo said pleasantly.

Chris scowled at him. Leo smiled back.

"No, at ECGC, in the afternoon," Rob said.

"Don't need witnesses for that at least. Vice will have the film," Shalonda muttered. "You at work yesterday?"

"Lawyer up, Rob," Leo said.

"Enough, Kladsko," Chris said.

"C'mon, Chris, what is this bullshit?" Leo asked.

"Hey, Hey! It's not like that," Rob said "Yes, I was here. Or rather I was running around."

"What times can you account for?" Chris asked.

Rob thought a minute.

"About all afternoon, come to think of it," he said.

"Witnesses?" Chris asked.

"We'll check that," Shalonda said.

"He knows, Shalonda," Hoss said. "Say Rob, what did you and Chloe talk about?"

Rob eyeballed Shalonda.

"She's okay for this," Hoss said. "She got released from sex crimes for it," Hoss said.

"For this, or for the other thing?" Rob asked.

"For this and the other thing."

The chirps of someone badging in interrupted their conversation. Steve Guerra, the Violent Crime Major Offender agent, arrived with a black tactical backpack slung over one shoulder, wearing a red-and-white checked shirt, blue jeans and scuffed cowboy boots. His face said he had a joke on his lips, but it faded as he gauged the situation. He nodded as he came to a stop next to Leo.

Rob thought a minute about trusting a detective he didn't know. He needed to trust someone in this and he wanted to keep trusting, and being trusted by, Hoss King. He peered at Chris.

Chris nodded.

"Chloe gave me Wee Willie arranging the meet at the murder scene between her and Matthew Simmons, the man Jimmy Tank says he didn't kill," Rob said.

"Why the hell didn't you say something, dammit!" Hoss asked.

"She was high as a kite," Rob said. "I planned to re-interview her when she was down. Then I wanted to get phone records from the night in question. Once I substantiated her statements, I was going to go for the grand jury or a signed affidavit from her when she was sober."

"Well, now she's dead," Chris said. "How come I haven't seen the three-oh-two?"

"Because I just finished it," Rob said.

Chris locked eyes on his monitor and worked his keyboard.

Leo laughed out loud.

"Leo," Kay admonished from behind both Leo and Steve.

Rob caught Shalonda asking Hoss a question by expression, and saw him nod slightly in return. Rob hoped he'd just been cleared of the murder.

"What was the time of death?" Rob asked.

"Midday to about supper time," Hoss said.

"Yeah, I'm covered," Rob said.

"What else have you got?" Hoss asked.

"I got Jimmy Tank moving a block of money around, but no source yet"

"Why not?"

"I have to subpoena the account-of-origin records."

"Well, get on it," Chris said, rejoining the conversation.

"Yessir. I've got Baxter's statement —"

"Not anymore," Chris said.

"And the banks and account numbers," Rob finished.

"Get the paper done," Chris said. "Get up to speed and be sure to stay clean with Headquarters. I'll call the ASAC," Chris said.

"Yes sir," Rob said.

With Chris in a mood, Rob would normally head to his cube and get to work, but he wanted to talk to Hoss, so he stayed put. Unfortunately, so did everyone else.

Chris surveyed the scene. Leo beamed as he, Steve and Kay blocked the doorway. Hoss and Shalonda waited patiently.

"You are all allegedly working you know," Chris said.

"Leaders lead by example," Leo said.

Chris flushed red.

"All right studs," Chris said, "while you're getting down to business, think about this: why did they have to kill Simmons in the first place? You're all big shot investigators, so investigate that instead of wasting taxpayer money. Now get out."

"Leo," Kay admonished, as they all filed out of Chris's office.

"What?" Leo asked, feigning innocence.

"Hoss, can we get in to see the crime scene?" Rob asked.

"Sure, come on, we'll head up there now. Let me ask you this, as a formality you understand, who are your witnesses for yesterday?"

"Oh, sure. Melissa Simmons. Her cell is —"

"For the love of God, boy, your alibi is the widow lady?" Hoss asked, throwing his hands up in exasperation.

"Well, yeah."

"Don't you see, this could be you and the widow doing the revenge thing," Shalonda said.

"I did not kill Baxter. And if your theory is true, wouldn't I kill Wee Willie? Baxter didn't have anything to do with the killing itself."

"But wouldn't y'all want to get everyone involved?" Hoss asked.

"Not me. Too much risk," Rob said. "Anyway, you're only assuming Baxter's murder is related to the Simmons matter. She was a freak, a stripper and a prostitute. Anyone could have come along and killed her. What was the cause of death?"

Hoss and Shalonda measured each other with a glance.

"Guess it's time to get on over there. Let's go," Hoss said.

The Perdido River meanders south in southwest Alabama, eventually forming the border between the tab of Alabama touching the Gulf of Mexico and Florida. Baulene County, Alabama covers the real estate between the river and Mobile and for Deputy Sherriff Messer Tate, the most important thing about Baulene County was the presence of Celia's, a breakfast and lunch café in Denetclaw City.

After four years in the Air Force Security Forces, including a tour running convoys around Iraq, and three years as a corrections deputy at the Baulene County Correctional Facility, Messer had finally made road deputy. He was almost done with his field training. Before he could work one-man, taking calls by himself, Senior Deputy Buck Holston had to sign off on his competence.

Thus, Celia's. Messer had to get Buck to Celia's at eight am, not seven fifty-nine, not eight oh-one, but eight, every morning, activity be damned, to get Buck's signature on Messer's rookie forms. Buck had coffee and smothered biscuits with Officer Charlie Tolder of the Denetclaw City PD every morning. Buck may have been old, but Ancient Charlie had been working Denetclaw City since "that damn Georgian shat up the White House," as Buck liked to say.

"See now, I'll tell you what, I voted for Trump. Proud of it, too. I liked the way he stirred things up," Buck opined. "That old boy was large and in charge. Ain't nobody pushing him around."

Buck picked the sausage bits out of the white sauce smothering his biscuits. At five-foot-ten, he did not carry his 275 pounds well, in Messer's opinion. Buck often told Messer, and anyone else within hearing distance, he picked the sausage bits out of the gravy in deference to his doctor and his wife. Both urged diet modification considering his most recent heart attack, which had nearly sent him off to the Holy Roll Call in the Sky.

"Buck, don't go getting' yourself all worked up. It'll ruin your day," Ancient Charlie said. "And why don't you eat like your partner here. Y'all can tell he's in it for the long haul." Ancient Charlie winked at Messer.

"I'd rather head on up to the Holy Roll Call in the Sky than eat that shit every morning," Buck said, referring to the bowl in front of Messer. "Oats is for horses."

"Buck, this here's a family place," Celia called from the back.

Messer spooned up the last of his oatmeal with raisins, enjoying Buck's rebuke.

Ancient Charlie wasn't doing too badly, thought Messer, with his one fried egg and single strip of bacon. Ancient Charlie had respect for his own heart attack and, as a result, was still around.

"I'll tell you what about that Biden," Buck started to say, but he never did get to tell them what about the President. The county dispatcher interrupted him.

"Two Car, y'all need to call the Sergeant," Becca the dispatcher said after a burst of static.

"Two Car, roger," Messer said, waiting for instructions.

"I better do it," Buck said from around a mouth full of biscuit. "It's never good when they want you to call in."

He leaned his bulk sideways to get at his cell phone and punched the quick dial for the Sergeant. Buck only mentioned to Messer a thousand times it was Buck himself who had signed off on the Sergeant at the end of his rookie field training years ago.

A moment later they were racing down Old Seminolacola Road with lights and siren. Messer drove. Buck tried to raise the complainant on his cell phone. "Turn here!" Buck shouted.

Messer drifted onto Louisville Road and floored it. He loved this, flying down the street with the light package going and siren blaring. He barely slowed as he turned with the road to the north, and ran at an honest 125 miles per hour for about two minutes.

"Slow it down a bit," Buck said. "There, see 'em?"

"Yeah, I got 'em." Messer could see the old Rustoleum gray GMC pickup parked up ahead.

Messer slowed down. He saw two white boys wearing t-shirts and jeans standing on the grass next to the truck. Messer put the cruiser in park. The boys were quite solemn.

"Boys, why ain't y'all in school this morning?" Buck asked.

They were barely old enough to drive. One was short, slight, blond and freckled. The other was taller, equally thin, with brown hair and pimples. They exchanged a glance with one another before responding.

"We're sorry, sir," the shorter boy said. "We skipped out on math to fish for a bit."

"Well, we'll talk about that later. Why did you call the sheriffs?" Buck asked.

"Sir, we found a dead lady."

"Where at?"

"Down this road at the hole."

"Can we get the car down there?"

"Yes, sir. There is a little road that comes up on a hill by the river."

"Close enough to fish from the truck?"

"Yessir, that was what we was going to do. Couple of casts from the bed and back for AP History."

"This here is a right serious pick-'em-up boys. I sure like these tires." Buck examined the tread closely.

"Thank you sir," said the shorter boy.

Buck ran his fingers over the raised patches of the tread pattern. Messer liked the aggressive pattern. It made him think of stacked stone. Buck whipped out his cell phone and snapped three pictures of the tread.

"Hop in this here patrol car and show us where," Buck said.

The road surface changed from asphalt to gravel to sand as they drove through a copse of oak. Recent traffic had kicked up darker loam along the wheel tracks.

"The hill is up there, sir," the taller boy said.

"Stop the car, partner," Buck said. "Boys, y'all stay here for a minute. C'mon, partner. Take the keys. Walk along here, stepping on the grass. Mind your feet."

After a few steps, Buck stopped and motioned Messer closer. Buck pointed at the road, no more than a sandy area of trampled growth at this point. He bent at the waist, studying the spoor. Messer did too, excited to feel like real police.

"See here, boy," Buck muttered, "this here is the truck tread and here is a different tread, performance tires or I'll be a fucking defense attorney. Now I can't tell for sure but them Crime Scene folks can, but I think this here is a Camaro or Corvette footprint, or something wearing that rubber. Let me take a few." Out came the cell phone. "Drive the boys' truck or our cruiser on this and there'll be nothing left to cast. Mind where you step. Try to stay in the grass."

They made it up to the crest of the gentle hill. A naked woman floated in the water near the bank under some bushes. She was a tall, thin, white female, barely more than skin and bone with small breasts. She was really, really old. Old and dead as shit, Messer thought.

"Fucker," Buck said. "Stripped her and got her all wet. Must have only been a few hours ago."

"Should I check her vitals?" Messer asked.

"You think maybe she's alive?"

"Shouldn't we ought to check?"

"She's dead as shit, boy. And you jump down there and mess with that crime scene and we could cost Nooker the evidence she needs to solve this bitch. We got real lucky to get on her before the 'gators and what not, so don't go rookie it all up."

Nooker was the lead detective of the department. Neither Messer nor anyone else in the office had the balls to call her "Nooker the Hooker." Not that he'd pay to sleep with her; she was built like an armored reconnaissance vehicle.

"Two Car," Buck said into his handset, "is our Sergeant at the station?"

"Sure is, Buck."

"Ten-four. I'm callin' in." Then Buck said to Messer, "We'll frustrate the holster sniffers listening on the scanners a little by calling in. At least we can get Crime Scene and the investigators here before all the weirdos drive down the road and block it the hell up." Buck regarded the dead lady and said, "I'll buy you smothered biscuits tomorrow if she weren't dragged up here from Mobile."

Rob rode up to the Baxter crime scene behind the Plexiglas partition in the back of Hoss's department issue, plain-skinned, dark blue Fusion. It stank of tobacco spit, sweat and fast food. Hoss drove and Shalonda rode shotgun.

Rob handed the young officer guarding Chloe's apartment his card for the log. He trailed Hoss inside. Shalonda maneuvered herself slightly behind and to the left of Rob. He knew she wanted to watch his face when he saw Chloe for the first time. Chloe lay on the floor, but Rob forced himself to examine the room before he started on the body.

The first thing he noticed was the odor. Not the odor of death, Chloe was too fresh, what with the air conditioning and all. The apartment had a musty smell with accents of spoiled food and trash.

The room where she lay was a combination kitchen and sitting area. The walls had been painted a shade of white, but were faded now. Grease and an unrecognizable black substance provided highlights in the corner kitchen. A mismatched set of table and chairs were over there too and, although originally white, they were dirty with stains and crusted food particles. A small maroon-turning-to-grubby couch Chloe must have grabbed from the front lawn of a frat house moldered against the far wall, offset from the front door. The

Crime Scene technicians had come and gone, leaving the sterile wrappings of their collection supplies on the floor.

There was no indication of any violence or disorder outside the parameters of normal in the front room. Except, of course, for the dead body.

Now it was time for Chloe. She had not done her hair or put on makeup yet. She wore a pink robe, synthetic playing at silk, with sweat stains around the underarms. Her tank top was grimy around the edges and her panties were stained yellow at the front.

The wounds tracked fairly straight. They appeared to be close range hits with something big, but the powder stippling was missing. Rob was sure they would find the bullet from the head shot in the floor, but was surprised there was nothing in the wall by the couch or the cabinet nearby. All things considered, Rob did not like the crime scene. He frowned.

"Me, neither," Hoss said.

"Reading minds now? How about this: someone she knows or expects at the door. Bang, down, bang again. It's over, *adios*," Rob said.

"Pro job," Shalonda said.

"Negative on the neighborhood canvas. Suppressor?" Hoss asked.

Rob sighed. Hoss and Shalonda needed a big break or they were going to focus on him again, he thought.

"Let's look at the bedroom," Rob said.

"No evidence of sex. Just dirty disheveled sheets," Hoss said, when they got there.

"You mean recent sex. Rob, what caliber pistol do y'all carry?" Shalonda asked casually, like she was curious or something, on their way back to Chloe.

Rob knew where she was going. The hole in the hard bone of Chloe's forehead was clearly caused by a 9 millimeter or .38 caliber bullet. Rob glanced at Hoss, who shrugged his shoulders slightly.

"Forties," Rob said.

Rob led them away from the uniformed officer. They formed a small circle.

"This is officially out of my comfort zone," Rob said. "This was too good; not some crazy john or admirer from the club. I have to go back to the office and let Chris know we have a professional on our hands."

"Yup, I agree. This here was done by someone who knows what they're about," Hoss said.

"Let's run back down to the RA," Rob said. "I have to do this in person."

The three of them were back in Chris's office. He dropped off a budget conference call to listen to the wonderful news about some professional shooters in his territory. Hoss shared what work had already been done by the police department.

"The canvas was a bust," Hoss said, in summary.

"First things first," Chris said. "I want you to do another canvass at dinner time. I want facts about the shooters. I want something on them; they weren't ghosts. Rob, where are we on the case-in-chief? Exactly, I mean?"

"I've got subpoenas in to the financial institutions I already know about regarding the suspected payment to Jimmy Tank; we'll have to do the analysis on them as soon as they come in, and hopefully that'll mean more subpoenas," Rob said.

Chris thought a financial analyst — full time for the foreseeable future — from Headquarters City would help.

"I've got telephone numbers," Rob said. "I need to do the historic investigation and analysis around both the Simmons murder and the Gubbs arrest on them."

Two Agents, full time, Chris thought.

"After that, I need to work D. Randall and Wee Willie. Hopefully, the bank and phone records will give us leads for follow—on subpoenas and also search warrants on them."

"As soon as he gets wind of 'em, he'll move to quash 'em," Hoss said.

"Hoss, he'll be in big boy court now," Chris replied. "Won't be as easy. We'll have to move fast though. Who do we think did the killings, Jefferson or Hargrove?" Chris asked.

Rob and the detectives silently kicked the question back and forth, saying nothing.

Great, Chris thought. They don't have a clue. Shit. He would have to ask for two surveillance teams. This was turning into a cast of thousands and the only way he could support it would be to ask for an office special, which meant as the Supervisory Special Resident Agent, he would lose control in favor of someone from Headquarters City or, even worse, Headquarters FBI itself way up in Washington.

"Do you have any idea who actually did the shooting?" Chris asked.

"No, sir," Rob said.

Chris thought for a moment. Clearly, Seminolacola would want to be involved, and possibly the State. He'd have to spend a few hours talking at the US Attorney's Office.

Pressure will come from Washington to make sure they got everyone, and to make sure this wasn't tied to criminal enterprises, whether the old La Cosa Nostra or the syndicates, or street gangs or narcotraffickers. There would also be pressure from Tallahassee and City Hall to work the case on the cops and wrap it up quick.

God forbid and Jesus help them if the gang down at the Seminolacola News Journal or any of the TV stations got this before they were ready. They would be in the middle of the shitstorm, should the case leak.

Chris thought about Elani and the kids. If he had to cancel out of their summer plans again this year he'd really feel like crap.

Chris heard a polite cough. He had unconsciously leaned back and rotated his chair to stare out the window at the distant Gulf, which had put his back to his guests. He spun back around.

"Here's what I want: subpoenas and financials first, get all your paper out. Rob, draft up justification text — you've got about five minutes. Then we're walking to the USAO. I'll call the ASAC and get a feel for surveillance teams TDY'd down here. Hoss, we need everything on these two officers."

"Chief will want to do it joint," Hoss muttered as he examined his fingernails.

"Done, but make sure it's you two. I'll call him."

They would need Title Threes; at least a wire up on each of the officers' cell phones. He stood up and leaned through his office doorway.

"Who's here?" Chris shouted.

Kay and Steve answered from their respective pods. After they joined the meeting, Chris went on. "Clear your desks as best you can. Rob's dog has turned into a case. Get ready. Rob will need help with financials and phone records. Prioritize justification for deeper subpoenas and search warrants. Also, we're going up on the wire."

Groans came from all present.

"Rob," he continued, "as case agent, make sure you get started on drafts of affidavits for T-Threes on each of the subjects' cell phones. We can't have these guys going around killing everyone they've ever worked with. Now listen up everyone, unsubs that know what they are doing have killed a witness. Start watching your own asses more than usual. That's it, get on it."

The detectives left. Rob wrote furiously at his desk. He could hear Kay and Steve working the phones to re-prioritize their day.

Only about 40 minutes had passed when Hoss showed up again. Rob let him in and Kay and Leo joined them.

"EvaJo's been killed," Hoss said. "They found her up on the Perdido on the Baulene County side. They ID'd her with prints."

"Shot like Chloe?" Rob asked.

"No. They can't discern the manner at the scene. No obvious signs. I'm heading on up there. Want a ride?" Hoss asked Rob.

Checking out the crime scene and possibly the autopsy beat the heck out of writing, Rob thought. "Let's go," he said. Rob had never seen an autopsy.

Kay put her hand on Rob's shoulder. "Rob, think about this," she said. "You're case agent on an investigation with three homicides attached to it, not counting the execution. The ASAC will be on

Chris's ass. You need to write. Hoss can check out the crime scene and the autopsy and let you know what he saw."

"Or you can run up there and do some real work," Leo said.

Kay scowled at Leo.

Adrenaline kicked ass on Rob's judgement.

"Don't worry, Kay. I can pound everything out when I get back."

D. Randall was on four to midnights and did not have to be in until later, which is why he wore his vintage baggy weightlifting pants in a blue vertical pattern and a gray t-shirt advertising a police 5K from 2002. He nursed a coffee in the Waffle House downtown, by the beach, while waiting for Wee Willie. Sunlight glinting off the Gulf made him squint.

Wee Willie sauntered in and joined him. "Man, you look like shit."

"Who are you to talk? Your uniform ain't never been ironed. And you stink like you're homeless," D. Randall said. "What'd you do with your Rookie?"

"His ass be at the station redoing an accident report."

"Y'all ready to order?" the waitress asked.

She was in her middle years and wasn't fat or skinny, tall or short, or otherwise notable to D. Randall. He glared at the menu as he spoke.

"I'll take the steak and eggs, grits, white with butter; and more coffee."

Wee Willie ordered a Texas Bacon Patty Melt with the hash browns and a Coke.

"EvaJo is gone," D. Randall muttered when they were alone.

"Yeah," Wee Willie whispered.

"I been thinking. She done gone to the Eye, and we don't have any damn idea about what she told them. I been thinking we need to tie this thing on off. Tie it off, you know? I think they'll have shit if the wife is gone too."

D. Randall wiped his mouth with the hand he was using to block the sun. He didn't want to see Wee Willie's stupid face. He put his hand back up between them.

Why doesn't stupid Wee Willie say something, D. Randall thought.

"See here D. Randall, the wife ain't no Smartphone whore. That girl is like a real person," Wee Willie said. "She works at a hospital."

"Why can't you ever see the big picture? Willie, she's the only one around who's going to complain about the dead guy and —"

"Jimmy Tank?" Willie interrupted.

"What? No, the guy we iced at the hotel."

Bam! The plates with D. Randall's food slammed onto the table.

"Shit, bitch, you made me spill my coffee!" D. Randall said, jumping to his feet.

"Sorry," she said, laying Wee Willie's plate in front of him before promenading away.

"How about closing these damn shades?" D. Randall shouted after her.

There were only four other customers inside. They abruptly stopped talking and started studying their food, their faces blank.

"Say D. Randall, why don't you sit down, man?" Wee Willie asked. "Now see here, man, she don't know nothing. She didn't know EvaJo or even Jimmy Tank. Let's leave her out of it, know what I'm saying?"

Randall accepted Wee Willie's invitation and then bent in close. "You the brains now? You the brains of this operation now? What the fuck do you know? You don't ever do any felony investigations. When was the last time you were in court for a felony? I know what's going to keep us clean." D. Randall quickly scanned the restaurant to see if anyone was checking them out. "She's got to go."

"Give me one good reason."

"There's more to this. It's bigger than what it is. With her gone, ain't no one going to complain."

"And the fed won't have no one to talk to no more," Wee Willie said, nodding slowly in the affirmative.

Finally, D. Randall thought.

"With no one to talk to, the Eye guy will move on and this thing can die down and all."

They ate. Wee Willie lowered his head to meet his sandwich instead of the other way around, an MO D. Randall found disgusting.

"Ah-aight," Wee Willie said, "I'll take care." Wee Willie used the last forkful of hash browns of sweep up the last of the fat and yoke on his plate. He shoved it in his mouth and said, before chewing, "I'm on it. I got it. I better get going."

Wee Willie stood up. He wiped his hands on one of those small paper napkins and threw it on his plate.

"You know, you look like shit. You eyes is red. You need some rest, motherfucker."

D. Randall scowled at Wee Willie's back as he headed out the door. Then he realized the shithead had taken off without paying.

"So the way I see it, EvaJo got done down in Seminolacola and dumped up here," Hoss said.

He and Rob were in Hoss's car, driving north fast. A high, hot sun overwhelmed the air conditioning and brought out the customary odors.

"You haven't even seen the crime scene yet," Rob said, "how can you develop conclusions?"

"See, first off, I already talked to the responding officers. Second, folks in this case are starting to drop, and to me, it's all D. Randall in the library with a wrench and shit."

"She was a meth whore, Hoss. Her last trick of the night could have done it. It could have been a coincidence." Rob wanted more facts before he came to any conclusions.

"Homey don't play coincidence," Hoss said.

Rob's BlackBerry rang. "It's Chris," Rob said. Long before the phone got to his ear, he could hear Chris yelling.

"Get back here NOW! The goddammed ASAC is in a fit! Turn your ass around and get back and start writing. Then go to the US Attorney's Office and get those subpoenas. DO YOU HEAR ME!"

"Yes Boss," a shaken Rob said, "but before I do, don't you think there is value in me seeing the crime scene? Maybe I can run up there and turn around real quick? Boss?"

There was nothing but silence in Rob's ear.

"Boss hung up on me," Rob said.

"Traditionally a bad sign in our line of work. I'm turning around?"

"Yeah. I don't think I've ever heard Chris like that."

Master Blaster had not seen Sniper Stefon since he paid him for the white bitch, which he was still pissed off about since the Sniper had cost him what Master believed would have been world-class oral sex. Now he had another job from Wee Willie at twice the fee, a total of ten thousand due to the rush and the fear in Wee Willie's voice, and the Sniper weren't nowhere to be found.

Master stood in the parking lot of the Jupiter Motel next to his black Tiburon in a white t-shirt and black Adidas training pants. He stood stock-still sweating under the high sun. If the Sniper wasn't here, Master would have to do the recon for tonight himself. Hell, he might hide in a bush, whack the bitch and keep all the fee for his own bad self.

The single-story L shaped hotel bracketed a sunburned asphalt parking lot. Master had parked in the middle. He didn't see Sniper's truck, but he did see a faded pink VW Beetle in front of one of the rooms. Only two other rooms had a vehicle parked in front. One was a jacked-up, beater pickup and the other was an old Delta 98, also sun damaged and dragging ass. If Sniper was here, he was fucking the Beetle 'ho for sure.

At the room, Master tried without any luck to see inside around the curtains. He banged on the door three times.

"Yo, Sniper, come on! It be Master," he shouted.

Master backed away a bit so Sniper could see him from either the peephole or the window. Master didn't want to get the business from Sniper's romping big wheel gun.

Master fought the urge to knock again. He could barely breathe in the heat. Bitch had to be here, he thought.

He finally saw the curtain move. The door opened a crack, exposing Sniper's head. Master stared into the Ray Bans.

"Yo, time to go to work," Master said.

"Yeah, man, ain't good right now," Sniper said, rolling his head back to indicate someone was in the room.

"'Ho?" Master asked softly.

"No man, the Sniper don't pay."

"Chick, bitch. I was asking if you had ass in there."

"Yeah man. Got me ass in here. B-T-W motherfucker, you got my shit?"

"Yeah, man, I gots it with me."

"Well, give it the fuck up, motherfucker."

"We got to recon a job. It be rush, you know? We gots to roll back on over to Seminola. You in?"

"Yeah, I'm in. Gimmie a minute."

Sniper's head disappeared into the dark room and the door closed. It was more like ten minutes by the time Master saw him again, now wearing a black tank top and black skinny jeans, holding a red shirt. Master had gotten the car. Ten more minutes and they were out of the tunnel, shooting over the bay on their way back to Seminolacola.

Rob worked his keyboard through lunch. He and Hoss were communicating by phone as Rob wrote. He wrote up four affidavits and applications: one for Chloe Baxter's telephone and email communications, one for EvaJo's, and he finished up another for her financials for the one bank he knew of. Then he wrote to Wee Willie, using the known numbers and emails provided by Hoss, and a separate bank where Wee Willie had his salary sent direct deposit.

Chris stormed up to Rob's cube. His tie drooped and his cuffs were unbuttoned.

"Rob, at the order of ASAC Katz I had to call the State and brief them up. I told Hoss about it already. This thing is about to get all crazy. You done?" Chris asked.

"Just about. Unless you want something for D. Randall," Rob said.

Chris gazed out the window for a moment.

"We don't have enough for anything on him," Chris finally said. "I don't think we have enough. All we have is his association with Wee Willie. All this could be on Wee Willie for what we can prove at this time."

Rob nodded.

"You ready? Send them to Pam," Chris said. "Make copies and let's go, she's waiting for us."

Shit, Rob thought, he couldn't remember Pam's email. Hell, he couldn't even remember her last name.

"Big cases, big problems; small cases, small problems; no cases, no problems," Leo said, materializing with Pamela Eswago's business card. "Need help?"

"Can you take care of the hard copies?" Rob asked.

"Yeah, send them to me and I'll set them up."

As Rob gathered his things to go, his phone buzzed.

"Got fresh fish dinner?" the text from Melissa read.

"Lawson, let's get it in gear!" Chris shouted from the front.

"Here," Leo said as he returned, dropping off a stack of collated and organized hard copies.

Rob scooped them up, stuffed a black nylon brief case and ran.

Melissa parked her Civic and yanked the hand break up. She liked to hear the clicking sound. She grabbed her gym bag, handbag and two grocery bags. She had stopped at the store in black Active yoga pants from Forever 21 and an oversized t-shirt for one or two items, which had spiraled into a fish dinner she hoped would include Rob.

The text she had sent him still embarrassed her. She had not yet heard back and hoped he'd make it. The idea had ambushed her when she saw the fresh trout on special. Jules ate fish sometimes, and ate mac and cheese all the time, and she needed almost all the fixings, hence two bags.

Home at last, she thought. She liked her condo, the second of five row houses in red brick with white trim and a gambrel roof of black shingles. The main entrance included a small concrete porch at the top of a short set of steps, with the porch area to the right and a large, circular four-foot-tall planting of thick green Jasmine bushes on the left.

Just as she was about to mount the steps, something shook the bush and startled her. She screamed and jumped back onto the grass. Her groceries thudded to the ground. The bush quivered, and with a flash of black with white trim, a bird with a large forked tail sped away.

Melissa caught her breath. She bent to pick up her things, relieved the pickle jar hadn't broken.

Pam Eswago buzzed Rob and Chris into the US Attorney's Office herself, as staff had already become scarce. Her brown hair had been pulled back. Large black horned-rimmed glasses complemented her round face and cheeks. She wore a red and white striped blouse (making Rob think of peppermint) and a matching red above-the-knee solid skirt.

"Hello, Chris," she said before facing Rob. "I'm Pam. I don't think we've worked together before, but I've seen you around." She stuck her hand out.

They shook. "Nope, first time," Rob agreed.

"Sounds like a doozy, too. Let's go to my office."

Pam started down the carpeted hall and the two men kept pace, taking up positions behind her. An ample derriere swung seductively as she strode forward, head high and shoulders back, on four-inch heels.

Pam entered her small office, crowded with a desk, stuffed bookshelves and a circular table. She used the chair behind her desk and the men sat at the table. Rob pulled the hard copies out of his bag.

"Rob, Chris told me a bit about what's happening on the telephone, but can you tell me about the case from the beginning?" Pam asked, her fountain pen and legal pad at the ready.

"I guess it started at the execution of Jimmy Tank Gubbs. He told the gallery while he was guilty of some of the murders he committed, he adamantly denied killing Matthew Simmons," Rob said.

"The murder for which he was being executed?" Pam asked.

"Yes."

"He pled out to that one?" Pam asked.

"No, convicted at trial."

"And you believed him?"

"Enough to want to look into it."

"Didn't you work the case?"

"No."

"Why were you at the execution?"

"I accompanied Simmons's widow, at her request." Rob couldn't believe he just said that sentence. The words sounded surreal, as though they belonged to someone else.

"Uh-huh. How —"

Pam was interrupted by a scraping sound from the hall. Chris moved his arm slightly toward his weapon. The three of them exchanged glances.

"Yes?" Pam called.

After a moment, Josiah Waller stepped into the doorway. He wore a white shirt with rolled up sleeves, a red tie, gray wool trousers and an expression of insincere good fellowship.

"I saw you all come in. A bit late for a meeting, so it must be important," Josiah said.

"Yes, we think so," Pam replied.

"What's it about? I mean, can I help?"

"I'm just learning about it myself, Josiah, but I appreciate the offer. Why don't we catch up tomorrow?"

"Wouldn't it be more efficient if I joined now?"

"I'm sorry. I know you're new, so let me say it this way: we're not like a regular prosecutor's office. Since we deal with intelligence issues, there are need-to-know rules in effect. But let me get caught up and we can talk tomorrow."

Pam smiled and made slight cheerleader nods as she delivered the bad news.

"Well," Josiah said with a shrug, "T-T-F-N."

Pam kept smiling.

Josiah waved and tuned his back.

Chris started to speak, but Pam showed him the palm of her hand. She pointed her chin at the door. Rob rose and closed it before sitting back at the table.

"What was that about?" Chris asked.

"The bar in this part of Florida is fairly small and I've known Waller all my career. Until we hired him, even when I was interning at the State's Attorney's Office, he never had two words for me. Now he's here and he expects us to be best buddies."

Neither man said anything.

"I know it sounds puny," Pam continued, "but there is more. Maybe it's his imperiousness, or maybe it's a chemistry thing, but still, this is pretty sensitive and for now I'd like to keep it between us."

"He prosecuted the case against Jimmy Tank," Rob said.

The three of them were silent as Pam and Chris digested the new information.

"Okay," Pam said. "Okay. We'll consider that later. For now, let's get back to it. Where were we? Oh, how did you meet the widow Simmons?"

Rob intuitively knew not to share the exact "how" of how they met. He'd be on the next flight to the New York office, spending the rest of his career re-assembling shredded Wall Street documents.

"We go to the same church," he offered.

"How retro!" Pam said. "I don't attend myself, although I'm very spiritual. Anyway, so you must have believed Gubbs?"

"Enough to be curious. The wife more so."

"She did? Why do you think that?"

"I think she reacted well to the way he sold it, with more weight than what a convict looking to rehabilitate his reputation would use. And another thing: he copped to the killings impacting the other witnesses present."

"What were they?"

"A gang-banging, a drug robbery, and the two kids who were hooking up at the State Park."

"I *remember* that. He was the shooter?"

"Yup."

"Sounds like he got what he deserved. So what got you curious?"

"He admitted the other murders. Why would he insist he was innocent of just the one?"

"But you weren't convinced coming out of the execution?"

"No, not all the way. The wife's opinion got me thinking about it. I agreed to look into it, and what I meant was I'd read the press coverage and get into the police file."

"So what did you find?"

"Nothing."

"Nothing?"

"There wasn't much for a case that went to trial. It appeared to not even have a detective assigned to it."

"Maybe they worked the investigation out of the State's Attorney's Office."

"Maybe."

"There's more," Chris said.

"I hope to hell so," Pam said. "Rob, go on."

"The arrest was downright lucky. The arresting officers observed Jimmy Tank in a car that clearly he didn't belong in. He ran, they chased. They caught him and, during a custodial search, they found the pistol used on the decedent. The file was very skimpy. There was nothing in there to indicate anyone had tried to interview him."

"So Rob, have you talked to anyone at the State's Attorney's Office? Maybe it's all in the trial file."

"Yes," Rob said. "They didn't have anything."

"Who'd you talk to over there?" Pam asked.

"Josiah Waller."

Pam leaned back in her chair. She locked out her arms and rested balled fists on the edge of her desk. She took a deep breath, filling her cheeks, and slowly exhaled.

"Let's put that aside for now. Did you do any investigating?" she asked.

"Yes, after the press reports and talking to a sympathetic detective, I tried to find the arresting officers. I was able to approach Officer William Washington Jefferson no hyphen and got my head bit off. Davis Randall Hargrove was out that day and I have not tried to approach him since. I spoke with Waller, negative results. Next, I interviewed the penitentiary chaplain, known universally as Father Clyde. Jimmy Tank found Jesus in the big house."

"The priest gave you something? Will he testify?" Pam asked.

"No and no. He did remind me Jimmy Tank had a mother and I went and found her. She recollected Jimmy Tank gave her a bundle of money, like about mid-five figures. There's a trail: a bank account and a rental agent, as well as motor vehicle lien records."

"Do you have them?" Pam asked.

"Applications ready for signature," Rob said, patting his papers.

Rob risked a glance at Chris, whose displeasure radiated off him.

"What kind of witness will she make?" Pam asked.

"The kind that's dead," Chris said.

"Dead!" Pam shouted in a high-pitched bark. She blushed and shot a glance at the door.

"As of this morning," Rob said.

"It's going to get worse," Chris said.

"How?" Pam asked.

"I developed a source that shared knowledge of a whore who worked the Crystal Suites," Rob said. "She was scheduled to meet with the decedent, Simmons I mean, the day of his murder. The meeting had been set up by Wee Willie."

"Wee Willie?"

"Washington Jefferson's nickname."

"Wait, she'll testify that she met the decedent on the day of his murder in a meeting set up by one of the arresting officers who caught Jimmy Tank?"

"Yes, that's the story, but . . . ." Only now did it occur to Rob how bad this all sounded.

"She's dead too," Chris said.

"Jesus Christ!" Pam mock shouted in a stage whisper. "Is anybody still alive in this case?"

"The widow Rob is sleeping with," Chris said.

"Goddammit! Rob, you don't do routine. You didn't take the prostitute to grand jury? No? Affidavit?"

"No," Rob said.

Pam inhaled deeply and exhaled forcefully with her eyes closed. Her lids rose, exposing hard black bullets.

"Stop fucking the widow or you're off the case," Pam said.

Rob didn't want Pam to clearly see his expression, so he looked at Chris.

"Chris, I'm not kidding," Pam said, "He stops or he's gone."

Chris nodded.

"Fine. Rob, what else did the prostitute give you? Was she supposed to turn a trick?" Pam asked.

"The plan was for her to meet the decedent and set up for the trick. Her understanding was the police would arrest them both. Her arrest would be a sham. She thought of herself as 'under cover.'"

"Was she there for the murder?"

"No. Willie called and told her not to come."

"How did she meet the decedent?"

"He was a regular at ECGC."

"ECGC?" Pam asked.

"Strip joint uptown," Chris said. "You need to get out more."

"You must be talking to my husband. Why aren't we questioning Washington Jefferson?"

"Number one, it was only a few days ago. Two, before I accuse a cop of murder, I want to be sure. Chloe was high when we spoke. I want to get her phone records and corroborate her story," Rob said.

"And now she's dead," Pam said.

"Yes," Rob said.

"Overdose?" Pam asked.

Neither man said anything.

"Talk to me," Pam said.

"Shot at point blank range with a large caliber pistol inside her apartment," Rob said.

"Any leads?"

"None. Even the bullets were wrecked. No usable ballistic information."

"So far we have a hunch and a statement from a dead prostitute connecting Washington Jefferson to the murder supposedly committed by Gubbs, who was executed by the State for it. What else have you got?"

"Our contact at Seminolacola PD says Wee Willie works for D. Randall Hargrove, who is supposed to be a criminal mastermind with extensive contacts and business dealings. Besides Wee Willie, we've got nothing on D. Randall. I need time to rope him in," Rob said.

"Why do we think he controls Washington Jefferson?" Pam asked.

"The locals say so. Our local contact says Wee Willie is dumb as a post."

Pam chewed her lower lip. The men waited.

"What are those?" she finally asked, pointing.

"Subpoena duces tecum applications. Known phones for everyone. Known bank accounts for the cops and I discovered one for EvaJo Moorer, Jimmy Tank's mom. I have requests for email and internet service, so I expect a second round once those are identified. By the way, electrons in your in-box."

"Hargrove, too?"

"No, but I want to write to him, too."

"On what basis?"

"Hearsay that he is the mastermind."

"From who?"

"Our local contact in the department."

"Hoss went on paper?" Chris asked.

"No, he told me and I'll be the affiant," Rob said.

"No way," Pam said. "You're the case agent. Get —"

"Look, let's concentrate on what we have here. More bad news, I'm afraid. At the direction of the ASAC, I called the State," Chris said. "We have to hustle."

"Shit!" Pam said.

"I know. Sorry," Chris said. "I expect tomorrow the pressure to lock up the dirty cop and close the case as "done and done" will be on. You know what they say about us, that we're always trying to find the conspiracy and all; whatever but we still need these records. We need to get this investigation rolling. There's more here."

"I see it. For now, we'll concentrate on getting these out. But I want a strategy meeting tomorrow before lunch. Rob, you and I have a date," Pam said, turning toward her computer.

"Yo bitch, you have to do that now?" Master Blaster asked.

"Keep me even," Sniper Stefon said, as he lit up a five-dollar rock of crack Master had fetched for him in a small glass tube.

They were sitting in a stolen Chrysler 300 on the street not far from the Simmons crib. They both wore dark shirts and trousers. Sniper wore fingerless gloves. They were each carrying their favorite pistols. Sniper had his big-assed revolver and Master carried a Walther nine millimeter, the old James Bond gun. It made him feel like a spy and shit. License to kill, motherfucker.

But now, as he watched his partner crack up, he only felt foreboding. He thought Army guys wouldn't operate high. It wasn't professional. Master covertly watched Sniper as he finished. With Sniper high and the hurried nature of the job weighing him down, all Master could think about was how this shit be messed up.

At least they only had to kill the woman.

They would leave the kid alone.

Wee Willie rode one-man in a marked Seminolacola cruiser. The lay of the single-family houses let him idle on a street two blocks away and still keep an eye on Master Blaster and the freak he rode with nowadays. He couldn't see the Simmons house, but at least he could see the two twits. He welcomed the setting sun, hoping for relief from the heat. The sunset put him in a marginally better mood until he saw the quick glow of the cigarette lighter from the front passenger seat of the Chrysler. He knew what that was about, and he knew who was doing it.

"Shit," he muttered.

Melissa tried not to be too disappointed at Robert's text about being late. She covered his plate with plastic wrap. Thinking about him made her a little nervous. Maybe if Lila left now and she could get Jules to sleep quickly, she and Rob could have some time alone, as in *alone*.

She finished clearing the table in the bright kitchen and loaded the dishwasher. The last little bit of orange disappeared from the sky. Melissa closed the vertical blinds at the balcony doors. Lila and Jules watched Teen Titans Go!

"About time Lila went home and we thought about bed, Jules," she said.

"'til the end of the show," Jules said.

There was a knock at the door.

"I'll get it!" Jules shouted, launching himself off the couch.

Melissa caught him at the door. As Jules turned the knob and pulled, she put her hand flat against it.

"At night we ask who it is and look out to make sure," Melissa said.

"But it's too high!" Jules whined.

"That's why I answer the door."

Melissa stood up straight and put her eye to the peephole.

Master knocked on the door again. Sniper's fidgeting annoyed him. Boy couldn't hold his crack, Master thought. Master rested the fingertips of his left hand on the door.

"Mrs. Simmons, delivery," he shouted.

She saw the two black men on her stoop. The one on the right glared around the neighborhood, twisting his torso and exposing the bright shiny gun with a long, long barrel he was hiding behind his back.

"Oh!" she said, stepping backward. "Oh!" She pressed her hands to her chest, her fingers splayed out.

"Fuck this shit," Sniper Stefon said. He squared off on the door and raised his leg.

"No!" Master shouted.

The loud bam against the door made Melissa jump. The shock jumpstarted her brain. Ten years of serious gymnastics, of running at vaults and flying around bars, and four more years of throwing herself off the seven-and-half-meter platform had conditioned her keep thinking when scared, and she was scared now.

"Take Jules and run out the back!" she shouted to Lila.

Lila stood stock still with her mouth open.

"Lila!" Melissa hissed. "Take Jules now! Run out the back!"

Bam!

Lila scooped up Jules and started running.

"Go to Reverend Nettles's!"

Bam! Melissa saw the toe casting part from the jamb. She checked on Lila and Jules. The vertical blinds were swinging. They were gone.

BAM! Melissa heard the sound of wood splitting. The casting barely hung on. The next hit would knock the door in. She felt like she was dithering, but she decided on her play, picked her spot and got ready. She bent her knees, raised her arms and focused on the door with competition concentration.

Master Blaster held his pistol out in front of him in both hands with his arms straight, like he'd seen on TV, and kept his back to the front door. He scanned the area wildly. Sniper Stefon had made him furious. The loud kicking must have got everybody off their screens by now. Not only that, the crack done made him stupid. After each kick he spun around and crowed a bit, like an NFL player in the end zone.

"Finish it, bitch," Master said.

"Fuck you," Sniper said as he kicked the door again.

The framing gave way and the front door toppled. It seemed to fall in slow motion. The two men tripped over the door and each other as they struggled to get in.

Melissa's plan was as old as motherhood: she would use herself as a decoy. She would blitz past the bad guys and run. Hopefully they would follow her.

She hopped up on her toes and started sprinting, hands high, elbows and knees prominent, and legs pumping.

The second man, almost on his feet, went down again, tangled in the first man's legs.

Melissa made seven solid gymnastic strides. She planted both feet in front of the door and bent her knees so she dropped into a squat. Momentum carried her forward.

She pushed off and the coiled strength in her thighs did not fail her. She cleared the tangle of male bodies in the beginning of a perfect arc out of the house, missing the head jamb by a breath. She figured she had enough height to tuck and roll.

She misjudged and hit the grass on her face and chest. She slid, the wind knocked out of her, but wasted no time in forcing herself up and taking off. She thought she'd lead them through the neighborhood and, when she had lost them, circle back to the Nettles place.

Over at the home of Reverend Coleman and Keisha Nettles, they dressed for dinner. Not intentionally, but their habitual wear, a suit and tie for the Reverend and a dress for Keisha, had influenced their children. Tonight Reverend Nettles ate in his shirtsleeves with Keisha, sixteen-year-old Rehema and twelve-year-old Issa.

Lila burst in the front door of their modest Victorian, dragging a crying Jules by the arm.

"Reverend, did you remember to lock up?" Keisha deadpanned, her annoyance plain to see.

Indeed, Reverend Nettles thought to himself, he had not. The kids were wide-eyed at the sight of Lila crying.

"Lila, what's going —" Rev. Nettles began.

"They have Melissa! They kicked in the front door! We ran!" Lila said as she tried to catch her breath.

Nettles saw Keisha working her cell phone. God bless her quick thinking.

To Lila, Nettles started to say "Dear, why don't you —"

Melissa Simmons charged in.

"Call the police! Two men broke in! They kicked in my door! They're coming! We have to run!" she said.

"Daddy!" Rehema shouted.

"Oh no. No, no. We don't run," Nettles said, as he jumped up and bounded for the stairs. "Keisha, take everyone to the back room!"

Nettles felt certain about what he was going to do. In a way, he had been preparing for this his whole life. Nettles ran into the master bedroom and jerked open the door to his closet. Short as he was, he picked up a volume of Erasmus from his hardwood end table and shoved it up on the inside of the closet.

There weren't no little girls going to get blown up in his church, nor no little boys killed, he thought. His church wasn't going to get burned down, either. No way.

The book pushed up on the recoil pad of a Browning side-by-side double-barreled 20 gauge shotgun. With practiced ease, he knocked it off the shelf and dropped the book. The weapon dropped straight down and he caught it by the checkered grip, his trigger finger automatically resting alongside the trigger guard.

"Reverend!" Keisha said, entering the bedroom.

"Keisha, don't start now sweetheart. You called the police?"

"On their way!"

"Take everyone to the back room, please!"

He wanted them there because the back room did not have a door to the wrap around porch. He had thought about this a lot, how he would handle it. He would wait out front to make sure no one got in. When the police arrived, when he saw the revolving lights, the shotgun would go back into the closet, or under the couch, or whatever.

He worked the breach of the shotgun with one hand as he opened at the drawer of his end table with the other. He found the cardboard box of buckshot. He put a handful of the shells in his pocket and two in their chambers, shutting the weapon with authority. He flew down the stairs, Keisha behind him, finding her voice, shouting they would kill him if they saw him with a gun.

Nobody had moved.

"Get in the back room, now!" he yelled.

The front door slammed open. "Listen hear, motherfuckers," yelled a young black man, dressed in black, pointing a large shiny silver revolver at them, "We want —"

Reverend Nettles did not think turning the other cheek necessarily applied to angry armed trespassers hell bent on causing harm. He brought the shotgun to his shoulder and fired, as fast as if a pheasant had been flushed.

He must have pulled it a little to the right because the intruder flinched to the left.

"What the fuck you doing?" the man dressed in black yelled, more startled than mad, Nettles thought.

Nettles adjusted his aim but before he could fire again, his target was gone. Nettles moved to the doorway and aimed the shotgun again. Two dim figures ran off into the night. The threat faded. There was no need to shoot.

Back in the house, he encountered a sea of shocked silent faces.

"Everyone all right?" he asked.

The question ended the incident. The house fill with a cacophony of crying, screaming and shouting.

Wednesday

Rob woke up on the floor of the Nettles's living room, next to the couch, still in his clothes from the day before. Melissa, on the couch, breathed evenly as she slept on. They had finally gotten Jules down in Issa's room on a second bunk bed, the novelty of which had distracted him after the scare. Lila had retired to a guest room and everyone else was where they were supposed to be.

Melissa had called Rob and he had bolted out of Pam's office. By the time the interviews and the crime scene investigations were done, the reporters gone, and he had finished nailing shut Melissa's front door, it was 3:15 am.

Rob checked his watch. 5:15.

Rob stood. Melissa slept on, peaceful as a child. He wanted to stay to show his support, and be there should the subjects try again. He wanted to crawl under the blanket next to her. He wanted to do a lot of things, but he knew the fastest way to ensure her safety was to work the case.

He padded out of the house on his socks, holding his shoes. He'd call her later.

The sun rose high enough to blast into the master bedroom of the Jemison household. They lived in a four-bedroom Florida ranch in Saintes, real close to the water on the northeast of Seminolacola Harbor. Eartha Jemison had decorated the room in light pastels. Alphonzo stood in front of their lemon dresser and mirror combination admiring himself. Alphonzo thought of his skin tone as Mocha or Hickory, but Eartha thought he was more Coffee or sometimes a Pecan, but don't bet on it under florescent light.

No matter. What he was, was in some shape; maybe the best of his life. He was all cut up and broad and shit, like the old days. He held his arms straight out and made fists, flexing his shoulders, biceps and triceps. Damn. He was radical, even if he was wearing bikini briefs in black and red paisley. Eartha insisted he ditch the white Army issue boxers after they first met.

"Baby, you hot," Eartha purred from their bed.

"Two hundred-twenty pounds this morning," he said.

"Two hundred twenty?"

"Well, 220 if I still had the leg. About, I figure. 204 actual this morning."

Alphonzo was six-foot-two.

A well-muscled six-foot-two from his close-cropped black hair with part cut therein, to his thin mustache, to his flawless physique, ready for a bodybuilding competition, awesome at his age of forty-two years. Except for his legs.

The right one ended below the knee. The scarring on his left leg started on the inside of his thigh and got worse as it went down, burns and cuts, culminating in a missing chunk of his calf. The foot was still attached and working. Thankfully, the Mujies missed that one.

"Just how hot am I?" he asked.

"Get yourself right here and I'll show you, baby."

Now Eartha herself could still stop traffic, Alphonzo thought. They were the same age. She threw off the covers and spread her arms. She was a hand-carved piece of erotic ebony hardwood. Alphonzo twisted and jumped onto the mattress, landing in her embrace.

"Mom!" Twelve-year-old Cedrik yelled, bursting in without knocking. "Damn, y'all. Y'all, they's making out again!"

The twins, younger than Cedrik, started laughing and yelling as they scrambled down the hall. Carrie and Edwin pushed around Cedrik and hopped on the bed too.

"Now y'all get out, Mom and I got some business, you hear? Get on out!" Alphonzo said.

"You done had sex twice, ain't that enough?" Cedrik said.

Alphonzo's cell toned and vibrated.

"You saved by the bell Cedrik, for running your mouth with disrespect in front of your Mother," Alphonzo said without a whole lot of force, while rolling and reaching to grab his phone off his night table.

"Jemison," he said.

"Yeah, hi, Alphonzo. This is Norm Gopher. You got a minute?"

"Yessir," Alphonzo said, sitting up and waving the kids out. Did he have a minute for the Assistant Chief of the Florida Law Enforcement Division Domestic Security and Investigations Section? You bet your ass he did.

"How you been doing? You coming along?" Norm G. asked in his whispery slow-moving voice.

"Yes sir, coming along." Alphonzo thought he was about to be fired. They couldn't tolerate the lost leg after all.

"That's good. Yeah . . . that's good. You have enough to do?"

All he'd been doing is working out every damn day since he got cleared for duty. No cases assigned.

"Enough sir, but always ready for more," Alphonzo said.

"I like that. Okay, because more is what we've got. What rank are you in the Army, Al?"

"I was a master sergeant, sir."

"Yeah, outstanding. To me, it means you can handle discretion. Can you handle discretion, Al?"

"Yes, sir."

"Al, you ever worked with the FBI up there?"

"A time or two. They change out a lot."

"Yeah . . . throughout the state. Al, we need a solid agent to go over there and help them out. This comes from the Commissioner and he got it from the Governor. We need you to go on over there this morning and help them keep their eye on the ball on a case they've got going.

"The Governor wants them to lock up a crooked cop they found. But you know them Al, they'll want to investigate the 'enterprise' and do 'link analysis' and dig out every little thing they think they can find before they actually do any police work, you know what I mean?"

"Yessir."

"The Governor is afraid they won't understand the impact of this on the public. The Governor wants the bad cops off the street, and so does the Commissioner."

"Yes sir."

"You go on over there as our liaison. This will be full time, so unload your cases. You help them out, Al. Yeah . . . you also help them arrest the dirty cop and move it along, you get the chance, you know what I mean?"

"Yessir."

"The Commissioner himself likes you for this."

Norm G. is slinging some fresh, pungent bullshit this morning, Alphonzo thought. The Commissioner couldn't pick him out of a lineup.

Al kept his mouth shut.

"We're all glad you're back, Al. Keep Region in the loop, but call me every day. And if you need anything, anything at all to move them guys along, just ask."

"Yes, sir. Thank you, sir."

"Yeah . . . you got this, Al. Go on over there and kick 'em in their slow-rolling federal asses."

FBI Assistant Special Agent in Charge Andrew Katz pointed his Ruby-Red Metallic Tinted Clearcoat Ford Fusion west on I-10 into an absolutely beautiful Florida day. Even though he had started from the Tallahassee Field Office early, he was shaved and wearing normal business attire. He favored white shirts, subdued suits and striped neck ties. His suit jacket hung on a hanger from the hook behind him in the rear seat area and his weapon and two extra magazines dug into his torso.

He belonged out in the field, he thought. This is where it was done. He'd much rather have been heading to the Seminolacola RA for a retirement or transfer lunch, or to present an award, but sometimes things go awry and the effective Bureau leader gets out there and confronts them head on. After Senior Supervisory Resident Agent Christopher Karas, a supervisor with a known light touch for the troops, called to tell him about a Civil Rights case with two connected homicides and a serious attempted homicide, he knew he needed to pounce on it.

That's why he was known as "The Cat." He enjoyed his reputation as someone who put concerns about his climate survey scores well behind doing the job. He was always ready to pounce, like a big jungle cat, when FBI personnel missed the mark. Some thoughtful subordinates had given him the nickname after a particularly necessary pouncing during a past investigation.

The Special Agent in Charge was in complete agreement. She talked him out of leaving mid-morning, pointing out bad news doesn't get better with time. He enjoyed having her trust.

Andrew relived the conversation as he used both hands to smooth down the hair on the sides and back of his head, up top being a non-issue, until he quickly grabbed the wheel again. Safety and policy mandated he drive with two hands on the wheel at all times.

The racket of keyboard clicks and ringing phones filled the RA. All the agents were at their desks. Rob had swung home, cleaned up and changed. He had put on the same suit he had worn to Jimmy Tank's because the local bank, White Sands, didn't accept electronic filing and he would have to hand deliver a hard copy after it opened. For now, he pounded away at his own keyboard, filing the subpoenas Pam had signed the night before.

"Hey, listen up!" Chris shouted. He had come out of his office with his coffee cup and set himself up at a location central to the cubes. "Clear up some time. Rob's case is going to get hot and we'll need everyone free."

"That's a great suggestion, Chris. I think we'll all get on that," Kay said.

"Rob, how is Seminolacola handling the new Simmons matter?" Chris asked.

Rob stood up to clear cubicle partitions. "I spoke to Hoss. They're selling an attempted push-in robbery, suspects unknown. The morning news is buying."

"How are the victims?" Chris asked.

"Still sleeping, Boss," Rob said. "They bedded down quiet enough last night."

"Hey Chris, the Asshole is on his way!" Leo shouted.

Rob and everyone else knew from the context Leo referred to ASAC Katz by his nickname. Furthermore, it was common knowledge Leo had an excellent source base in the front office. He and the ASAC's Secretary in Tallahassee had worked together in the Brooklyn-Queens RA, up in New York Division, in the past.

"When did he leave?" Chris asked.

"The SAC chased him out at a quarter to eight," Leo said.

Chris consulted his watch. "Well, we have some time. That reminds me, anyone know Special Agent Alphonzo Jemison from FDLE? Didn't he deploy and something happened?"

"Uh, yes Boss," Steve Guerra said, standing up. "He deployed as a reservist with the 20th Special Forces, to both sandboxes, I think. Had some trouble at the house when he got back from the second one and switched to the 53rd Infantry Brigade to slow down bit; trying to keep his wife happy. Deployed again with them and got blowed up running convoys. I didn't know FDLE would let him back in – he lost a bit of one of his legs, I think."

"Which bit?" Leo asked.

"The bit you stand up on," Steve said.

"How do you know all this?" Chris asked. "You do anything with him?"

"Not professionally. I know him from the Special Forces Association and Wounded Warrior."

"What's his story?" Chris asked.

"He's all right. Sherriff's Department from before and then FDLE. Worked lots of drugs, gangs and homicides. Last I heard, he was getting into Cyber, but I don't know if he officially changed over yet."

"Alright. Rob, he's rep-ing FDLE on our new 'joint' investigation. We all know he's coming to push us to lock up the cops and close the case. Careful what you say around him; it will go straight back to the Commissioner and from there to our SAC, with negative spin, no doubt."

The bell rang, announcing a visitor.

"Probably not the ASAC. Let him in," Chris said.

"How do you know it's a 'him?'" Kay asked.

"Lunch says it's Jemison," Leo said, on his way to the door.

"No bet," Kay said.

They all started moving to the front, by Chris's office, and met Leo escorting in a tall, muscular black man. He wore a tan alpine dress style cowboy hat, a white shirt with light brown stripes tucked into tan Dockers and shiny brown cowboy boots. His shield, pistol, handcuffs and an extra magazine were on a belt secured by a mid-sized oval silver rodeo buckle. He regarded everybody with a steady, clear-eyed gaze out of worldly eyes. The trimmed mustache went with the outfit.

Too bad we aren't in Texas, Rob thought.

"Everyone, this is Special Agent Alphonzo Jemison. Alphonzo, this is —" Chris said.

"Hello, Al," Steve said, interrupting Chris and stepping forward with his hand extended.

"You up here now, Captain?" Al said.

"Yup, transferred up from Tampa a few years ago. Heard about the leg."

"Yup."

"Doing good?"

"Making it, making it. How you doing?"

"*khá tốt.*"

Alphonzo smiled in a closed-lip, guarded way.

"Done with the reunion?" Chris asked, eyeing his watch again. "This is Rob Lawson. He's the case agent. Rob, why don't you get Special Agent Jemison some coffee and then bring him up to speed. After, I'd like to see both of you in my office."

Chris walked away.

"Special Agent —" Rob started to say, extending his hand.

"Make it Al," Alphonzo said, smiling and taking Rob's hand.

"Coffee?" Rob asked.

"You bet."

Rob led Al to the break room. Kay, Leo and Steve joined them. Rob handed Alphonzo a clean-enough Eglin Air Force Base Security Forces mug. They fixed their coffees.

"Al, have they filled you in?" Rob asked.

"In the best tradition of FDLE, I don't know crap," Al said, grinning.

Rob summarized the nuts and bolts of the case and where he hoped to go with it.

"And how about last night?" Al asked.

"Hoss King from SPD is on it. They're carrying it as an attempted burglary, like a home invasion type of thing," Rob said.

"Anything on that?"

"Not really. No vehicle, no usable evidence. The only piece of luck was Reverend Nettles, who had a shotgun and knew how to use it."

"No kidding?"

"No kidding. He had a 20 gauge side-by-side loaded with number three buckshot."

"Is that like ours, Leo?" Kay asked.

"No, smaller," Leo said, "but more of them, traveling a little slower. I think there are 20, let's call it about 25 caliber pellets in a 20. Our 12 gauge buckshot is nine 32 caliber balls."

"Shot them?" Alphonzo asked.

"Uh-huh. He got off one round and hit one of them. Hoss thinks Reverend Nettles got him in the left shoulder area. They only pulled four pellets out of the wall. Odds are the subject has eight to fifteen or so in him," Rob said.

"I'm planning to stay awake during his sermons. How did he get involved?"

"The victim, who goes to his church, lives nearby and ran over to his place, bring the shitbirds with her."

"What are parishioners for? Which church?"

"Maritime Methodist."

"We go to Beth-El AME up in Donne. Seminolacola put out the emergency room watch?"

"All state for the tri-state."

"On the cops, you got zip, I expect," Al said.

"I wouldn't say that. I've got leads," Rob said.

"Why don't we bring Wee Willie in and sweat him?" Al said.

Leo laughed out loud, becoming the center of attention.

"Governor give you those marching orders?" Leo asked.

"Uh-huh," Al said with mock seriousness, "and the Commissioner likes me for this assignment. I'm hand-picked."

The group murmured in ironic agreement. They all sipped their respective coffees.

"You know we aren't going to pop the one and call it quits, right?" Leo asked.

"You can't blame me for trying. Be advised though, we're going to be under pressure from Tallahassee to arrest Wee Willie and wrap it up, with a press conference telling the people they're safe and everything."

"You guys wouldn't have anything on this, would you?" Kay said.

"Funny you should ask. We know about Wee Willie. He's easy. What's going to be tough is D. Randall."

"You have something on him?" Rob asked.

"Nothing concrete, lots of innuendo and speculation, but nothing to go at him with for real. You know he's connected?"

"We've been told. I was also told to make sure my life insurance was paid up," Rob said.

"Yup. Witnesses have a habit of disappearing when you start on D. Randall's trail. Bodies rarely turn up and when they do they're clean, but really, other than that, we don't have anything either."

"I do have something," Rob said. "Wee Willie was hanging around Melissa's neighborhood last night."

"How do you know?" Leo asked.

"Who's Melissa?" Al asked.

"The victim of the push in. I saw him. He was in uniform, parked in a marked unit, about two blocks away from the crime scene. I drove by him close enough to spit," Rob said.

Coffee cups up. Sips. Coffee cups down.

"He's there to watch?" Leo asked.

"He's there as a tourist, maybe," Al said.

"Watch, like a hit?" Kay asked. "Like it's a hit? Could be. If not, why didn't he help with the call?"

"Lazy?" Rob asked, playing devil's advocate.

"He's lazy . . . why show up at all, though?" Al asked.

"Just curious?"

They contemplated issues regarding Wee Willie's character while they drank more coffee.

Master Blaster was beat to hell. He had not slept even a wink. Sniper Stephon, the big Army guy, wouldn't shut up. Back in his girl's crib, all night long it was "it hurts" and "help me."

And the house was a mess. They camped out in the boy's bedroom with Sniper face up on the bed. Master had cut away Sniper's shirt and sweater, but he was in the same pants. Master had showered and changed into baggy blue jeans like jail pants, and in layered t-shirts, brown and white.

Since Sniper would not let Master's vet work on him, Master had been using sheets to try to stem the bleeding. When they got soaked he dumped them on the floor. The little motherfucking God squad prick put lots of pellets into Sniper. Maybe even broke his shoulder. Master could not be sure because the pussy wouldn't let Master touch him.

This ain't how no Army acts when they gets shot, Master thought.

"Yo, Sniper, let me get the vet, man. People is animals and he can do 'em all. He's good. He fixed me up more than once," Master said.

201

"Fuck no. Man, get me some Cotton, bitch," Sniper said.

First of all, he didn't need to be talking like he the man I be a piece of shit, Master thought. Second, Master was not sure oxycodone was the way to go. What if it killed the little pussy? If it did, Master would have to do something with the body.

Master surveyed the room. When his girl gets back, he might have to do something with two bodies, he thought. She will definitely try to kill him because of Sniper and the mess. In the meantime, Sniper was sick.

"See here man, I don't know if Cotton is the way to go," Master said.

"Get me some blow. Or crack. Get me something motherfucker! This shit hurts."

"You don't need to be talking to me that way. Frap bitch, I'll go get you something."

Master grabbed his keys and his Walther and slammed the door behind him.

Wee Willie lived with, rather spent most nights with Lyra and her children in a three-bedroom bungalow in north Navarre county. He had children of his own, but they lived with their mother in Fort Walton. Lyra had gone off to her job and the kids were at school. Wee Willie lay on the king-sized waterbed wearing a t-shirt and cotton sweatpants cut down to shorts, nursing a headache and ignoring his cell phone. He knew it was D. Randall and he knew the man would be pissed.

That shit last night was crap, Willie thought. How it went so bad so fast eluded him. Master Blaster was a prime contractor.

It must be freaky Sniper's fault. Lighting up some Crack just before a job. He hated Army guys, and Navy worse. The Air Force sucked too.

Willie swung his feet onto the floor. He hated the room. It had been done in cedar shake several decades ago. The offender must have been some white snowbird from Ohio, he thought. Willie got up and tottered to the kitchen, the buzzing of his phone chasing him.

He saw the orange juice container on the counter amid the breakfast refuse. Willie reached out for it with shaking hands. How the hell did he get in this situation? he asked himself. The container was empty. Willie grabbed the milk from the fridge and poured himself a glass. He drank it down quick.

He was in a bad way. Either he was going to go to jail for a long time or D. Randall was going to kill him.

"Shit," he said.

It had been so sweet, and sweet for years. Willie had been a main service provider for D. Randall in the Community and it had paid. Willie collected rents, did a little enforcing and supervised the talent they hired for jobs. Now though, he needed to think things through. He needed to keep everything cool.

He needed coffee.

ASAC Katz rang the bell at the door to the Resident Agency. They buzzed him in. He walked confidently to Chris's corner office and caught him coming around his desk.

"Thanks for meeting me at the door," Katz said, sitting down in a chair.

"I was on my way to let you in," Chris said.

"But you didn't make it. So, you know your case agent on the Simmons matter hasn't finished his Blood Borne Pathogens training yet. Opened it, yes, but not finished it. I'm fooled, Karas. Are you fooled? He fooled me."

Katz caught Chris's wince. At least he has the decency to be embarrassed, Katz thought.

"He's been a little busy," Chris said, taking his own seat behind his desk.

"Too busy for an SAC's evaluation item? One that directly impacts the SAC's bonus?" Katz asked.

The SAC had made it clear to him she *would* bonus this year.

"It's an OSHA requirement," Katz said. "The division, hell, the FBI could be embarrassed," Katz continued.

"Yes sir," Chris said.

Finally, Katz thought.

"Where do we stand on the case? Three murders now? Has Victim Witness been notified?" Katz asked.

"Two murders occurred, and there has been an attempted home invasion. We're trying to tie them together," Chris said.

Chris's obtuseness annoyed Katz. This was why he had cultivated the reputation of staying on top of the troops. It was the only way to get anything done in this organization.

"If you say so. Bring me up to speed," Katz said.

Chris did, up through last night's incident. Katz grew more and more perturbed as the narrative went on.

"So, what I am hearing is you are only assuming this is a civil rights violation. You cannot link anything to these cops, but you're going full bore on them anyway. You are embarrassing us in front of Seminolacola and now the state. And I can't believe you let an agent who can't even finish some computer-based training keep a prominent case," Katz said.

Laying down the law was quite satisfying, Katz thought.

"And another thing, isn't this the agent I told you to get rid of? The one on leave without pay for a year? Why is he still here even?" Katz asked.

Chris seemed to be unwilling to look him in the eye.

"This is on you, Chris. This is why you have to stay on the troops. If you had terminated him, we wouldn't be in this position."

"Boss, we need some manpower out here. Records will be coming in and we need to go through them fast. If we can't substantiate the allegation, we can close it down. Give me some help and we'll wrap it up quicker than shit."

An idea swam in ASAC Katz's consciousness but he couldn't grab it. "I suppose you want a financial analyst too. I'm not going to pay for it. Get your money from HQ," Katz said.

As Chris responded, the idea pushed its way in. Katz had never run an office special. He could get this mess designated an office special and run the shit out of it. How about that for his SAC application package? He wished Chris would shut up, his yammering distracted him from his planning.

"It's not like I'm asking for a major case designation or an office special or anything," Chris said.

"I'm declaring this an office special," Katz said. "We need manpower and resources. There is probable cause to believe there has been an egregious violation of the civil rights of, of . . . ah . . . ."

"Jimmy Tank Gubbs."

"The victim. I can clearly see the direct link to the murders and the home invasion, which from now on we'll refer to as an attempted murder of three people, including a child. I think we need ten agents and two financial analysts. How many computers have you got? Never mind, order enough for all the task-force officers. Be sure to call up to HQ and get us some funding. I'll call the SAC."

"Yes sir."

"Get everybody together."

What a stroke of luck, Katz thought. With a little bit more, like arrests, maybe even a dismantlement, this could make him SAC before the year was out. The death penalty angle was great. Activist involvement and everything. Maybe he could get Denver. It wasn't so damn hot in Denver.

Rob worked frantically at his desk to get organized. Al was talking Army with Steve. Rob expected to get called in to brief the ASAC any minute. He decided to use notes. As he double checked his facts, he thanked God he was in a suit.

"Everyone up front," Chris announced.

ASAC Katz waited for them. He had male pattern baldness, a narrow face and a thin frame with pot belly who's shape reminded Rob of half of a bowling ball. He rested his hands on his waist thumbs pointing down, and studiously avoided making eye contact with Rob.

"Alphonzo, this is ASAC Katz. Everyone, please pay attention to the ASAC," Chris said.

"Thank you, Chris. The SAC wanted me to tell you she thinks you are all doing a phenomenal job on this case. I don't have to tell you the FBI takes civil rights violations seriously. Chris and I are in the process of getting more agents and resources en route to the RA. Also, we are in the process of getting this designated an office special. For those of you that have never worked one, you'll get to see how the FBI handles a serious matter.

"Accordingly, there will be some changes. To enhance on-site supervision, I'll be staying. There is no word yet if Headquarters is going to designate an Inspector. Chris will continue to run the RA and handle administrative matters while Kay —"

Leo could not keep a straight face and snorted to cover up his laughter, with minimal success. He morphed it into a cough.

"Kay will take over the case agent duties," Katz finished.

Rob felt like he had been punched in the solar plexus. He peeked around expecting to see shocked faces, but instead, everyone showed expressions of studied indifference.

"My phone ringing?" Leo asked no one in particular, heading to his cube.

"Lawson," Katz said, "pass your notes to Kay. Kay, get up to speed. I want an executive case brief in an hour. I'll be in Chris's office."

ASAC Katz nodded to Chris and returned to Chris's office. Chris shrugged and followed along.

Kay winked at Rob and relocated to her cube as if she did not have a care in the world.

Rob's phone went off. He had a text from Leo.

"Meet at the 'buck in 5," it said.

"Boss, sir," Kay sang out cheerfully, "I need a latte. You all want anything from Starbucks?"

"Let's go Roberto," Steve said from Rob's elbow, startling him. "You too, Alphonzo. It is time for the 'bucks." Steve hurried them out the back door.

Within minutes the group filled a table in the farthest corner as they could find in the coffee shop.

"So fuck the Asshole," Leo started off.

"But Kay . . . ." Rob said, pointing at her.

"Don't worry, Rob," she said. "You're the case agent. I do Counterintelligence. OSI at Eglin or NCIS at the Air Station do my heavy lifting. I haven't run a criminal case since San Antonio."

Leo leaned back. "I called Hoss. He's on his way. Rob, where do we go from here?"

"Oh. I . . . what about the ASAC?"

"Rob, didn't you hear Leo?" Steve asked in his quiet measured way.

"ASACs come and ASACs go. Field agents are forever," Kay said.

"Oh," Rob said. "Okay, then. I think there are three major issues: linking D. Randall and Wee Willie to the murders and last night, and linking them to Jimmy Tank. For the first, we need phones and for the second, we need money. We follow the money, right? So let's do the bank records as they come in. D. Randall can maybe hide a financial transaction, but I bet Jimmy Tank sure as hell couldn't. Third, why did they go through this goat rope in the first place? What was the point?"

"Perhaps we will find out when they are interviewed," Steve said.

Hoss and Shalonda arrived. Shalonda went to order and they made room for Hoss.

"Hey y'all. We hear ASAC Asshole is in town. Man, you breed 'em that way or what?" Hoss asked, slapping down a file folder.

"All your bigshots are superhip, are they, Hoss?" Kay asked.

"You know it. Don't think nothing of it Robbie; they ain't pulling you from a case, you ain't trying hard enough."

"What's in the folder?" Leo asked.

"Shalonda will tell it, she found it," Hoss said, smiling.

Shalonda brought over her large milky iced drink.

"Hey, you guys know Alphonzo Jemison from FDLE?" Rob asked.

"Sure, sure. That thing, the international thing?" Hoss asked.

"Yup," Al said.

"Shalonda, before your time. We'll have to tell you about it over adult beverages," Hoss said as they shook hands all around.

"So, what's in the folder?" Leo asked again.

"You all like to follow the money? It's what you do?" Hoss said.

"What's in the folder, Hoss?"

Hoss grinned.

"For God's sake, Hoss," Shalonda said, with an eye-roll. "You all know we've been looking at D. Randall now and again? I knows a friend and her brother got roughed up on a beef with D. Randall some time ago. She a realtor. She's been working on D. Randall on her own and she done figured out a lot of the real estate D. Randall is attached to. He don't own anything in his own name, but the companies and such. There's a lot in there."

"No kidding," Leo said, sounding impressed.

"Really?" Rob asked. As the white-collar agent in the RA, he had the most experience with this end of an investigation. There could be rich vein of gold running through their file.

"Great," Kay said, "Let's divide up the work. Rob, what needs to be done?"

"Why don't we start with last night? Hoss?" Rob said.

"We are carrying it as an attempt burglary and nobody has questioned it yet. We got all the traps out, but nothing has come up local vis-à-vis a shooter. Hospitals in the tristate are all negative for unexplained gunshots and no reported buckshot wounds at all. We're querying surrounding departments for IDs on similar MOs. We got twenty-four hour now on the Reverend Nettles's house manned by picked officers and I talked all of the vics into staying there today," Hoss said.

"About all we do have is the description of the revolver the suspect had," Shalonda said. "How big it was. It occurs to me Baxter was killed with a thirty caliber, like a nine, .38 or .357. No brass. Could be related. Oh, and we ripped her phone. I'll send the results," Shalonda said.

She tilted her head down to work her own phone and started tapping.

"Next," Rob said, "we need to link Jimmy Tank and D. Randall. I'll start with the financials. I'll run to the bank and serve them and get started there. Alphonzo, you want to come with me?"

"Sure thing. Hoss, can you pull inter-car chats from the SPD server for the two of them?" Al asked.

"Shit, I wish I'd have thought of that," Hoss said, tapping a note into his phone.

"I think the second thing we should concentrate on is the link between the decedents and the officers," Rob said. "Lastly, I think we should start tailing Wee Willie. Who wants to do what?"

"Me and Steve will take Wee Willie," Leo said.

"I'll take the phone records as they come in," Kay said.

"I'm about ready for a look at them there phone records. Can I help?" Hoss asked.

"I'll pitch in with the tail," Shalonda said.

"You are very welcome," Steve said. "Does Willie know you?"

"Nope," Shalonda said with a shake of her head, "we never met. And my car is new to the department, too. An Enclave we got in a seizure."

"Let's get on it then," Rob said.

"I'll need a summary of results for the ASAC at noon. Rob?" Kay said.

"I'll get one together and get it to you by 11:45."

Chris watched ASAC Katz, behind Chris's desk, inspect his grooming. Cuticles, fingernails, a dig for eye jam.

"Boss, don't you think we should have discussed removing Rob from his case before you announced it?" Chris asked.

"I don't see why. He is clearly too much of a lightweight for this." Katz adjusted the stapler. "Besides, he needs to get started on other things."

"Sir, he —"

"Do you really believe I should have kept him on as case agent? May I remind you he has done about nothing while all his witnesses were killed? And how about the perception issue?"

"What perception issue?"

Katz let his hands fall to the desk. They landed on their palms and made a loud slapping sound.

"The perception he was sleeping with the prostitute?" Katz said. "You know when this gets up to Headquarters, people will go ahead and assume he was."

Finding the idea absurd, Chris could not even think of anything to say in response.

"He could have killed her because she was carrying his baby," Katz continued. "The seventh floor will certainly believe she was. Perception is reality at Headquarters. Chris, we need to distance ourselves from this mess. This Lawson can't be allowed to pull me down. I want you to call the police and have them check to see if she was pregnant. It could have been Lawson's child."

Katz nodded slightly as he brushed at a small stain on his French cuff.

D. Randall was on midnights and should have slept until two, but a low-grade headache and cotton mouth kept him in bed staring at the ceiling. What had gone down at the Simmons residence made him profoundly unhappy with Officer Washington Jefferson. Said officer refusing to answer his phone only added to D. Randall's dissatisfaction.

D. Randall swung his feet out and parked them on the floor. He rested his elbows on his knees and propped up his head with his hands. He grabbed bunches of hair and rocked gently. He knew what he wanted, but he knew he shouldn't.

He pushed himself onto his bare feet and padded into the kitchen. He told himself he only needed a beer. He twisted the cap off a cold bottle and quaffed a third of it. He drank some more at his worn kitchen table and didn't think about the glass jar behind the coffee at all, well, only for a moment or two.

After a few of those moments he told himself he was worried the pills might be gone. Maybe Cessy, the Cleaning Spic, helped herself or maybe a user had broken in or something. He thought he might check on them. Just to make sure.

Once in the freezer he reached around the can of coffee. He felt the cold glass and knew they were still there. His little voice told him everything was cool, he could leave it and go, and even as he agreed he pulled the jar out. He noted the lid was askew. He opened it, just to reset it, to check, and everything seemed all copacetic. He stood there a minute, examining the jar.

Then he helped him himself to two pills, washed down with beer.

D. Randall put the jar away. He carried the beer back to his bedroom and sipped at it as he lay on the mussed bedcovers, his head propped up by the pillows. The knot in his chest started to loosen. He breathed easier. The beer tasted first-rate.

Things were spinning out of control. He thought about the different ways he could get away from a situation that was becoming a leaky bag of shit. He thought about the Mobile shooters, but he didn't know too much about them and they didn't know anything about him, by design.

EvaJo was gone, Little Chloe was gone. Jimmy Tank was gone and that hadn't cost him a thing. The only one still around who knew anything about his involvement at the working level was Wee Willie. D. Randall calmed down even more.

Only Wee Willie.

The knot in D. Randall's chest came undone and his eyes grew heavy. He thought of the only person who knew and drifted off to sleep with a smile on his face.

The bank occupied several floors of an all-glass office building close enough to walk to, but Rob and Alphonzo had driven anyway. They waited in a conference room on the fourth floor painted and wallpapered in muted browns and tans. Complementing watercolor seascapes featuring the sugary sand dunes and sea grasses of the Emerald Coast hung on the walls. They were able to see the Gulf through floor to ceiling windows. Rob lost himself for a moment in the deep blue water, until his phone buzzed.

"How r u? R u tired?" Melissa texted.

"ok how are you?" Rob sent back.

His phone rang.

"I'm scared, Rob. They're making us stay here with the Reverend. They said it was a robbery, but we don't have anything. Why would they rob us?" she asked in a small shaky voice.

Rob felt terrible he could not be with her. He wanted to tell her what he thought. This was not a burglary. It was murder for hire, and she had been the target. But he knew there was nothing to gain by disclosing what was probably going on. It would only cause panic and make the situation worse. If he went with the burglary story, he'd likely be lying. On the other hand, he needed her calm, safe, controllable and in one place.

"Rob, are you there?"

"Yes, Mel, I'm here," Rob said. "I think it was a pair of drug addicts trying to grab your TV to trade for Crystal uptown. Just to be sure, we would like you to stay put. The police still there?"

"Uh, let me check . . . yeah, they're here. But Rob, why did those men follow me?"

Smart, he thought.

"Pride, I bet," he said. "Once you beat them, they couldn't let it go for pride's sake."

He hoped she would buy it.

"Do you think so?"

She sounded uncertain.

"Sure I do," he said, owning the lie. "Let's face it, you're not very big and you are very hot. What man can stand the thought of you whipping his ass? One minute they were on top and the next you had embarrassed the hell out of them. I bet they were completely on automatic pilot when they ran after you."

"Really?"

Rob could hear as Jules screamed for her in the background.

"I have to go, Rob. When can you come by?"

"Soon."

"Call me."

"Yes, honey, really," Rob said into the dead phone.

Alphonzo reclined in one of the leather seats. The backrest propped up his head and tilted his ranch low.

"Man, you must got it for her bad," Alphonzo said from underneath the brim.

How embarrassing, Rob thought.

"How do you mean?" he asked.

"You were smooth as silk, bro. Even I started believing you. You known her long?"

"No."

"Must be killing you to be here and not with her."

"Yes, it is," he said.

"Don't worry, we'll get 'em. This got the ass-clown tag big time. I agree with you though, it's connected."

"So where would you start?"

Mary Alice brought in a manila folder that dashed Rob's hopes due to how thin it was. Rob and the blonde Mary Alice, sexy in a Nordic way for a forty-seven-year-old, were on a first name basis from previous investigations.

"This is it, Rob," she said, handing him the folder.

"Anything?" Rob asked.

"Just flip past the top two pages and start reading."

The $75,000.00 check jumped out at him.

"What?" Al asked.

Rob laid the folder on the conference table. He spun the records so Al had a better angle to see and kept his finger on the entry.

"You got to be kidding," Al said.

"Look at the date," Rob said.

"When was the murder?"

"Two weeks before."

They had it. Rob could tell Al thought so, too.

"Mary Alice, can we get a front and back copy? Also, we'll need the actual check," Rod said.

Mary Alice leered at Rob as she clasped her hands behind her and arched her back slightly, emphasizing her not inconsiderable bosom. She released her arch with a sigh.

"Back trouble. You know, for all the work I do for you, the least you could do is buy me a drink," she said.

Thankfully, Rob did not have to say anything. A white man in his mid-twenties wearing a sweater and skinny jeans showing his sockless ankles walked in. He handed the copy to Mary Alice. She passed it to the investigators.

"Here you go, boys. Rob, why don't I call you when the check comes in? Let me know if can provide any other services," Mary Alice said as she left.

An embarrassed Rob thought he should say something, but Al saved him.

"When it rains, it pours. What you got there?" Al asked.

"Check copy, front and back," Rob said. "Bingo. It's made out to Jimmy Tank and drawn on an account of a check cashing place. And here's the address. The place is local."

"I got a hunch. Let's see if it's in the real estate file. We'll also think of another way to come back to this here bank so we can see your groupie again."

"Wonderful," Rob said.

Wee Willie felt better after a Big Breakfast and Sausage McMuffin with Egg. He drank his coffee with his ass going numb from the plastic seat. He paid little attention to the young mothers ignoring their ankle biters crawling around in PlayPlace.

Wee Willie did study the surrounding countryside. The restaurant had been built on the southwest corner of the intersection of County Road 71 and Fire Lane Road; nothing but trees and fields all around. Willie wanted to run away into the forest, never to be seen again.

His cell rang. He knew who it was without looking.

Willie wanted to throw it out and drive away. He wanted to drive to Marathon where he had a great time fishing that one time. He picked it up.

"Yo," he said.

"Yo, bro. Last night a bitch, huh?" D. Randall asked.

He sounded sympathetic, which was not regular.

"Yeah, man. It was a bitch," Willie said carefully.

He never knew what would set D. Randall off and what wouldn't.

"Yeah. Hey, let's talk, man. We got to fix this. Come on up to the ranch. We can hang at the fish camp. We can do this," D. Randall said.

Shit, the fish camp, Willie thought. Not good.

"Got to work, bro. Let's meet for supper at the mall," Willie said.

"Call in sick man. Get on up here," D. Randall said without anger or haste. "Come on up. We can fix this."

"No can do. Hey, Lyra just walked in. I'll call you," Willie said, hanging up.

He contemplated the forest outside and sipped his coffee.

Rob and Al were in Rob's car. Rob prepared the updates for the ASAC briefing on his phone.

"Next time we're taking my car. I don't think your air conditioning is all that," Al said.

"It's definitely hot," Rob said.

"FBI, can I help you?" Kay said.

"It's Rob. I have what everybody has been doing. Do you want it for the ASAC?"

"Email it?"

"Sending it now."

"I have something for you." She sounded pleased. "Shalonda sent over Baxter's phone information. Nothing from what numbers we know about, but one number jumped out at us. It was a recent addition to the call activity. The calls lasted longer than her everyday business calls, starting from only a few days ago. I asked Pam for another subpoena and got registrant information."

"Wonderful, Kay. Who does it come back to?"

"It's a prepay phone linked to a prepay credit card, so the subscriber information is iffy."

"Got the account number?"

"And card vendor, but get this, the name on the phone is Bill Jefferson."

"You're kidding!"

"Nope. Oh, there's the ASAC. Lemme go."

"Interesting development?" Al asked.

"Listen to this," Rob said. "The throw away phone calling Baxter was registered to a 'Bill Jefferson.'" Rob felt a surge of melancholy in his chest as he thought about Chloe.

Al's brows went up. "No shit?"

"Can you believe it?"

Rob felt himself grinning.

"Say man," Al said, "you going to call Wee Willie in?"

Rob nodded. "Soon. I want to get the financials in and correlate the information. I also want the records on the pre-pay card to see if there is something firm there, like automatic payments from one of his personal accounts or something."

"Uh-huh." Al wiped the sweat off his forehead. "Say, the AC in this thing work? I'm hot as hell. How about 'afore we go to lunch, we switch to my car? She's as cold as ice."

Master drove into the heat of the day in his Tiburon. He worked his cell phone with one hand and the wheel with the other. No one he knew good was up yet and as he ran by the usual corners, none of the entrepreneurs were out driving the economy.

He thought of Secrets. He picked up Government Boulevard and headed out of town. Master meandered, driving with the flow of traffic.

Bitch can fuck himself if he wasn't fast enough, Master thought, regarding Sniper.

So can Willie. He hadn't heard from the cheap bastard. Master wondered if Willie was going to stiff them the half he owed them. It had been so fast, they had not had time to plan it good, like to do the business. Double true since she was like white bread people and shit, Master thought.

He crossed the city line. Government shrank to two lanes of patched asphalt. Before Grand Bay he made two quick left turns.

He rode up on a cinderblock building with a shingled roof and dirt parking lot. The faded red residential door was the only visible way in or out. There were no windows. A sign with "Secrets" written in black cursive on a light background had been baked bland. The bullet holes didn't make anything better. There were three cars parked by the door.

He slid out from behind the wheel and stood there, surveying the red dirt lot and the trees shielding the building from the main road. Row upon row of new soybeans surrounded the property. He really didn't like Secrets. Mylon did though. It was like his office or some shit. Master pushed past the door.

He waited a moment to adjust to the dim lighting. He nodded at the black bartender, a young guy in a black shirt and slacks. He was in charge of a chewed up, dinged up bar of darkly varnished pine running the length of a wall.

One customer had parked himself smack in the middle of it; a white dude in a red flannel shirt with cutoff sleeves, a dirty Deere cap and a no-shit red neck. The redneck's world had devolved down to the highball in front of him. He showed no signs of noticing the saggy-titted black stoner who danced listlessly to some House on the center stage.

Master wondered what was up with the redneck, but no one else appeared to care, so he let it be.

Mylon was at the far end of the bar with his back to the wall. A watchful muscled-up brother stood a respectful distance away.

Ethiopians be fat next to his dog Mylon. Mylon wore sunglasses and dreds and a wispy little goatee. His head pivoted toward Master who could see his reflection in the mirrored Ray-Bans. Mylon raised his hand, heavy with gold rings and a highball. The glass held reddish liquid with fruit in it.

"Master, what bring you out here man?" Mylon whispered, before he downed a mouse-sized taste.

Master could barely hear him.

The bartender asked for his order.

"Red Stripe," Master said, sitting down next to Mylon. "Came to say 'what up,' you know?"

Mylon smirked and then laughed. His laugh sounded like a deflating tire.

The bartender placed a bottle in front of Master and waited a moment. When nobody said anything, he drifted away. Master drank before speaking.

"So what up brah?" Master said.

"The customary. Not like you, my man," Mylon said.

"It's cool."

"Cool you all missed last night. Cool your new partner got hit. Cool." Mylon drew out the final "cool."

"You hear shit out here," Master said.

"Oh, yeah. Some real shit. Like you need like ampicillin and shit."

Master's frustration bubbled up on him. "Yeah, I need some shit like that, but the bitch only wants white. You happen to have any?"

"Ho, what you saying, bitch? I don't do that no more. You knows that. Man, take your bitch to the Family Parenthood he needs fixing."

Mylon got up and reached around the bar. He placed a small glassine baggie with white powder in it near Master. Master recognized it as twenty-dollar bag of cocaine.

"I's just asking, you know," Master said as he stood and reached into his pocket.

"Say man, beer's on me as you had a bad night," Mylon said. He jutted out his chin at the bag. "I know you got business today, so don't think you need to stay around here jerkin' the gherkin, know what I'm saying? Go on, it be chilly."

Master pocketed the baggie. "Thanks, yo," Master said.

"Not for nothing yo, but you know you hit a man of God?"

"Wasn't the intent, Mylon."

"Shit, I knows that, but my advice be stay away from the Reverend Nettles. Sometimes it like God be on his team and shit," Mylon said, back in his seat, reaching for his cocktail.

Al waited for Rob in his Malibu in the Resident Agency parking lot. They were eating lunch when Rob had been called back in. Al passed on the opportunity to listen to some more upscale, high-priced federal ass chewing. This Rob boy was all right, Al thought, even though so much of a type. The car idled and blew cold air. A bracket anchored Al's Smartphone to the windshield with a heavy duty suction cup. He punched in a number.

"Lieutenant Joel Cheeks," said a deep voice coming from the phone.

"Ass Cheeks, what you doing?" Al said, smiling.

"Watching the paint peel instead of writing a DHS grant. How about you, Stumpy? You got some high-speed, low-drag state case rolling or what?"

"Now you know better than that. I'm on FDLE welfare, just saying."

"Heh heh. I'm sure there be some payback in that. You ain't feeling guilty or anything?"

"Hell no! Getting paid back for more than a few extra hours, know what I'm saying? You still drilling?"

"Yeah, actually getting ready to wrap it up. I got my twenty by a longshot. We both earned some of that shit."

"Yeah, you know it. Say, I need to talk to Wee Willie Washington."

"You gonna lock him up?" Joel asked.

Al wondered if the news about the investigation had gotten to Joel by now.

"Nah, a few questions only, back to that drug thing, you know?"

"Yeah, sure. Say man, you do what you got to do with that motherfucker. Don't worry about me."

Joel's comment told Al volumes. Bless you, Joel, Al thought.

"What do you need me to do?" Joel asked.

"If you text him to coffee, will he show up?"

"Shit yeah."

"Do it, please. I want him sitting in the Mason's Bar up by I-10, sweating, like yesterday."

"I'm on it, bro."

"Thanks man."

Rob stood tall in Chris's office. Chris sat in one of the armchairs, gazing at the floor, forearms resting on thighs and hands clasped between his knees. He wore a white shirt, his striped tie loose around his neck, an empty holster on his leather belt.

"Furthermore," ASAC Katz continued "I am not pleased at your conduct in this case. Especially in the time since I relieved you as case agent. My expectations were you would stay in the office and, as a first order of business, finish your Blood Borne Pathogens course. Yet, you have not done so. Even if the excitement of the moment overcame your judgement, and you had to do something on the case, you should have been spending your time organizing the records and entering them into the case file."

"Not reading them?" Chris said to the floor.

The ASAC fixed what he must have thought was a fierce stare on Chris.

The ASAC's ass-chewing was as underwhelming as the figure he cut. Kathryn could teach him a thing or two, Rob thought.

Rob realized the ASAC was scrutinizing him. He only caught the end of his question.

". . . listening to me?" ASAC Katz shouted.

"I'm sorry, sir?" Rob said.

"That's it! That's it! Karas! Get your man out of here. I am sick of this. You run one heck of a squad."

ASAC Katz threw his hands up and stepped around Chris's desk, stopping in front of Chris. He crossed his arms and frowned.

"Get back to work Lawson," Chris said, continuing his investigation of the floor.

"Yes sir."

Rob thought Katz was treating Chris particularly shitty today. Rob concluded the best course of action in the present situation was to stay in the RA, so he slipped out and made for the stairs to tell Al. ASAC Katz had a point. He did need to finish his mandatory training and the incoming records did need a thorough examination.

Rob pushed out the doors into the bright, bright heat. Al had parked on the curb with the passenger side of his white Chevy opposite the building. The Chevy could be nothing other than an unmarked police car, down to the rims. They were black utilitarian steel with small silver hub caps in the middle. The passenger window rolled down.

"Come with me to an interview," Al said.

Rob rested his forearms on the sill put on the best aw-shucks grin he could muster.

"I've got to run back up there," Rob said. "I'm only here to let you know I've been grounded. You can come up, if you want to."

"ASAC chew on you some?"

"You know it. You want to call it a day?"

"Say man, he's had his fill. He won't be interested in you for an hour or more. We can run up and back 'afore he sees you're gone. Come on, get in."

Rob thought about it.

"I see you thinking about it," Al said. "Get on in here and think about it. If you ain't getting yelled at, you ain't working hard enough. You can text your girl."

Rob felt a grin spread across his face. He jumped in the car.

Jules continued whining. He whined about being bored and about the heat. He whined about the food and about not going to school. The available games were poopy and TV was boring. Melissa wanted to whine herself. She had gone to her condo and gotten fresh t-shirts and shorts for them, as well as her computer. They were alone at the Nettles house. The police were still there, in a marked cruiser idling in front at the curb. All the members of the Nettles family were out. Even Lila was running an errand.

"Mommy, I'm hungry," Jules said.

"You're not hungry, Jules. You just ate half a Dominos."

Melissa searched the internet for Rob. Lots of Robert Lawsons, but none of them were him. Nothing on LinkedIn or Facebook or anywhere else, either.

"I want dessert," Jules whined.

Then Melissa searched for Kathryn. She turned up in some professional posts and a Facebook page with high privacy settings. She did not feel like digging in too deep there.

She thought about texting Rob, or even calling, but she didn't want to bother him at work. She thought about posting, but didn't want to worry anyone. She thought maybe Rob would catch those men soon and then she could let everyone know how it turned out in the end right from the beginning.

"I want to go outside," Jules whined.

And really, she asked herself, how bad could it be if her only protection was in a car by the curb?

"You want to go outside? So do I," Melissa said.

If she hadn't heard anything, they must be caught or on the run, Melissa told herself. She wasn't going to sit in here and sweat. She wasn't going to raise Jules as a prisoner.

"I want to go to the pool. Do you want to go to the pool?" Melissa asked.

Jules squealed with joy as she led him by the hand, out the back door of the Nettles's house.

Traffic had picked up. Al used speed to exploit spaces in traffic to get around slower vehicles and position himself at the lights.

To ignore his being jolted forward, backward, and sideways, Rob concentrated on emails and thought about texting Melissa. He could not come up with something reasonable to say. He thought about Kathryn. It would be decent to check in with her and maybe even see her before she went back to Indianapolis, but he had nothing to say to her either. It was as if signing the papers had closed the book.

"We here," Al said, parking.

This Mason Bar was one location of a chain of fake saloons. The exterior included a Hollywood western type storefront of a spray-on material shaped and colored to mimic weathered wood, and included the expected swinging doors. Once out of the car, Al put on a brown linen jacket with western detailing.

"Hey, Al, what's this about?" Rob asked.

"Stand by. Keep your shit together when you see him. Try to look tough," Al said, pushing through the swinging doors and scanning the bar.

Al tensed up and focused. He stepped out at the quick-march, weaving through tables. Rob had to run to catch up.

"Wee Willie? That you? Man, you remember me! I'm Al! Alphonzo Jemison!" Al said to a black man sitting in front of a large mason jar full of Coke with lots of ice.

Both were sweating.

Rob broke out into a sweat himself at the sight of Wee Willie Washington Jefferson, a named subject in his investigation, a police officer, presumed armed, implicated in recent violent acts, sitting there in front of him. And they were going to talk to this man! Without an Operations Plan! Wee Willie wore a gray t-shirt and blue cotton sweatpants cut down to shorts. He had not shaved in a while, leaving a ratty mess, not fashionable bristle.

A square table jammed Wee Willie onto one of two perpendicular benches. The backs of bench were five-foot-high partitions of fake distressed wood. The panels met at one corner, forming an alcove. Single seats were positioned at the other two sides of the table. Al flopped into one as he deftly drew his blue steel semiautomatic pistol from under his jacket. He had palmed his badge in his left hand and showed it surreptitiously to Wee Willie.

"Hands on the table. I'm FDLE and my heat is pointed at your guts. This is my associate Special Agent Lawson of the FBI."

"Hey," Willie said, pointing a finger at Rob, "you said you was a reporter from the Miami Herald."

"And he's giving me one chance to work this case before taking over and seeing to it you get what Jimmy Tank got," Al said, almost at a whisper.

Rob sat across from Wee Willie. He wondered if he should draw his weapon too. He wondered if he came off as tough enough.

"Hands on the table Willie or I'll cut you in half, no hard feelings. Last warning," Al said.

Wee Willie did as he was told, trying hard not to cry, Rob thought.

"I ain't saying nothing," Wee Willie said.

"Listen then. We got the Jimmy Tank check. We got little Chloe Baxter's cell phone. We got your credit card and your cell phone, the one you been using this little bit. We got you. We got you for Baxter and we got you for Jimmy Tank," Al said, barely loud enough to be heard.

"Hi, y'all. Can I get you anything?" A bubbly, chubby, white college-aged girl in a yellow tank top with a Hello Kitty tattoo on her shoulder asked.

"Yeah, Miss, my friend and I will have sweet tea. Can we get some chips and salsa, and maybe some of those mozzarella sticks, you know, the fried ones?" Al said.

"Sure thang. I'll be back in a minute."

Rob did not like sweet tea; too much sugar, but, now that it had come up, his mouth was as dry as Southern California.

"I'm here to give you one chance and that's because I remember when you were a good cop. I know D. Randall is behind all this. You work with us and we'll work with you. Otherwise, you go down for the girl for sure."

"Fuck you," Wee Willie said without much energy. He reached for his drink.

"No, fuck you fat boy. Rob, tell him where he stands," Al said.

"Murder under the color of law, officer," Rob said, trying hard not to drop the ball, "is a federal capital offense. Even if you get life, there is no parole. Ever."

Rob congratulated himself for the last little flourish.

Willie snorted and choked a little on his Coke.

"No parole, even if you don't get the needle. Ever. It's D. Randall or you my friend," Al said. "What's it gonna be? You in the federal pen in general population with the life expectancy of a no-see-um, or you dealing and D. Randall carrying the load?"

Willie's hand shook so bad some Coke sloshed out of his jar.

"He should carry the load. You know the Mother fucker got most of the money," Al said.

Rob had caught up. He put aside thoughts of how much trouble he was in and how he was going to get out of it. He leaned in and touched Willie's hand. Willie remained fixated on the table where the drink had spilled.

"You used to be a good cop. Don't let D. Randall take that away from you," Rob said.

Wee Willie met Rob's gaze.

Rob had the impression Wee Willie was measuring his sincerity.

Wee Willie nodded curtly. "I want a free ride," he said.

"You know the lawyers will work out the specifics Willie. I ain't got to tell you that. I will tell you this. Time is of the essence, my man. We got work to do tonight and you got to help us do it," Al said.

"Jesus Christ," Willie muttered as he put his elbows on the table and rested his face in his hands. "First the fish camp and now this."

"Where's your gun, Willie?" Al asked softly.

"Hey y'all," their waitress said, delivering jars of tea. A young, thin Hispanic man slipped around her and put down two platters of salsa with chips and the fried cheese before disappearing. "You ready to order?" She asked.

Rob deferred to Al.

"Say baby, can we get all this to go?" Al said, without taking his eyes off Willie.

No clouds provided relief from the bright and blazing sun this fine hot afternoon. Kathryn, behind big sunglasses and wearing an AEO patterned sleeveless wrap romper in purple, brown and white, walked on the thick grass down the row of plaques at Aumale Memorial Gardens. She held a lace trimmed handkerchief with "KEL" embroidered in the corner balled up in her hand. She stopped at the plaque engraved for Benjamin Kelleher Lawson, noting the pitifully short time between the dates of life and death did not add up to even three years.

She felt the tears coming so she concentrated on the field of deep green grass and the row of mahogany trees. An African-American caretaker used a loud weed trimmer a few rows away. There were no visible debris from the recent hurricane. Her little red rental baked on the narrow cemetery road. She was taking it to the airport. She wanted to visit Ben before flying back to Indianapolis.

She made a sound of equal parts of sadness, discontent and contempt. She had been so out of it after Ben's death. She had depended on Rob to take care of the details. All he had managed for the stone was Ben's name, dates and "loving son."

How utilitarian. That was Rob for you. All he was about was numbers in a column. And here she stood, sweating, about to drive away in her sub-compact to sit in an economy seat, going home without a son or husband.

Had it come to this?

She wanted to connect with Rob before her flight but remembered routine social media was not available. She couldn't pull him up on Instagram or check his Facebook or even read his tweets – agents didn't do social media. To connect with him, she would have to call him. Maybe he would answer a text.

Yes, she thought, this is what it had come to.

She could not hold it back any longer. She cried into her handkerchief, sobbing for her son and her marriage, and wondering how all this was going to play online.

D. Randall padded around his dark trailer in white skivvies, drinking a beer to cure his headache. The curtains were closed to help the air conditioning fight the heat. He had been dressing for work when he spoke to Wee Willie earlier. Their conversation had knocked him off track, stopping him the underwear level and giving him his headache, which multiple beers had not yet mitigated.

Fuck it, he thought. He called in and told the duty sergeant he'd be out sick.

D. Randall finished his beer and opened a fresh one. He stood swaying in the kitchen when his cell phone rang.

It was Wee Willie.

"Hey," D. Randall said.

"Yo. Say, man, why you want me up at the ranch?" Wee Willie asked.

D. Randall wasn't one-hundred percent sure he was going to kill Willie up there.

"Yeah man, come on up and let's talk things out. We got to make sure we're on top of things. Let's meet up there now. I called in sick," D. Randall said.

"What things is that?" Willie asked.

"You know, things."

Although come to think of it, it was getting easier for D. Randall to see himself shooting the fat bastard and cutting him up for the 'gators. He would junk Willie's car in Mobile.

"Like how we're going to handle the Simmons woman thing from last night?" Willie asked.

"Yeah man, like that," D. Randall replied.

It wouldn't be the first time he done fed 'gators up there, D. Randall thought.

"I don't want to handle her like you handled EvaJo," Willie said.

"You don't want? Who the fuck are you now, the god dammed Chief?" D. Randall yelled. "Listen Willie, don't sweat her none," he continued in a speaking voice. "EvaJo wasn't long for this earth anyway. Jimmy Tank did what he could for her but she was a psychonaut, man. You know that. What's gotten into you anyways?"

"That Jimmy Tank thing. You know what D. Randall? Why'd we even do that shit? I don't see as it resolved nothing and here we are still dealing with it. What did we do that for?"

An idea punched through his headache and blew up in D. Randall's head. The wooden way Willie sounded, the questions when he never asked questions before, his wanting to talk; the motherfucker was recording the call.

D. Randall about pushed his thumb through the touch screen cutting Wee Willie off. He threw the phone onto a recliner as if it had become too hot to hold.

ASAC Katz liked Kay's look. He considered it as she briefed him up on the investigation. She wasn't too fat or too thin, and she was short enough to make him feel tall. He liked her face, something about her hazel irises and her lively, innate optimism overcoming the effect of her big nose. Katz decided if he had not had a policy of complete faithfulness to Amelia Ann, he'd sleep with her. Katz found it more pleasurable to think about sleeping with Kay than listen to her droning on about a case.

". . . records are coming in and they're voluminous. I recommend a financial analyst full time, TDY'd to here," Kay said.

Now that caught his attention. There were damn few financial analysts in the field office. Their supervisor would scream and the agents whose cases they were working on now would bitch. Besides, a TDY cost money.

"Don't we have any special agent accountants around here?" Katz asked.

"Yup. He's out on surveillance. Unless you're also counting Rob. He's one, but you pulled him off the case," Kay said.

He did not appreciate snark from his agents. He produced his best supervisory scowl, one he'd practiced to be sure those around him knew when he was displeased.

Kay smiled sweetly. Katz would have considered it insubordinate, but there was the chance she wanted to sleep with him. A man in his position had to be careful. One could never tell what a disappointed woman would do, considering him and Amelia Ann and all.

"I'll tell you what Kay, after he finishes his online Blood Borne Pathogens, he can get back to work on those financial records. It's an inspection item, you know. Linked directly to the SAC's bonus," Katz said.

"The financials?"

"No, the Blood Borne Pathogen training."

He hoped a little smugness seeped into his comments. He hated to show emotion, but he needed to let the troops know who was in charge from time to time.

"Oh, he's not doing Virtual Academy. He's busy," Kay said.

"Pardon me? What is he doing?"

"Making a consensual with Wee Willie in the conference room."

"WHAT!" Katz jumped to his feet. "Karas! Get in here! Did you know about this?"

Katz only had one thing on his mind now: blood, the real kind. He stormed out from around the desk and blew by Kay on his way out of the office.

"God dammit Karas! Where the hell are you?"

Chris trotted up from the back.

"Know about what?" Chris asked, stopping in front of Katz.

"Did you know they picked up that dirty cop? Did you authorize it? You're in violation of about fifty policies, Karas. I'll have your ass for this," Katz said through clenched teeth.

The Cat will pounce, Katz thought.

Lawson stepped into the hall from the conference room.

"I don't know what you're smiling about, Agent Lawson, but you are going to regret —" Katz began.

"Yessir," Rob said, interrupting him. "Wee Willie turned himself in," he said to Chris.

The insubordinate son of a bitch! Katz thought.

"Boss, he's given us a boatload of stuff and agreed to a call," Rob continued. "We just finished with D. Randall."

"You have violated about ten serious policies," Katz fumed, "including recording a US citizen without permission."

"I filled out the emergency authority. I'll get it to Chris in a minute, sir," Rob said.

"That is inappropriate and you know it. I'm right here and I have delegate authority. You are being, being, inappropriate. Karas, this is on you."

"What did Wee Willie give you, Rob?" Chris asked.

"He gave us the push-in robbers from last night and some shooter jobs they've done for him and D. Randall in the past, including locations," Rob said.

"Local?" Chris asked.

"Mobile."

"Get on the horn and get paper as soon as you can. I want – what are the names?"

"Master Blaster and Sniper Stefon."

"Oh for God's . . . Sniper? That sounds like there is some military training there. Anything to worry about?"

"Possibly," Rob said. "Willie puts him as having been in the Army."

"Better call Hoss," Chis said.

"Karas, I'm —" Katz said.

"And I'm calling the SAC," Chris said, facing Katz.

A stunned Katz didn't see any merit to any position Karas could articulate, but still. Perhaps it would be better to back off a little. As Katz was about to say something, Karas stepped around him on the way to his office. Katz thought he better hurry before Karas did something rash and hustled on after him, ignoring Lawson.

D. Randall obeyed his powerful instinct to change locations. He had dressed, packed fast and pointed his pickup inland for a night at the ranch. Adrenaline had cleared his head and gotten him moving. The setting sun moved lower than the visor and burned into his left eye. His mind raced as his truck crawled in the after-work traffic. He thought and thought and decided he needed some help. He started dialing his cell phone.

The call from Chris Karas in Seminolacola had brought Special Agent in Charge Maebh Rowe to her feet behind her desk on the fourth floor of the Tallahassee Field Office headquarters building, a new structure as sleek and lithe as the SAC herself. Congressman Miller had cancelled tomorrow's visit, leaving her free to drive by and order Katz back to headquarters city for "coverage," thus separating the children.

Maebh wore black knit pants and a matching matador jacket with a lime blouse. She had to have her clothes traumatically tailored for fit and even added belt loops so she could wear her pistol instead of carrying it in a purse. She kept her curly red hair short, barely down to her neck, to simplify cleaning up after her workouts.

Deeply into training for an upcoming triathlon, the SAC had two-a-days scheduled for most of the work week, before and after her long office days. A drive out to Seminolacola would mar her workout schedule. Workouts did not really interfere with her home life, seeing as she didn't have one.

She thought about her marriage. It had been before the FBI. She and her husband had worked in Hartford, she as an insurance executive and he in private banking. He had always known her sights were set on the FBI. He always assured her of his support. He even got high scores in the spouse interview during her application process.

It wasn't until she had her orders to the FBI Academy at Quantico, Virginia, the problems started. He became distant, sending infrequent emails and texts. Their conversations on the phone became shorter, and then stopped. It wasn't until after she reported to her first office in Milwaukee, leaving him in Connecticut, she learned the bastard had been fucking his favorite Cross-Fit instructor the whole time.

Then there had been the long-term relationship with another agent in the management program. They had stuck it out, using up some of the important years in her life, keeping the relationship going. Sometimes they served together and sometimes not. She was on a year-long TDY in Pakistan when he ended it, claiming the separations were hard on him. A month later the bastard married a twenty-six-year-old intelligence analyst, already pregnant with their child.

At least she had met Peter. She could see his full head of straight gray hair, his smiling round face and his barrel chest. She liked his altitude; he could look right at her when she wore heels. Peter favored polo shirts, slacks and a Rolex as he ran his fast food empire, fourteen restaurants from Mobile to Jax. He was safely divorced and his kids were at university or on their way, and atypically civilized toward her.

Her direct line rang. Caller ID made it Saint Peter himself. She felt a nervous flip at the top of her stomach as she reached for the receiver.

"I was thinking about you," she said, sitting down and spinning to enjoy her view out the windows.

"Well I hope it was about how happy you'll be joining me on the boat for the weekend. By the way girl, how *are* you?" Peter asked.

Maebh liked his voice, a mature baritone with a wide range he used fully even in routine conversation.

"Just peachy and ready for a weekend afloat," Maebh said, twirling the cord around her forefinger, feeling the slightest bit giddy.

"Well that's great. We'll drive a bit and drop the hook. How about we leave Friday after work, and I plan for steaks on the grill?"

"Sure, sounds delicious."

"Say, Maebh honey." He pronounced it May-AV-uh. "You know I would never interfere in your work —"

Her smile froze in place.

"Seeing how real important it is to our country and all, but a little bird done told me you all was taking a swing at a good old boy over in the western parts by the name of D. Randall."

"Oh? Who might have told you that?" she asked.

"Now, Maebh honey, don't make me into a snitch, but I will tell you this, that old boy does some fine police work out there. It can be rough in those parts and it takes tough men to take care," Peter said.

Men? Maebh asked herself.

"Now see here, Maebh, honey, can't you make a call and let D. Randall come in with this little shyster he knows and maybe answer any questions you all may have? It sure would be a better use of taxpayer resources to nip this in the bud before it gets all, like, uh . . ."

Maebh's mouth straightened into a grim line. She swung back and stood up again. "Like before we make a federal case out of it?" she asked, lightly and with a touch a humor she did not feel.

"Why sure. Can I pass on you'll do it? Make the call?"

Maebh stopped breathing. She wondered what kind of leverage this D. Randall had on the Bastard Grant, his new identifier in her life, to get him to make this call.

"Well, I'll tell you what, Peter," she said, forcing herself to relax. "I need to call out there anyway as I don't recognize the name. I'll find out what's going on and see what I can do."

"I would really appreciate that."

"On Friday, will you have the marinated Black Angus with you again?"

"I sure will."

"Can we anchor out again at the same place, by Saint George?"

"We sure can."

"Well, why don't I call you as soon as I figure out which way is up, oh, here's Selamta waving at me from the door," Maebh lied, "I've got to go."

"Okay baby girl, I'll see you soon."

"Bye-bye," she said, hanging up quickly. She hated that "baby girl" shit.

Maebh rested her fingertips on her desk and bowed her head. Peter Grant had been okay. She was even willing to tolerate being called "baby girl." But there would be no call, no vacuumed packed steaks out by Saint George Island and no post Bureau life of companionship and ease financed by billions and billions served.

Maebh decided to drive on out to Seminolacola in the morning and shove this case up that cop's ass. She would go to work on Grant next. She had been briefed the subject was "connected." She would make the RA find out how connected.

Her intercom buzzed.

"Congressman Miller's office called. The meeting is back on for tomorrow, but they want to move it to 8:30. What should I tell them?" Selamta asked.

Shit! Maebh thought. She pressed the button.

"Can you explain the Rule of Threes, Selamta?" Maebh said.

"Sure can. What about the Congressman?" Selamta asked.

Why is she the one who has to give in all the time? She was the fucking boss. The ball should bounce *her* way. At least occasionally. She pressed the button.

"Yes, 8:30 is fine. Can you call Chris back and tell him he has to live with Katz by himself a while longer?"

Josiah Waller had wrapped it up and was about to walk out of his cramped office for the night when he heard Pam talking to a man.

He adjusted his blue bow tie and buttoned the jacket of his seersucker suit. He heard them speaking but could not make out what they were saying. He ran his fingers through his hair and thought about stepping out into the hall to see if he could hear more. Not too risky. Most of the staff had left for the day. Not that any of them had stopped in to say "good night."

With his one hand flat on his stomach and the other dangling, he peeked down the hallway, alert for anyone who might still be around. He had not made any friends yet. They were a little standoffish here, Josiah thought. One casualty of their lack of collegiality was his inability to pick up on office gossip. He felt out in the cold and now he wanted to hear a little of what Pam was cooking in her hot little kitchen. He crept closer to her office.

". . . the paper on the shooters," he heard Pam say.

"Thanks," the man said, "to confirm, I'm going to send these to Mobile now."

"Do it. Let's get them interviewed. This thing is messy and I want to clean it up."

"You got it."

At first, Josiah could not place the voice. Then it hit him. It was Robert Lawson from the FBI; the agent poking around Jimmy Tank.

"For now, we have him. They are still at the office, but we want to hold him. He's cooperating. Do you have —"

"Hi Josiah!"

"Whaah!" Josiah shouted as he jumped, unable to stop himself. He spun around to see Andrea the happy intern smiling up at him.

She was all long dark hair and brilliant white teeth. Even her eyes smiled. She wore a tight clingy pink blouse stretched by her ample breasts, a short tight black skirt and lots of bracelets on each wrist.

"Whatcha doing?" she asked.

"Getting ready to go. I wanted to check in with Pam to see if I could lend a hand."

"I *know*! She has been working super hard. The FBI has been in and out all *day*! Isn't it exciting? Do you know anything about it?"

"Nope," Josiah said.

He thought he heard Pam's door latch.

"But I did hear there were homicides involved," he said.

"Homicides? Wow. Have you prosecuted a lot of homicides?"

"I sure did. You know what? I was thinking of a drink on the way home. Why don't we go together? I'll tell you about them."

"I feel like I can't really *technically* drink, like, in a bar yet, but . . . ."

"Oh, I wouldn't worry about that," he said to the girl, thinking he was old enough to be her father, "after all, I'm an assistant US attorney. What could happen?"

"Cool! I'll get my purse."

Now this was a benefit of divorce his lawyer never mentioned, he thought, watching her rock her skirt down the hall.

Melissa had Jules in front of Nick Jr. so she could concentrate on cooking up some grilled chicken, wild rice and broccoli for herself, Jules, Lila and the Nettles clan. She wanted to be back in her own kitchen where she knew where everything was. She wondered if she should ask the officers if they wanted some. Her cell rang.

"I've got warrants for the robbers," Rob said as soon as she picked up.

"Thank God," she said.

"We know where they are, and I hope we'll have them by tomorrow. You and Jules will be able to go on home after."

"Oh, that would be great." Melissa did not like the way her comment came out. "Not that the Reverend and Keisha aren't great, but I really want to go home." When Robert didn't fill the space, she grasped for something to say. "I'm cooking. Want to come for dinner? Everyone will be here." Then she realized she invited him to someone else's house. She probably sounded like an idiot, she thought. With her elbow on her hip, she dropped her face into her hand.

"Just parking. There, finished. No, I really want to and all, but I'll be here all night probably. Sorry. Hey . . . I miss you."

"I miss you, too," Melissa said, meaning it.

"Um, do you think we could take Jules to Buccaneer Bob's when we get this behind us?"

She wanted to laugh and cry at the same time and resisted both. "Yes, I think we can do Buccaneer Bob's. It would be super."

In the small brown Florida Cracker with the long driveway near where St. Stephen's meets up with Dr. Martin Luther King, Tiesha Kenshaw did her best to keep her four-year-old quiet. Master had just ended an argument with Stefon by demanding silence, so television was out of the question. Ra'aed was whining because he missed Daniel Tiger. Tiesha hated to do it, but she shut him up with another Snickers.

She also hated Master now. At first, she didn't know what he was. He charmed her and showered her and Ra'aed gifts and slithered in like a snake. Once he was in, his work became clear and she was fucked.

Now this.

His friend was bleeding on her sheets and blankets and stinking up the place. She thought the po-lice would not be long in coming. She needed to get herself and Ra'aed out. Master and the shot boy had plenty of guns. She knew she and Ra'aed wouldn't be worth shit when the cops come and the shooting started. She started to cry because it did not seem likely both of them would get out of there safely.

The doorbell rang.

Tiesha pulled herself together. "You hush now, and I'll get you on the TV soon," she said to her son as she went to the door.

She cracked the door and saw a thin, swaying old lady with matted hair wearing a ratty old sweater and a black dress stained with white powder. She held a bottle in a brown bag.

"See here, Leroy in there?" she asked, slurring her words.

"Ain't no Leroy in here. Go on now; no reason to be here," Tiesha muttered.

The old lady garbled some words and fell forward against the door. Tiesha let go of the door and caught her. The old lady regained her balance gawked around Tiesha.

"Leroy?" she called out, "You be here?"

"What the fuck is going on?" Master ran up from the back. "Shut the motherfucking door!"

"She looking for Leroy. He the mans renting me my house," Tiesha said.

"I don't care if she's looking for Barry-fucking-Obama," Master said. He pushed the old lady. "Get off my property, bitch!" he shouted, slamming the door.

The old lady dropped her bottle, landed on her back and shouted something unintelligible as she rolled onto her side. After pulling her legs up under her and somehow getting upright, she staggered to her bottle, picking it up. She made her slow shaky way down the drive.

She wobbled to the next block where she crossed the street. As she passed out of sight of the Florida Cracker, the standard three bedroom, one bath model she had noted, her walking steadied. She picked up the pace and made some turns until she waited by an intersection.

The light turned red. A faded green Toyota minivan with smoked windows stopped curbside. The side door slid open and the old lady gracefully jumped inside, over the legs of a large white man, muscular and in his early thirties, who shut the door. The middle seats had been removed and he sat on the floor facing backwards. The van started moving.

"She there?" the white man asked.

"Yeah, her and Ra'aed. There and scared shitless. Pass my bag," she said, joining him on the floor with her back to the van wall.

He handed her a backpack. She put it in her lap and worked the zipper. She put her bottle inside. Good bottles were hard to come by. She slid her wig off and jammed it in as well. She removed some clips from her hair and shook her head. Long straight black tresses cascaded down.

"They in there?" the driver asked. He was older, about forty-five or so, black, with an afro and expedition quality sunglasses.

"Yeah. I saw Master Blaster. The other one was definitely shot. I could smell it from the door. He's going septic, I think."

She went to work on her face with makeup-removing wipes. She quickly morphed into a South Asian woman of some twenty-six-years, thin-faced with high cheekbones and a pointy chin. She slipped off her sweater and shimmied out of the skirt.

"Better," Investigative Specialist Neysa Singh said with a sigh. After disrobing, her slim figure sported a white tank top and navy tennis shorts. "Do we have time to write it up?"

"No," Tavis Holly, the driver, rumbled. "They need us now. You'll have to brief the team in prime time, you know what I'm saying?"

Tavis was her surveillance team leader and had taken her under his wing since her transfer from the Salt Lake City field office.

"You up for that?" he continued "I know you are. Hey, when are you going to hang with Andy here?"

Neysa considered Andy. She thought he was cute and he did have a great body, being tall and broad shouldered. He had blond hair, blond stubble he blushed under a bit right now, and a few piercings. Today he wore a red plaid shirt with the sleeves roughly cut off, exposing a Celtic Warrior armband tat on his left arm and knee length tan cargo pocket shorts. She also knew him to be somewhat nice and a little shy.

"You waiting for an act of congress? Maybe a subpoena or something?" Tavis said.

"I'm waiting for *Andy* to ask!" she said, laughing.

"I texted you two nights ago," Andy said.

"Which was about as vague as could be. I didn't even know what you were talking about. I went ahead and ignored. My sisters and I don't do those texts and we don't hook up. You want me to come out? Say it straight, you know what I'm saying? You could say it now, you know."

Tavis laughed. "What'd I tell you, boy? That's old school right there," he said.

Andy blushed again. They stopped at a light. Neysa caught him checking her and when caught, he quickly developed an attentiveness to the nothing happening outside his window.

Neysa thought she might have been too hard on him, tender male ego and all. Maybe, she thought, but it was true. Amma didn't approve of text dates for her and her sisters and Neysa hardly had an issue with it.

Neysa started writing notes for the briefing. They drove in silence and as they were pulling up to the field office, her phone rang. She fished it out of her bag and saw Andy's contact info on the screen.

"Andy!" she said.

"Hi Neysa," Andy said, as if she had answered it, ringtone still sounding off. "I was wondering if you wanted to get something to eat with me after the briefing tonight?"

Tavis roared with laughter, even hitting the steering wheel with the heel of his hand, as he drove through the gate into the parking lot of the Mobile Field Office of the FBI.

"Everyone, listen up. Listen up!" Radley Lewis shouted.

Radley, the FBI Mobile SWAT Senior Team Leader, hated to shout and rarely did, so this got everyone's attention.

Radley liked to make believe he was back home in Hawaii. As soon as he cleared probation years ago he lost his suits, except for a classic blue single breasted hanging in his cube for court, in favor of his Hawaiian shirts, washed out blue jeans and boat shoes.

Rad was a large and rubbery pokiki, six-foot tall and almost portly; with thinning black hair and a nascent double chin. But his build disguised a constitution of immense strength and endurance.

Rad spoke in the SWAT room with its green linoleum tile, white boards in front and metal gear lockers painted dark green along the walls. SWAT team members called out for tonight's job and his mates off the Violent Crime squad used black folding chairs to sit around gray plastic folding tables.

"Here's what we got," Rad briefed, "warrants on two shooters who did the job the other day in Seminolacola. It went down as an attempted push-in robbery. In reality, they were hitting a witness and her kid. They're witnesses in some civil rights/public corruption bullshit out of Seminolacola RA. The subjects are persons of interest in that case, and they're linked to other murders. Definitely known shooters.

"We got a cooperating witness putting them in Gorgas in a one-story single family on a bigger than average lot. So far, our only information is pistols; however, one of the unsubs has the street name of 'Sniper Stefon.' Anybody got anything on a Sniper Stefon?"

"Nah, Rad. Never heard of the guy. Any intel on his being an actual trained sniper?" one of Rad's own snipers asked.

"Nothing yet. Nobody's heard of him that we know of. The other guy is Master Blaster," Rad said.

"Oh yeah, a shooter for the black gangs and some freelance. Outside of a few bits here and there, no one can touch him. He uses Frances O'Connor," another agent said, naming a respected criminal defense lawyer in town.

"Yeah, yeah, I remember. Knows how to keep his mouth shut, that one," Rad said. "Anyways, we got surveillance out there now."

"Hey, we're in the house, y'all," Tavis said, walking in with his team.

Tavis wore a black t-shirt under denim overalls around his broad girth. Sunglasses dangled off a lanyard draped around his neck. Rad knew Andy and he couldn't remember the name of the new girl. She was petite with notably long black hair. She seemed very young to Rad.

"How'd it go?" Rad asked.

"Neysa got all the way in," Tavis said.

"You go, girl," Rad said. "What can you tell us?"

Rad saw she held a pad and her hands shook.

"I put eyes on Tiesha Kenshaw but not Ra'aed, her four-year-old son. I did hear a child calling out for his mother. It sounded about the right age. I did see Master Blaster but did not see the other unsub. Kenshaw was scared and Master was angry. He had a pistol in his right hand, but mostly hid it behind her back," Neysa said, addressing the room.

"You didn't say nothing about that. You see that, you get out," Tavis boomed.

"I didn't exactly stay, Tavis."

"Was he pointing the pistol at her or hiding it from you?" Rad asked.

"More like hiding it," Neysa said.

"Go on."

"Kenshaw is larger than her pictures, like five-one, one-fifty. The house, it's a Florida Cracker, standard for the neighborhood, with no visible alteration to the usual floor plan, living room in front of the kitchen on the left and one bedroom on the right; the other two bedrooms and the full bath in the back."

"How do you know what the usual floor plan is?" Rad asked.

"I studied the real estate in the area after I got here," Neysa said.

"Not bad."

"Thanks," she said with a radiant smile.

"Anything else?"

"Only odor. I could smell the other one. In the briefing they said he was possibly shot? I'd say definitely. Probably no medical assistance either, based on the smell."

Sharp as she was, Rad decided to risk a judgment question in front of God and everybody.

"Neysa, I'd like to call out Tiesha and Ra'aed before we go in. If I can get her to answer the phone, do you think she will come out?" he asked.

She scrunched up her nose and squinted in concentration.

"Yes," she said.

"That was definitive. What makes you think so?"

"Sir —"

The SWAT operators interrupted her.

"You're a 'sir' now, Radley!"

"Promoted by a rookie!"

"Don't get a swelled head, Rad. Zoomers say 'sir' to old men all the time. When are you KMA?"

"All right, all right," Rad said to the group. "Neysa, you were saying?"

It shook Neysa up a little, but she collected herself fast.

"Raadddleyyyy," she said, gazing around the room. "I searched the address and the vehicles registered there, the Sentra. Everything is in Tiesha's name. Utilities too. That's her house and her life. I don't think she's with, I mean *with* Master Blaster. She's like a real mom and I don't see a subject like the one we have fitting in with that kind of responsible life. I think she'll do anything to keep Ra'aed safe. That's why I think she will come out."

"We've got a job for you in the FBI," Rad said. "Well done. Tavis, you guys going back out?"

"We got another team watching. These kids got to go get some eats and some rest. They been out since before dawn on a Counterintelligence thing."

"We'll need them all night."

"I got that, but I'll need your supervisor to call mine, you know the dance, man."

Rad wrote it down so he wouldn't forget. "You got it. Listen up," he said to the operators, "John, you got enough for tape drills. Let's practice sticks on both sides of the front door and I'll make the call from there.

"Practice both ways: our getting her and the boy out and our going in and covering them. Run it until you're comfortable before knocking off. See you all here by zero-two-hundred for a zero-four-thirty hit. Alibis?"

Rad gave the crew a last chance for questions, comments or complaints. He visually checked with everyone in a slow scan: the SWAT operators, squad members, and the surveillance crew. The room was silent. Rad nodded with satisfaction.

"I'm off to deal with the bosses," he said. "Ready, break!"

Long after sunset, Alphonzo parked Wee Willie in the care of two FBI special agents at their safe house, a bungalow about a block in from the bay FDLE had not known about. Until now, that is. He sighed as he cranked up the air conditioning and headed north, to go around the bay to his home. Traffic had long since thinned out. He pushed the Chevy's accelerator to the floor.

Only a few blinking navigational lights punctured the inky darkness of the bay. As he topped the river bridge, with its clearance designed to facilitate commercial traffic and sailboats, he saw lightning far out on the Gulf. The sharp flashes were over the horizon. He did not hear the thunder.

He called Eartha and let her know it was him pulling onto their concrete driveway. This practice of theirs, his calling as he drove up late at night, had begun the very next day after one night when she almost blew his head off with his Colt .45 Gold Cup, early in their marriage. He had taught her to shoot it the weekend before.

He locked the door and set the alarm. She waited for him in the kitchen. She wore her silk pajamas, a button front short sleeved shirt and shorts, not a garment traditionally associated with evening fun in the lexicon of their relationship. Two of those itty bitty glasses and a bottle of amaretto were in front of her.

"You look beat," he said.

"One of these and off to bed," she replied.

They had their drink. Al listened to the news of the day. Then Eartha stood up.

"Come to bed," she said, holding out her hand.

"One call baby, and I'm there," Al said.

"Only one, Alphonzo Jemison. Just the one."

"Just one, baby."

"Just the one."

Al watched closely as she went, enjoying the sight. Eartha could make a burlap sack sexy. He picked up his phone.

"Call Lowery King," he ordered.

"Yeah?" Hoss came on the line sounding newly roused from sleep.

"Hoss? This is Al Jemison from FDLE. How you?"

"Woke up," Hoss said.

"Yeah, sorry. Hey, you were talking about that Mullur thing, the German tourist thing, the last time we worked together?"

"Yeah, that's it." Hoss yawned.

"That was something."

"Wakes me up sometimes. Sorry about your leg."

"Yeah, shit happens. Thanks. Hey, what do you think about me getting a state warrant for the D man?"

"The D guy? The one we all are working? You getting ahead of yourself?"

"Not really. Why do you think that?"

"We got nothing on him yet."

Alphonzo chewed on Hoss's comment for a moment. A thought struck him.

"You get a call today?" Al asked.

Hoss did not come back with anything right away. "Maybe not the one you're asking about," Hoss finally said.

"Somebody came in. You were supposed to get a call."

"Somebody?"

"Somebody near and dear and I don't want to say, you know what I'm saying?"

Al listened to dead air again.

"You mean . . . ," he finally said.

"Yup," Al said. "Listen here, my bosses are chafing for results. They're —"

"Fucking federal mother FUCKERS!"

Well, Al thought, Hoss was wide awake now; probably most of the neighborhood, too.

"Yeah," Al said. "Hey, my bosses are chafing for results and are afraid the Bu will take a month of Sundays poking around and linking things to terrorism and shit."

"You think they were hiding it from me?"

"Oh hell no. I think they got busy is all. Anyways, my bosses, they want to call up the US Attorney himself and clear it at the highest levels. They want a warrant and the turds off the street and are willing to use all sorts of political capital to get it. Can you be ready for an interagency state arrest by midday, assuming FDLE gets SPD agreement?"

"You got the evidence?"

"Yup."

"Your bosses call my bosses?"

"First thing in the am."

"Then I say yes. The climate here has turned very against the D man. We can use our CP and shit. We'll be ready. You get the paper," Hoss said.

"Done," Al said around a yawn of his own.

"I won't say anything until I hear from you. I don't want him to run."

"Well, can you move fast once you hear?"

"Yeah," Hoss said. "I'll stage it up with some friends, you know what I mean?"

"Cool."

Hoss hung up.

Al yawned again as he pushed himself away from the table. He needed sleep. Tomorrow was setting up to be a big day.

Thursday

Tiesha Kenshaw had had a very bad night. She "slept" in a bed not her own. She missed the queen-size she and her baby daddy had bought before he cut.

She sighed.

Really, she bought it. Her baby daddy was there at the store with her, but no more. He cut after Ra'aed was born.

Tiesha tried to rest on a cheap double in the front room. She wore a long t-shirt with a statement on the front: "Stacked Like That Cause I'm Black Like That." She couldn't sleep. After the incident at the door, Master had smacked her around a bit.

She had gotten Ra'aed to sleep but the stress churned up her insides. Curious about the time, she checked her phone.

It rang! She answered it quickly to silence her ringtone.

"Who this?" she whispered.

"Tiesha Kenshaw?" a white man asked.

"Yeah. Who this?"

"Hi Ms. Kenshaw. My name is Rad Lewis and I'm a Special Agent with the FBI."

Oh shit, she thought; oh shit, oh shit, oh shit.

"Ms. Kenshaw?"

"Yes?"

"Are Master Blaster and Sniper Stefon in there?"

"Yes."

"Good. What is the chance you and Ra'aed can come to the door without waking them?"

First she asked herself how they knew Ra'aed's name. Fear suddenly gripped her good. She did not know what Master would do if she tried to leave. She did not think she could get out without waking him. She needed a minute to think.

"Tiesha? Can you come to the door with your boy? We need to get you out right now."

Shit, shit, shit, Tiesha thought.

"Ma'am, now is the time. Are you safe right now?"

"Um, I don't know," Tiesha said.

"Okay. Is he near you?"

"No, he be in the room in the back."

"Ra'aed is in the back?"

"No, he in the bed."

"Near you?"

"Yeah, with me."

"Okay, good. Pick him up and bring him to the door now, please."

Oh God, Tiesha thought. Oh God, Master will kill them if they move.

"Tiesha, we have to start this. Can you come to the door?"

"I don't know," she said.

The man did not say anything. Tiesha felt the anxiety thing and could not catch her breath. She was certain she and Ra'aed were going to die.

"Tiesha, are you still there?" the man asked.

"Yeah."

"What room are you in?"

"The front bedroom. Master gots my room."

Now she was having diarrhea of the fucking mouth. Stop running on, she told herself.

"Okay, can you and Ra'aed get in a closet?" the man asked.

"I don't know."

"Can we play hide and seek? Can you and Ra'aed hide under the bed?"

"Yeah, we can do that."

She felt okay to move now. She softly skooched closer to Ra'aed and got on her knees. She lifted him as gently as she could. Tears came but she was able to avoid outright sobbing. She placed Ra'aed on the floor and lay next to him. She wrapped him up in her arms and shimmied herself and Ra'aed under the bed.

"Momma?" Ra'aed said.

"It be 'k honey bear, it all right," she said. "Let's go to sleep."

She lay on her side with Ra'aed next to her in her arms. She realized she'd left her phone on the bed.

She heard the sound of wood slowly splintering, followed by quick, quiet footsteps. Suddenly the bed was lifted up and thrown to the side. A large man landed on the floor next to her. He got his arms around them both. He covered Ra'aed's ears with his hands.

"Cover your ears," he said to Tiesha.

"Wh —"

Bright flash, BANG! Bright flash, BANG!

Ra'aed started screaming. The man held on to them both, hard.

"Room three clear, one in custody!" a man shouted.

"Room two clear, subject in custody!" another man shouted.

Running footsteps.

"Doc up to room two!" someone shouted.

"Wait Doc! Get in here, room one!" The large man yelled. He let them go and stood up. He turned on the light. He wore all green and a vest and a helmet. He had an army rifle. He said something to her, but she couldn't hear him. Her ears were ringing.

"What?" she asked him.

"Ms. Kenshaw, hi, I'm Special Agent Lewis. We were speaking on the phone a moment ago. How is Ra'aed?"

She adjusted her position. She got up to her knees to examine Ra'aed for injury. He jumped up into her arms and continued to scream.

"I think we good," Tiesha said.

"This agent here is our team ADCAP medic. Doc, check 'em out before moving to the back. Subject back there is shot up, but it's historical.

"Two in custody, no injuries," Lewis said into his radio.

Then he called out "who's buying breakfast, *hoaalohas*?"

Melissa found herself in the Nettles kitchen again, whipping up some Bisquick pancakes for the mob. Sunlight streamed in and she could hear the air conditioner's compressor running against the heat. She wore a long t-shirt and shorts, her hair tied in a casual ponytail. She yawned so broadly, she almost missed her ringing cell phone. She ran into the living room and scooped it up off a wooden table done in dark stain. She saw it was Rob, the call making her feel warm inside.

"Hi!" she said.

"Hi, I have some good news," Rob said.

"You got them!"

"Not me, but the Mobile office. Both men are under arrest."

"Oh God, that's great. Can I go back home?"

"Yup, you can go on about your business."

"Should I tell the officers out front?"

"Yeah, but I bet they're gone already."

Melissa skipped to the front.

"Yeah, no car. There was one there last night."

"There you go."

"Can we celebrate?" Melissa asked in a rush, then apprehensive she might have put too much out there.

"I'd love to, but not yet," Rob said. "The case is kicking into high gear now. We've got tons of communications records and financials to review and it looks like there is another person we have to pick up."

"Who is that?"

"It seems like two people conspired to set up Jimmy Tank, and this other guy might have been part of it, too."

"Oh? Who is it?"

"Can't say, but we think the leader is still out there."

Fear grabbed Melissa again.

"Would he come to get Jules and me?" she asked.

"I don't think so. I wouldn't worry about that. He's working big issues having nothing to do with you. Getting ready to run, no doubt."

"So I can get back to my life?"

"Sure can, as long as I'm still in it."

She smiled and shifted her weight from one foot to the other.

"If you behave," she said.

"We'll have to discuss exactly what you mean by 'behave.' I have to run. I'll call you later."

The team had grown as temporary assignees filed in from around the division. They crammed into the conference room in the RA, filling the seats and standing behind those sitting. Chris stood up front and ASAC Katz beside, and slightly behind, him. They were both in suits, while the majority of the group wore casual clothes.

Rob had worked overnight, gone home and, after a nap, cleaned up and put on a suit, as he expected to be back and forth between Wee Willie and the courthouse. Alphonzo was there next to him, dressed much as he had been the day before. Rob detected a new flavor of tension between Chris and the ASAC. Chris was clearly out front, and started the meeting.

Chris cleared his throat. "I spoke to the SAC several times yesterday and she asked me to thank you for the great job you are doing on the case," he said. "She wishes she could come out, and possibly will do so soon, but today she had a meeting with Congressman Miller. She especially thanks those of you who have had to leave home and join the team. Rob, where are we?"

"At about four forty-five this morning, Mobile SWAT successfully executed our arrest warrants on two unsubs, also known as Master Blaster and Sniper Stefon, without incident. Mobile will handle the interviews, although Hoss is on his way."

"I didn't authorize that," Katz interrupted.

"Rob?" Chris said, ignoring Katz.

"We're working a civil rights violation where a known felon with a history of capital crimes allegedly was put to death for a murder he didn't commit. A problem area in the original arrest was the arresting officers. Yesterday, one of them came forward and started cooperating. He gave us the unsubs.

"The investigation so far has revealed questionable payments to the executed individual from accounts controlled by another one of the subject officers through cut-outs. Today we'll put together link analysis to show communications patterns. We have identified three additional potential homicides which we hope to connect to the case. I'm predicting we will be able to connect the other subject to the whole scheme. Surveillance is out but so far can't lay eyes on him."

"Where did he put his head down last night?" Chris asked.

"We couldn't find him yesterday. He was supposed to work evenings, but never showed up. Kay has gone out. She can find people," Rob said.

"I didn't authorize that," ASAC Katz said.

"Everyone, it's time to make the case. Let's make it," Chris said. "We all know what we're doing? Then let's get to work. Rob, see you a minute?"

Rob and Alphonzo stayed as the room emptied.

"Rob, you personally focus on the financials. If you're not at court, work the books. Al, can I get you anything?" Chris asked.

Rob watched as Katz did not even bother to hide his gloating.

"Naw, Boss, I'm good. I'll partner up with Rob here," Al said.

Rob's morale ticked up a bit.

"Did you major in accounting?" Katz asked.

"Nope. Women's Studies," Al said.

Katz froze.

Chris sighed. He nodded slightly, dismissing them.

"Women's Studies? Really?" Rob asked as they got in line for break room coffee.

"Hell no. Criminal Justice. Let's blow this joint and get coffee on the way to the courthouse," Al said.

"The courthouse?"

"Pam is ready to give us a warrant for D. Randall."

"Pam? She wants the results of the Mobile interviews. Besides, she won't be in until nine."

"She thought about it some and changed her mind, and she's waiting for us in her office. She wants a skinny caramel macchiato. Did I hear you say you were buying?"

D. Randall drove in with the morning rush after a breakfast of tranks and beers. He couldn't sleep at the ranch. The little ole missus of the dead Matthew Simmons preyed on his mind and kept him awake. She stood out like a nail needing to be beaten in. Like a nail on a dock you step on with your bare feet. Like unfinished business.

He wore the clothes from the previous night and had not shaved or otherwise cleaned up. He decided to swing by and take care of the Simmons woman before getting ahold of Wee Willie. Time to find out what game Willie was into these days. For that, he would need privacy. On the off chance Wee Willie had been caught by internal affairs, D. Randall had borrowed a maroon Jeep Cherokee from a neighbor up river, a reliable old rust bucket perfect for running around under the radar.

Too bad he couldn't use the Corvette. It was long gone, via a scrap place in Alabama.

Kay had gotten into the case in a big way. She organized the sub files and reviewed almost all the initial incoming records, made all the assignments and briefed up the bosses. She was ready for a day out of the office after flying the keyboard for hours. She liked surveillance in general and was lucky more often than not during such operations.

First, she enjoyed dressing for the op. Today she wore her hair back, a charming pair of peach Hugo Boss sunglasses and a super large Auburn t-shirt. She needed it large because of her Bureau issue ballistic vest. On the belt of her lightweight green Columbia expedition pants she wore her weapon, three extra magazines, two pair of handcuffs and a one-handed folding knife with a notably thick blade. Her husband called it a 'BFK.' She may be working spies now, but she had a plethora of gang experience from her first office agent time.

Speaking of spies, she was behind in all her matters. She'd blown off meetings with colleagues at the Naval Criminal Investigative Service and the matter at AMS Tech was getting hot. She did not want to miss that opportunity, she thought. In the meantime, they were searching for D. Randall.

"So if I were D. Randall, where would I go?" she asked out loud, although she was alone in the car.

Two of Rob's witnesses were dead, three if you counted Jimmy Tank, but let's not, Kay thought, because Jimmy Tank's situation wasn't normal. She tapped the steering wheel in time to some Beyoncé playing on the good-time radio.

All ladies, she thought.

"What if he won't leave it alone?" Kay said out loud.

She parked and dug through her notebook until she had the address of the Simmons condo. Kay put her Bu ride in gear.

D. Randall had some time to think, as traffic kept him inching along and Wee Willie would not be up yet.

D. Randall did not really want to kill the Simmons woman. He couldn't remember her first name. She was merely unfinished business. He remembered her as a strong little thing. Not too much in the chest department, but a worthy diversion should an opportunity come up. Maybe he should swing by her place, he thought. Like to kill time before catching up with Wee Willie. Then he laughed.

"Kill time? Get it?" he asked no one in particular.

Kay glided into a great spot on a street running diagonally southwest from the front of the Simmons home. She had a small pair of binoculars, only the rising sun washed them out at this time in the morning.

Can't have everything, she thought.

The sun would be higher in a minute anyway. She put the car in park.

D. Randall got tired of fighting traffic so he exited I-295 and weaved his way south. He thought of checking to see if Wee Willie's car was parked at the station, but then he thought that motherfucker would not get anywhere near work this early. He headed south and east. D. Randall felt for his off-duty pistol to check if he had it. He felt for a drop gun he'd picked up, an old five round Chief, which he'd already wiped clean.

Kay liked surveillance. She used it as time to work things out. She was thinking about her daughter, wrapping up her sophomore year in high school, who had been quite moody lately, when she caught sight of a middle-aged white man driving a rusted out, mud-spattered, maroon four-door 2000 Jeep Cherokee. She raised her binoculars and saw he had sidewalls and wore wrap around Oakley sunglasses.

He stopped at the curb in front of the Simmons condo. He showed Kay the back of his head while he scrutinized Melissa and Jules's home. Kay kept the glasses on him. His arm casually rested on the steering wheel.

Finally, he rotated his head.

She had him. Adrenaline amped her up. She loved the way she felt when she caught up with a subject.

"All units, the subject is in front of the Simmons residence," she radioed.

D. Randall slowly scanned the area, his head rotating, not too far, enough for a furtive peek around the area, nothing more.

"Too late," Kay said aloud. "I've got you, shithead."

The Jeep started rolling, gradually picking up speed. Kate put her vehicle in gear.

"Northeast on Bayou," Kay said into her radio.

The others let her know they were rushing her way.

Pam had skipped her makeup regimen and wore a simple scoop-necked beige blouse and a brown skirt. Rob and Al were in her office watching her type. A headband kept her red hair pushed back out of her eyes, if not totally under control.

"Washington will have my ass for this, Al," she said.

"You love it, Pam," Al said.

"Rob, now you wouldn't lie, would you? Al is giving it to me straight?" Pam asked.

"Huh?"

"You get this today and you'll execute immediately? The only way I'll survive this is if you guys go out and get him," Pam said.

"We'll get him today, promise," Rob said.

He was way behind on reporting to the Civil Rights Unit at Headquarters and with an ASAC sitting in the local office, right here, he knew he had no authority to represent to a federal prosecutor when they would roll on the warrant. Locking up a cop, no matter how dirty, required loads of "coordination."

"Sent. Let's go," Pam said, jumping out of her chair.

The three of them charged out into the hall and bumped into Josiah Waller. An open file folder absorbed his attention.

"Hey, y'all are in an awful hurry. What's going on?" he asked with the usual forced sincerity.

"Search warrant Josiah. Gotta run," Pam said, charging forward as she made sure her two investigators kept up.

D. Randall noticed the Ford with the older, but still hot, blonde in it as it made a couple of turns off Bayou. Even though she finally went away, her having made three turns with him made him nervous. He dialed Wee Willie and the call went to voicemail. He hung up.

What if the fucker went to Internal Affairs? he asked himself.

Mutt and Jeff, D. Randall's names for the Department's two Internal Affairs detectives, couldn't find their collective backsides with the help of a fudge-packing ass doctor backed up by the Queer Eye crew carrying flashlights, but they could cause trouble. He didn't want them sitting up on his house trailer yet, so just in case he drove down to the beach to hole up in the condo.

His condo building had parking decks and he pulled the Jeep in and grabbed a spot near the center, so it would be less visible from the street or the beach.

Once inside the elevator, he jabbed the button for the seventh floor and jabbed again, this time the second floor. That blonde had hinked him up. There was a balcony off a common room on two. He wanted to check the street before he went up to his place.

He crept up to the railing and checked up and down the street. He almost tossed his cookies when he saw the blonde in front of the salon one block east. She stood next to her Ford talking to a guy he did not recognize but the other woman there, she was Jackie from HR for sure. He knew she hadn't been out on the street in years. Maybe those IA assholes were getting some smarts. He was going to have to call in and get the lay of the land when he got a moment. Now he needed to get to a safe place and start building his defense.

D. Randall rode the elevator to the ground floor. He exited onto the beach. He sweat through his shirt before he walked ten yards. He thought about what Wee Willie could have given Mutt and Jeff. He was not overly concerned. He had gotten out of tighter spots in the past. For now, being lost and making calls was the order of the day.

"Now see here, Robbie," Al said. "There ain't no thing to it. You tell them if y'all don't arrest D. Randall, FDLE will." Al faced him diagonally from the driver's seat with his left arm resting on the steering wheel. They had stopped curbside on Battery Boulevard. Rob sensed Al wanted him fully sold on this idea before they got back to the FBI office.

"I don't know, Al," Rob said, "they aren't going to take it well. Chris is going to have to get out of joint with the ASAC. I don't think I'll have much of a shelf life after this. Besides, there is far more to do. We haven't even identified all of D. Randall's associates."

"Rob, this ain't about associates. It's about dirty cops needing to be cut out of the body police like tumors. I need you —"

Al's phone rang. "Oh shit," Al said, "the boss." Al swiped right. "Yes Mr. Gopher," Al said, "Yes, sir . . . no, we have it . . . not yet . . . just getting a key wit . . . give me a chance to . . .," Al's jaw set. "But sir, this will set back . . . yes sir . . . yes sir. We're on our way."

Al terminated the call. "Well, it's out of our hands now," he said. He centered himself and put his seatbelt on.

"What happened?" Rob asked.

"The Commissioner is calling the SAC. At least it will come from the top down."

"What will?"

"We're arresting D. Randall Hargrove on state charges today. One way or another he's going down."

Chris glared at Rob and Al as they entered the RA. So the fuckaround twins have arrived, Chris thought. He was pretty sure they had colluded to create this state-federal tension point. He couldn't touch Al, but he would deal with Rob later.

Chris had called the team together. There were about twenty-five people present, some in chairs they had rolled out of cubicles and others standing. Some were RA personnel and others were from around the division, sent to Seminolacola to assist in the investigation.

"Where the hell have you two been? Never mind," Chris said.

The situation made him cranky and he didn't care who knew. Not the fuckaround twins and certainly not the ASAC, who stood next to him and would not sit down.

"As I was saying," Chris continued, "here's what we've got: SAC Rowe in communication with the Commissioner of FDLE and the United States Attorney has made the decision to arrest our main subject, D. Randall Hargrove, on multiple charges including violating eighteen USC section two-forty-one. Our two erstwhile princes-of-the-realm have only this minute returned from the US Attorney's Office with our arrest warrants, yes? Gentlemen?"

"Yes, sir," Rob answered.

"Very nice. Leo, bring us up to date."

Leo had been standing. He stepped forward. "This case kicked off with the execution of Jimmy Tank Gubbs, a known felon with a propensity for violence, for killing a local businessman, ostensibly during a robbery. We now have strong reason to believe he either did not actually kill the decedent or if he did, he did so at the direction of two Seminolacola police officers, William "Wee Willie" Washington Jefferson and D. Randall Hargrove. Wee Willie is currently cooperating. Unfortunately, he claims not to have been in on the whys and wherefores of the matter, and, surprise, surprise, puts everything on D. Randall Hargrove. Wee Willie will not be available most of today as he is in conference with his lawyer."

"No shit," Chris heard someone mutter.

"Who said that?" ASAC Katz asked. "Karas, take that name."

In spite of the ASAC stationing himself on Chris's last nerve, he ignored Katz.

"Go ahead Leo," Chris said.

"For those of you that don't know Jim, he's a financial analyst from headquarters city. Jim, can you talk a bit about the financials?" Leo asked.

"Sure." A thin young white man with whiskers and a full head of black hair stood up. He wore a blue Counterterrorism polo and khakis. "The check recovered earlier was drawn on the general account of a check-cashing business in town. With subpoenaed records we were able track the flow of funds and, for a small business, it's quite complicated, with instruments and cash coming in and moving around. We're doing the analysis now, but we did discover the subject has authorities on the account."

"Nothing on the funds coming in?" Chris asked.

"No sir, not yet. Everything is comingled anyway. We'll trace everything in and out. We're working on a six-month window, three before the check and three after. What do you think?"

"Better than good, Jim, thanks. Anything else?"

"Not pertinent to the actual arrest, but this guy is everywhere. I can already see the tentacles."

"Great, Jim, keep it up. Leo?"

"Jenny, you're next. She's an Investigative Analyst working the real estate. Jenny?"

A middle-aged white woman in a gauzy pink short-sleeved blouse and stretch pants stood up. Her thick glasses rested on her nose and her brown bob had the occasional gray strands.

"With the records from Detective Hodges, we were able to locate multiple businesses affiliated with the subject. We have the known bank accounts and are fairly certain there are more. We've already identified four that will need subpoenas for Jim. We may have some aka's as well. Using our list, we found an additional residential property in town titled in a business name affiliated with the subject. It's a beach condo on the Gulf. Leo has the address. Hi, Chris," Jenny said, sitting down.

"Thanks for coming, Jenny," Chris said.

"As far as locations," Leo said, "we're going to recommend hitting both the known house trailer and the beach condo Jenny mentioned at the same time," Leo said. "Kay picked up the subject early this morning in front of the Simmons home. It should be noted Matthew Simmons was the decedent Jimmy Tank Gubbs was executed for. What the subject was doing there is not known at this time, however, there has been the one previous attempt on her life. Kay and the team out there now have tailed him to the condo."

"Get me an arrest plan," Chris said. "Any —"

"It's going to be a SWAT job. Call HM and let him know," Katz said.

Chris had had enough. That was it. He was ready for a public throw down with ASAC Asshole. Chris started to turn to face him when out of the corner of his eye he saw a slight wave from Leo.

"What?" Chris barked.

"Already done sir. HM is on his way," Leo said.

Overtaken by events, Chris thought.

The doorbell rang. Someone activated the electronic lock release. It buzzed. They all wanted to see who was joining the party.

"Howdy, y'all," Hoss said.

Hoss wore whiskers, blue jeans and a department polo tucked in, exposing his pistol and badge.

Recognizing the SWAT issue was dead, Chris asked Hoss to brief up the Mobile arrests.

"Sonny Melvin Johnson," Hoss began, "also known as Master Blaster, has both lawyered up and thrown his associate Andrew P. Clarkson, aka Sniper Stephon, under the proverbial bus. Johnson has stated in the presence of his lawyer Clarkson had taken Johnson captive and held him against his will. He also advised the drugs found at the arrest location were Clarkson's. He offered to testify against Mr. Clarkson in the Baxter murder as Johnson was under the impression they were going to party with the decedent, a known stripper, whore and all-around sex worker, not shoot her in her head. Lastly, he advised he could not recall knowing any Officers of the Law named Washington Jefferson or Hargrove."

"Film at eleven!" someone yelled from the back row.

"Settle down," Chris said. "What did Clarkson have to say?"

"Very little as he was under sedation, allowing our medicinal colleagues to finish fishing the holy buckshot out of his dirty law-breakin' body, same munitions having been introduced therein by a certain country preacher by the name of the Reverend Nettles, who has an interesting interpretation of 'doing unto others.' I expect Clarkson is still under the knife as the medicos mentioned gangrene. Honestly, I believe that is a first for me. Gangrene."

Someone started clapping and the applause spread. Hoss bowed.

"Quite a presentation, Hoss," Chris said.

"Hoss, was Clarkson ever in the Army?" Steven asked.

"One of the Mobile agents called an Army CID contact who could not find a record. I'll put in an official request as soon as I get to the office."

The door buzzed again.

"What the hell is this, a sad sack convention? Hello Chris." Howell 'HM' Trotter burst in, his muscular frame barely contained by an olive drab flight suit. His sidewalls were freshly cut and his flattop was perfect. "Sir," he said to Kratz, with what Chris thought of as a fair amount of sarcasm, although he couldn't say exactly what made the comment sarcastic. "You all got the paper?"

"Sure. You want a brief?" Chris asked.

"What's to brief? We got two dirty cops, one's cooperating, the other requires a daytime arrest. We'll hit two locations. Oh, and I should 'dig my own grave' before I head out or some such bullshit. I read that in the file. Where's the rally point for the Team? They're about twenty minutes behind me."

"We'll use the SPD command post," Hoss said.

Chris thought the situation was getting away from him. The ASAC would surely object.

"Great. Gear up, sunshine, you're with us," HM said to Rob.

"He is NOT!" Katz yelled. "He will stay here and do his Blood Borne Pathogens training. He is off this case."

"Really?" HM said.

Chris wondered how this was going to end.

"Really," Katz said.

HM met the ASAC's stare until Katz looked away. Even so, Chris knew HM would abide by the ASAC's order.

HM moved on. He pointed at Hoss.

"Can we get started? Time's a wasting," HM said.

"Um, yeah." Hoss silently checked with Chris and the others. There were no objections. "Let's go," he said.

The group broke up. Chris let the troops drift away. He waited for the ASAC to say something, but Katz pretended to read a document he found on an unoccupied desk.

Rob made his way to his cube, embarrassed by the exchange between HM and Katz. He did not feel like discussing his being benched with anyone. Besides, he really needed to put his head down and get to work, his online training being the first order of business. Clearly, he was in hot water; hotter than he had previously estimated. Someone sidled up behind him.

"D. Randall is a police officer," Al whispered in his ear. "You really think he's sitting at home waiting for us to come along and kick in his door?"

"You heard the briefing. Surveillance followed him to the building and we can connect him to the property," Rob said. "What do you think?"

"I think he ain't where we think his is. Let's run on out there and talk to the surveillance team."

If I've jammed myself up, Rob thought, I might as well jam myself up all the way. Besides, it beat the shit out of following the ASAC's orders.

"Let's go, this way. The back door," Rob said.

Employees from throughout the division filled up the Resident Agency. Some people were doubling up in cubes. Everyone was busy. Rob and Al worked their way toward the exit. They were almost at the door when Steve Guerra approached them from between a row of cubes. Steve wore a tan CIRG polo and green expedition pants. A blonde woman was with him. He waved them down.

"Rob, a word?" Steve asked.

The four of them huddled up.

"D. Randall is a police officer. You really think he's sitting at home waiting for us to come along and kick in his door?" Steve said.

The woman behind Steve was striking. Her round face held evenly spaced features. She wore a Redskins ball cap and her straight blonde ponytail had been threaded through the opening in back. She also wore polo shirt, blue with a Ferrari shield on her breast, and tan tactical pants. She radiated an aura of extreme fitness and easygoing confidence.

"Rob?" Steve asked.

"Yeah?"

"I see your target acquisition radar picked up Kerri. Kerri, these reprobates are Rob Lawson, he's assigned here with me in the RA, and this is Alphonzo Jemison of FDLE," Steve said.

Rob nodded and Al reached out to shake hands.

"Kerri is a new agent. Just graduated the Academy." Steve stepped in a little closer and whispered: "She's former CIA."

"Oh?" Al asked. "Ops officer?"

"GRS," Kerri said.

Al nodded like he knew what she was talking about. Rob didn't have a clue.

"Rob, I'll bet the entirety of my Thrift Savings Plan D. Randall isn't at home," Steve said.

Kay entered the back door carrying a pink backpack and her radio.

"Hey everyone," she said.

"Kay, what's the likelihood D. Randall is still in the building?" Steve asked.

"Very. The Jeep is still parked."

"Could he have —"

"What are you saying Steve? I had a good eye. The Jeep is still there. It's not like I could have missed it leaving, all muddy like as it was. Now, if you all will excuse me," Kay said.

"See, that's what I mean," Al said. "He's done walked on out of there. He's got country property. We need to run on up there and check it out. I don't think he's gone to ground yet."

"Al," Rob said, "Didn't Wee Willie say something about a fish camp at the restaurant? I meant to ask him about it in the interview, but it slipped my mind."

Al shrugged and was about to say something when Steve cut him off.

"Fish camp? I spoke to Jenny about property already and she mentioned something about a riverside ranch and a shrimp farming business."

Steve led the way. They snaked back through the crowded RA to where Jenny had set up shop.

"I cross-referenced the tax documents and found the addresses. I was able to Google them. I made up some arrays out of the images. The main house, out buildings and the fish camp are marked. Sorry, all I have is an inkjet," Jenny said as she handed out the photos printed on paper. "I'll see what I can do about getting you glossies."

"Thanks, Jenny," Steve said.

"This is the Perdido," Al said.

"Pretty rural area," Kerri said.

"Wasn't EvaJo found here, near Denetclaw City, south of the property?" Rob asked.

"Was she?" Steve asked.

"Sure was," Al said.

The three of them wore solemn expressions. Rob wondered if he did as well.

"We take it to Chris?" Rob asked the group, though the question was mostly directed at Steve.

"I don't know," Steve said. "I can't imagine HM would want to split up the SWAT team even more, and I also can't imagine ASAC Katz is in the mood to hear us out."

"What if we don't say a thing? What if we go on up and poke around?" Al asked.

"We need signed plans to make high risk arrests," Rob said.

"Y'all don't need permission to do a site reconnaissance, do you?" Al asked.

"We don't," Steve said, starting to smile.

"I don't feel like spending the day at a desk or watching the SWAT boys run around, even if this is nothing really. Let's drift on out of here real tranquil like and meet in the lobby," Al said.

Moments later they stood downstairs in a close group in a quiet corner. Those with business in the building came and went, paying them no mind.

"So what do we want to do? Four to a car? Two cars?" Rob asked.

"Two cars, I think. I don't like driving right in the main gate though," Steve said, studying the inkjet photos of the property.

"You see any other way in?" Kerri asked.

Steve shook his head.

"Let's drive up and scope it out. Come on, we're burning daylight," Al said, heading for the main exit.

"Too bad we don't have a helicopter," Kerri said.

Rob laughed out loud at the idea.

Al snapped his fingers. "You want a helicopter? I can get a helicopter," he said, making a call. "Hey, stop pulling it up there, you perv. You need a partner to get in the Mile High Club. Solo don't count. It's Al. You flying today? Call me back."

He dialed again, winking at them as he held the phone to his ear.

"Hey, it's Al Jemison," Al said. "No man, I'm back working . . . thanks, Doug around? Okay. Hey, you guys flying today? No, got a deal going . . . no, with the Eye, but this has to be on the arm . . . not that far. How about Denetclaw City? What do you mean when? How about right freaking now? Yeah . . . yeah . . . a local drop and you're free . . . okay . . . extraction by FDLE cruiser, no worries . . . okay . . . roger . . . Fairgrounds? Yeah . . . thirteen hundred? Roger." Al terminated the call profoundly satisfied.

"How about you all gear up and meet me at the Fairgrounds in an hour?" Al asked. "Make it on time and it's flying the friendly skies. If you're late, they will split and you're walking."

"Roger, Fairgrounds in an hour," Steve said as he pointed at Rob and Kerri.

"What gear?" Rob asked.

"Helocast?" Kerri asked.

"Yeah, of course," Steve said.

"Sure, helocast," Al said.

"There's gators in the Perdido," Rob muttered.

"Relax. You're the top of the food chain, big guy," Kerri said.

"I like her," Al said. "Hey, I'm Al. Fly me."

Kerri squinted, carefully measuring Al of the broad shoulders and big pecs, bringing her right forefinger to her chin in contemplation.

"You're a little scrawny for me. Why don't you hit the gym and then give me a call?" Then, back to Rob, she said, "besides, take another look at the photos. No place to touch down due to trees."

And with that, she skipped off in the direction of her car, ponytail bouncing.

"Ouch, she tagged me. I'm I bleeding?" Al brough four stiff fingers pressed together to his nose in a theatrical examination for blood.

Steve shrugged and walked away.

"Appreciate the sympathy Steve," Al shouted. "Rob, about them gators, it will be only small ones. Want me to drive?" Al asked.

Rob had Al take him to the storage locker. Rob sweat buckets as he dug through his stuff in the cinderblock unit. Al waited outside where one could merely fry an egg on the concrete. Rob found his tactical bag, a large duffle made of black rip-stop nylon and rifled around until he found his tactical gun belt, a small day pack and a two-foot square waterproof zip-lock pouch made out of thick olive drab plastic.

"Hey Rob, c'mon, we got a plane to catch," Al shouted.

After ten minutes of continued searching and sweating, the only pertinent clothes he could find were a blue FBI Academy polo shirt and a pair of tan Royal Robbins with holes in them. He grabbed a low profile ballistic vest out of the big gear bag and shut the unit door with authority.

He could feel his adrenaline beginning to run.

"Let's go," Rob heard himself say.

Rob and Al arrived at the Fairgrounds first. They parked deep in a large lot where the pavement ended and the grass began. Al opened the trunk and Rob started to get organized.

He had changed into his trousers in the car. Now Rob focused on his tactical equipment. He used the Velcro straps to secure the vest and put his polo shirt on. He unloaded his pistol and put it and his magazines in the pouch with an FBI radio and his cell phone. The pouch went into the day pack.

Rob put on his belt, a black tactical nylon Sam Browne, with a drop holster and two sets of handcuffs. He checked the miscellaneous equipment: a military Individual First Aid Kit, robust folding knife, flex cuffs, his Asp expandable baton. He had just checked his mirror on a stick when Steve parked next to Al.

Steve wore an old Army woodland camouflage battle dress uniform without markings. He carried his Glock with an empty magazine well in a nylon holster. His boots were low profile and civilian. Rob could see no evidence of a ballistic vest.

"Let's see those pictures again," Steve said, closing Al's trunk and spreading them out on top. "I also have a map."

Kerri drove up and completed the rank of parked government cars. She exited ready-to-go in a high-speed camouflage pullover with matching pants under a ballistic/load-bearing vest combination. Her pistol was in a cross draw holster in a clear plastic covering. She also had magazines and other equipment secured to her vest with MOLLE clips. Her pony tail was under a camouflage do-rag and she wore mirrored Oakleys.

"Girl, that is one big fucking knife," Al said, pointing to her foot-long LHR Combat Knife, worn handle down off of MOLLE straps on her vest.

"Rob here mentioned the gators," she said. "Love your outfit by the way." She blew a large pink bubble of gum and popped it.

"How do we want to do this? Al, what are they flying?" Steve asked.

"Lakotas. They can handle range and weight," Al said.

"Here we are," Steve said, pointing to the map. "What say we fly down from the north, deploying to hit this area here and scout on up to the main house? What about a rendezvous for extraction?"

"Walk down the road?" Kerri suggested.

"I thought I'd drive on up and pick you all up," Al said.

"You aren't coming?" Rob asked.

"Bum leg," Al said.

Rob had forgotten. Embarrassment and regret for having brought it up torqued up his stomach.

They heard it before they saw it. Not the whup-whup-whup of yesterday's helicopter but a turbine-like whine accompanied by a staccato smashing of the air into submission instead. A stubby olive-drab Florida National Guard helicopter sporting a red cross on a white background rushed into their piece of the sky, spinning a four-bladed rotor. It rapidly grew and, after flying above the nearest strip mall, banked sharply over the four law enforcement officers and landed on the grass. It was a fatter, stretched Little Bird, with three vertical stabilizers on the tail and runners on the skeds.

One of the pilots hopped out, a large forty-year-old white man in a desert tan flight suit, sweat flattening his thinning blond hair. He jogged up to Alphonzo.

"You gimped up crippled son-of-a-bitch. What are you still doing sucking the government tit?" he asked as they shook hands.

"Adult supervision, motherfucker. Dodds, meet your new best friends," Al said, pointing to the agents. "Friends, this is CWO-3 Randy Dodds, only the best bird driver in the Army."

"He says that about all the girls. I understand you need a ride. What's the play?" Randy asked.

"How about dropping us riverside at this ranch on the Perdido?" Steve asked.

"Right here, this Perdido? Yeah, let's do it," Randy said.

"That's it?" Rob asked, surprised.

He could not fathom getting to use a helicopter without asking permission from a cast of hundreds and filling out a mountain of paperwork.

"Yeah, we're on a cross-country boondoggle today, so that's all we need. Don't talk about it to anyone, though," Randy said. "No good turn goes unpunished. Where's the LZ?"

"Uh, they were thinking of helocasting," Al said.

"Whoa. Al, what are you getting me into here?"

"No, it's cool. Everyone is experienced and qualified."

"Why not Dope-on-a-Rope then?" Randy asked.

"Not good to hang out in the area. It's faster to cast," Steve said.

"All you guys good to go, qualified, I mean?" Randy asked the group.

"Yeah, I'm good," Steve said.

"Roger," Kerri said.

Rob had helocast exactly once before, into Lake Lunga, during his FBI SWAT training, much longer than a year ago, time-wise, clearly putting him out of scope.

"Sure thing," Rob said, hoping his nerves were not showing.

"Is the bird certified for it?" Al asked.

"You all want to jump out of a perfectly good helicopter that's still flying, go ahead. It don't hurt my feelings at all," Randy said easily.

"Fine. They do," Al said.

"They?" Randy asked. "You ain't coming?"

"Nah man, the leg thing and all. Besides, I'm the extraction plan. I'll drive on up and get 'em after they're done. You get to do the drop and go on about your business."

"Sorry dude, forgot for a minute. Tally-ho and all that shit. Show me where you want out exactly," Randy said.

Josiah Waller worked at his computer, his reading glasses low on his nose. He wore a crisp white shirt, striped silk tie and tasseled loafers, doing his best attorney-from-central-casting. His drafting of a rebuttal to a motion to exclude firearms evidence concerning one of his cases needed his complete concentration, so Andrea surprised him when she slipped into his office and closed the door behind her.

There wasn't anything wrong with Andrea slipping into his office and closing door. They had gone out for a drink that grew into dinner. While she had proven adept at ducking out on him at the door to her apartment without so much as a kiss, she had agreed to go sailing with him on the weekend. An exciting prospect. She had a lush figure, highlighted by today's A-line in blue.

"Have you heard?" she asked, enjoying their conspiracy.

"No, what?" he asked.

"The FBI is going to arrest a *police officer!*"

"No! How did you find out?"

"Pam went running out of here. In her office recycles was a draft of an affidavit and I read the front page."

"Did you get a name?"

"Uh-huh. Randy Hartgrove or something. Do you know him?"

"No, not that I recall. Did you grab it?"

"No. I tried but I almost got caught! I heard Toni and got out of there. It's so exciting!"

"It sure is," Josiah said. He locked his own computer and stood up. He glanced quickly at his desk and in his own recycle container. Nothing sensitive. He started rolling down his sleeves. "I have to run an errand. See you later?"

"Sure. I'll keep zeroing."

"Ah, great," Josiah had no idea what she meant. "You can fill me in over a drink."

She gave him a last arch glance as she left the office.

Josiah reached for his jacket.

They flew upwards, turning until the rotors were vertical, left side down, then pivoting hard until Randy crossed the Perdido, after which he yanked it onto its other side for a moment and, now on course, leveled out.

Kerri and Rob faced forward on a bench seat. Steve had a rear-facing jump seat and had put on a headset.

Steve held up five spread fingers. He made eye contact with Kerri and mouthed the word "five," and then again with Rob. She replied with a nod and a double thumbs up. Rob nodded also.

Kerri slid open her door. They had decided she would go out first.

The cabin filled with rushing air. Rob's nerves kicked into high gear. He began to have second thoughts.

Steve opened the door on the other side. Randy swung it around in a large circle and flared it to drop both speed and height. Soon it flew much slower at about ten feet.

Steve pointed at Kerri.

She showed them her pearly whites. In one smooth motion, she unbuckled, pivoted on her backside, placed her boots on the runner and let gravity take her without a backwards glance.

Crap, Rob thought. He was going to drop like a bird turd compared to Kerri.

Steve jumped. Rob hesitated.

The bird flew on.

He made up his mind and tried to imitate Kerri. First, the straps hung him up. Once clear of those, he shimmied himself out to stand on the runner. He stopped there.

The helicopter had stopped moving forward. He was thinking about taking advantage of the near stop to go ahead and jump when

Randy sped up and banked the helicopter, Rob-side down. Rob fell forward.

Rob slammed into the brisk up-river water in a near belly flop. He sank into a maelstrom of green and bubbles. Water pushed up into his nose. He experienced the events like an observer, noting his tumbling only as a passing thought. When he saw his feet between him and the surface, he realized he needed to do something.

He sorted himself out and pulled for the surface, braking through, the sound of the helicopter fading. He tried, and failed, not to think about getting bit by an alligator. He expected sharp teeth tearing at his rib cage any minute but managed to keep his head, swimming slowly using a quiet breaststroke.

He had missed his chance to follow the others out at their planned spot but did see the fish camp, a weathered unimproved cabin on stilts about four feet up. Steps led from a wraparound porch down to a floating dock. He decided to clear the camp and then catch up with the others.

Rob swam up to the dock. The gray wood had been long ignored and felt rough and splintery. He carefully rolled up on top and froze, concentrating on sounds and smells. The buzzing and chirping of the river resumed. He inhaled the rich loamy odor of the slow-moving river with its faint highlights of decay. There were no vehicles on the rutted muddy slash through the thick vegetation leading to the camp.

D. Randall wasn't here, Rob thought.

Rob reached for his equipment pouch. He retrieved his pistol and pushed a magazine into the handle, forcing it until he heard the click, working the slide slowly. With his pistol in his holster and extra magazines in their pouches, tension he had not previously recognized drained away.

Rob started up the stairs, keeping to the edge, shifting his weight from step to step. He paused at the top. Birds called and the river gurgled. He turned a corner. The camp did not have glass in the windows, only screens.

He made the first corner and kept up his pace, carefully placing each step to avoid causing the wood to creak. He studied the large room making up half the cabin. It was rustic inside, unfinished, bare wood and no ceiling, only the underside of the roof overhead. Rob saw a wood burning stove made out of a fifty-five gallon drum, a wooden picnic table with fixed benches and work counters along the walls. Across the room, two closed doors led somewhere. Probably bunkrooms, Rob thought. He passed the next corner.

He reached out for the handle of the front door; he saw a flash of silver and felt a sharp constriction around his neck. A powerful blunt force pressed into his back.

Garrote!

"Choke out, you son-of-a-bitch!" a man yelled.

Rob arched his back and shoved with his legs. They fell backwards and the constriction around his throat loosened a bit. Rob pushed his chin down to his chest and clawed at the wire.

"No you don't shithead," his assailant growled through gritted teeth.

Rob tried to roll but the man wrapped his legs around Rob. Rob reached for his pistol but the other man shifted them to trap it between Rob and the split planking of the porch. Rob tried to throw a few punches and a few elbows, but he felt himself fading, felt the cabin receding into a bright white. His neck hurt less.

Rob moved in the sea of white. He saw a young man sitting on something, on some of the white. He rested comfortably with his elbows on his knees and his feet on the floor or what would have been the floor had the floor not been part of the endless white. The young man, Caucasian, wore black jeans and a brown long-sleeve button-down shirt. The cuffs had been rolled up to his mid-forearms. He had an athletic grace to him, even at rest. Loose waves of thick brown hair covered his ears and stopped at his collar. As if he knew what Rob was thinking, he flipped up his brown bangs. He smiled at Rob, showing neat white teeth with one incisor slightly out of place. The young man reminded him vaguely of Kathryn, of all people.

"Hi, Dad," he said.

"Ben?" Rob asked.

"Yeah, Dad, it's me." Ben-at-twenty years old stood up.

Handsome, Rob thought. Healthy, too; build like a soccer player, or maybe tennis.

"Dad," Ben continued, "I've been allowed to come to tell you it's okay. It was my time. It was my time to go."

"You look good, Ben. We would have taken care of that tooth."

Ben beamed broadly.

"How could it be your time? You were three," Rob said.

"Dad, it's okay. It was my time, back then. We all have a purpose. It was my time. But it isn't your time now. You have more to do. It was my time, though. You know, you taught me what to do in this situation."

"I did? You were three."

"Don't worry about that, Dad. We were sparring and you told me, but we didn't practice it. You thought I would use it at school and get suspended."

"You didn't go to school. You were three."

"It was another time and another place. Now listen Dad, you have to go back. It isn't your time, so take your thumbs like this," Ben slid his hands out of his pockets and made fists with his thumbs sticking straight up.

"Ben, you were three."

"It was another place. Dad, stick out your thumbs."

Rob's neck started to hurt again. He had no air in his lungs.

"What?"

"God damn it," Ben yelled. He grew larger, morphing into a nightmare version of Ben. His skin turned gray, his teeth grew sharp, his hair wayward and he glared terribly. "Throw your thumbs over your head! Throw them up, UP! Dig in, DIG IT IN!"

And suddenly Rob was on the porch. He could breathe. He sucked in a great gulp of warm wet air.

Someone screamed. Rob's left thumb felt something squishy. His right one hurt.

He was on the porch! The legs were loose and so was the wire. Rob jabbed his attacker jab in the eye with his thumb again and spun out. He got up on all fours.

He recognized his assailant as one D. Randall Hargrove, who tried to hold on to the wire, wipe his injured eye on his shoulder and kick Rob.

Rob punched him twice, breathing deeply between hits. D. Randall, eyes closed, let go of the wire and swung at Rob, missing.

Rob hit D. Randall twice more before rolling him onto his chest. After fumbling briefly, he had D. Randall in handcuffs.

"You are under arrest, asshole," Rob said.

"Fuck you, motherfucker! You blinded me!"

"Shut up," Rob said, swinging at D. Randall but missing him.

The punch pulled him off his hand and knees and he fell on his side. He crawled closer to the cabin, too tired to stand, ending up with his back against the wall and his boots resting on D. Randall's back. He sucked in gallons of fresh air, as refreshing as a glass of cool water. The sky was so blue. The leaves were so green. He felt like he was seeing everything for the first time. He did not see any sign of Ben.

Alphonzo drove north on Quarry Road, which paralleled the Perdido on the east bank, roughly, from Seminolacola to the town of Quarry Springs, near the Alabama border. This far north the road was a two-lane. Thick vegetation grew wild in the protected Perdido River Water Management Area on one side of the road, across from fields of green cotton plants sporting their squares.

Al followed the roadway into a turn and had to jam on the breaks because Kerri stood on the double yellow line, arms hanging down and hip cocked. Al twitched the wheel and the car came to a sliding stop with the passenger door next to her. Kerri lifted the latch.

"Hit it," she said, sliding in and buckling up, "we can't raise Rob by radio or phone."

"Shit," Al muttered. He floored the accelerator.

"Thirty-two oh four," Steve called on the radio, using Kerri's call sign, "I got him, it's all good. Location secure. Come on in, forget the main house and come up to the camp. What's your ETA?"

"Minute," Kerri said.

Kerri had Al turn down a nearly overgrown gravel driveway.

Steve ran toward them, waving. Al stopped and lowered his window.

"D. Randall jumped Rob and tried to garrote him. Rob about gouged D. Randall's eye out."

"How's Rob?"

"His neck is chewed up and it scared him shitless, but in general, he's fine."

They called it in and if Chris was mad, he hid it well. The Asshole was not heard from at all. They decided Steve and Kerri would secure the location, Al and Rob would transport D. Randall and the balance of the team would get and execute a search warrant on the property.

The sun beat straight down on the car as Al tore up Quarry Road. Rob had put a battle dressing on D. Randall's left eye. When they crossed the town line, Rob's phone rang.

"You on your way with the guy?" Leo asked.

"Yeah," Rob said.

"Don't say much, he'll pick up a lot from even just listening to you. You coming to the office?"

"Yeah."

"You have a dust up with him?"

"Yeah."

"He need medical care?"

"Eventually."

"You're interviewing him now?"

Rob hadn't given it much thought. He felt very tired.

"Yeah," Rob said.

"I'll get you guys something to eat and meet you in the interview room."

"Thanks."

Rob thought about Ben, or his hallucination of Ben. Ben would have grown up to be a prince of a man. Rob missed him, but Ben seemed content. There was solace in that. Of course, it could not have actually been Ben, Rob told himself. Perhaps his oxygen-starved brain tried one last trick before checking out. Nevertheless, the thought of a content Ben calmed Rob considerably.

Upon arriving at the office, Al took a quick lap around the building for security's sake. Al stopped at the back entrance to the lobby. Rob opened the car door, stretched his legs, and stood up into the heavy air. He shuffled like an old man around the car to get D. Randall.

"You up for the stairs?" Rob asked.

"Yeah," D. Randall said.

The two tired men trudged up the stairs together. Rob hustled D. Randall through the back door and straight into the office interview room. The small chamber had beige walls, chairs with taupe plastic surfaces and chrome supports, and a table with a fake wood veneer. Rob guided D. Randall into a chair.

Chris appeared. "You search him?"

Rob scanned the area behind Chris.

"SAC called him back to headquarters city. He's gone." Chris nodded to D. Randall. "You search him?" Chris asked again.

"Yes, me and Steve both," Rob said.

"Your neck looks like shit. I want him shackled. I'll watch him."

On the way to the storeroom, Rob basked in the silent admiration from the agents, task force officers and professional staff. He lifted a set of shackles off their hook and bumped into Leo at the doorway.

"Hey, I got something to eat," Leo said, showing him a large McDonald's bag and drinks in a gray paper tray. "You need a partner for the interview?"

"Uh," Rob said.

"Great, I'll do it."

Leo's excitement was palpable.

"Sure Leo," Rob said.

Rob figured he should have been as eager as Leo, but for some reason he wasn't.

"Great!" Leo said. "Let's try this, we give him something to eat and the three of us just eat. Don't ask him anything. We let him piss and everything. This guy, he's not going to be expecting that. He's waiting for us to try to out-tough him. What do you think?"

Rob felt his stomach growl at the scent of the fried beef. "Yeah, let's try it."

"Shackles, great idea. You go in first. Offer him a choice of a Big Mac or a Quarter Pounder with Cheese."

Back in the interview room, Rob secured D. Randall's ankles by running the chain between them and through an eye bolt in the floor. Chris made himself scarce. D. Randall stared at the shackles. Rob stood up and sighed.

Leo arrived with the McDonald's bags.

"We have Big Macs or Quarter Pounders with Cheese," Rob said. He sounded run down even to himself.

D. Randall glared at Rob with his unpatched eye.

"Hey," Leo said, "we're gonna eat. Want some?"

D. Randall aimed his eye elsewhere and shrugged. "I'll take a Quarter Pounder," he said, after a minute.

Rob re-cuffed D. Randall so his hands were in front.

"You can take them off asshole. I'm shackled," D. Randall said.

"You tried to kill me. You can eat while cuffed," Rob replied without any heat.

Leo passed the bags around and set the drinks down. Rob helped himself to a sandwich and a red box of fries. Leo handed him a drink. Rob popped the lid off and drank down about half of a very large Coke. Swallowing hurt. He opened the cardboard box and bit into a Big Mac, still hot. It tasted fine, familiar and fantastic. He couldn't remember fast food ever tasting this good. He jammed some fries in his mouth.

"You shitheads have got to be kidding. I'm not talking because you bought me a Quarter Pounder," D. Randall said.

Rob kept chewing.

"So don't," Leo said.

"Aren't you hungry?" Rob asked around a mouthful of food.

D. Randall started to say something, but suddenly stopped. Then he shrugged again. His face relaxed. He reached for the bag and brought out the fries first and then the sandwich, which he positioned neatly on the table.

"Got any ketchup?" D. Randall asked.

"Shit," Leo said. "I knew I forgot something."

D. Randall nodded, mostly to himself, and started to eat. They finished their meal in silence. Rob started to feel better. As they nursed the last of their Cokes, D. Randall spoke up again.

"There, I ate. I still ain't talking," he said.

Rob found the phrasing interesting. He had not asked for a lawyer. He only said he wouldn't talk. Rob sipped his Coke.

"Okay with us," Rob said. "We have Wee Willie in a room in the officers' quarters on the Navy base." Rob lied. They had him in a civilian safe house, but he wasn't going to give D. Randall any help at all in having Wee Willie killed. "He's been talking a mile a minute. He gave us Master Blaster and Sniper Stefon, who are both locked up and talking, tripping over themselves to give up each other and Wee Willie. They know about you, by the way. So, here's where you sit: everybody's pointing at you."

"Talk," Leo said, moving the drink tray and putting an Advice of Rights form down by D. Randall's hand, "or don't talk." Leo placed a black push-button Skilcraft pen on top of the form, which had a space to initial by each of the four usual Miranda warnings: to be silent, anything said could be used against D. Randall, he could have a lawyer and that lawyer could be free of charge; and a place to sign at the bottom. "We don't give a shit. If you do nothing from now on, you're going to get the same needle you arranged for Jimmy Tank Gubbs, you son-of-a-bitch."

D. Randall's mouth opened but no sound came out. He put his hands, palms down, on the form and glared at Leo and Rob.

"Oh no. You can fuck that shit and fuck you, too, you cock-sucking faggots," D. Randall said. He licked his lips. "I got to know you ain't going to screw me," he said.

"We won't screw you D. Randall. We're here to help you not screw yourself. What you get depends on what you give," Rob said.

D. Randall bored into Rob with his good eye. Rob met D. Randall's eye-fuck and held it, keeping his breath even and his shoulders down.

After about three long minutes of "mine is bigger than yours," D. Randall snatched up the pen and signed the form, initialing by each of the four statements.

He started talking. He talked for two hours straight. He talked until the Agents finally stopped him. There would be more talk later.

Tonight, they had work to do.

Chris, back behind his desk, with the telephone handset at his ear, resigned himself to another hungry Friday night on the jay-oh-bee as the sun settled into the perfect late spring angle necessary for it to burn his retinas out. Happened twice a year.

He forced himself to listen to the conference call, to the arguing Headquarters supervisors from the Public Corruption Unit and the Civil Rights Unit as they respectively claimed ownership of Rob's case. As they yammered on, Chris authorized subpoena expenses in the computer.

Rob and Leo burst into his office, hollering at a mile a minute. Chris calmed them down and as he grasped what they were saying, rose to his feet, incredulous, so much so he hung up on the very people he had to talk to.

Josiah could not believe Andrea didn't want to come with him. The little bitch had texted something about a sudden cold. Fine. He wrestled grocery bags down to the galley of his 1985 Tartan T-3000 custom sloop moored in the Seminolacola municipal marina. There were other plastic bags of non-perishable food on the deck, next to two fully-packed canvass LL Bean duffle bags, one green and the other brown. He'd have to store everything later. He was losing his daylight. Once out of the marina, he would be fine. He'd taken this boat to Yucatan before and heading off at night did not bother him at all.

He scanned the marina from the cockpit. Rows of finger slips filled with expensive floating hardware were up ahead. Beyond the boats were the rock jetties protecting them. The City kept the marina up and the taxpayer-subsidized slips were highly sought after. Josiah checked the time. He needed to get to the fuel dock before it closed.

Al drove. Leo rode shotgun with Rob in the back.

"You calling the Coast Guard? I got a number for 'em," Al shouted over the siren.

"No, I got something better: Jeannie Brice the Queen of ICE," Leo said, worrying his phone.

"What, she won't go out with you?" Rob asked, winking at Al.

"Not ice, cretin, Immigration and Customs Enforcement. She's the last of the old Customs peeps running a boat. It's a really monstrous go-fast. It was an old seizure and I bet she keeps it running out of her own pocket. She's going to love this one." Leo held up his hand. "Jeannie? You there? You busy?"

Jeannie loved nothing better than a hurry-up. She had cut the boys loose, it being Friday and all. She texted them to come back. They had only been on the road a minute, so she expected them soonest. Jeannie had set up a folding chair on the broad battleship-gray foredeck to settle down with a cocktail and watch the sunset, but alas, duty calls. Excited, she started waking up the old girl. She and her Sonic were used to this.

Jeannie had been a proud US Customs Service special agent running boats back in 2001. Here she was, all these years later, still running boats. She'd outsmarted the dissolution of the Customs Service, the creation of ICE, the Department of Homeland Security order moving all non-Coast Guard boats to Customs and Border Protection. She knew every trick Logistics could throw at her to survey her Sonic, with the goal to junk her or sell her or otherwise shut her down permanently.

One thing she could not survive was her mandatory retirement at fifty-seven, which crept closer each day. She did not like to think about that, so she scampered about getting ready to start her three 900 horsepower engines.

"Overall, the collective 'they' could kiss my broad white ass," she muttered as she worked.

Jeannie was from the Panhandle originally and was mostly Caucasian with some Native American mixed in. Sun and salt had etched canyons in her face and she wore her gray-blonde hair butch. She stood five-feet-seven-inches tall in her tactical black law enforcement boots, and was fairly stocky, especially lower down. Her forearms were comically large and well defined. None of that stopped her from moving gracefully around her forty-five-foot Sonic go-fast with its triple 900s and the muscularly curved hull presenting the very image of movement, even when still.

Jeannie saved her cocktail and stowed her chair. She checked the fluids in the engines and the transmissions. She ran the blower, engine cover up and all. She pushed the start button on number one. It roared to life and settled down to a low rumble after a second. The boys made the lot as the third engine got comfortable.

"M-4s, boys! It's show time!" Jeannie yelled.

Josiah cast off his lines, leaving them in pile. With the engine in gear, he moved away from the fuel dock. He had to get around a row of slips before he could motor out to the harbor. He'd be heading into the low sun at first, but then it would be south into the Gulf and away. He could not help smiling. He liked to be on the water. He did not think about abandoning his life or losing his law license. The worst of it was giving up the municipal slip. This was such a great marina, he thought.

Josiah heard some shouting and chose to ignore it. In response, he pushed the throttle forward a little. He would be out in the dark and lost in a huge expanse of Gulf before they could get a search going. He planned to head out to open ocean at first, then adjust course later, to avoid giving them clues. He knew what he was about. With all his experience, and native intelligence, too, they would never catch him. He was admitted to practice law, after all.

Josiah turned to starboard around the end of the dock, looking away from the men who were trying to get through the gate. They were calling his name. His phone rang, which reminded him to turn it off. He'd throw it overboard as soon as he cleared the harbor.

Josiah decided to stay on the engine as the sun went down. He would not have much speed with this slight breeze if he unfurled his sails. Maybe there would be more wind outside, he thought. In a few minutes, he'd turn to port and leave the marina. The sun hung low and full in the thick air.

Then he heard it.

It sounded like one of those big Air Force propeller planes always taking off from Hulbert Field at first, as if it were flying along the wave tops. Josiah even craned his neck trying to spot it. Its roar grew louder.

"Some dumb-assed stinkpotter running around," Josiah said to himself.

It was time to turn to port. A siren blared. He saw a flare, a white flare, even though there was plenty of daylight.

A black speedboat popped out from behind the jetty. It barreled down on him, throwing a huge bow wave of white phosphorus, soon to smash into him in the marina exit.

"Get out of the way, you dumbass!" Josiah shouted.

A spotlight snapped on.

"THIS IS THE DEPARTMENT OF HOMELAND SECURITY!" a contralto voice announced over a loudspeaker.

The engines of the speedboat revved and Josiah watched the bow dip, its forward motion violently checked. Only when the back of the boat rose as its own stern wave overtook it did he notice the two armed men in the cockpit. They were fully equipped with helmets, vests bearing CBP placards and assault rifles. The passing stern wave pushed the speedboat, now at a loud idle, forward. The sharp bow kissed his Tartan. The men were kneeling on the flat foredeck now, with their rifles aimed at him.

He wondered about damage to his gelcoat.

Josiah decided righteous indignation was the way to go. He could bluff his way out of this one. CPB officers weren't too bright, he thought.

The passing wave rocked his sailboat, knocking him off balance.

A loudspeaker crackled. "SAILING VESSEL BLUEBERRRY TART HEAVE TO AND STAND BY TO BE BOARDED!" the driver said, using the loudspeaker even though she was right there. The men leapt aboard, landing with practiced ease on the rolling deck.

Josiah started shouting something about jackbooted thugs when the first officer reached him. The officer released his rifle and let it hang by a sling. He threw Josiah to the deck.

"Get down, get down, get down," the officer shouted afterward, as he flipped Josiah onto his stomach and roughly cuffed his hands behind his back.

He felt them shift his boat into reverse. The speedboat helped her about, surely scuffing the gelcoat more. The officer at the wheel put it in forward. They headed back to his slip.

Shit, he thought.

"You are making the worst mistake of your lives," Josiah finally said. "I am an Assistant United States Attorney."

"Shut up," the officer at the wheel said.

"You have us confused with the FBI," the other one said. "They might care, but honestly, we don't give a fuck."

They were waiting for him at the slip: Robert Lawson, that asshole Leo Kladsko and some black guy in a cowboy hat. His temper broke. Josiah kicked the deck. He kicked out at the officers and cursed them. He hated the sound of his own voice, the way it came out so high and shrill.

They laughed at him as they changed out handcuffs. Josiah lost his words and shouted like an animal in a trap until someone grabbed him in the old schoolyard hold, one hand around the back of his neck, squeezing hard, causing him more pain than he had felt in a long time.

"Stop, Josiah. This isn't helping," Lawson said from behind him.

The fight left him. His energy dissipated. He deflated, collapsing into the deck as if his very bones had dissolved.

"I want a lawyer," Josiah muttered. "Call Q. Burnham Ingersoll. He'll come out. He's between wives."

It had been full dark for some time when the doorbell rang. Chris pushed himself away from the plate of warmed up meatballs and spaghetti he had been eating in the breakfast nook of his ranch. He was alone, save for Skylos, a furry mop of a mutt hoping to share. Elani and the kids were out.

Chris still wore his pistol and, despite the sauce, his necktie. He slowly chewed a piece of the crusty daktyla Elani made from time-to-time as he contemplated the door. Kind of late for unannounced visitors, Chris thought. He put his fork down to free up his shooting hand. He decided to wait a moment and see what happened next.

His phone rang with an incoming call from Leo.

"Yeah?" Chris said.

"It's me at the door, Chris."

Chris hung up and let him in.

"What's up? Hungry?" Chris asked.

"Famished. What have you got?" Leo said, following him into the kitchen.

"Meatballs and spaghetti."

"Elani cook it or store bought?"

"Please, Elani's."

"Great, I'll have some, if you please. Anybody else home? I don't want to intrude."

"No, nobody. They're out running around. How do we stand?" Chris asked as he fixed Leo a plate.

"Some of that bread, too. It's yellow?"

"Yeah, daktyla. How do we stand?"

"They're searching the boat. We've got Waller's phone and laptop. We squirreled him away in a hotel," Leo said.

"A hotel?"

"Yeah, who thought of another safe house? I sure as shit didn't. Waller lawyered up."

"Big surprise."

Chris put a plate down in front of a chair and motioned for Leo to sit.

"Drink?" Chris asked.

"Uh . . ." Leo pointed at Chris's glass, a short plain tumbler holding red wine.

"You got it." Chris produced another glass and poured.

They both sat and Chris waited for Leo to have a bite. Before Leo could get the second one to his mouth, Chris spoke up.

"So you drove over to tell me Waller lawyered up?"

"Oh, he lawyered up. Ingersoll."

"Hell, Leo, I'd use Ingersoll. So?" Chris asked, forking up some food.

"Ingersoll came out."

Chris's fork froze in midair.

"They talked for almost an hour and then Waller started talking to us. They're still at it," Leo said.

Leo twirled up some spaghetti.

Chris ate a bite of meatball. Not something you see every day, he thought.

"What's he saying?" Chris asked.

Leo told him.

Friday

Rob woke in his own apartment with a start at 4:30 am. He had better get up and get ready, he told himself, but he did not move. His four hours sleep did not feel like nearly enough.

After Waller spilled it all, Chris had deployed his forces. Agents were on surveillance. If necessary, Rob and Kay would interview Chucky Dauphin, of all people. Waller had mentioned Chucky, former employer of the decedent Matthew Simmons and current financial advisor to Melissa Simmons, and the working theory was if Chucky heard about Waller's arrest, he might run.

Rob dragged himself out of bed and cleaned himself up, including a fresh shave. He had slept through fourteen emails; he handled those on his phone. He made his bed and then used it to lay out his clothes and equipment.

The rep tie, red with narrow silver stripes, went through the button down collar of the white dress shirt. Rob skipped his ballistic vest. He did not see Chucky as the type to shoot his way out of an interview, no matter what was at stake. On went the summer weight wool trousers from his off-the-rack blue suit, his socks and his shined black oxfords. He slipped on his shirt and tucked it in neatly. He threaded the reinforced dress belt through the loops, adding handcuffs, empty magazines pouches and an empty holster as it went around. He thought of Melissa as he tied his tie. He hoped he'd have time to call her today.

Rob filled his pockets from where he had put his wallet, keys and everything else down last night. He went to his nightstand for handcuffs, two full magazines and his pistol and holstered up. He put his jacket on and placed his FBI credentials just so in his right breast pocket so he could pull them out and present them perfectly.

He bought a fast food egg sandwich and coffee on the way in. Kay arrived dressed in a business pantsuit, the same shade of blue as his, carrying a brown Newport handbag from Woolstenhulme with its integral pistol carrying system for her Glock 23. Her breakfast bag sported Krispy Kreme colors.

The case had earned itself round-the-clock shifts, and four TDY'ers worked on their summary, due to Chris and Headquarters first thing. After Rob ate, he spoke with the overnight financial analyst and got caught up on developments. The analyst told Rob they had found several payments from a Channel Islands bank deposited into one of the business accounts associated with D. Randall.

"Sounds like you need a trip to London," the analyst said.

"Sure," Rob said. "I'll buy you lunch if I ever get that past Headquarters."

"Oh, you better taking me with you when you do."

Rob returned to his cube and powered up his computer. He had a minute, so he thought he might get to the emails waiting for him on the classified system. Then the phone rang.

"Robert Lawson?" a confident male voice asked.

"Yes," Rob said.

"I'm Jimmy Thibault, in from C-7 on the TDY for your case? We were overnight on Dauphin. Well, he dragged two big duffle bags out to his car and now he's heading to town. By the way, he put fourteen bags of shredded paper at the curb on his way out. We were told you'd do the stop?"

"Uh, yeah," Rob got up and searched for Kay. "Does it look like he's heading for the airport? We'll use TSA to grab him."

"We're westbound on Ten almost to 295. Hang on and we'll tell you if he turns. Wait one."

Kay was at her desk, also waiting for her classified computer to load. He filled her in. Kay started gathering her things.

"He's picked up 295," Jimmy said.

Rob could feel the adrenaline entering his system. He felt energized, and chills passed through his chest.

"He's on 295," Rob told Kay. "Let's start heading to the airport."

Kay nodded and picked up her handbag.

"He's pulling into the mall," Jimmy said.

"He's going to his office," Rob said into his phone and to Kay. "He's got a place in the high-rise. We're on our way."

Ten minutes later, Rob and Kay parked next to Jimmy and his surveillance partner in the nearly empty lot facing the street entrance to Chucky's office building.

"Parked and went straight up," Jimmy said after introductions.

"Did he bring the duffels?" Rob asked.

"No, but he did bring a bag, like a gym bag, all loose and shit like it was empty. He's not dressed for work though. Casual green and white plaid button down and light blue shorts. What are you going to do?"

"We're going to do a knock and talk," Kay said. "Let's go, Rob. Let's shake the tree and see what falls out."

Kay positioned the handle of her bag into the crook of her arm and strode off to the door.

"Guys, can you call Leo and ask him to collect the shredded documents? Ask him to treat them as collected evidence," Rob asked, running catch up to Kay.

"How do you want to play it?" Rob asked.

"I was thinking we could act like we were informing him of Waller's arrest and see where it goes," Kay said. "Like a courtesy call or something."

"Sounds like a plan to me."

Soon Kay and Rob were standing at the frosted glass entrance to Charles Dauphin and Associates.

"Ready?" Kay asked.

"Should we knock?" Rob asked.

"Nah, let's surprise him."

Kay tried the door. It was locked.

"I've only been in here once. I don't know if there is another door," Rob said.

"I'll knock," Kay said.

She paused, probably to give him time to suggest another idea if he had one, but he responded with a sharp short nod of his head.

Kay knocked on the glass.

They waited. Time crawled for Rob.

"Do you think we missed him? Maybe he shook the tail," Rob said.

Kay violently shook the double glass doors and knocked again, this time with insistence.

Rob heard someone behind the door. Keys jingled. The lock turned. It was Chucky himself.

"Yes?" Chucky said with no small measure of stuck-up annoyance.

That pushed Rob's buttons.

"Why Chucky, that's no way to greet an old friend," Rob said. "You don't mind if we come in?" Rob pushed his way in past Chucky's mild resistance. Kay joined him.

"Hey, you can't come in here!"

"Going somewhere, Chuck?" Rob asked.

"Uh, yeah. I'm taking a trip."

"Where?"

"None of your business."

"Now Chucky, there's no call for snippiness."

"I'm *not* being snippy! What's this about?"

"We're here as a courtesy, Chuck, to give you some news, but if you don't want to hear it," Rob shrugged, "well . . . Kay, let's go." Rob made a move for the door.

"What news?"

"Not like this, out here like we're the hired help. Let's go to your office. You know, I haven't seen it yet. Does it say 'financial genius' on the door? It's this way?"

Rob walked around the receptionist's workstation.

"You can't just barge in here," Chucky said, raising his voice.

"You don't want to show it off? That's not normal, Chuck. What's going on?"

"Nothing is going on. Okay already, follow me."

Chucky trotted around Rob and walked at a fast clip down the carpeted hall with his head down and shoulders up. Kay smiled and Rob smiled back. They stepped it out to catch up to Chucky. Even so, he rounded his large hardwood desk as Rob made the door. Rob swung out to see around the desk. He ignored the floor to ceiling windows with views of the town, beach and Gulf.

There were two cabinets on the bottom of the credenza behind the desk. Chucky's gym bag lay on the floor in front of the right cabinet, with its doors ajar. The gym bag was open a crack, showing a visual slice of banded stacks of cash. Rob caught a glimpse of a safe inside the cabinet, also unsecured, with another narrow angle on more blocks of cash. With a quick brush of his hand and push of his toe, Chucky closed the bag and the cabinet.

"Have a seat," Chucky said. "When my people get in we'll have some coffee."

"Thanks," Kay said.

"Great office, Chuck," Rob said.

"Thanks." Chucky offered him the nearest chair with a gesture. For no reason in particular, Rob crossed the desk front to the other chair, the one on Chucky's right, nearest the door. "What news to you have?"

"We arrested D. Randall Hargrove yesterday. He's the officer —"

"I know who he is," Chucky snapped.

"So you know Melissa is out of danger?"

"She was in danger?"

"Oh yeah. D. Randall was on his way to kill her."

"No kidding? Really? He wouldn't do that," Chucky said, with no more concern than a passerby at a minor traffic accident.

Chucky's shoulders were down and he slumped in his chair. He inhaled and exhaled evenly. Pretty calm for someone who professed to care for Melissa, Rob thought.

"Oh? Do you know him?" Rob asked.

"Ah, no. How would I know him?"

"Then how do you know he wouldn't kill her?"

"Well, he's a police officer for God's sake."

Something is off here, Rob thought. Chucky's detachment was out of place.

"You said you knew him," Kay said.

"I don't know him, I know who he is in relation to the situation. If that's all, I'm very busy —"

"Are you going somewhere?" Rob asked.

"Huh?"

"You said you were traveling, but now you're saying you are busy. Which is it?" Rob asked.

"Busy traveling."

"You're packing up a lot of cash there. You know, it's not really a good idea to keep that much cash around. It might get out and the next thing you know some bad guys will come around and take it. Do you normally keep lots of cash on hand?"

"Uh, is it illegal?"

"No. But if you take a sizable amount out of the country, odds are most of it will get seized in the country you are going to. Why are you holding so much?"

"It's none of your business. I don't have to tell you. It's not illegal. I have a real estate transaction this morning and I need cash for the closing."

Rob scooted up to the edge of the chair and leaned forward. "You're going to a closing with cash outside the country?" he asked.

Chucky's eyes darted up and then back to Rob. "No, here. It's a rather large closing and you know these good ole boys, they like their cash."

"What 'good ole boys'? Aren't you going to Mexico today? Is this the deal that is going down in Mexico City?" Rob asked, completely shooting in the dark.

Chucky's face froze. His chair squeaked as he rocked back slightly.

"No, Crestview. Why would you think I was going to Mexico?" he asked, rocking forward and loosening up again.

"Isn't that why you have your passport?"

Chucky's left hand moved towards his left front pocket before Chucky stopped it cold.

Got you, fuckface, Rob thought.

"D. Randall told us you'd head there when you got jammed up," Rob said.

"He told us a lot of things about you," Kay added.

"We don't know each other! Why would he say that? We never even met!"

"He knows Josiah Waller," Rob said, watching Chucky's face.

He watched Chucky's focus change to somewhere behind Rob, as if Rob wasn't even there, as if a ship far out in the Gulf had his attention. He watched Chucky's mouth sag and his head lean slightly. Chucky's right shoulder came up and his torso leaned a bit.

Something was wrong. Rob's heart started pounding.

"Chucky? Are you all right?" Rob asked.

Chuck looked at Rob, smiled and quickly pulled on the top right drawer of his desk. He reached inside. Instinctively, Rob stood and leaned forward. Chucky's right hand cleared the drawer, revealing a large stainless pistol: a Beretta 92.

"GUN!" Kay yelled.

Rob only had a moment to decide on a course of action or he'd take at least one in the chest. He decided to go for Chucky's pistol instead of pulling his own. He threw his hands forward, grabbing Chucky's wrist with his left hand and the barrel of the Beretta with his right.

"GET DOWN!" Kay yelled.

Rob immobilized Chuck's wrist at the same time he twisted the barrel up and to his left. Rob leaned deeply to his right in case Kay started shooting.

Chucky shot first.

The round went up and into the ceiling. The crack hurt Rob's ears; they started ringing. Rob fought against the action and slowed it enough that the weapon failed to chamber the next round. He pushed the pistol and Chuck's wrist in opposite directions.

As the pistol came free, the barrel hot in his hand, he teared up and his eyes began to violently sting. Rob had to cough. The odor caught him. Rob knew that smell.

Rob kept a death grip on Chuck's wrist. He stepped back and hauled, yanking Chuck onto the desktop. Then he had to bend at the waist and cough again. Snot ran out of his nose and he wanted to throw up. He kept a hold on Chucky while he beheld Kay in action.

She stood in front of her chair with her handbag in the crook of her arm. She sprayed a stream of Oleoresin Capsicum into Chuck's face from the largest can of OC spray Rob had ever seen. It was black and the size of his mother's hairspray cans from when he was a kid. Kay was no more concerned than if she were spraying water on flowers back at the house.

"Enough," Rob croaked. "Cuff him!"

"Oh, sure," Kay said, putting her spray back in her handbag and coming out with her handcuffs.

Chucky coughed, cried, dry heaved and drooled saliva and snot all over his hardwood desk.

Rob coughed some more, spit and blew snot onto Chucky's thick crème carpeting.

Rob heard Kay call Chris on her cell. He heard her tell him as soon as the boys stopped voiding various bodily fluids all over Chucky's luxury office, they would be bringing Chucky in. He heard her say "Oh, and because Chucky tried to shoot us, could you please send the Evidence Response Team? Someone needs to get up into the drop ceiling and dig out the bullet."

That night, Rob had a date with Melissa for dinner back at Emerald Oyster and Steak in the Seminolacola Historic District. He paced outside as he waited. He had showered and changed clothes and then spent the day processing Chucky and writing search warrants for Chucky's house and office. He would have ran the search operations, but . . . .

The nature of Dauphin's arrest had made Pam highly irate. The gunplay did not seem to make her any more sympathetic. She kept going back to the Waller operation. She truly relished chewing Rob out for not calling her in when Waller started talking.

"Get Dauphin in custody," Pam had said. "Then, first thing you're going to do is help me clean up the Waller mess. He's asserting he was given immunity. We'll have to convince Ingersoll he wasn't, and if we can't I mean to repudiate and file for the death penalty. Maybe after that we can have a meaningful conversation with Mr. Douche."

Rob had spent the late afternoon dodging Headquarters (the one in Washington) supervisors, on a dog and pony show for Ingersoll and dealing with the fallout of the Dauphin arrest. At first, Chucky had wanted Ingersoll to represent him too, causing no end of bullshit.

Chris got between FBI HQ and Rob just intime for the SAC's arrival. She needed briefings. For whatever reason, she was especially interested in some guy named Peter Grant the Fast Food King, whoever the hell he was. But Rob knew the worst of today was about to occur.

Melissa came his way with a spring in her step and a grin on her lips. She wore a white, long-sleeved blouse un-tucked and short green shorts with brown leather sandals. She had rolled up her sleeves. She carried a white sweater and clutch purse. Her expression changed to one of concern.

"What happened to your neck?" she asked, reaching up to touch the damage.

They embraced and kissed.

"It looks worse than it is. I'll tell you inside. Sorry I rushed you out. How did it go at the house?" Rob asked.

"Nothing boxed mac and cheese with Lila in front of a movie couldn't fix," Melissa said.

"Well, thanks. Hungry?"

"Sure," she said, smiling again.

Rob had reserved a table against the weekend crowd. They were seated in the back, in a booth with a little privacy. They caught up on the last few days as they ate, with Rob having steak, fries and a tossed salad, and Melissa opting for broiled grouper and mixed vegetables.

"Let's get a coffee. We have a little business to discuss," Rob said.

"If you want to, but I'll have water. I don't want to be up all night."

A fresh icy glass of water and a steaming cup of coffee were quickly delivered. Rob added some milk and began.

"Melissa, we locked up Chucky Dauphin this morning," he said.

"Oh my God! Really?"

"Yes. Mel, I want you to hold on, this is going to get rough."

"What is?"

Time had flowed solidly into the dinner hour, but they were still fairly private in their booth.

"We think he had Matthew killed."

Melissa went pale. Her mouth opened several times without speaking. When she found her voice she said, "What? What are you talking about? Not him, he couldn't do something like that."

"Based on everything we know so far, it appears he was running a Ponzi scheme."

"A what? What's that?"

"A Ponzi scheme is a con where the subjects committing the fraud pose as investment brokers or money managers. They attract investors and use money from recent investors to make fraudulent payments to earlier participants creating the impression of fantastic returns. In fact, the returns are merely the principle from the investments themselves.

"While those payments are being made, keeping investors happy, the subjects are stealing the rest of the money. They encourage the first victims to recruit new victims. The goal is to amass a fortune and eventually disappear with it, leaving all the investors picked clean."

"No," Melissa said, sitting up straight with her shoulders back. "No. Matthew would not do that."

"Well, Mel, we think Matthew figured it out. It started with real estate investments. I think Matthew put it together and once he did, he wouldn't play along."

"You mean driving around, visiting those construction projects, was Matthew investigating?"

"Yes. We think he challenged Chucky, or Chucky learned Matthew had found out. One of Chucky's original investors, who we believe became a partner in the fraud, was a lawyer with contacts in the police department who were less than honorable. We think we'll be able to prove they conspired to kill, and then killed Matthew to keep him quiet. We'll know for sure in a few days."

"So Chucky killed Matthew?"

"Had it arranged, I'd say. I think the officers did it or hired the shooters from your push-in attack to do it."

Melissa put a hand over her mouth and leaned forward as if she'd been kicked in the stomach.

"Mel," Rob said gently.

She recovered and sat up primly. "No. No, he did not. If he did, then what was Jimmy Tank Gubbs all about?"

"I believe they paid Jimmy Tank to take the fall."

"The fall?"

"The blame, to act as a cut-out essentially."

"A cut-out?"

"Yes, the trail would cut out at Jimmy Tank. If anyone had started following the trail, no one would look any further than Jimmy Tank."

"Why would he agree to do that?"

"To keep anyone, police, regulators, anyone, from recreating Matthew's work and figuring out what was going on."

Melissa shook her head. "No, I mean Jimmy Tank."

"I don't think we ever will know for sure," Rob said. "I think maybe there was something of a conscience acting up in him. Like what motivated him to work with Father Clyde, maybe. I think his conscience led him to speak up at the execution."

Melissa put her elbow on the table and rested her forehead in her hand.

"Honey, there is more. I'm sorry, but you are a victim here, too."

"Don't you think I know that?" She came off her hand fierce and angry. "He was my husband!"

"Yes, of course. I mean financially. You are the victim of a financial crime." Rob hated breaking the news. It put a hard pit in his stomach.

He watched the news change her face, first crimping the skin between her brows, then screwing up her features, ending with a quiver on her chin.

"What? What are you talking about now?" Melissa asked. "You're not making any sense. I'm leaving. You're sick." She grabbed at her purse.

Rob moved next to her, blocking her way. She twisted away from him at the waist. He put his hand on her shoulder.

"Go away," she said to the wall.

"Mel, Chucky didn't help you with Matthew's life insurance money, he stole it. All of it. Your investment accounts are a fiction. Rather, the accounts exist, but they have no funds in them. I have to see your copies of your mortgage papers, but as of right now we think those were all counterfeit and in fact, Chucky has been paying rent on the condo you and Jules live in. You don't own it and there is no equity in it."

"The condo?"

"Yes honey, the condo too."

"We had a closing."

"Staged. Completely fake. Title vests in someone else, and he has owned it for 9 years. I wanted to ask you, how did you come across the property?"

"Chucky . . . ." Melissa swallowed hard. Tears welled up. She coughed. "Chucky showed it to me. He said it wasn't on the market yet and the seller was motivated. He took care of everything."

"Uh huh," Rob said sympathetically.

"You have to understand, it was crazy, with Jules and everyone pulling at me. I was glad for the help."

"I understand."

"Chucky said he was paying the mortgage, taxes and insurance."

"He lied."

"He said he took care of those things for me. He had me come by and sign things all the time."

Rob shrugged.

"How do you know?" she asked. "You don't know that. You don't know any of this."

"We know, Melissa."

"No. You're doing this because you hate him. You're jealous."

"No honey, I'm not. We're doing this because we did our jobs. We followed the money. We do know. It's gone."

"That's not possible. Those are good firms."

"Yes, Fidelity and Vanguard are and you have a little left there. But the bulk of your money was in Foremann Investments. Those statements are false and all the money has been transferred out."

"Gone?"

"Gone."

She looked away again. Rob reached for his cup. He sipped his coffee to clear a lump in his throat.

"Shit," Melissa said. "My mother said so. She thought the whole thing had been too easy, after Matthew was killed. She told me and told me and I wouldn't listen. I just went along with it." She faced Rob. "It seemed legit to me. It was Matt's old boss, a financial professional, taking care of things. I thought I was lucky. Shit."

Melissa worried her hands. Minutes passed.

"What are we going to do now? Are you saying I'm homeless? Me and Jules? We're homeless and have no money?"

"Not yet. in fact, I've located the owner. We might be able to get him to rent it directly to you."

"I can't, Rob. I can't afford it. I know what they rent for. I don't have any other money than the money Chucky is managing for us. Was managing, I guess. I can't . . . that was the whole thing, so I could work part-time and live there like that. I can't . . . what am I gonna do?"

"You can move."

"Rob, I need more money. I don't even have enough in my checking account to put money down on a new apartment. Everything was with Chuck. All my savings were with him. I can't, Rob, I can't. I can't do anything."

Melissa leaned in to him and rested her forehead on his shoulder. She burrowed her face down to where his neck met his chest and started crying. All he could think to do was to hold her and kiss the top of her head.

"Now I have to call my mother and tell her she was right," Melissa said between sobs.

Rob kept quiet. Melissa's crying wound down. She excused herself and went to the bathroom.

Rob paid the bill.

Melissa did not want to go home, so they strolled down the brick sidewalks in the fading heat. She held on to him with one arm around his waist and sniffled into a napkin. She did not want to talk, so Rob peered into the shops they passed. When Rob spotted Gulf Creamery, he almost suggested an ice cream, but caught himself. Not now, he realized.

Inside, there at a table, he saw Ali Bakr and Kelly Ann MacDonald sharing a milkshake. He wore a concert t-shirt and she wore a pink tank top. She had pulled her hair back. They made googly eyes at each other as they sipped through their straws until Kelly Ann started to laugh.

Rob and Melissa walked on. Kelly Ann and Ali made him feel better. It made him feel like he and Melissa would work this out, that everything would work out.

Then he had an idea.

Three Months Later

Rob sat next to Leo and across from D. Randall at a plastic table. The dull green chairs clashed with the lighter green floor tiles. The walls were white, as were the ceiling tiles and the window blinds. They had closed them for privacy and to help the central air handle the midday heat. D. Randall wore a Bureau of Prisons' khaki shirt and trousers. Leo and Rob were in bowling shirts.

They had worked a deal to get him in the Federal Prison Camp on the Navy base, pre-trial. D. Randall was a miserable pain the in the ass over the two weeks he needed to dry out, but sobering up helped him analyze his situation. Now, he was all about cooperation.

"I know I'm fucked, boys," he liked to say to them, "but I want a good rep so I can serve in a good place, and if I knock a few years off the back end, that'll put me a little closer to getting laid before I die, maybe."

D. Randall was providing so much information, Rob had to interview him several times a week. The cooperation was so complete D. Randall's lawyer had stopped coming and accepted Rob's summaries after each interview.

"Okay for him," Rob said, closing the folio and wrapping up their current discussion. "Next time we'll start on Peter Grant."

"That guy," D. Randall snorted, "the Fast-Food King."

"You remember him?" Leo asked.

"Oh yeah. He got one sick-assed sport fish, definitely over sixty foot. Slick as snot, that one. Don't worry, it won't be too much, but there's stuff, like the time he paid me to get the health inspectors to close down a little spick burger and taco joint. Competition. And I had to motivate a guy to sell the right corner of some fucking empty intersection somewhere. Oh yeah, the occasional mad dad of one of the underage cuties working for him, too. Fucking dog, man. Hell on them high school girls."

Rob and Leo shared a glance.

"Grant wanted a lot of service, and paid," D. Randal continued, "but if we ever saw each other around, he pretended not to know me. Forget about getting a piece of one of those franchises. He bragged about his tax guy, though. You know what that means? It means —"

"About those mad dad's," Rob said.

"Don't you worry. I didn't need to kill even a one of them."

"Yeah, but how many did you smack around?" Leo asked.

D. Randall chuckled.

Rob pulled four cans of mackerel out of his briefcase and passed them under the table to D. Randall. Rob put Bureau informant money on his books, but D. Randall really liked getting the contraband mackerel. He had specifically instructed Rob to be careful at the hand off. He did not want the corrections officers to know. Rob tapped his knee with the cans.

"Put one over on the man, man," D. Randall said, checking the door over his shoulder.

Rob felt D. Randall take the fish.

"We are the man, Randy," Leo said.

"No way, Leo. You guys are the bomb."

"Thank you," Leo said. "Hey, you on the pile? You're looking better."

"Yeah, on the pile and walking laps. Eating better, too."

"Keep it up."

D. Randall fairly beamed at the compliment.

"Randy, got to go," Rob said, standing up.

"'Kay brah, stay safe."

They shook hands. D. Randall set off alone. Rob and Leo gave him time to get away before walking toward the office of the Special Investigative Unit.

"Hey," a tall thin white man with an extravagant salt and pepper mustache, who wore plain clothes, met them on the sidewalk. "Problems?"

"Nope. We gave him four cans," Rob said.

The Special Investigative Unit supervisor laughed. "He started a store, you know."

"You going to shut it down?" Leo asked.

"Nah. He's keeping it under control. Unless he starts making hooch. Then we'll have to. I'll call you if any big infractions come up."

"Thanks, man," Rob said.

Out in the parking lot, they stood next to each other by the open trunk of Rob's car, squinting against the glare and instantly sweating. They reconstituted themselves: pistols back in holsters, knives back in pockets, cell phones back on.

"So, what you gonna do with another spin-off? You should go into business and sell them to slackers who need the work," Leo said.

"Grant, yeah. I can't wait for the full story," Rob said.

"Going to interview some cuties?"

"They ought to be in college by now, don't you think?"

Once in the car, they cleared the Camp and the base.

"You must be getting real popular at IRS CID at this point" Leo said.

"Their supervisor bought me lunch yesterday," Rob said.

"No kidding! How goes D. Randall's forfeiture?"

"It will be huge. We know about a million plus right now if we can liquidate at market rates, and we're nowhere near done. Forfeiture Fran is working on Headquarters to give us a budget for TDYs. I may be able to preserve something resembling a life if we get a budget."

"You did a hell of a good job on this one, Rob," Leo said.

"Thanks." Rob felt good hearing it from Leo, whom he respected.

"I think the best part was how you got Katz to sign off on that big-assed one-time source payment for the housekeeper who identified Chloe Baxter. No shit, I've never heard of one that big."

Rob laughed.

"None of my business," Leo said, filling the silence Rob left hanging, "but how's it going with the widow lady?"

"I expected it to be rougher. I was really worried she would resent it and all, but after a few days, it was normal. It helped a lot Jules was all into me moving in."

"You get out of your lease?"

"No worries there. I was in it month-to-month."

They parked at the RA and trudged up the stairs. They badged their way in the front. Chris used the intercom to call everyone to his office. Rob caught up with Steve and Leo.

"What's up?" Leo asked Steve.

Steve shrugged.

Chris came in and put a bottle down on the table. Kay followed with five plastic flutes.

"Champagne?" Leo asked. "What's the occasion?"

"Prosecco," Chris said, working on the bottle. "I have an announcement." He unwrapped it and eased the cork out with a soft pop. "We're toasting the ASAC's transfer to Headquarters."

"Oh, hell *yeah* I'll drink to that," Leo said. "Where's he going?"

"Inspection Division."

Chris poured. They held their cups up.

"May he be well up there, and may he spend all his time inspecting Anchorage!"

"Here, here."

They all drank.

"Leo, I'm surprised you didn't pick it up, with your network," Kay said.

"So am I. I'll have to check up on it."

"Rob, you have somewhere to go?" Chris asked.

"No, just watching the clock," Rob said. "It's Melissa's first week of classes and I'm picking up Jules tonight. I don't want to be late."

"Oh?" Chris poured them each a little more, killing the bottle. "How is she doing?"

"She's excited to be back at school."

The party ended with the cups empty and the team going back to their cubes. Pending work swamped Rob. The main case, spin-offs, unrelated leads and financial Suspicious Activity Reports, plus a new background were stacked up on him.

He checked his watch again. In addition to getting Jules, he had committed to cooking. He knew he needed to write up this most recent interview, but he thought of something else he wanted to do first.

He figured he had time to do both before he had to leave. Rob logged on to his computer and went straight to Virtual Academy. A message in bold red letters let him know about his long overdue course. He clicked on the link to get back to it.

"Best of luck to you, Asshole," he muttered, starting on the first Blood Borne Pathogens slide.

Acknowledgements

Novelists tend to recruit others to their projects as unwitting co-conspirators. I'd like to thank several of my victims, whose generosity I greatly abused. First and foremost, Betsy Glick of the FBI's Office of Public Affairs, for her advice and support. Marta Sprout, author, most recently of KILL NOTICE, for all things editorial. Ron Chillemi, former state prosecutor and Assistant United States Attorney, New Jersey state official and overall attorney extraordinaire, for comments and perspective (although all mistakes and misrepresentations are my own). Kimberley Howe, Interim Executive Director of Thriller Writers International (thrillerwriters.org), for more of her time than she could afford. Rebecca Stinson created the cover art and I used the services of editorworld.com. Thanks to Dale and Julia Dye (warriorspublishing.com) for their close reading of the text. Saving the best for last, many thanks to my wife Susie, who lets me write fiction when I should be fixing stuff around the house or driving the kids somewhere.

The Resident Agent

About the Author

Mitch Stern is a lawyer and consultant in private practice. He served as a special agent in the FBI for twenty years. He is a graduate of the Jacob D. Fuchsberg Law Center of Touro College. Before law school, Mitch served as a police officer in Dallas, Texas and as an investigator for the City of New York. Prior to attending SUNY Stonybrook as an undergraduate, he served in the US Marine Corps. Mitch and his wife Susie have three children.